THE STREAM

LOST IN THE SAND

MICHAEL SMITH

"The idea here is, that travellers in a caravan
would approach the place where water had been found before,
but would find the fountain dried up
or the stream lost in the sand;
and when they looked for refreshment,
they found only disappointment".

Albert Barnes, Notes on Job, circa 1835

ONE

April 1994

Benjamin Bone, his face unshaven, long arms hanging loosely, was staring out of one of the floor-to-ceiling windows running along the south wall of the terminal building. Eventually he looked back at a young woman sitting behind him, stabbed his finger at the glass and snapped. "Look. Over there! Who is that man on the runway?"

"I told you. I don't see anybody." She sighed irritably.

"Stand up…, please..., look…" Benjamin pointed again. A running man was just visible in the shimmering haze.

The woman gazed into the distance, still unsmiling. "Yes, I see him. I don't know who he is. Why should I?"

But Benjamin could see him better now. Although he was high on the second floor he could make out the man's greasy, red hair curled around his chubby, freckled cheeks. In a sky blue shirt soaked in sweat, he was stumbling across the concrete, gripping a red briefcase tightly against his chest.

Germaine grunted softly as she sat down again, grabbing her bag from the floor. She was smartly dressed. A green tight blouse tucked into a white knee-length skirt. She looked younger than Benjamin. Her skin was smooth and tanned, and she had long, dark and wavy hair.

He was still staring through the glass. "Yes, it's the other man at the interview."

Germaine looked up at her husband. "Why should he be out there? You couldn't possibly recognise him from here. And you are always wrong." She smiled thinly as she said it.

"I'm right this time." He pressed his face against the window, cupped his hands around his eyes and looked down past a muddled collection of baggage trucks and electric cars, parked in anticipation of the arrival of the morning plane from London. Yes, he was sure. The man's red hair and podgy, freckled face, freckles vivid beneath a flushed complexion, were unmistakable. And the red case, he remembered that too.

Yesterday, he had left Earl Rittman's office after his interview, briefly confident. He had glanced at a man sitting in the plush reception hall of the Outland Oil Company, gripping a red case. The man's hands and bloodless fingers were wrapped round its red leather shell.

Benjamin had nodded at the receptionist sitting behind her high desk, and muttered a goodbye. She had nodded back and beckoned the man over. "It's your turn now," she had said. "Don't be nervous." Benjamin remembered. The dishevelled, red-headed man had looked at the floor as he spoke. "I mean to get it, I mean to get it," he had muttered as he stepped towards the door of Earl Rittman's office.

Benjamin wanted the job badly but he knew he could not compete with such certainty. Success required passion but he was cynical of the motives of his peers and uncertain of why anything could matter so much. Everywhere he went, everyone he met, he struggled to care. And interviews were just an exercise in lying. Although appearing cool, confident and carefree, he was none of these. He worried about money, he worried about his marriage, and he worried about the future. He was a worrier. And he wished Germaine had stayed at home.

The red-haired man stopped running just below the window through which Benjamin was staring. The man looked up at him, shouting inaudibly, waving his briefcase in the air, its shiny red cowhide swinging up and down like an air traffic controller's paddle.

"I can't hear you," Benjamin said aloud, even though he knew that he was inaudible the other side of the thick glass pane. "What are you doing out there?"

The man shouted back, pointing at his case as he did so. "Mickey Mouse did it."

"Mickey Mouse did it?" Benjamin read the man's lips and mouthed the words back to him.

The man nodded repeatedly. "Yes, Mickey Mouse."

In the distance Benjamin spotted four men appear from behind the far wing of the terminal. They were running. The red-haired man turned to look too, and turned back, eyes wide with terror. He tossed the case into a luggage trolley and ran left along the wall of the building. Benjamin strained to see, pressing his face hard against the window.

The four pursuers divided. Two headed off left before disappearing behind a parked plane. The other two continued towards the building. They both glanced up at Benjamin before they too disappeared from view.

"Germaine…," he said, looking back at his wife who had her handbag open on her lap and a compact mirror in her hand. "He was trying to talk to me."

"Really," she said in a careless tone. "I'm going to the ladies room, and then I'm going to look around the terminal for a bit." She closed her bag and slung it over her shoulder, stood up, smoothed her white skirt and walked off.

Benjamin said nothing. He watched her go, then dropped into the seat his wife had vacated. He was wearing a crumpled grey suit and white open-necked shirt which pushed up around his neck as he slouched in the seat. Weathered lines ran down each of his cheeks, cutting into a prominent chin. His light brown hair was thin on top, cut short on the sides. He looked very tired.

To beat the traffic along the Eastex Freeway, which runs north directly into Houston Intercontinental airport, he and Germaine had checked out of their downtown hotel at six in the morning. He had always been an early riser but his wife, waiting on the kerb, had complained vigorously while he had loaded their two suitcases into a taxi.

He closed his eyes. His mind drifted away, calmed by the hum of air conditioning and the faint sounds of birds and traffic from outside. He was in a transient, meditative state of semi-sleep, both aware and unaware of where he was.

After what seemed like just a moment he felt a gentle tap on his shoulder and jerked forward. "What's going on?" He stammered.

A man's head moved into his line of vision. It was a large, round head, with close-cut grey hairs sparkling like optic fibres. He had a bulbous blue nose and fat red cheeks and wore the blue uniform of a security guard. "Why were you signalling?" The head spoke with a Texan accent.

Benjamin forced his eyes wider. He saw two men. The other to his right was short and thin-faced, wearing a dark suit. They were both staring at him slouching in the seat.

He stood up before replying. "I was asleep. What do you mean signalling?"

"I saw you signalling to the man outside. Why are you here? The London flight doesn't leave for hours."

"I like to be in good time… early…, what man? Who are you talking about?" Benjamin spoke defensively. He knew that he sounded unconvincing. "How did you know which flight I was on?"

"You're English…aren't you?"

"Why were you chasing him?" Benjamin interrupted.

"Why are you here," the Texan repeated, "why were you signalling?"

"I was not!" Benjamin raised his voice but his tone took on an unfortunate squeaky timbre. "Who are you?" He squealed back at them.

"My name is Bauss." The squat, weasel-faced man in the sharp suit spoke for the first time. "Here is my card. Now please tell us how you know that man?" He had a gentle voice at odds with his sharp, squinty features.

Benjamin took the card, glanced at it briefly, then glanced at it again as both men stared at him. He felt pressured and anxious.

"I don't know who he is," he said. "I was looking out the window and saw him running this way. He disappeared over there." He waved his arm in the general direction the man had gone. "Followed by you two I suppose." He pointed at them both in turn.

"You say you have never met him. You weren't trying to talk to him?"

"Yes. Of course I've never met him."

"I'm sorry we bothered you then. Please accept our apologies. Come on Jim."

Jim, the Texan guard, turned and squinted at his colleague. The weaselly man repeated the words softly and firmly. "Come on Jim. Leave the English gentleman in peace. He doesn't know anything."

Benjamin watched them walk away, uncomfortably certain that neither of them had believed him. Why had they left so abruptly? He didn't know. But he did know why he had not told them the truth. He looked at the business card in his hand. "Mick E. (Micky) Bauss" it said. He mouthed the words the red-haired man had said. "Mickey Mouse… did it." Say it silently. Micky Bauss. He watched the two men disappear behind the closed duty free shop and wondered what the red-haired man thought Mickey Mouse had done.

Three hours later Benjamin and Germaine's DC10 aircraft was humming softly as it crossed the Newfoundland coast, beginning its journey over the Atlantic. They had not spoken since the plane had taken off in Houston. Benjamin was wearing headphones. A plastic cup half full of beer, two more empty cups and several foil wraps that had contained peanuts littered his tray table in front of him.

Germaine turned to her husband, tapping his arm. "Benjamin, I've been offered a position in our head office in Paris."

Benjamin turned. "What," he shouted, spraying grains of peanut from his dry lips.

"The office says I can move back to Paris." Germaine repeated, wiping her cheek self-consciously. "And we are over, I think." Benjamin removed his headphones. He had been listening to rock music on his Discman and, for the moment, had been content. He liked sitting in the dark in planes, eating peanuts and drinking beer. It was cosy and peaceful. Germaine knew he liked it and it bothered her. She had never been able to come to terms with the five mile drop beneath her feet. Exasperated at Germaine, he grumbled, "what? I was listening to my music."

"It's over!" Germaine raised her voice. "I'm going back to Paris."

Benjamin stared at her in the dim light and took a sip from his beer. He attempted to appear nonchalant, glancing back at the movie screen on the seatback in front of him. A wildlife documentary was flickering, unmindful of this drama. Lions were devouring an antelope, peeling off the skin and fur with their teeth. It made him think of Germaine removing her yellow rubber gloves midway through washing dishes. She would complain bitterly about England, the hard water, the cold, and the dirt. "What's it doing to my hands," she would scream? The picture on his screen changed to a grass covered plain, a single statuesque tree. The antelope was gone.

"No it's not." He finally said. "Why come with me on this trip?"

"I came because I wanted time with you. And to tell you this. I hoped you would be happier, with this job and everything. But that's not the point. It is over."

"No it's not," Benjamin said again.

"You always contradict me, Benjamin."

"Yes I do."

"What's that supposed to mean?"

"It was a joke."

"Be serious can't you? We are not comparable."

"It's compatible."

"Whatever it is, I must go home now. You have no job. I am not happy either. It's nothing to be ashamed of."

"OK, if you want to leave, then leave. Blame me, blame Benjamin Bone." Benjamin spoke the words in French, with a lump in his throat and glistening eyes. He roughly rubbed them with his fingers. Replacing the headphones over his ears, he mumbled to himself. OK then. You go to your boyfriend in Paris. Don't think I don't know about him. He stared fixedly at his tray table, counting in his head the number of scattered nuts that lay there. There were twenty two, although a couple were just fragments. Of course he knew it was over. It had been for months. Since before he had lost his job. I don't care, he thought. He did care though. He was going to be lonely. I don't even like Germaine and she doesn't like me. If only the baby had been born. No, it's good we don't have children. Fuck, I don't know what I want.

It was true that Benjamin was perpetually anxious, often about nothing at all. And the fact that he did not know what he was anxious about made him feel guilty. Guilty of a secret he should be ashamed. Benjamin was depressed by this guilt but tried to pretend otherwise. I only don't become suicidal because I know today is not as bad as it could be tomorrow, he thought. Tomorrow, he knew, would be even more depressed. On his seat-back screen one of the male lions, now replete, its face smeared with blood, was roughly mounting the backside of a stooping lioness.

They hardly spoke for the remainder of the flight. Benjamin couldn't sleep. His thoughts were all over the place. He had lost Germaine, he needed a job, and who was that red-haired man back in Houston? Trying to be optimistic he dwelt on good things to look forward to, but failed to come up with anything more than a freshly-made bed with clean sheets. The cramped economy class seat tormented him with its design, permitting brief periods of succour cut short by long periods of pain. When Benjamin achieved his ambition of ephemeral comfort he dozed until one of his limbs became numb, then began to throb. A fat man behind him jerked the back of Benjamin's seat every so often, jerks uncannily timed to coincide with his fitful naps. When breakfast finally arrived he was red-eyed, sore and itchy. His stomach was bloated and his mouth tasted like a stretch of the runway on which they landed in the early spring morning.

After a long wait, stooping in the aisle of the stationery plane, and an even longer walk down the bleak, cold corridors of Heathrow airport, they cleared immigration and Benjamin collected a luggage trolley. Together they waited for the baggage. They didn't speak. So I have to carry your case, he thought. Who will carry it when you fly to Paris? The carousel trundled around. My bag will be last. It always is. He leapt forward to inspect a label on a case barely resembling his own. Another passenger grabbed it. They waited some more and the choice diminished.

"There is mine," shouted Germaine, "get it!"

Benjamin stepped forward. His own case appeared a few bags along and he dragged them both onto his trolley as Germaine headed towards the customs hall. He was about to follow when he spotted another bag come out through the rubber curtains at the end of the now almost empty carousel. On the rubber belt of the carousel a small red briefcase was trundling towards him.

He stared at it. It was the red-haired man's case. He was sure of it.

He looked around at the few remaining passengers. Would anyone take that case? He waited some more. No one did. He watched it circle, then disappear through the rubber curtains on the far side of the carousel, and reappear through the curtains on his side. He gazed at it, memorising its details like a prize on a game show. Perhaps it was full of drugs, or arms, or a bomb. He dare not take it and carry it through customs. He let it circle one more time checking again to see if anyone was watching. The carousel jerked to a halt. The case lay there in front of him, all by itself.

Shaking slightly, a nervous sweat on his skin, Benjamin picked it up. His bowels were loose and his stomach was empty and nauseous. He placed it on top of the bags on his trolley. The case was light. It couldn't be drugs, well not many anyway. His heart was beating faster. He could hear its thump, thump in his ears as he pushed the trolley to the exit gate, his legs weak with anticipation.

Trying hard to cover up his nerves he walked through the doorway into the customs hall. From the corner of his eyes he could see three uniformed men talking together. Another man was inspecting the contents of a bulging suitcase, rummaging through the neatly folded silk garments of a well-dressed Asian couple.

The exit door lay around the corner and he pushed the heavily laden trolley in a broad arc towards it. But he pushed the trolley too fast, cornering too sharply. His bags shifted and the small red case slid off the top and dropped onto the resin floor. It spun before thumping into the wall.

Benjamin stopped. One of the customs men was standing nearby. The man looked at Benjamin, then looked at the bag and picked it up. Benjamin froze, gripping his trolley handle, his nails digging painfully into the palms of his hands. He was now convinced the red case was full of heroin. The officer walked towards him. He walked very slowly indeed, and he was grinning, grinning like he would soon get a big bonus. He stopped in front of Benjamin who stood very still with the trolley in front of him, his mouth clamped shut.

"Here you are, sir." He handed the case to Benjamin.

"Er, thank you." He knew he looked guilty, like a boy with a toffee in his mouth caught running from a sweetshop. He unclenched a greasy wet hand from the trolley and took the proffered bag. The customs man smiled again and turned back to continue his conversation with his colleagues. Benjamin stumbled away, pushing his trolley with his left hand, clutching the case under his right arm as tightly as the red-haired man had done yesterday.

Outside in the arrivals hall Germaine was waiting in the crowd. "Where have you been?" She said, sounding a little angry. And then, in the same tone, "you don't look well."

"This bag was on the carousel. I'm sure it's the one the red-headed man was carrying. I took it." His voice was shaking a little.

"You took it? What's in it?"

"I don't know. I haven't looked. Let's get the car."

They caught the feeder bus to the long term car park where Germaine's small Toyota was parked. As he stowed the two large suitcases in the back Germaine picked up the red case but Benjamin grabbed it back. "Let me have it," he said. "You get in the car. I'm going to look inside before we go."

TWO

The locals liked to boast that the town of Karim was the most important settlement on the flank of the widest, longest and deepest wadi in Yemen but there were several larger towns lying on the edge of the plateau. Karim was certainly powerful, dominating the surrounding lands, looming over fields of millet and grain, grapes and dates and, of course, qat bushes planted in neat rows on the slopes of south-facing hillocks below the cliffs. The cultivated land was irrigated by the falaj, a series of culverts in the rock, mud conduits and metal pipes, carrying water from the shallow aquifer below the jebel. Fertilised by effluent trickling down the cacti-covered hillside beneath the town's crumbling walls, Bedouin tribes had fought long and costly battles for control of these few thousand acres of productive land.

Under a sinking sun two young Bedu men rode from Karim, side by side, along one of the sandy tracks leading away from the fields. The red sandstone cliffs towered on either side of them, tapering off into the distance. The men wore blue jeans and coloured nylon shirts with loose, chequered scarves around their heads. Rashad, who rode the larger and stronger of the two horses, was in a foul, indignant mood. His face was smooth and handsome, his eyes bright and brown. He cursed loudly as clouds of dust whipped up on the hot wind stung his cheeks.

"We did it, younger brother…" he shouted angrily in Arabic, spittle flying in a fine silver cloud from his lips, "nobody can change that...." He paused for a moment to look back at the town. "And we'll do it again whatever the old man says. You'll see!" His voice was a trembling whine.

Mahmoud, his wiry half-brother, listened to the words placidly, his broad mouth stretched, his dark eyes squinting in the sun. He looked at Rashad sadly, steadied his horse, and spoke solemnly. "You are impatient Rashad. Do not show your emotions. It is a sign of weakness."

Rashad stared back at him, still angry, but without malice. "He did not thank us, not a word. We brought him the Land Cruiser. We could have sold it ourselves...," He stopped, expecting his brother to nod in agreement but Mahmoud simply smiled.

"It's worth ten thousand dollars," Rashad went on. "We should have taken it north to the border. To Saudi. Next time we will do that, eh, Mahmoud?"

"Forget the cars Rashad!" Mahmoud replied sternly, brushing away the frilly corners of his headscarf flapping in the gusts of warm wind funnelling through the valley. "It is better we stop taking cars. The Americans will soon start drilling for oil in Wadi Qarib and we don't want to scare them off. I know I can get jobs for our men at the camp and they will give us all the baksheesh we need." He stopped and looked around at the cliffs to the north. "Yes and there are other things too, worth much more than cars."

Rashad ignored him, lost in his inner anger. "It's our history, it's our tradition. There is no certainty in oil..." His horse tripped on a boulder and he tugged at its reins, then cantered ahead, bored by his brother's foolishness. He knew the tribe must rely on itself alone, not on those heathens from America.

Mahmoud had different ideas as he watched Rashad canter away, not smiling now for he was saddened by his brother's ignorance. I will make a fortune selling water to the Americans, truly a fortune, he was thinking. Then he blessed his own mother for bequeathing him the business sense his half-brother lacked. Only last month he had negotiated a deal with the American engineer to supply water to drill the oil well. With the nearest water forty kilometres from the American camp only he could get it to them, only he had leased every flat-bed truck in the region. Paid in dollars he would be a rich man very soon.

Rashad had reached the asphalt road and, as Mahmoud drew nearer, he shouted back at him, as if reading his thoughts. "The drillers will come and go like the Russians did in Shabwa. There's no oil here and, even if there is oil, the government in Sana'a will take it all. We won't see a single dollar." Rashad rubbed his thumb and forefinger, fingering an invisible note. His stubby fingers were deep brown, with chipped blackened nails, dirt ingrained into the skin beneath. "We have to think of the future... of our people." He pointed back at the town, "the sooner the old man hands over leadership to me the better for us, for Karim, and for the tribe."

"He's not going to do it," Mahmoud interrupted him angrily. "You'll have to wait till he dies," but he knew his half-brother was even now tempted to hurry the process along.

"And I hear the oil company has been dynamiting a hole in the floor of Wadi Qarib," Rashad said, ignoring his brother's words, "and the track they have bulldozed is scaring the wild horses." Mahmoud had seen the graded track running along the wadi from the new airstrip in its mouth right into the American's camp.

"And a drilling rig has arrived on a ship from Africa," Rashad went on. "They will find oil, for sure."

Mahmoud had also been impressed but he hid it. Instead of agreeing, he was wondering about other ways to make money from the rich drillers who seemed to have so much money to give away. I don't care, he thought. I don't care if they find oil or not. I will make my money whatever happens.

The new blacktop road started outside Sana'a, Yemen's capital, and ran northeast towards Marib Governate, then eastwards along the edge of the plateau, winding its way for three hundred kilometres along the valleys, sometimes beneath plateau walls, sometimes far into the sandy plain. The road ended in the city of Marib, a bustling town on the edge of the Empty Quarter. Marib, the capital of the former kingdom of Saba, was once a rich trading post on the incense route from China used before a shipping channel through the Gulf of Aden and Red Sea had been established. But it was destroyed by war and neglect fifteen hundred years ago when the dam built to help irrigate its agriculture finally collapsed.

The crumbling buildings and walls of old Marib now attracted tourists from Sana'a and the blacktop road had been built to expand this trade with money loaned by the World Bank. However, still deterred by repeated carjacks, few westerners, even in Land Cruisers driven by Yemeni drivers, dared speed down the highway past the slow-moving trucks and battered saloon cars of the local people.

From Marib a pitted old road ran east through the desert for another hundred kilometres before entering Wadi Hadramawt along its northern cliffs. Only rarely did vehicles from Sana'a reach this remote region but the old road was a vital conduit for the Bedouin tribes of the valleys.

Beneath the northern wall of Wadi Hadramawt, Mahmoud and Rashad now trotted westwards over the broken asphalt of this old road. In the near distance a dusty square tent stood on a low hill, its canvas flapping untidily. Below it a mound of stone and cement and a tatty white flag marked a primitive checkpoint. Three dishevelled soldiers in dirty green uniforms were resting on the ground in the shade of the tent and the brothers headed for them, reined in their horses, and dismounted to squat in the sand.

"Anything happened?" Mahmoud asked perfunctorily.

One of the soldiers looked up at him and grinned, before opening a toothless mouth to speak. "We found this in the sand after you left." He held a brown leather wallet which he tossed over.

Mahmoud picked up the wallet, opened it and took out several plastic cards and a piece of paper which he unfolded carefully to read. "He is a tourist. The paper is stamped by General Geshira, authorising him to pass through your checkpoints." He read the name written in English. "Gary Turnbow," he declared guilelessly, not mentioning that it said 'Dr Gary Turnbow'. "Was there no money?"

"No just the wallet," said the toothless soldier. The others nodded in agreement.

Mahmoud ignored the lie for he was intrigued by the American's permit, surprised to see the authorisation by Geshira. "Why were you going to kill him," he said? "He has a permit signed by your General." And why was he here, he thought, so many kilometres from Marib?

"Orders," said the toothless soldier, a spokesman for the rest. "We follow orders from Captain Abdullah." He paused and looked in the direction of the army camp, hidden behind a low hill to the west of Karim. "You should not have stopped us, Mahmoud. You will be in trouble with the old men."

"I can look after myself." Mahmoud snapped back and spat in the sand. "It is you who are in trouble." It was true. He was not worried about the town elders. But as he spoke he glared at the soldiers and then looked over at his sullen half-brother squatting silently, running sand through his fingers.

'Dr Gary Turnbow', he read again the words to himself on the crumpled permit. Why would Captain Abdullah give orders to kill an American tourist. An American doctor? A shiver ran through his body despite the heat. It had been weak to save the life of that man. Would it be a deed he would live to regret? And could he ever achieve his dream and leave the desert for good?

THREE

Benjamin Bone and Tom Fetters, a rangy, bony man with rare wisps of blonde hair, sat amongst the early evening crowd in a noisy pub in West Kensington in London. Benjamin held a slim stapled set of quarto pages open in his hands.

"It's a brilliant idea," Tom was saying. "You drink some Coke from a big plastic bottle which is so much cheaper than Coke in the small glass ones. The bottle has a concertina-like surface which collapses to fit the space of the remaining Coke. Then the fizz can't escape. You know how annoying it is to find half a bottle of flat Coke in the fridge."

"No, I don't," Benjamin said irritated. "Anyway get to the point. What about this company?" Benjamin waved the papers in his hand.

"I told you, it's a normal company," answered Tom, who liked to think of himself as an inventor but was actually an accountant. A decade previously he had shared a flat with Benjamin at Exeter University. "It makes no profits. All its assets are high risk. It needs to grow."

Benjamin flicked through the pages. It was a draft of the annual report and accounts of Outland Oil, detailing its assets, finances and plans for the future. The report had been the only thing in the red-haired man's briefcase.

Early yesterday morning at the long term car park of London's Heathrow airport Germaine had sat in the car while Benjamin had opened it, standing alone away from other cars. He had told her to stay where she was should the bag contain explosives. Germaine had been unimpressed. "Or nerve gas," she had said.

The case was not locked and it flicked open smoothly. Inside was the report, with a bright photograph of an oil rig at sunset glued onto its cover page.

"How can Outland Oil grow with no profits?"

"They have licenses to explore for oil in different parts of the States. They are hardly looked at before, so cheap to buy. Small companies add value to exploration areas by studying them. Then they look for partners. These will be oil companies with cash who they persuade to fork out the money to drill a well or two and maybe find oil. It's called a farm-out."

"I know. And Outland will keep a share."

"Yes, if the wells find oil, a share in the profits without having to take the big risk."

"Is the company solvent? They must need funds. Where do they get them?"

"Outland has a little oil production in the States and small amounts in the North Sea too but not enough to pay all the overheads. It relies on shareholders putting in money in the hope of a big strike. There is big money in oil if you can find it."

"Why should anyone want to invest in a company like this? Surely a big oil company would be more likely to find something. I've never understood how small ones survive."

"Big companies have bigger overheads, but you are right I wouldn't invest my money." He sipped his beer, reflecting for a moment and then went on. "Of course once in a while someone does make it big. The big oil companies were small once weren't they? They get lucky and find an oil field. Of course, the oil price has to go up as well."

"Its reports like these...," he pointed at the papers in Benjamin's hand, "...that try to convince investors to come up with the cash. The accounts are audited before they can be printed but most of the stuff in the front is bullshit. Just advertising."

"Why the hell was that man so agitated about this report?" Benjamin spoke more to himself than to Tom. "So Outland is an ordinary oil company?"

"Yes that's right...." Fetters paused as a group of rowdy youngsters left the bar, "...but there is one thing." He took the pages from Benjamin and flicked them open to a photocopied picture of a sandy plain and a solitary camel. Embossed on the sky was a map of the Middle East. "Here it is. It's called Wadi Qarib. It's in the Yemen."

Benjamin took it back and looked at the picture. "What thing?"

"Outland is going to drill a well here. On its own. No partners. No outside money. It's going to need a lot of cash. They will never be able to borrow the money for something like this. But someone must be financing it."

Benjamin was interested. "I applied to be the operations geologist on that Yemen well."

"Oh," Fetters looked surprised. "Lots of companies take long shots once in a while...."

Benjamin frowned.

"Oh gosh, I didn't mean you were the long shot, I meant the exploration license. I'm always putting my foot in it."

Benjamin nodded, remembering how his friend had once asked Germaine if she wanted to borrow things for her baby while complimenting her on the size and shape of her belly. It had been three weeks after her miscarriage.

"Anyway this license in the Yemen would have to be very good to justify putting the company at risk. The company is valued at forty million dollars. Just one well could cost over ten million."

"At risk?"

"If it doesn't strike oil the shares will plummet. They'll never be able to raise money again. The stock market will remember this for years. Unless of course the oil price shoots up and then every back-street oil company is hot. When I joined the business money was pouring into all kinds of cowboy outfits. Take the job if you can get it."

"Yes I will. But is there nothing exceptional here. Is that what you believe?"

"Belief is what people use to justify an opinion where there is not enough evidence," Tom said smugly. "So I don't believe anything. Anyway it looks OK to me, but really risky." He flicked through the report once more.

After a pause he said. "There's always someone with more money than sense, particularly in America. Outland must have the cash from somewhere. Can I keep this? I'll have a close look at the figures. Its weird how you got it."

"Yes, of course, it's probably nothing anyway."

A clock chimed on the wall and Fetters glanced at his watch. It was seven o'clock. "Look I've definitely got to get back. Sally is going to aerobics tonight and I'm supposed to baby sit. She'll give me hell if I'm late."

"At least you have someone to go back to."

"Germaine's not coming back then?"

"No," Benjamin answered gloomily. "But I'm over it now," he lied.

"Good for you. I always found her…" he paused "too glamorous for you."

Benjamin ignored him. "Go on, have another drink."

"No I must go. It's OK for you, but I've got a wife at home waiting for me." He got up awkwardly. "You get yourself another girl, Benjamin. You can't live on your own." He rose and put on his jacket.

"Yes, Tom. Thanks for your help. I'll be seeing you." He watched his friend leave then drank up and left too, not knowing what he would do for the rest of the evening. He was lonely and bored.

He arrived back at his empty flat a couple of hours later after taking a long walk along the Embankment. It was a cold, dry night for the time of year, the wind coming from the northwest. Chilly gusts were blowing through the open window of his living room. Germaine's house plants were already wilting and he knew they would all die. His answer phone was flashing and he pressed the red button.

"Bonjour Benjamin." It was Germaine's voice. "I have something to tell you urgently. Please call me back when you get in. I'm at the house of Gilles Duval. The number is in our address book. Please call as late as you like."

What does she want now? She's not coming back here. Of course he knew she had no wish to come back and, what's more, he probably would have welcomed her. She wants me to send her electric shaver, he thought. He had found it in the bathroom cupboard that morning. Contrary to English public opinion on the French, she had been obsessive about her armpits.

He looked up Gille's number and dialed.

"Allo!" A Frenchman answered.

"Gilles, its Benjamin here, Benjamin Bone. Germaine asked me to call her."

"I am very well thank you. I will get her right now. Hold on to the telephone please." His voice, in English was heavily accented and polite. Gilles had been Germaine's boyfriend before she and Benjamin had met.

After a moment the receiver was picked up and Germaine spoke.

"Why did you take so long? I have something urgent to tell you." Her voice sounded anxious.

"What is it? I've only just got in."

"Where have you been so late? You should be there....at home."

The logic escaped him. "What is it?" he said again.

"A dead man was found in the cargo hold of an Air France airplane when it arrived in Paris yesterday. The plane came from Houston. There was a photo in the paper Benjamin. It's a red-headed man. He was the one you saw."

Benjamin's mind was racing. "He must have hidden in the plane," he said after a moment, "you can't survive in the cargo hold. It's too cold...no air."

"Yes, Benjamin," Germaine interrupted. "The paper said the same thing, but after what you saw...." Her voice trailed off.

"Could you post me the cutting?"

"OK. What about the papers in the red case? Did your friend find anything?" There was an edge to her words. Germaine had never liked Tom Fetters.

"No, it's just a photocopy of the annual report of Outland Oil. God knows why he stowed away on a plane."

"But those papers must be important."

"Well they're not." He spoke sharply but did not know why.

She was quiet for a moment. "It was an accident," she finally said. "He hid from the police, what a silly thing to do? Why don't you ask the oil company if they know anything?"

Benjamin wasn't convinced. He remembered the face of the red-headed man, the fear in that face, and the weasel-faced Micky Bauss and the big Texan guard called Jim. "Yes, I'll ask Outland Oil."

"Call me if you find out anything please."

"You're not coming back then?" He regretted saying it immediately.

"No I'm not. I don't want to come back and you don't want me. I know it."

"I don't?" The red-haired man was forgotten.

"We have changed and now we can meet the rest of our lives with a new beginning."

"You French are so pretentious."

"Benjamin I'm quite happy," countered Germaine. "You should be too. It's been difficult these last two years... since the miscarriage. Once you get a job you will know everything is for the best." She spoke in a congenial tone. "Take more care of your appearance, comb your hair."

She stopped abruptly as if diverted. "Oh by the way," she went on, "could you post me my shaver? I think I left it in the bathroom."

FOUR

Nest morning Benjamin Bone decided to pay Outland Oil a visit. The company ran a small office in Lincoln's Inn Fields in Central London and he rang to make an appointment with the Managing Director. Wearing his best grey suit he left his flat at ten and walked up the street to Notting Hill Gate to take the Central Line to Holborn.

At Holborn he took the escalator to Kingsway and walked to Outland's office on the second floor of a Victorian terrace overlooking the square. He climbed the narrow staircase, nervously combing his hair with his fingers. A girl with fat cheeks and dyed blonde hair swept high over her forehead, sat at reception. The room was small. One door led off to a small kitchen, the other was closed. The girl looked up from her screen, "Hello, what can I do for you?" Her voice was friendly but sharp. She spoke with an American accent. She had a hint of moustache above her upper lip.

"I'm Benjamin Bone. I spoke to you earlier. I have an appointment with Mr Greaves."

"Yes, Mr Bone. Please take a seat and I'll call him. Would you like something to drink?"

"No thanks," he answered nervously.

Her plump figure was crammed into a short blue denim dress and a tsunami of cellulite rippled over her thighs as she crossed the room to the closed door.

Benjamin perched himself on the arm of a richly upholstered armchair in the reception area. Magazines lay on a low table next to it and he flipped through the pile, looking for a copy of Outland's annual report. He tried to plan what he would say but nothing came to mind. He didn't find the report so he picked up a copy of the Oil and Gas Journal and flicked through it without reading anything. Moments later the girl returned.

"Go in. Mr Greaves will see you now."

Greaves' office was large but dimly lit stuffed with lush oak furniture. Its walls were hung with expensively framed lithographs. A sash window flanked by heavy curtains overlooked the Law School on the other side of the square. There was an oval desk and a leather chair below the window alongside two easy chairs. Greaves, who looked to be in his early fifties, was standing, staring at a file in his hands. He wore a dark suit and had black, thinning hair. His high forehead was disguised by a greasy quiff that swung carelessly in front of his bright, deep-set eyes. Typically for tall men his shoulders were rounded, his upper back arched. His eyes gleamed. With the arched back Benjamin thought of an angle poise lamp illuminating the gloomy room.

"Please come in and take a seat Ben. How did the interview in Houston go?"

Benjamin moved to sit opposite the desk but Greaves shepherded him to an easy chair facing the window. Greaves sat opposite, silhouetted in the dim light.

"It seemed to go fine. Haven't you heard from them?"

"No. I never get told anything. We aren't important in this office."

"So you can't tell me whether I have a chance?"

"Of course you have a chance. We wouldn't have paid for a flight for you, and for your wife, if you had no chance. Would we?" He spoke patronisingly, in a clipped English accent, like a disappointed father. "No, I can't tell you anything new. I'm sure Earl Rittman will get you a response soon."

"He said he would call me. I haven't heard anything."

"Come on Ben. Rittman is a busy man. He has other things on his mind."

"Yes of course. So I can expect an answer soon?"

"What exactly do you want Mr Bone? You won't be working for me so Houston has no reason to keep me up to date." An impatient tone had entered his voice but he was still smiling.

Last night Benjamin had lain in bed wide-eyed. He had decided to visit merely for something to do. It had seemed a good idea at the time but now he was regretting it. Greaves was staring at him.

"I'm anxious you see…" Benjamin said eventually. "…I just thought I'd ask." He paused a moment but Greaves maintained his gaze. "You see I was reading your annual report," Benjamin went on. "I thought the finances for the exploration program in Yemen looked...well, risky." He tried to paraphrase Tom Fetter's words.

For the briefest of brief moments Greaves reacted. A merest widening of the eyes and a protruding of the jaw, but it was gone so swiftly, Benjamin, who had an eye for these things, dismissed it. "We don't handle any of the finances of the company from here. We oversee our UK interests. You will find the company is well regarded in London. And New York. Are you a finance expert, I thought you were an operations man?"

"I'm not an expert. I'm sorry. It's just…, I have to work on the project...It's better to be sure..."

"You can always turn the job down. Or I can call our people in Houston and say you no longer wish to be considered." His pained voice was withering.

"I still want to be considered. Don't do that…"

"Ben, if you worked for us you would be privy to highly confidential and sensitive information that can make or break a company. What we want from you is not only vision but also professional conduct. Do you appreciate what I am saying?" He stopped and stared again.

Benjamin waited for a moment, hoping it was a rhetorical question as he had no clue what he was supposed to say. Greaves just stared. Evidently an answer was expected. "Yes, of course," he finally said weakly.

"Is that all then?" went on Greaves, apparently happy now.

"Er yes, thank you. Thank you for your time." Benjamin rose from his chair. He was now sure that everything he said was a mistake. But he looked back at Greaves regardless and asked. "Did you meet the other man interviewed?"

Greaves stared. Even his smile had disappeared. "Other man? You were the only shortlisted candidate. Rittman was interviewing no one else."

"But after me ..."

"No one else. If you can do the job, you will get it. Thank you for coming, but I am a busy man." He got up and extended his hand. "Goodbye, Mr Bone."

Outside in the lobby a Chinese girl was talking to Greaves' secretary, leaning against the reception desk, clutching a large envelope. An airline ticket lay on the desk. She looked at Benjamin and smiled, her red lips apart. Benjamin smiled back.

She was small and slim, wearing a black, tight fitting dress. Benjamin was instantly attracted to her. Her eyes transfixed him. They were large and round and deep blue.

"You are Chinese but you have blue eyes?" he said stupidly, nodding his head as he spoke.

"Yes I am," she laughed and glanced sidelong at the plump secretary.

Benjamin felt himself turning red. "Goodbye," he said, unable to look directly at her eyes, instead looking foolishly at the secretary.

"Goodbye." Both girls answered at once.

As he descended the stairs the nape of his neck tingled. He was sure they were both laughing at him?

Back in Outland's office Peter Greaves stood looking out at the green square. He had spoken brutally to Bone, but it had been necessary. It was a way of speaking he had mastered in America. It was designed to be authoritative whilst commanding respect. Unsurprisingly it had a different effect on his colleagues, engendering dislike and fear. But Greaves was satisfied, fear and respect were interchangeable to him.

But he was worried too. Why did Bone say the finances were risky? What did he know? The finances were not risky at all.

FIVE

It was early in the day and Earl Rittman, the Chief Executive of Outland Oil, was bellowing at his secretary through the open door of his thirty sixth floor office in the west of Houston. He spoke in a haughty, condescending tone.

"Yes, Earl. What now?" Claudia, his receptionist and personal secretary, replied with just enough volume to be heard. She had worked for Rittman for over six years and, for her at least, the arrogant voice disguised a benign nature.

"Get me Kraill on the phone. I can never get through."

"OK, sir."

Claudia Pasquale secretly adored her boss. She was from Mexico and had big brown eyes, thick black hair and smooth dark skin. But she was not blessed with the voluptuous beauty of so many of her compatriots. Her head was a little too large and her frame a touch too long.

Although she was proud of her Mexican roots she was indebted to her boss for getting her a work permit and green card in the States, allowing her to get a job and help her parents. But this was not the main reason for her adoration. It had begun after her husband had been arrested for forging travel documents and smuggling immigrants across the border near El Paso.

Rittman had offered bail money and a defense attorney but her husband had skipped bail and disappeared. Although he had been re-arrested a year later and was summarily deported back to his home town of Caracas, Rittman had not got his money back. To Claudia's surprise and gratitude he had not once complained to her and never even hinted at blaming her.

So she dialled the twelve digits for Yemen, smiling as she did so, cradling the receiver on her shoulder and doodling on her shorthand pad as she waited for a connection. The line clicked repeatedly, there was a short low whistle followed by an extended ringing tone. Finally a distant American voice answered, "Outland, Kraill speaking." The voice was businesslike and fortunately this time the line was free of noise or feedback.

"Hi it's Claudia. Mr Rittman would like to speak to you. Are you free?"

"I'm always free for Rittman. What's he want? Did he get my fax?"

"Yes he got it, he sounds mad."

"You can cool him down?"

"Are you scared of him Emmett?" She spoke good-naturedly.

"No, Claudia. But I don't worship him, like you do."

Claudia cut him off straightaway and buzzed Rittman. "Emmett's on the line."

Inside his office Rittman picked up his phone, leaned back on his chair and perched his feet on the desk. "Kraill, what have you to report today?"

"A lot," he said after a pause, "you saw my fax about the riots this weekend?"

"Yes, what do those Muslim fanatics want? They lost the election. They should shut the fuck up. I read in the Wall Street Journal the international observers thought the election was fair."

"Don't worry. The people don't want those fanatics in power any more than we do. But the real problem right now is in the south. The leaders in Aden are unhappy. A civil war would screw us up."

"Will there be a war?"

"I was speaking to Dick Collins at the Embassy a couple of hours ago and he said the southerners don't have the capacity to do anything. He said be careful and carry on as normal. None of the expats are evacuating. Everyone's gonna have to compromise. The government's got no other option. The Embassy's putting pressure on the president to deal with them."

"I hope he's right Emmett. These guys are fucking crazy." Rittman rarely swore and was conscious of how his language changed when he spoke to operational staff. He knew he was a little afraid of them.

"Yeah life goes on as normal. Actually you are right about the riots. It's the fundamentalists who could screw everything up. And of course the tribes out east with their own little armies."

"Any news on the missing American?"

"Collins tells me he was a doctor on a mercy mission. The name's Turnbow. The Yemenis are keeping it quiet. Bloody idiot, he had no guard and hadn't even told the Embassy."

"Where was he going?"

"To Marib. To see the old city ruins we presume. A Russian doctor at the hospital told Collins the guy had been planning a trip before flying home. Our Embassy didn't know he was missing for three days. Can you believe it? They only found out when his wife reported him missing when he didn't turn up in Denver. The Yemeni army's out looking. The area is mostly desert but there are a dozen big towns out there. He could be anywhere."

"Does this Collins guy think he had an accident or what?"

"Someone would have found him by now."

"Make sure all our personnel only fly to our airstrip at Qarib. No driving."

"The Twin Otter will fly twice a week and all our crew changes will be by plane."

"Good. And the rig?"

"It's arrived from Somalia but its junk. It's got a bunch of bullet holes."

"Fix it up. I don't want any delays."

"Sure. The road up the wadi is ready. We'll truck it in a couple of days. We're going fine. But what about the operations geologist you promised. Bob Janek's a great driller but he can't handle the technical stuff. Nor can I."

"Sorry, Emmett. You and Bob have gotta handle it. We're not going to hire an ops man now. Call Ray Bowes here if you need any advice."

"What!" Kraill burst out angrily. "You were interviewing someone from London. You know as well as I do Bowes has no idea what goes on outside Texas!"

"It's decided Emmett. Have you anything else to report?" Rittman spoke with finality.

"No… nothing," he said, "but we don't want more problems... I advise you to reconsider. Anyway, you're still flying out for the party?"

"Yes of course."

"OK, I've asked Teri to take care of it."

"Ask her to call me. I'm bringing a VIP guest."

"Who's that?"

"That's all for today." Rittman ignored Kraill's question. "I'm relying on you for a smooth operation. This well is important to Outland."

"I won't let you down," Kraill replied, accepting the responsibility, knowing he was paid to do that but still angry about the geologist. "I'll talk tomorrow."

Rittman hung up and placed the copy of Emmett's fax into his out tray. A few moments later Claudia came into the office. She sat on the corner of his desk and Rittman noticed at once the shortness of her skirt, the suggestive way she crossed her legs and, not for the first time, his heartbeat quickened. He wanted Claudia but he wouldn't cheat on his wife.

"Jason called while you were on the line. He wanted to speak to you about his exams. He thinks he's flunked them." Jason was Rittman's son, twenty three years old, a handsome boy whose laziness was legion. "He says he's going to Europe if he fails,"

"Call him back and tell him I'll meet him for lunch to discuss it."

"Let him go, Earl. He can look after himself."

Rittman was about to disagree when the phone rang, its shrill tone making them both jump. Claudia reached for the receiver, her hand brushing his.

"I'll take it, Claudia," Rittman said quickly, picking up the receiver. "Yes. This is Earl Rittman," he said as Claudia slid off the table and left the room.

"This is Congressman Steeples. What's the latest?"

"Oh Congressman, of course, sorry," he said. "It's all running smoothly. We expect to spud on target."

"You expect? Is it or isn't it?"

"It is, but in this game delays are always possible. Yemen isn't an easy country to work in."

"I know about Yemen."

"It will probably be on time. OK." Rittman was deliberately evasive. "And about the trip next week…?"

Steeples interrupted him. "We'll talk tomorrow." The line went dead and Rittman cursed into the receiver.

Claudia put her head round the door. "Mr. Bauss is here. He's waiting in reception."

"Send him in." He paused, "No, let him wait five minutes and then send him in."

Rittman rose from his chair and looked out at the city beneath him. His office had a broad view of the flat, sprawling suburbs of west Houston and beyond. In the haze he could see the downtown area surrounded by forest. To the north behind acres of red-roofed suburbs a plane was landing at the international airport. The only other visible movement was from the neighbouring tower. Through the windows he could see neon-lit offices, men in white shirts and women in sharp suits shuffling papers, tapping on keyboards or simply staring back at him through their own windows.

He was worried and wanted a moment to think. I know about Yemen, Steeples had said. How does he know? Congressman Steeples was risking his reputation on this Middle East well. There was money to be made, huge amounts of money, but Steeples was already rich. He didn't need money.

The fax from Greaves in London had stung him. The English geologist had visited the office, asking peculiar questions. Why? Of course he knew why. It must have been Brad Brockley. That red-haired idiot had walked in moments after the interview with the Englishman, opened his red case and pulled out that ridiculous report. What was he trying to achieve by threatening him like that? Rittmann was uncertain of himself all of a sudden. The consultant's reports were unequivocal, oil at Wadi Qarib was a certainty, but any unexpected thing could go wrong, not to mention the risks that were self-evident. Riots, terrorism, war even. He hoped that Dick Collins at the US Embassy knew what he was talking about?

And Micky Bauss, how to handle him? Rittman had an intense dislike of Bauss. He's a control freak, definitely not to be trusted. He turned from the window, scratching his bottom vigorously, uncaring of the watching eyes in the tower block opposite.

He shouted for Claudia and she put her head round the door again. "Can I show Mr. Bauss in now sir?"

Rittman nodded and moments later Bauss entered. "Hi, Earl. How's the well going?"

Rittman sighed to himself. He couldn't stand the man's abruptness. What business was it of his? "We haven't started drilling yet, Micky. I'll keep you informed."

"OK. But I'm afraid I have bad news." He sat down.

"What bad news."

"That Bone guy you interviewed. He's been asking questions in London."

"What sort of questions?"

"He went to your offices."

"I know. Greaves told me. How do you know?"

"We decided to have him followed. I didn't trust him. Bone could have spoken to Brockley...," he paused, "...after your meeting."

"Why didn't you tell me you were following him? Who was following him anyway? You're an accountant."

"We do what is important for our clients." Bauss spoke tersely.

"Greaves told me that Bone just wants the job. I'm sending him a rejection letter and that'll be the end of it."

"Brockley must have talked to him."

"Claudia told me he didn't. They never spoke."

"At the airport, I mean. Anyway can you trust her?"

"Of course I can," Rittman.

"Then why was he at the airport so early. Looks like they were going to meet."

"You said he couldn't have met him there."

"Maybe so, but we are going to have to do something about Bone if he asks any more questions."

"Do what?" Rittman found Bauss's detachment unnerving.

"We'll think of something. Got any ideas?"

"No of course not. Is that all?"

"There's one more thing." Bauss's weaselly face stretched into a sneer. "Your son Jason will pass his management exams in the top five of his year. It's fixed, we'll give him a job."

"He definitely doesn't know you fixed them?"

"No, he doesn't know." Bauss smiled thinly at Rittman, "and he won't...." He paused for several seconds, "...unless I tell him."

When Bauss had gone Rittman picked up the phone and dialled. A woman answered.

"It's Rittman."

"Yes Earl. What can I do for you?"

"Buy Outland. One hundred thousand. Use your usual nominees."

"Are you sure? That's nearly a million dollars and your stock's weak today. The oil price has slipped a dollar since the OPEC meeting broke up last week. The market thinks most of them are gonna cheating on the new production quotas."

"Maybe so, but the oil price can continue to drop and Outland's shares will buck the trend. They were at 8.48 this morning. They'll be 10.00 by close. You trust me don't you?"

"Of course I do, you're the one who knows what's going on. You want me to spread it around your shares are hot?"

"What do you think? And sell Buckfast Energy short. Twenty thousand to start. Give me fifteen days."

"That's a lot of money. They're at 34.60."

"I won't need the money. Buckfast's collapsing. Domestic oil is at a twenty percent discount. The oil price is weak isn't it? You said so yourself. And they have no upside. We have."

"You mean the Middle East? Yemen? Come on Earl, its high risk."

"Our geologists know what they're doing."

"Sure, Earl. If you say so. I'll put it around?"

"Just say its speculation. Our shares are gonna skyrocket...," he paused momentarily "...and when Buckfast drops below 30 sell 20,000 more."

"I'll have trouble borrowing the stock."

"Do your best. They'll get good commissions. You will too. If anyone asks, you don't know what's going on and neither do I. I'll call you back after close." He hung up and looked at his writing pad. While speaking he had written Buckfast Energy in black ink. He picked up a thick pen and carefully and determinedly crossed through the letters. The nib of the pen crumpled under the force of his hand.

SIX

Sheikh Achmed, Rashad and Mahmoud's father, lived in near the centre of Karim in a huge mud-brick building with over three hundred stained glass windows. The Toyota Land Cruiser his sons had hijacked was parked in the walled yard, where bare-foot children usually played. Sheik Achmed had cursed his sons for taking the car, accusing them of being no better than bandits and shouting at them for jeopardising the future of Karim. But he had inwardly admired their nerve.

Achmed had called together the leaders of Karim and now, late in the evening, they were sprawled on the floor, leaning on hard cushions, in his diwan in the upper chamber. The room was large. It had line of decorated windows on two sides, a floor mostly covered by expensive but dusty rugs, and walls of white stucco plaster. The group of men, seven in all, were patiently waiting for dinner before discussions and chewing qat, the amphetamine-rich leaf, could begin.

Sheikh Achmed sat by the door, resting his bony limbs on a plump cushion. Although now an old man his bearded face looked strong and his eyes were bright. "We are all here. It is time to eat," he said.

Aluminium trays loaded with plates of hot food had been laid out on a cloth on the floor. Circles of yellow-brown bread blistered in the tannur oven were piled alongside pyramids of steamed rice and two bowls of oily soup. A pot of boiled mutton, plates of chopped tomato and red onion salad and small dishes of hulbah completed the feast. The men converged around the meal and began to tear themselves pieces of the bread. Hussain, a merchant who controlled the local marketplace and ran the cartel who set the yearly price of grain and rice in the region, poured a bowl of soup into the mutton pot. Grey chunks of meat and bone with globs of yellow fat slopped to the surface beneath an oily mist. The men plunged in their spoons. Hussain used his fingers to remove a glistening strand of meat soaked in oily gravy. He sucked the meat into his mouth, smacking his lips with pleasure.

Two boys appeared with a tin plate heaped with chopped goat meat, roasted to a golden brown. To make space the diners pushed half empty dishes aside and at once began to tear chunks of the stringy meat from the plumpest limbs, passing the choicest fragments to their neighbour. Dr Khaled, the town's only doctor, dressed in an ill-fitting polyester safari suit, sucked his teeth noisily, a scrap of goat meat lodged in his molars.

Ali finished first. He rose with a belch and stretched his legs. Ali was the head of the second great family, a rich man and director of the Investment Bank of Arabia, a family bank headquartered in the capital. He was dressed in a full length thawb, the gleaming white robe worn by many rich men in the desert, but he wore an ill-fitting grey jacket over his robe and the handle of a curved jambiya knife of carved rhinoceros horn jutted from a scabbard in his belt.

Replete, the men returned to the places on the floor at the far end of the room, leaned on the cushions and lit cigarettes. Bundles of qat branches thick with fresh leaves, green and shiny, had been placed next to each of them. Hussain was the first to tear the youngest shoots from the tip of a branch and shove them into his mouth. He chewed whilst dragging on his cigarette. Soon the right cheeks of all the men had swelled with masticated leaves. Sheik Ahmed's qat, with its powerful amphetamine kick, was grown in the most fertile plantations in Wadi Hadramawt.

The boys returned to clear the plates. Many of these, still piled with food, were destined for the women to enjoy at a more leisurely pace in their own room at the other side of the house. These women would laugh together, joking about their husbands and boasting about their children, in stark contrast to the serious atmosphere in the men's room.

After taking a drag from his cigarette, Sheikh Achmed spoke, his voice muffled by the damp, leafy bulk in his mouth. "You have all seen the car I am sure," he grunted. They all nodded except Dr. Khaled who was still digging meat from his teeth with the end of his grubby forefinger. "But you don't know we got more than a car...." he went on, then pausing to revel in the moment, "...we also got an American."

Hussain, the merchant, arched his eyebrows, his head tilted away. This deformity gave him a sinister appearance leading even his closest friends to distrust him. "What do you mean an American?"

"He was in the car, you fool," interrupted Ali, "and Achmed's got him locked up."

"How did you find out?" snapped the Sheikh.

"You think I don't know what's going on in my town. Get on with what you have to say."

"My sons, Rashad and Mahmoud, were out along the highway with your soldiers, Captain Abdullah."

Abdullah nodded. He was the head of the small army post but a local man whose allegiance was to his cousin, the Sheikh.

"We all know what young men are like," went on Achmed. "One of your soldiers killed the driver…he had not stopped at the checkpoint…" he looked at Abdullah without anger, "...and my sons took the American. The killing was wrong but it's done." He stopped, remembering how he had shouted at his sons angrily.

"We can't lock up an American," said Hussain. "There will be terrible retribution." His own son was rotting in an army jail in Sana'a following his arrest last year. He had also been hijacking cars.

"We must kill him," snapped back Ali. "There is no option. We can't let him go." He spat into a spittoon at his side.

"Why can't we let him go?" Latif was another of the Sheikh's cousins and a rich qat farmer. He was a tall gentle man with high cheekbones and a fat drooping upper lip. His wife, renowned for her humour amongst the women, compared him to an ancient camel, especially his eating habits and the odour of his farts.

 "Of course we can't, you fool…," Ali said.

"Let me tell you..." Abdullah the soldier interrupted, his piercing blue eyes staring at Latif. "The American knows a soldier killed his driver. Our government needs the Americans. They will have an excuse to raid the town. No, we can't let him go." He spoke slowly and carefully like a teacher in a primary school.

"We didn't kidnap him, Achmed's sons did," said Latif.

Achmed sat up smartly. "Captain Abdullah and Ali are right. We can't let him go." His words were spoken with finality. He looked across at Mutara. "You are quiet, Mutara, what do you have to say?"

Mutara's black face was impassive. He was a migrant from North Africa who imported silver jewellery from India to sell on to tourists and expatriates in the central souks of Sana'a and Marib. The vendors marketed them as local pieces sculpted by the few remaining Jews left in the country. He had also known about the American before coming to the meeting.

"I am thinking perhaps this man may be useful. With the oil company in Wadi Qarib we can use him wisely. But I am also thinking..." He spoke slowly and carefully, looking hard at Achmed, "...your sons are stupid and they should be punished for their stupidity."

"That is for me to decide," interrupted Achmed. "What then should we do with the American?"

"I've got it," butted in Hussain before Mutara could reply, "we will trade him for my son. Perhaps we could send the American Ambassador an ear... or something like that... to prove we have him. Yes, a white ear would be enough."

"Shut up, Hussain you are mad," shouted Achmed. "An ear! Are we barbarians?"

They talked for hours, chewing on qat and sucking smoke from bongs at their feet. Each had a point of view. Each was influenced by his own agenda. But at last Sheikh Achmed waved his arms at the windows where a blood-orange light was appearing as the new day dawned. "We have talked enough and are no nearer to a decision."

They turned to look across the weathered plain where shafts of morning light were striking through a deep ravine in the cliff face.

"We must vote," he exclaimed as if the idea had just come to him. "Like the Americans." There was a tired humour in his voice but only Hussain sniggered edgily.

"Yes!" said Ali. "Democracy. The Americans tell us to be democratic. A vote for everyone." He hawked and spat into the spittoon. "My vote is to kill him and leave his body on the highway so the American oilmen know what happens when they steal our oil."

"We have gone over this too many times," Hussain interrupted. "You are wrong. They will send troops to the town and we will be the first to pay for the man's death. We should trade him for my son."

"The position of your son is irrelevant to the vote," interjected Mutara.

"But we must think of him." He paused but no one spoke.

"No!" thundered Ali. "Kill him."

"Quiet." Achmed spoke softly but firmly. He slowly got to his feet. All the men's eyes followed him. He crossed to the window and stood for a moment staring out at the plateau, wishing he could decide on his own the fate of the pathetic American in his cell. I should have been decisive at the beginning. Now I am both cursing and protecting my sons. I am a weak, old man, with no ambition left. Ali and Mutara are strong. Money runs this town these days. Once I had a purpose. I wanted to make our tribe powerful but I lost my idealism when Rashad's mother died. Such a beautiful woman but she gave me such a stupid son. The government in Sana'a, supported by American money and influence, are too strong for us and our old ways. Without turning he muttered in a soft, sad voice. "We will vote then. Kill him or not?" He paused before repeating louder, "kill him or not?"

He turned to look at Dr Khaled, who had been asleep for much of the night but was now idly picking his nose, surreptitiously tasting its contents it on his tongue. "Khaled, what is your vote?"

SEVEN

The single entrance to the US Embassy in Sana'a was blocked by iron gates and a steel hump painted with yellow stripes. Guarded by Marines, even black limousines with flags on their hoods were thoroughly searched. But a sports club, swimming pool, six-hole golf course and four all-weather tennis courts were all crowded into the grounds and officials automatically became members of this club. Guests of members could come and go as they liked so Embassy employees attracted many friends. In return the Americans got invited to all the dinner parties and hotel functions in the city.

Today Marine Sergeant Cutler was in charge of the guards. He was standing a few metres behind the gates and had just waved through four white women in tennis dresses. Cutler was a tall muscular man with a thick neck and shaven head. His face was expressionless. He had been in the country only two months and was proud to be a Marine, proud to serve the greatest country in the world, proud to be associated with a group of men with a courageous history. You will work hard, his recruitment sergeant had told him, but you will party hard.

He cupped his hands over a match, a fresh cigarette dangling from his mouth. But as the match spluttered he saw a dirty saloon, its chassis barely off the ground, drive up the slip road to the entrance. Two of Cutler's guards, local men in smart American uniforms, were standing behind the gates staring through the bars at the car. It stopped by the kerb and a small dark man in torn jeans and a dirty T-shirt climbed out. Instead of coming towards the gates, he walked away.

Sergeant Cutler eyed the man curiously, blew out his match and replaced the cigarette carefully into its packet. "Hey, you can't park there," he shouted in English. The Arab did not turn around. "Are you deaf you moron, move that car!" The Arab began to run.

"Son of a bitch...," mouthed Cutler, "...get the fuck out of here...." he shouted to his guards as he threw himself to the ground. But just as he did so the car exploded.

Fortunately the two guards had also spotted the threat early and had been darting from the gates before Carter had opened his mouth. The explosion however, would not have thrilled a child at a fireworks party. The windscreen of the car did collapse due more to years of unattended cracks and chips than the effect of the blast. The driver's door flew open, along with the boot flap, and a cloud of dust billowed out, but the car remained intact, looking at least as road worthy as the majority of vehicles driving around the city.

Cutler stood up and wiped the dust from his lips. He took out his box of cigarettes again. The two guards crept out from behind the guardhouse and retrieved the rifles they had thrown to the floor in panic. The driver of the car was nowhere to be seen.

Two hours later, in a large windowless room in the Embassy building Dick Collins, the Embassy Security Officer, met with the Ambassador. Collins was just short of six foot with a sharp face and dark hair hanging limply over his large ears. His torso was long and straight but his legs were rather short.

"Only the detonator exploded," he was saying, "…if it had been wired correctly the blast would have been big enough to blow in the gates." He spoke firmly and confidently.

"Which group was it?"

"We don't know but I expect it was one of the northern tribes. They don't like us selling arms to the government."

"Well fortunately they seem incompetent," said the Ambassador.

"A stroke of luck. Our guards weren't much better."

"Who was in charge?"

"Sergeant Cutler. He's only been here a couple of months but he couldn't have done anything. There should have been guards outside the compound as well as behind the gates."

"Reprimand Cutler. Put him on one of the private houses instead." He reflected a moment. "Second thoughts he can guard my wife, Sergeant Hagler upsets her. That'll be punishment enough." He smiled at Collins. "Yes. And put two Marines at the gate at all times and two local guards outside. We can't have any more of this. It's your responsibility you know Dick."

It's your responsibility, Ambassador, he thought. I need more Marines in the Embassy, right here, not out ferrying wives around town. Collins lived alone in Sana'a. Divorced, he had little patience with men who brought their families to Yemen. It was a dangerous country and not a place for dependent women and children. But he said nothing.

"I need to talk to you about Turnbow, Ambassador. The doctor who has disappeared."

"Yes, what are you doing? I'm being pressured from the States. You better find him fast and get him out." The Ambassador sat behind his large desk, hunched forward, cocking an eyebrow and steepling his fingers. His name was Erwin Shelterman Jr. but everybody called him Ambassador, even his wife. What was striking was his hair, huge quiffs of grey shot from either side of his head like flying buttresses.

"Its my top priority," answered Collins angrily, "you know we've been approached by a Yemeni. We need you to meet this man."

"Can you believe him, do you trust him?"

"He's a powerful man and it's the only lead we've got. He wants to see you. I need you to make a decision."

"Are you saying we talk to him or not?" The Ambassador snapped back at him. He spoke with a husky, almost feminine voice and Collins winced again. But he hid his feelings, badly wanting a good appraisal and a transfer. Collins first choice would be Europe, preferably Paris, somewhere civilised. He had little dignity left after what had happened in Indonesia. And now he was sure his relationship with Teri Mayes was over.

"We should talk to him," Collins answered, "he's a powerful man."

"If you say so, Dick. You're the expert. We don't want another Lebanon, do we? But don't go inventing wheels that have already been invented."

"OK," Collins said, ignoring the idiotic remark. "When are you free to meet him?"

"What me? I don't want to meet him. You're in charge of security."

"He expressly said he wants to meet the Ambassador."

"These Arabs always make demands. Curt will do. Ask Curt to be there."

Collins held back his temper. Curt Gawain was the Deputy Ambassador.

"I don't think he'll do. You know Ambassador, it would be much better..."

"I'm too busy. Now find that doctor and get him out."

Collins flesh crawled. Too busy! He was sure the Ambassador's afternoon was booked for tennis.

Later in the day Collins drove his Ford four wheel drive through the imposing gates of a stone-brick house on the edge of the diplomatic sector of Sana'a. He parked in a gravel yard surrounded by a garden of cacti and miniature palms. A gardener stood watering the plants from a leaky hose. Curt Gawain, the Deputy Ambassador, driving a smaller Japanese saloon car, followed him through the gates and stopped with his rear wheels car parked on the hose strung across the yard. He got out of the car, slammed the door and walked to the house.

Gawain was a big man with short dark hair. It had mostly vanished from his shiny, round head so only a small patch of black down perched on the centre of his skull. He had a matching moustache and his walk was unsteady, duck-like feet pointed outwards, voluminous trousers draped over an unwieldy bottom. His physique made him look inept and much of his reputation stemmed from his looks. He actually had a sharp mind but few could discern it.

"Hey, Dick," Gawain shouted, "you nearly lost me in the traffic."

Collins ignored him and pulled the bell handle sharply. The door opened and a smartly dressed Arab servant ushered them into the lobby.

"Come this way please sirs."

They were led into a bright, carpeted room. At the far end was a rough wooden desk above which hung a framed black and white photograph of an extraordinarily impressive Arab man posing in uniform. They looked round the room then crossed to gaze at the photo. After a moment a deep voice behind them said, "He's my grandfather. He was a great man....."

They both turned. A tall, bearded Yemeni walked in through the doorway. He was wearing a brilliant white robe. His teeth were also brilliant white, shining through the dark fuzz of his beard. A a much younger man, wearing Western clothes, walked in behind him.

"...a great man, but unfortunately murdered when I was a boy."

"Murdered?" Gawain said.

"By the government. My grandfather dreamed of democracy. He had many followers but he was executed in the city square."

"We are sorry." said Collins.

"There is nothing to be sorry about. It was a long time ago when the fundamentalist government ruled the country under sharia Islamic law. They terrorised intellectuals like my grandfather, but he died bravely." He smiled proudly. "Most men kneel for the sword but my grandfather stood. Look I have a photo." He pulled open a drawer of the desk below the picture and took out a dog-eared, black and white photo. It showed a fierce-looking beard Arab standing in a crowded square. He held a curved sword embedded in the neck of another man, also standing, but with his head bowed. A gush of black blood was clearly visible.

Collins looked at the picture. "What about your father?"

"Oh, he was killed too. I was imprisoned but escaped to the town where my family comes from. That's Karim, in the east, near the border with Saudi Arabia. "I am Ali and this is Rashad, the son of my friend, the Sheikh. Please sit gentleman." He motioned to cushions lining the room. "Would you like tea?"

The Arab returned his photo to the desk drawer and sat cross-legged on cushions opposite them. He coughed and spat a gobbet of phlegm into a silver bowl by his feet. Rashad, who had not spoken, sat next to him.

The four men waited for the tea. They talked about the traffic, the unusual heat for the time of year and the quality of local restaurants. It was impolite to immediately embark on business. Ali regularly spat into his bowl, Rashad said nothing and Gawain added tactless comments.

"Shall we discuss Dr Turnbow?" Collins finally said.

Ali smiled and passed round the tea cups. "It's quite simple. America gives millions of dollars of aid to the government each year. Where does this money go? It leaves the country as fast as it enters. To Switzerland, to Cayman or somewhere else, but never to a bank here. Either you Americans are stupid or do not care. Our people never see the money...."

"We monitor funds tightly," interrupted Gawain.

"Tightly?" He spat again into the spittoon and Collins wondered where all his saliva came from. Pavlov could have used this guy.

"As I said it's simple. The Investment Bank of Arabia is a small bank. A bank for the people. I am one of its directors. I want half the aid budget to be paid into an account to be used directly for projects in the eastern desert. Where my people live. I did not kidnap your American doctor but I know who did. Do what I ask and I will find Dr Turnbow and bring him back."

"Where is he? Why should we trust you?" Gawain interrupted.

Ali spat again. "Can I trust you? You told me the Ambassador would be here."

"I have full authority to represent him."

"I don't trust you at all," said Ali forcefully, "but I can get Turnbow back to his family and I can distribute aid fairly. I am a good man, Allah be praised. Take it or leave it."

"We would need authorisation," Collins said, "and we will need to see evidence before we could do anything."

"My word is evidence. You get your permission, but get it fast. I will try to keep him safe but for how long I do not know. I do not control him and it will be dangerous for me to get him out."

Collins did not trust Ali. And the younger man, Rashad, also made him uneasy. With his hard face he was sure Rashad was not an educated man like Ali. He knew there was no way the aid money could be diverted, but perhaps these men would lead to Turnbow anyway.

"OK," he said, "we will do what we can to meet your demands. Won't we Curt? Keep Turnbow safe. You know how to reach us."

"We will expect your call in three days, no more." Ali spoke sharply, with a rasp foretelling another spit into the spittoon. But he didn't spit this time. He just rose and showed them to the door.

When I get my hands on that money, Ali thought, after the Americans had left, Sheikh Achmed will be unable to stop me. I will run Karim and I will rule the eastern tribes. Despite his long private argument with Sheikh Achmed, the old man had cast his deciding vote in favour of keeping the American alive. Achmed was so weak, believing in American democracy at the expense of common sense. How could stupid men like Dr Khaled and Hussain, who know nothing of politics, be allowed to vote? Latif too, caring about human life, even an American's. Democracy doesn't work when voters are stupid, in Yemen or anywhere else. But Ali was pragmatic. If the American was to live he could be used. And with Rashad involved, Sheikh Achmed would do nothing.

Rashad, standing by his side, was still angry that his father had refused to let him move the Land Cruiser to the border. So when Ali had suggested he come to Sana'a and negotiate cash for the American he hadn't flinched at betrayal.

The telephone rang later that day in an office of the Al Hadda army camp on the south-western outskirts of Sana'a. General Geshira removed his reflective sunglasses and picked up the receiver. Geshira was from Aden in the south and was taller than most of the other generals but he was fat and his face was pink and soft. After listening for a moment he said into the phone, "on the first day of next month I will order my men to attack the presidential palace. Provided I get the help you Americans are offering the battle will be short."

"Get it right Geshira" the man said on the other end of the line. "Everybody in Yemen knows about your troop movements. Are you incapable of doing anything in secret?"

"There have been leaks I know…"

"You'd better plug them. If you don't you'll be dead in a month. The President is not stupid."

"That's why I'm bringing it forward. Keep your part of the bargain."

"I'll keep it," said the American, "we'll put you in power and we'll support your army. Aden will win, but this thing has got to be timed right. I'll get back to you with the date."

"And the money?"

"You'll get your money in cash," the American voice said, "and another one million dollars will be transferred to your Swiss account as soon as the President is gone."

"Why?" Geshira said. "Why are you doing this? The President has allowed American companies to invest here, tobacco, the soft drink factory, oil exploration rights. He's no fundamentalist."

"No questions. You have what you want. We have what we want. This must be kept secret."

"But my officers must know."

"Nobody is to know about my involvement," the American said roughly.

"Of course, nobody knows about you. Why should I tell? And what about the kidnapped doctor?"

"General, he should be dead. He was supposed to be dead. In the States they care about this man and should your Government recover him perhaps public opinion won't be so supportive of you."

"I ordered him killed. My men made a mistake. Anyway what do I care about public opinion in America? America is not my home."

"Perhaps not. But you have a house in Washington and your boyfriend is studying in California. It would be a shame if he lost his visa."

"Don't threaten me! Do the rest of your people know what you are doing?"

"I'm not threatening you. I'm pointing out you need me as much as we need you. Where is Doctor Turnbow?"

Geshira smiled. "He's being kept in Karim. My man Captain Abdullah is in charge of the army base there. He's the one who messed things up."

"Why are they holding him? What does Karim want?"

"The usual I suppose. A share of the oil revenue...."

There was a pause before the voice on the phone said, "...but there are no oilfields near Karim."

"Surely you know," said Geshira, surprised, "an American company is drilling in a wadi, just forty kilometers from the town. There are rumours they are going to strike a huge oil field."

"If you are in power the money from the oil can be put to good use then."

The General smiled. He would soon have power over the northern Yemeni ministers paying his meagre salary. And money too. He could buy any young boy. "What do you want me to do about the doctor?"

"I've already told you, better he had never existed, better he was dead."

Across town in the diplomatic sector of Sana'a where the offices of the few western companies investing in the country were located, Emmett Kraill, General Manager of Outland Oil, was meeting his two expatriate staff after the local employees had gone home. They sat around a large teak table in a well-lit meeting room, decorated with local antiques and potted plants.

Kraill said, "give us a run-down Bob." Bob Janek was Outland's Drilling Engineer.

"Not much has changed. The rig's still moving east and should arrive at Qarib tomorrow. I've sent over four maintenance guys in the Twin Otter to meet it and they'll do repairs. Cosmetic only, the derrick can't be repaired. It'll be lucky if we can get below five thousand feet, the fucking state it's in." Janek spoke sneeringly, spitting out his words. He was a tall, bony man from Oklahoma with sharp, angular features and deep-set eyes. His mouth looked as if he had swallowed his lips, sucked in by a tiny vacuum cleaner fixed inside his trachea. Cavernous dimples in each cheek and a drooping nose added to this effect. What was left of his face was orange and lined from years in the sun.

"We don't have to go below five thousand feet. Ray Bowes has sent in a drilling programme. In fact the reservoir we are drilling is supposed to be only at around three thousand."

"Seems shallow?"

"That's the program. I guess it'll take two or three weeks to reach it."

"If Bowes is right about the rocks, there shouldn't be any problems. But you know as well as I do Bowes couldn't find oil in a fucking gas station." Janek swore freely. "Why aren't we getting anyone for operations?"

"We've been over this. I don't know. It's too late now anyway. Teri, if we drill for only three weeks we are going to be a couple of million dollars under budget. Haven't we already got the money in the country? We're losing thousands in interest every day." Teri Mayes was Outland's Finance Manager.

"Who said anything about saving money?" Janek was looking at Teri as he said this, believing her to be inept.

"You're the drilling engineer. You're the one who should have told me?" Teri snapped back. "If you don't like what Rittman is doing you should give him a piece of your mind, but that would not leave you with much left." She was a mousy blonde of medium height with clear fair skin.

"I just do what your buddy Rittman tells me," returned Janek, ignoring her laboured joke.

Kraill interjected, "you do what I tell you, Bob. It's my responsibility. Teri wasn't to know the well would be so shallow…. Now Teri, transfer all the excess cash back to the States. Did you call Rittman about the party?"

"Yes. It's arranged, the Yemeni Oil Minister is coming. Security will be tight."

"Who is the VIP that Rittman is bringing?" put in Janek who, despite his bluff, was always up for gossip.

"I'm not supposed to say," said Teri, "Rittman said don't..."

"What the fuck is that all about. Tell us," interrupted Janek.

"We can't tell the staff or it'll be all around town." She was deliberately trying to rile him. Janek had always been opposed to her posting here. She was inexperienced and a woman, which would put her at a disadvantage in a Muslim country he had said. Rittman, with Kraill's backing, had overruled him and, in fact, quite the opposite had been true. Her Ministry contacts were polite and respectful. It was the expatriates who had given her the problems.

Janek looked at her angrily. "Fuck it Teri. Stop messing around and tell me."

Kraill looked at them both and sighed. What the hell am I doing working for this cowboy company in this shithole of a country. But he kept his emotions to himself. Instead he said calmly, "Rittman asked Teri not to tell anyone about the guest and she is right to keep it secret. However Bob, we have to discuss arrangements at these meetings so perhaps it is better you know. He's bringing Congressman Jack Steeples."

"Oh," Janek said surprised, glad the stand-off was over. For all his macho image and abusive tone he was an old-fashioned man and didn't like to argue with a woman. "Isn't he the guy who rages about American oil policy and the danger of relying on imported oil?"

"Yes," answered Teri. "The Government here will not be impressed by his presence and the Oil Minister would probably refuse to come to the party."

"It doesn't make sense to me. Why risk upsetting the fucking Minister."

"It doesn't make sense to any of us," said Kraill "but Steeples is coming and we've got to make arrangements."

"Except for Dick Collins and the Ambassador," put in Teri, "no one knows about him so don't go shooting your mouth off in the Embassy."

Janek gripped the side of the table. If she wasn't a woman I'd smack her in the teeth, he thought. He turned pointedly towards

Kraill. "This company's fucked up, Emmett. When the well is finished I'm gone." He got up and walked out.

"At least we can agree on one thing." Teri said after he had left.

EIGHT

"I'm sorry we have to close now," said the short, stout librarian, her jet black hair dragged back over her head into a tight pony tail.

"Sure, I'm going," Benjamin replied, closing the map rack and collecting his notes together into an untidy pile. He picked up the old leather bound book from the desk

"Here let me take that," said the librarian. She grabbed it and hurried off.

He had spent the day in the library of the Geological Society in Piccadilly in Central London. It had been a fruitful day but he was bewildered by what he had unearthed.

It had not been difficult to find articles about Yemen but locating geological information on Wadi Qarib had been a laborious exercise. It was hardly surprising. This part of the country had seen no oil exploration and few Westerners had ventured up the wadi, let alone published information on the rocks exposed along its banks. It struck him that Outland Oil had chosen the most difficult piece of acreage to drill in the whole of Arabia.

After searching for nearly three hours he had walked to Gerrard Street to buy lunch. Typically he kept his lunches frugal, not wishing to diminish his shrinking bank account, but today he needed an excuse to visit Chinatown. After eating a bowl of noodles he strolled along the back streets, past crowded Chinese restaurants and well-stocked grocery stores and deserted English strip-joints with shuttered windows and dark interiors. During his third traverse up a narrow lane a matronly Chinese lady with bow legs and a beach ball stomach had shrieked at him. "You want girl. I get one for you."

"Oh no," he answered, "I'm looking for someone I know." It was a long shot, he knew but he was looking for the Chinese girl with blue eyes he had seen in Outland's office in Holborn.

"Ayeeyah, why so shy? I arrange."

Benjamin had left hurriedly, the woman cackling behind him shouting to her colleagues in Cantonese. He had walked quickly back up Shaftesbury Avenue and Piccadilly to the library, annoyed with his stupidity.

After another hour of flicking through old, barely readable manuscripts with tiny script he had found a brief description of an overnight stay by a Victorian geologist in the desert town of Karim. The account figured in a history book describing geological surveying in Arabia before the presence of oil reserves had ever been recognised in the Persian Gulf. The exploits of the Society fellows in those days amounted to little more than an expensive hobby but they took their work very seriously.

The librarian located a dusty bundle of papers referred to in the book. They were tied in red ribbons and he undid them cautiously while she watched over him. Fragile and brittle, they had seen no light for years. It took over an hour to inspect them before he finally found what he had been looking for, the actual hand-written field notes of the trip in 1884 the English geologist had made. Although the notes contained little of use to him, including descriptions of the flora and fauna, the meteorological conditions and careful observations on the psychotropic effects of local plants, they did refer to a field map the man had drawn while walking in the region.

The librarian found the map in an oak drawer in the chart room. It was badly torn, but an original hand-coloured chart of the area around Karim, covering all the main wadis, including Wadi Qarib. It depicted, in painstaking detail, annotations of every rock type and every surface feature encountered on his expedition. Since wadis have high rock walls the geologist could see much at the surface and, even in those days, could make an excellent map. The information was sufficient for Benjamin, with his modern knowledge of oil exploration, to make predictions about what lay below the ground.

The search for oil is a risky business, you can never be absolutely sure oil is present a mile or two below your feet. Only a well will do, and even then sophisticated engineering equipment is required to recover the oil so you can see it for yourself. Oil exploration is educated guesswork. There are certain types of rocks more likely to contain oil and certain types of rocks less likely. In many areas you can guess there is a good chance of finding oil but most oil wells will still fail. It is never possible to be one hundred percent sure of its presence. Conversely you can be sure of there being none and in these places oil companies never drill wells. They know the rocks are not suitable and there are no uncertainties.

And so Benjamin was bewildered. If the map was right Wadi Qarib had no oil beneath it, none at all. Around Wadi Qarib, and indeed around all the wadis near Karim, lay a pavement of hard metamorphic rock. Deformed by high temperatures and pressures, any oil ever existing would have been destroyed long ago. He had double-checked the co-ordinates of the map and they seemed correct. He had re-checked the map legend. It was faded but clear. Outland Oil were about to drill a multi-million dollar well in a hopeless location. What on earth for?

It had been a stroke of luck he had found this map. It was unlikely Outland Oil, a small company in Texas, was even aware of its existence, but an Outland geologist in Yemen should have studied those rocks in the wadi. A geologist couldn't fail to be aware of their importance and, if they knew anything of oil exploration, they would come to the same conclusion as he had. Wadi Qarib was just a dry valley in the desert. Of course the old map could be wrong but Benjamin did not think so.

He left the building as the librarian was turning off the lights. Outside the spring sun was hotter and he removed his jacket. He breathed a deep draft of warm air before turning right up Piccadilly towards Green Park tube station, tucking his pad of notes under his arm and extracting his train ticket from his wallet. As he did so his notepad fell onto the pavement and he stooped to pick it up. A man following twenty paces behind turned to gaze intently into the window of a shop selling Afghan carpets.

Benjamin would not have noticed the man at all but for his shoes. They were green canvas sailing shoes. Sitting on the cramped train in the morning Benjamin had seen similar shoes worn by a man in the opposite seat. They had thought they were unusual and he would have liked a pair himself. Benjamin walked on, turned into the station gates and descended to the platform.

It was crowded but he managed to stand on the platform edge directly at the spot where the doors of the train would open. He could barely see anything around him. The station was full of commuters on their way home. He stooped down and saw, amongst the crowd waiting further along the platform, those green shoes once again. Despite the warmth of the station Benjamin put on his jacket, folded his pad and stuffed it into the jacket pocket.

The man was wearing blue jeans but Benjamin could see little else of him in the crowd. A train arrived and when the doors opened he jumped on, waited a moment and then unsuccessfully tried to get off again. The doors were blocked solid by passengers entering behind him.

Whereas most city transit systems whirr and hum, perhaps with an occasional shriek, the London Underground system clatters and thumps and bangs, shaking its contents with no rhythm at all. Benjamin listened to the noise, clutching a hand rail and unable to see past the people surrounding him. At the next station he quickly stepped off the train, looked up and down the dimly lit platform, and stepped on again. No green-shoed man had emerged to follow him. Only now, strangely disappointed, did he suppose it was a coincidence.

He arrived back in his flat to find a letter from the United States on the coir door mat. It had been delivered by a courier service and he tore open the big plastic envelope;

"Dear Mr Bone – Re: Operations Geologist, Yemen.

Thank you for attending an interview in Houston for the above position. After careful consideration we wish to advise that we are unable to proceed further with your application. We thank you for showing an interest in our company and wish you every success in your future career. We will be pleased to keep your details on file for any requirements more suited to your expertise. Yours sincerely,

Manager, Personnel Services Division".

What do they mean more suited to my expertise, he thought angrily? The job was exactly what he is qualified for. But he was only briefly upset. There was no oil, and now it wasn't his problem any more.

He walked into the living room, switched on the TV, and sank into an armchair. A copy of the telephone directory lay open on the carpet by the sofa. He normally kept it propped by a bookend next to the phone and he put it back in its position. He thought once again of the blue-eyed Chinese girl he had seen at Outland Oil's offices and had searched unsuccessfully for in Chinatown. He remembered she had been standing at the reception desk holding a letter with the name of a travel company printed on it. Two words. Hee Ho or something similar. He flicked through the business section of the directory until he found "Travel Agents." Scanning the listings he stopped on the name Hi Ho Travel Company. Its offices were in the Strand, close to Outland Oil's.

He dialled the number. It rang twice and a women's voice answered.

"This is the Hi Ho Travel Company...."

"Could I speak to the Chinese girl with blue eyes?" He went red with embarrassment even though he was alone.

"...if you would like us to ring you back please leave a message after the tone."

He quickly replaced the receiver without leaving his number.

Almost instantly the phone gave a shrill ring. He was startled by the sound and his heart, already beating faster than usual, began to race.

He picked up the phone again. "Hello, yes," he stammered.

"Hi, Benjamin it's me." It was his friend Tom Fetters. "I would have called earlier but we promised to take Amy out for her birthday. She woke us at six this morning. Anyway that's not relevant is it? What I'm ringing about is that annual report you gave me."

"Have you found something?"

"Yes, actually I have. I was at a client's office yesterday afternoon. A broker. I was waiting in reception and they had a shelf of annual reports from most of the oil companies. I checked if a copy of Outland's was there." He paused for breath. The phone was quiet except for shouting in the background.

"Well was it?" Benjamin finally asked.

"Oh sorry, Amy burst a packet of crisps over the floor. Yes, yes it was." Another pause.

"So."

"I flicked through it and it was obvious immediately. The balance sheet and the cash flow statements were completely different. All the figures. Completely different. The same year, the same assets but their value was far more. Over two hundred million dollars more."

"What do you mean? Which was more?"

"The report in the broker's office of course. It showed Outland having assets of around two hundred and fifty million dollars based on an independent valuation prepared by a firm of accountants. Like mine. The same valuations in the report you gave me were just forty million dollars."

"How could that be?"

"I don't know. But the Middle East project in Yemen was valued at two hundred million in the broker's report, instead of barely anything in yours!"

"So what does it mean!?"

"I don't know. Why two different valuations? But I can tell you the number in the broker's report is wrong."

"But what do they mean?" Benjamin said again. Tom could be slower than a snail in a slowest-snail, snail race.

"Anybody who buys shares in Outland Oil will think this Middle East thing is big. I would stake my life on the fact your report is close to the truth."

"And if it is?"

"It's a can of worms. People will have invested in that company on the basis of the published valuation. And if they find oil out there, or anywhere exposing them to the market, the shares will go through the roof."

"And if they don't?"

"They're stuffed. A two hundred million dollar valuation for blue sky acreage is ridiculous."

Benjamin understood. He was absolutely sure the published report Tom had picked up was a fraud. What's more even the red-headed man's photocopy had overstated it. Wadi Qarib was worthless.

"Don't do anything Tom. Just write down everything you can think of."

"Sure, I've done some calculations. I'll get them to you Monday. I'm busy tomorrow with my family… unlike you," he sniggered, "I suggest you show it to …. I don't know who… the police."

Benjamin decided not to tell his friend about the map at the library. Tom seemed over-excited and he didn't want to give him a coronary with a family to look after. "I'll look forward to seeing you," he said, barely able to conceal his own excitement. "On Monday. Don't tell anybody."

"Mum's the word, Benjamin."

He replaced the phone and went to the kitchen. On the work surface was a letter from Germaine. It had arrived in the morning and he took out a number of press cuttings from French newspapers and re-read them carefully. The red-headed man had been found in the hold of the Air France flight from Houston. He had been jammed between two luggage crates. He hadn't died of cold or asphyxiation, his neck had been broken. One of the newspapers discussed his injuries at length. It said stowaways usually die of hypothermia, their bodies unscathed. It was unusual for cargo to move around and it was dangerous. It could make the plane unstable. The Houston baggage control should be investigated.

As Benjamin sat in his kitchen reading the articles another possibility flitted through his mind. Perhaps the luggage had in fact been perfectly stowed. Perhaps the man had been dead before the plane had even taken off.

NINE

Congressman Jack Steeples' speeches were renowned in the oil field communities of the southern States. His words were enthusiastic, controversial and, above all, patriotic. As he entered the hall where the annual dinner meeting of the Oil Club of Oklahoma was taking place, an expectant hush settled on the massed diners. The hall was packed. The chief executives of most of the oil companies with offices in Tulsa and Oklahoma City were present and many of those from Dallas and Houston had travelled up especially for this keynote speech. Journalists, politicians and other oilfield personnel made up the rest of the audience. A number of men and women, unwilling to pay for dinner, had also waited patiently outside and were now filing noisily into the rear of the auditorium.

Earl Rittman, with his secretary Claudia, sat near the centre of the room at a table for ten. Three oilmen and their wives, a young journalist from Denver called Richard Clapton and a retired geologist from Austin with thick grey hair and deeply lined features, were also at the table.

Rittman was speaking to the journalist about Dr Gary Turnbow. "We don't know if he's been kidnapped, there have been no demands. Kidnaps have been happening ever since Outland Oil was in Yemen. It's only because this one is an American we have all the fuss. The British had a guy taken in the south a couple of months ago. He was held for nearly four weeks. As far as I know the British Embassy did nothing to get him out."

"Sure but Turnbow's from Denver. He may be unimportant to you but he isn't to his folks." Richard Clapton was tall, with curly brown hair and a gentle, youthful face. His nose was rather large but, despite this, he was a handsome man and his good looks made him confident and easy with people.

It had not been mere good fortune that the Chief Executive of Outland Oil was sitting at Richard's table. Following up the Turnbow story for his Denver paper, it had seemed obvious he should try to interview Rittman. His company was exploring in the region where Turnbow had disappeared. Clapton had swapped his seat with a young engineer who had been happy to move next to Richard's colleague, an attractive female intern.

"The kidnapping doesn't affect your exploration in Yemen then?"

"No, of course not," Rittman replied earnestly, "our well will be spudding soon."

"Yes I know. Your shares were up forty five cents on Friday. The market's anticipating a strike. You think you've got a winner?"

"It's an excellent area." Rittman smiled. He had already made a paper profit of ninety thousand dollars and next week his shares would skyrocket. He looked up to the stage. The Congressman was about to begin his speech.

Congressman Steeples was in his late fifties, seriously overweight with grey hair and a greasy pallor. He wore a blue suit with roomy trousers, hitched up over his waist in a manner common amongst aging Americans. "Ladies and gentleman," he shouted, accompanied by shrill tones of acoustic feedback. "I am privileged to be here in Oklahoma and to talk to such an esteemed collection of oilmen. You and men like you in Texas and California, in Alaska and Louisiana, you are the men America relies on to maintain her position as the most powerful and influential country in the world. But her pre-eminent position is being jeopardised by actions close to your heart. It is the Democrat's policy, Democrat's who care nothing about the common people of America, Democrat's pressured by so-called environmentalists, the Democrat's policy to kill our oil industry and allow the import of cheap, subsidised, second-rate oil from the Middle East. Fools and charlatans have been entrusted with our future. Sooner or later those Muslims will control us, tear us apart." He paused and a murmur of approval rippled round the audience. "Meanwhile the Chinese look on and laugh as they steal our industries and our American technologies."

Looking around the room Richard Clapton was thinking that Steeples had summed up the main problem with democracy. It was 'fools and charlatans' who had voted this guy into power.

"You all agree with me, don't you?" Steeples continued. He stared accusingly at his audience. "You all agree with me and do nothing. Despite your own disgust at the way your historic industry is being treated you have so far been spectacularly unsuccessful at convincing Washington that oil imports, a decimated domestic oil producing infrastructure, and a declining productive capacity constitutes a threat to our nation."

Steeples slammed his fist onto the podium, knocking the microphone which generated another piercing whistle of acoustic feedback. "Do we have to pray for hurricanes in the Gulf of Mexico? Do we have to pray for freezing winters? Do we have to pray for wars in the Middle East before Congress will get up off its fat ass and do something about cheap oil imports? Don't sit back and accept it! Fight it! Lobby your congressman. Lobby the President. Let us explore. ...."

"You're destroying the earth." A loud voice boomed from the back of the auditorium and the audience turned their heads as one. A short, dark man stood alone in the central aisle. He had his hands on his hips and was staring at the stage.

Steeples peered over his reading glasses and microphone into the audience. "What did you say?" He spoke in a solemn tone, but his voice betrayed a fierce temper. The audience could see he was livid at the interruption and most of them let out a cumulative gasp of dismay. This was Oklahoma City and heckling at a dinner meeting, particularly the annual dinner meeting, and especially against the sanctity of the oil business, was viewed upon with as much distrust as atheism. Freedom of speech was not high on anyone's agenda.

"Oil burning heats the atmosphere. It will kill our children." The heckler shouted.

"There is no such thing as global warming," shouted Steeples. "Show me the evidence. There's none. The double-talking alarmists spread such nonsense..."

"If you wait for proof, it'll be too late..."

"Eject this man now!"

"Does no one care about God's earth..?"

Three muscular men in tight gray suits appeared from the left, roughly pushed away a waiter who was serving coffee at the rear tables, and grabbed the man's arms. "You must listen...," he shouted as he was dragged out through the swing doors.

At Rittman's table the old oilman was visibly shaking with fury. "Disgusting manners," one of the wives said loudly as the others nodded in agreement. Richard Clapton looked at Rittman and smiled wryly, for the moment forgetting their earlier conversation. He noticed that his secretary Claudia, who sat next to Rittman, was looking intently at her coffee cup. She seemed afraid to look up.

Steeples however, continued his speech undaunted. Citing examples of where the good men of Oklahoma City had received a raw deal, he tore into the government and especially into environmentalists, which he prefaced with the term 'so-called', for another fifteen minutes. He answered a couple of supportive questions and, to thunderous applause, walked resolutely from the stage before circulating round each of the dining tables, shaking hands and accepting congratulations for his positive and brave stance. Being a consummate politician he milked the emotions of the audience.

As he passed the table where Rittman was seated he paused to pump the hands of the oilmen and kiss their wives. Rittman rose and extended his hand, "Congressman, can I have a word later in private?"

Steeples took his hand and shook it violently. "Ah, Earl, good to see you again."

"I need to check with you about next week."

"I'll call you." He turned and looked at Claudia who had not stood up. "This must be your good wife. Pleased to meet you," He put out his hand to Claudia.

"No, I'm Earl's secretary."

"My wife couldn't come," Rittman interrupted.

"What's your name then?" Steeples said.

"Claudia." She gave a tight-lipped, insincere smile.

"Well Claudia, I represent the future of America. You Hispanics are lucky to have the United States as your ally but the border controls should be tighter. The more who come here, the fewer jobs available for you people already here, eh?"

Claudia said nothing.

"Good." Steeples went on, "must talk to the rest of them. Call me at home tomorrow Earl." He left for the next table.

"What have Outland Oil and Congressman Steeples got to talk about?" Richard Clapton put in. "You're trying to find oil in the Middle East after all."

"We're on a number of the same committees back in Houston. Everybody knows him anyway."

Rittman replied breezily but Clapton noticed uneasiness in his voice.

The room was emptying. Delegates were departing for hotel bars and the Petroleum Club bar to discuss the speech and decide what to do about the federal government. Rittman and Claudia stood up by their table as the crowd thinned. A voice boomed out from across the room. "Earl, how are you old boy? I haven't seen you for years. How's your cowboy outfit in Houston doing?"

Rittman turned to look at the speaker. A thick-set man in his fifties was approaching. He wore a grey suit hanging from his body like a sack. Next to him, and in complete contrast, stood a slim handsome woman in her forties, elegantly dressed with permed blonde hair. She smiled with fixed lips.

Rittman looked nervously at Claudia and beckoned her to accompany him to the door. "What do you want, Buckfast," he said. "We have nothing to talk about."

"I don't want to talk to you about business. I would like to meet your charming girl friend."

"Hello," Claudia said, "I'm Earl's secretary."

"I'm Sam Buckfast and this is my wife."

"My name's Richard Clapton," the journalist interrupted. "You must run Buckfast Energy."

"Yeah, and I've got damn good deals out now. You interested?"

"Oh no, I'm a journalist." Clapton answered.

"Oh really," the wife spoke innocently in a tone perhaps copied from the voice artist of Pinocchio. "How interesting. Which paper do you work on? Or is it television?"

"A local Denver paper."

"That guy murdered out in the desert, out where Outland Oil are exploring comes from Denver, doesn't he?" Buckfast said, looking back at Rittman.

"He has not been murdered, he's missing. We hope he'll turn up."

"Don't count on it. These Arabs would kill the lot of us if they could."

"Nonsense. You're more likely to be murdered in this city than over there."

"If you say so Earl," he looked at Claudia and went on, "Earl and I were partners once but unfortunately when the oil price dropped in '84 we had to split up."

"You double-crossed me you bastard."

"Careful Earl, that's slander." He turned again to Clapton. "Earl took me to court but there was no case. You lost everything, didn't you Earl?"

Rittman glared at him before saying, "I noticed your stock was down on Friday. Looks like Buckfast is suffering from the low oil price."

"Temporarily, yes. There's been selling but our production is solid and we have just acquired new production leases north of here."

"You must have overpaid."

"It was a good deal." Buckfast snarled. "Don't go spreading rumours or I'll sue you, Earl."

"Since when have rumours been a problem for you? Everybody knows your deals are rotten. Clapton you check up on this man's deals and you'll see a list of sucker companies who have found bullshit in place of oil."

Clapton was surprised at Rittman's aggression. Although their own conversation had been short and he hardly knew him, this outburst seemed totally out of character.

"Don't shout at me Earl. Outland Oil with its chicken shit Middle East exploration is no match for Buckfast. I own my company. You own nothing. They can fire you tomorrow and I can make sure they do."

Rittman took Claudia's arm. "Come on, we've got to go."

She followed him willingly, muttering a cursory farewell to Clapton and nodding implacably at Buckfast and his wife.

When Earl and Claudia were outside Claudia asked "I don't know why do you hate Buckfast so much but I can fully understand. He's a pig."

"We grew up together. He took my company and he took my girl. I'll get my own back soon. You wait and see."

"The woman, was she your girl?"

Rittman ignored her. "Don't mention his name again," he said with hostility, and then added. "Sorry, it's not your fault, let's go."

Rittman was in no mood to talk to his business colleagues so they caught a taxi back to their hotel. The weather had turned blustery and he recognised the signs of a spring thunderstorm brewing to the east. The sky was dark and ominous, the warm winds picking up.

At the hotel, Claudia said, "I'd like a drink before I go to bed. Will you join me Earl?"

Rittman wasn't tired. His mind was still buzzing from the meeting with Buckfast and he was angry with himself for losing his temper. A drink was a good idea. He needed to calm down.

"Sure, Claudia," he said. "Let me buy you one."

They walked to the dimly lit hotel bar. It was busy but they squeezed into a seat in the corner. He ordered a neat Jack Daniel's for himself and a Campari for Claudia. Her stockinged leg softly touched his thigh, and they both pretended not to notice.

"So what do you think of Steeples?" Rittman asked.

"I don't like him. He's racist and he's ruthless too."

"No one likes him. But he helps our domestic oil industry. How do you mean ruthless?"

"When he commented about the Mexican border I'm sure he knew it would upset me. He wanted me to react so he could argue. Politicians always win arguments. What is he to do with us anyway? Outland Oil must be the sort of company he detests."

"He's on our side. I don't know why, but money is money."

"He seems like the sort of man who'll do anything to get his own way."

"How do you mean?" Rittman trusted Claudia's intuition. Her brazen opinions about his business partners had saved the company money in the past. He was a hopeless judge of character himself.

"Please, let's not talk about him. Let's talk about ... something else." She had been about to say "about us." Instead she pressed her leg against Rittman's and the mutual pretence of ignorance made her feel horny. A shiver went up her spine.

"Steeples is financing the Yemen well," said Rittman.

"What? Why?"

"To make a political point I suppose, demonstrate America has become totally dependent on Middle Eastern oil. Show how easy it is to find and how we should be controlling it directly. He's coming with me to Yemen for the party out there but we are going to keep it quiet until we leave, so don't mention it to anyone." He paused. "Steeples is a powerful man and Outland will be big after this."

"I wondered why you took this Middle East license. We've done nothing like it before."

"It wasn't my idea but it's going to make me a lot of money."

"Whose idea was it then, Steeples'?"

"No, of course not. It was a board decision."

Rittman was now well aware of Claudia's stockinged thigh against his. He had asked his wife to accompany him on this trip but she had refused. She was depressed again and couldn't travel. She had been disturbed for years and only their son, Jason, kept her from breaking down completely. He had no intention of encouraging Claudia but he couldn't help enjoying the sensation.

"Claudia, have you got any savings?"

"Yes, some, why?"

"You'll make money if you buy Outland shares on Monday. I'll tell you when to sell."

"Isn't that insider trading?" Claudia said, not for a moment doubting the veracity of his advice.

"No it isn't. You are not a director of the company."

She didn't want to do anything dishonest but was happy Rittman cared, and trusted her. He must be taking a risk to tell me this, she thought. "I'll do it then." Claudia said, and finished her drink. "Let's go to bed." Seeing Rittman's look she smiled, adding, "I don't mean together."

Rittman nodded and rose from his seat, leaving a large tip at the table as he did so. He was surprised to feel himself shaking imperceptibly and his heart pounding unnaturally.

They walked to the elevator. Rittman, behind her, stared at Claudia's full bottom in her tight white linen skirt. There was no one else in the elevator and they stood side by side looking upwards at the illuminated numbers above the door pass by. Claudia's floor came first and as the doors slid open she looked straight into his eyes. She didn't speak but her expression was enough. Her hand brushed the front of his trousers and his knees weakened. "No, Claudia. My wife..." His mouth was dry.

"Never mind Earl. She won't know. Come to my room for a night-cap, nothing else." She had put her foot against the elevator door to stop it closing and it shifted impatiently.

Rittman stepped out of the elevator without speaking while Claudia fumbled for her keys. They walked to her room and she unlocked the door, pushed it open and went inside. Rittman followed, letting the door swing closed behind him. He failed to notice a man standing by the fire door at the far end of the corridor.

The man walked up to the room door, paused for a moment, and then continued on to the elevator.

TEN

Benjamin was having Sunday lunch with his older brother and sister-in law.

"I still can't understand why you left her," said Charlotte, "she was such a nice girl. And good looking too. Too good for you." Charlotte Bone was a plump, middle-aged woman with greying hair coiled round her head like an anchor rope on the deck of a ship.

"Thanks," Benjamin replied scornfully, "I've told you before. She left me. And I'm perfectly capable of looking after myself without Germaine or anyone else." Benjamin looked back at her, regretting he had come. Charlotte was critical of everyone and everything, although she seemed unaware that this sometimes hurt people.

But she was a jocular woman, very different to her husband who now looked up from his dessert, a frozen Pavlova covered in raspberries that were still rock hard. "I think it's a good thing," he said grumpily, "she was too bloody bossy for my liking. Remember how she kept complaining about my smoking at your wedding. None of her bloody business."

"Don't swear please Bertie. And you were blowing smoke all over her mother."

"Well I didn't know."

"You know I don't like you smoking, especially while you're eating. By the way Benjamin how is Germaine's mother?"

"She died of lung cancer."

"That's shit."

"Bertie I asked you not to swear. She died did she Benjamin?"

"No, I was lying."

"Benjamin, your incorrigible. Bertie, go and make the coffee."

Bertram rose from the dinner table. A sloppy paunch under his shirt hung over his trouser belt His bald head was yellow and shiny. A smoker's head thought Benjamin. Instead of going to the kitchen his brother crossed over to the television and turned it on. An advert for shampoo was showing and he looked at it for a moment.

"I don't understand this," he said, "the girl is gorgeous and she's rejected because she's got dandruff. I wouldn't reject her if she was covered in flies."

"Hurry up Bertie, Benjamin's been waiting for ages. It's so terrible for poor Benjamin..."

"...I can wait for coffee," said Benjamin quickly.

"You loved her didn't you?"

Benjamin didn't answer.

"OK, I'll go and make coffee then."

Charlotte ignored her husband. "What are you going to do Benjamin?"

"Nothing."

"You should try to win her back. She's probably just doing it to make you guilty."

"She's not coming back. I need a job. Are you going to ask at your place?"

"You are both stupid. Your marriage was perfect and you just messed it up. Yes, I did. Personnel say we've got nothing suitable." Charlotte was a computer manager with a big UK oil company. Benjamin had once worked on a contract with them and Bertram, who was an antique dealer, had met Charlotte at a work drinks party in a pub when he went to pick Benjamin up.

"I didn't expect anything."

"What about the interview in Houston. How did it go?"

"I didn't get the job. The company rejected me." He reflected a moment and then added, "...something's weird with that company."

"What do you mean?"

He told her about the annual report, about Tom Fetter's call and about the death of the red-head. He was talking about his detective work in library the when his brother returned with the coffee.

"When Benjamin was a kid he wanted to be an undercover agent so he could stay in bed all day."

"Shut up Bertie and listen to what Benjamin has to say."

He retold the story, completing it this time. "Wadi Qarib is hopeless. I'm sure of it."

"Sounds strange." said Charlotte, "I'll ask in the office tomorrow."

"No don't. Tom promised to get numbers to me tomorrow. Maybe I'll take them to the police."

"What the hell can they do, eh?" said Bertram. "Anyway, come to the warehouse. Finish your coffee. I've got new pieces to show you. Are you coming Charlotte?"

Benjamin spent the rest of the afternoon with his brother and sister-in-law in Bertram's warehouse. An old lacquered Chinese sideboard caught his eye. Bertram told him it was English, early 20th Century and not worth a lot but it reminded Benjamin once again of the Chinese girl he had seen at Outland's offices.

He left after five, catching the tube to Trafalgar Square. It had been raining and the evening was overcast but now the air was clear and fresh. He walked up the Strand, found the building easily and looked up at the second floor. There were fluorescent lights glowing from a number of windows. There would be no one there on a Sunday evening he was sure but he decided to go up anyway.

The offices of the Hi Ho Travel Company, on the 2nd Floor of Peninsula Plaza in the Strand, were small but ideally located for city business. The building, a shopping cum office complex, was built in the 1960's but had recently been renovated with a shiny glass fascia and marble entrance. The new appearance belied the antiquated nature of its utilities and Natalya Cheung shivered at her desk, chilled by the damp draft of an air-conditioning unit blowing at her neck.

She had been writing airline tickets for a party of Chinese restaurateurs. She liked to work on Sundays as it got her out of her cramped house in Ruislip which she shared with her brother, her mother and father and his mother. The office was a haven. She was tired of the nagging at home at weekends, mostly about getting a boyfriend before it would be too late.

She completed a ticket and was taking a sip of her Chinese tea when she heard a knock at the glass entrance door at the far end of the room. The view through the door was obscured by stickers and she got up and crossed over to see who it was. A tall, well-dressed man stood outside. She was sure she recognised him but couldn't immediately place him. "We are closed," she shouted, pointing at the sign.

"Can I come in?" the man called back his voice muffled.

"No. Come back tomorrow."

"I called you. Did you listen to my message?"

"You left that message. Why did you want me?"

"Let me come in and I'll explain."

"Why should I?"

"Please..."

Although to her the man seemed friendly, she was hesitant. But she did eventually open the door.

The Chinese girl was as beautiful as Benjamin had remembered. About five foot six, slim and elegant in a long white blouse, draped over cotton leggings. Her blue eyes were large and round, with darkened lashes.

"Hello," he said innocently, my name's Benjamin. I saw you in the offices of Outland Oil on Thursday. Do you remember me?"

"No I don't." she lied. After Benjamin had left Outland's offices on Friday she and Louise, Peter Greaves' secretary, had talked about him.

"You don't?"

"No. Why should I. Did you leave the message? How did you find me here?" She sounded irritated.

"I wanted to meet you. Your blue eyes are so striking. How did you get them. Sorry, that's stupid. That's a bad start. I should go out and come back in?"

Natalya Cheung couldn't help but smile. "You're half right," she said.

"Good answer. But blue?"

"My grandfather was British. He was a prisoner-of-war in Changi jail... in Singapore. It's a mystery though. The blue gene is recessive. There must have been a white man on my mother's side as well."

"I've been to Singapore. I stayed there often when I was working in the South China Sea."

"What were you doing?"

"I'm an operations geologist."

"What's that?"

"I make sure that the exploration runs smoothly when oil wells are drilled. Collecting rock samples, checking for oil in the samples, that sort of thing."

"Like Peter does at Outland Oil?"

"You mean Peter Greaves I suppose. Well, not like him at all. He's a sort of manager. He doesn't do anything. You said your grandfather was in Singapore. Are you from Singapore then?"

"Yes, but I've been in England for nearly 6 years. It's changed, changing all the time."

69

"Singapore?"

"Yes, of course. England never changes."

"Why did you come here?"

"I like England. Except for the cold. My father works in a Singapore bank in the city, I stay with my family."

"It's hotter in the summer."

"You call them heat waves. They last less than a week and the rest of the year is freezing."

"In 1976 the heat lasted all summer. Old people were dropping like flies."

"Because they won't take their cardigans off, and those crinkly stockings." She laughed as she said this and Benjamin did too.

"Can I buy you dinner?" he said.

"I have to finish these tickets."

"I'll wait."

"OK then, but I'll pay half for the dinner. You haven't a job."

"How do you know?"

"Louise told me. Peter's secretary."

Benjamin grinned. She did remember him after all.

While she finished her tickets he flicked through travel magazines on a glass table. Half an hour later she took a black cotton raincoat and white handbag from the hat rack by the door. She ushered Benjamin out before locking the office. They walked side by side up the Strand to Trafalgar Square then north to Leicester Square where Benjamin selected a restaurant in a side road.

"Do you speak Chinese?" he said when the waiter had gone.

"I speak Mandarin, yes and my dialect is Hokkien. I also speak Malay and I learnt Arabic in England. We do a lot of business in the Emirates and my boss thought it would be useful. Do you speak any other languages?"

"No," he said. Of course he spoke pretty good French but he did not tell her.

"Why did you want to see me?"

"I don't know. I suppose I liked the look of you, your smile, your eyes."

She blushed and changed the subject. "Will you get the job?"

"No, I was rejected. Anyway the company is fiddling its accounts. Your friend Peter probably knows all about it."

"He's not my friend," she said. "How do you mean fiddling its accounts?"

For the second time today Benjamin found himself telling his story. This time however he didn't mention the death of the red-headed man. Not so much to avoid upsetting the girl. If he told her about him he would have to tell her about Paris. And then he would have to tell her about his wife. Of course I'll tell her next time we meet, he thought. There's nothing to hide.

When he'd finished his story he said, "how long has Hi Ho Travel been working for Outland Oil?"

"Ever since they opened an office in London. About four years. Almost as long as I've been with the company. They're good clients."

"You were doing tickets at Outland on Thursday. Who's going where?"

"Peter Greaves is going to Yemen. Actually I'm going with him."

"What. Why?" Benjamin's face reddened, embarrassed by his tone.

"My boss asked if I could go. They give us so much business. Outland is having a party to celebrate a well they're drilling. Peter said I could come if I interpreted for him."

"What's your boss think you can do?"

"I can get business for Hi Ho Travel at this party. He wants me to look for a joint venture partner. If Outland discovers oil there'll be lots more business flying Americans over to Yemen."

"Greaves told me he had nothing to do with Yemen. What's he going for? And why should he need an interpreter? They must have locals working for them."

"And my Arabic's not very good. He wants some company I suppose. He needed an excuse.....to tell his wife."

"You be careful."

"I know Greaves a lot better than I know you. You English men are always giving out advice but don't know how to take it."

"I am not an English man, I am an individual."

"That's ridiculous."

They talked until well after the meal was finished. Benjamin then walked with her to the underground station. He would have liked to kiss her goodbye, at least on the cheek, but he could not bring himself to do it. It was past midnight when he finally waved her off on the last train to Ruislip. He ambled home through Hyde Park, past Kensington Gardens and along the High Street. It was a chilly, clear and moonless night and the street was quiet. As he mused on the evening, for once feeling satisfied with himself, he tripped over a bundle of rags lying in the gutter. An old vagrant looked up and cursed him foully.

He crossed the road. A taxi, hurrying home, angrily tooted. The noise made a flurry of pigeons, picking at bins on the kerbside, take flight and clatter into the sky. A policeman on the corner of Holland Road looked at him. But Benjamin didn't care. For the briefest moment he had not a care in the world. He did not know it yet but his good mood would not last for long.

ELEVEN

Next morning Benjamin sat down to eat his breakfast in front of the TV. He was thinking of Natalya as he prepared a breakfast cereal left uneaten by Germaine. Was it the B-plan oat supplement or the oat plan B-supplement? It crackled pleasantly as he poured in some milk. Such a demanding woman, Germaine had wanted both nourishment and noises from her breakfast cereal.

The phone rang before he had a chance to eat his first spoonful. He picked up the receiver. "Hello, this is Benjamin Bone."

"Is that Benjamin?" It was a woman's voice and the words were accompanied by a loud sob.

"Yes, it's me. Who is it?"

"Sally Fetters." She gulped out the words.

"What is it Sally? What's wrong?"

There was a long pause. He could hear a child's voice in the background.

"Tom's dead," she finally said.

"Tom's dead? What! Are you sure?"

"Of course I'm sure."

"When? How?" Benjamin was too stunned to think.

"This morning. I was at a friend's house. His office at home was ransacked. He'd been hit over the head..." Benjamin could hear her sucking in gulps of air.

"I'm sorry." He could think of nothing else to say.

He heard a whining voice of a child say, "I'm hungry Mummy."

"Shut up. I said shut up," screamed Sally. And then, "I'm sorry." And more crying.

"Can I help?"

"I'm going to my parents in Manchester tomorrow. The police took me here.., to a hotel. Tom gave me some papers for you. I was going to drop them off before this happened. Tom said it was urgent."

"I'll pick them up at your hotel. Is there anything you need? Anything I can do?"

"No. I'm staying at The Venice Hotel in Kensington, Room 1215. It was the last thing he said to me. 'Give Benjamin these'."

There was silence now. "Won't the police help you? A social worker or someone?"

"I don't want anyone." Her voice became irritable.

"Shall I come over right away?"

"Don't keep asking questions," she shrieked. "I don't know. Come then. Get your fucking papers."

"No I was thinking of you."

"Sorry.... It's not your fault."

"Don't apologise, Sally."

"Come when you like," she said, "but I'm leaving early tomorrow." She cut him off.

Benjamin slumped on his sofa. His mind was numb. But there was a nagging voice in his head. Was it his fault? The report in the red case? But how could anyone know Tom had the report? Did he tell anyone about it? That it was important and huge amounts of money were involved. Tom had said he wouldn't tell anyone. No, Benjamin sighed, it must have been a burglar, nothing to do with Outland Oil.

Benjamin still had the telephone receiver in his hand and he got up to return it to its rest on the shelf. As he did so he saw the directories next to the phone. He remembered a directory lying on the floor when he had got back from the library on Saturday.

He took the telephone and placed it on the sofa as far as it would stretch. The wire connecting it to its socket was taped to the wall behind the books on the shelf. He tugged at it and the telephone directory slid forward slightly, but didn't fall. He returned the phone to its position.

He needed to use the toilet. He left the room and crossed the hall to his bathroom. After relieving himself he returned to the living room. The directory was face down, open in almost exactly the same spot as it had been on Saturday. Half pushed from the shelf supported only by its pages, it had splayed open, sagged forward and flopped to the floor.

He picked up the phone and looked at its base. He wouldn't have a clue bug but he did see the heads of the two screws holding the back of the phone to its body were scratched. He went to the kitchen to search for a screwdriver. Someone could have come in on Saturday while I was out and tampered with his phone. When Tom called they would have heard everything. They would have known

74

Tom had discovered something important....and they could have gone to his house to look for the report. Who would do that?

"Shit!" he said aloud dropping the screwdriver onto the floor. If the phone is bugged then whoever is listening could have been listening just now. They would know Sally Fetters has got papers for me. If they were looking for the report at Tom's they will still be looking. Now they know exactly where to find it.

It took Benjamin just twenty five minutes to run from his flat to the lobby of the hotel in Kensington, guessing that running would be quicker than the Tube. It was another five before an elevator arrived to take him to the 12th Floor. Room 1215 was half way along the dimly lit corridor. He sprinted down it, reached the correct room and knocked. A peephole was set in the door at eye level and he saw a shadow cross over it.

Sally, her eyes puffed with tears, opened the door. He could see the foot of two double beds and a wide vanity table against the wall, littered with papers. A cartoon was showing on a television in the corner but there was no sign of Sally's daughter. He said "Hi" and she stepped backwards, flinching.

He walked through the door and two men appeared. They had been hidden from view next to the one of the beds. They rushed towards him and grabbed his arms, pinioning him against the wall. Another man, wearing a hat, was sitting on the other bed.

"What's going on!" he shouted, the muscles of his upper arms were squeezed in a powerful grip. The pain was excruciating. "Let me go."

Sally, her tear-stained eyes streaked with make-up, shouted at him. "You bastard. You killed him, you bastard."

"What do you mean?"

"He knew about you and that company and you killed him."

"Knew what?" Benjamin shouted out the words, panic engulfing him, "What have they told you?"

"These men are from Scotland Yard. They found your fingerprints all over Tom's office. They found your fucking wallet on the floor."

"My wallet?" Where had he seen it last?

The bearded man on his left released his grip and spoke for the first time.

"You are Benjamin Bone?"

"Yes, of course I'm Benjamin Bone."

"We are detectives with the Metropolitan police. We are arresting you. Come with us now please."

"What do you mean? Tom was my friend."

"You murdered him you bastard. He was my husband. You murdered him. Your friend, bullshit!" Sally spat in his face.

The two policemen gripped his arms and hauled him out. He heard a child's voice. "Can I come out now Mummy?"

"No, not yet," and then she said to the man on the bed, "what shall I do now?" Benjamin stared at Sally as she looked back through the door. Her face was twisted with grief. One of the men holding him kicked the door closed and he was dragged backwards along the corridor.

He was dazed. He tried to think straight. How could the police blame him? And why was his wallet at Tom's? "I didn't do it, Sally" he shouted back at the closed door. The policemen were gripping his arms painfully and Benjamin went silent. He bowed his head.

What struck him at once were the shoes.

The bearded man who had spoken, whose grip was the tightest, who was making Benjamin's left arm throb, was wearing green canvas shoes. Benjamin had seen them before. The two men were acting like thugs, not policemen. They could not be policemen. But if they weren't policemen, they were probably murderers. Benjamin needed to escape but for now he relaxed his tired muscles and said nothing.

The elevator doors opened. An elderly couple moved aside and he was shoved inside. The doors closed behind them. Benjamin said. "My room's on the 9th Floor." As he spoke he wrenched his left arm from the bearded man's grip, and reached for the floor buttons. The man tried to grab back his arm but not before the elderly woman, standing by the button panel, pressed the number nine and smiled at them both. Benjamin shoved his captor on the right, simultaneously wrenching his other arm free. The old woman was swept aside as both men tried to restrain Benjamin. He was ducking and diving, punching his arms wildly. The elevator was shaking and bouncing. Both men were aiming punches at Benjamin's head. One caught him a glancing blow on the temple but most of the punches missed. Unfortunately his own swing landed squarely on the back of the old lady's head as she cowered in the corner. She screamed and dropped sideways to the floor across the doors. The old man, pinned in the back corner, shouted out furiously as an elbow lashed his face.

The elevator halted on the ninth floor and its doors slid open. Benjamin leapt over the woman on the floor, tore his jacket from the fingers of one of his captors, and sprinted up the corridor. As he heaved open the fire door he glanced over his shoulder. One of the men, the clean-shaven one, was chasing him. Benjamin had no time to ponder his predicament. Instead of running down the fire stairs he leapt over the guard rail and jumped the eight feet to the floor below.

Hardly noticing the pain in his ankles from the jump, he tugged open the fire door of floor eight and slammed it shut behind him. A fire extinguisher stood in the corner of the corridor and he rammed it beneath the bar jamming it closed. Drawing in gulps of air, he ran up the corridor to the service exit adjacent to the elevator shafts. Inside there was a trolley piled with dirty white linen blocking a flight of concrete stairs and the entrance to a service elevator. He shoved the trolley aside and sprinted three steps at a time down the stairs. Near the bottom his speed started to flag and he drew deep breaths of the dry, dusty air.

Double swing doors on the ground floor opened into a service area, brightly lit and packed with trolleys heaped with dirty linen and racks of untidy trays. An uneaten bread roll caught his eye and Benjamin took it. It was soft and stale but he was hungry. He walked across the room to a door marked fire exit and gently pushed the pressure bar. The door swung open and a piercing siren cut the air. He listened in horror. For a moment he held back but already he could hear shouts and running feet. He stepped out and found himself surrounded by people.

The fire door opened out into a porch adjacent to the main glass doors of the hotel. He was standing between two potted conifers in full view of everybody at the entrance. A uniformed doorman and several arriving guests were looking at him. A well-dressed man appeared from the main doors followed by the bearded man wearing the green canvas shoes. Benjamin stared at him and he stared back but Benjamin moved first, tearing across the driveway and into the road.

"Stop him, he's a murderer!" he heard someone shout. He dodged a taxi door flung open into his path and sprinted into the traffic. Over the road he ran through double doors into a crowded department store. A large lady wearing a tee shirt with the words 'Here to help' written on her breasts was talking with a customer. Other customers were trying to squeeze past her. He shoved past them all and ran up the escalator arriving in the ladies clothes department. He saw a sign marked changing rooms and headed in that direction. He stepped inside one of the cubicles and fumbled to pull the door closed behind him. His hands were shaking and he tried to breathe as quietly as possible but his heart was pumping like a steam hammer.

He had qualified as a paramedic years ago, the course financed by an oil company so he could double up on jobs when on drilling sites. As he struggled to get his breath back at first he massaged his ankles where they had jarred on the concrete floor and then he checked the rest of his body. He ached all over, especially his ankles. He decided to return to his flat to get his telephone with the bug and take it to the police. He was convinced now. He had been watched ever since he had visited Greaves at Outland's offices on Friday. He was also convinced of the importance of the annual report. He still had no idea what it all meant but he was sure Yemen and Wadi Qarib were critical.

The report was gone but Sally Fetters would support him as soon as she found out the truth. And the police would believe her with all those witnesses at the hotel. They would have to investigate. Sally would soon accept he was innocent when she found out those men were not policemen. But he worried about his wallet. The last time he had seen it had been at the restaurant with Natalya the night before.

It was nearing five thirty when he ventured out, leaving the cubicle and walking back through the shop. Outside two police cars with blue flashing lights blocked the driveway to the hotel and Benjamin guessed they were there on his account. He had coins in his pocket and decided to take the train back to his flat. The newspaper vendor at the exit from the station was setting up his stand to sell the latest edition of the Evening Standard. The headline, scrawled in black ink on a sheet of paper wired to the vendor's trolley said, *'Death In Venice - Mother brutally murdered in Venice hotel as daughter looks on.'*

Benjamin stared at the headline and started to shiver uncontrollably. He pulled up the collar of his shirt to hide his pale face.

Not far away two men were arguing in a hotel room in Russell Square.

"They lost him," said one of them. He was wearing green shoes.

"How did an amateur like Bone get away? They are useless idiots."

"He took them by surprise."

"Shut the fuck up. Did you deal with the wife or did she get away too?"

"I strangled her as you told me to. And I've destroyed the report. The daughter was in the bathroom. She thinks it was Bone. The police have got all the evidence they need. There must have been a hundred people saw him at the hotel. He'll get picked up soon enough." He paused. "But what about the Chinese girl? He was with her last night when I got the wallet."

"Leave her alone. Greaves is taking her to Yemen."

"What do we do now?"

"Find Bone and kill him and never mind if the police get to him. He won't get bail. We can kill him in jail."

"I'll tell them. My men are watching Bone's flat. We'll get him I promise."

"Don't make a mess of it this time."

The man nodded and left.

The other man took the phone and dialled. There were clicks as a connection was made.

"Hello, who is it?" The response was gruff on a crackly line.

"This is Bauss. We've got him. Everything's under control."

"Good. I want you back in Houston. Take the first flight tomorrow. You need to talk to Rittman. If he hears about Bone he's gonna work something out. Tell him the guy's gone mad or something."

"I can handle Rittman."

"Good. Call me when you get back to Houston."

Bauss replaced the receiver. Perhaps I should have told him about the hotel foul-up. No, there's no point, there'd been enough mistakes already. Bone's got nowhere to hide. He's as good as dead.

Deep in the Yemeni desert on the outskirts of Karim Doctor Gary Turnbow lay motionless on a camel-hair mattress on a metal bed in a small, windowless room. He was wearing only khaki shorts and lay flat on his back, eyes shut trying to ignore the heat and dirt. His bare chest and shoulders were covered with a damp matt of kinked, almost transparent hair.

The last light from the sun that had shone through the gap beneath the door was gone but he could still picture the grey walls of unplastered brick, the bare cement floor and the dirty bucket in the corner of the room. He remembered the hijack, his car careering into the dune as his driver tugged at the wheel to avoid the gunshots. Being dragged from the stalled vehicle and the single shot echoing off the cliffs as his driver had been shot in the back of the head. Worst of all, he remembered his own hollow fear as the gun was aimed at his own head. A sheen of sweat glistened on his forehead, dripping down his cheeks to form wet pools in the blonde hair at the nape of his neck.

Turnbow hated to travel alone. He had been sent to Yemen on a sabbatical by the hospital where he worked after an inquiry about a patient who had died during a routine appendectomy. He was innocent of the mistake, it was the anaesthetist who would take the blame, but it had been better to disappear for a few weeks while the case blew over. An American cigarette company was opening a factory outside Sana'a and they had donated three hundred thousand dollars to the General Hospital. Turnbow had agreed to deliver medical kits and inspect the facilities to advise on how best the money should be spent. A pragmatist, he did not dwell on the fact that the American factory was also providing the means for the locals to poison themselves.

Before returning to Denver he had been encouraged by his embassy to visit archaeological sights near Marib and a car had been arranged. It had been spectacular but on his own he was lonely. He longed to return to his family. Throughout his stay in Sana'a the phones in the hospital had been unreliable, usually with only crackles interrupting the silence. The one time a call did get through to his home no one had picked up. He had not spoken to Margaret, his wife of nearly twenty years, for many weeks.

He was not an emotional man but he was sad as he remembered the last time he had seen her. Margaret had a stern face as always but their two daughters of six and twelve had been laughing excitedly. "I'll be gone for only a few weeks," he had consoled his eldest daughter who had not needed consoling.

"Will you call me?"

"Yes of course and I'll get you both a present."

He had lifted them up, carrying each around their narrow waists so they could plant kisses on his cheeks. Margaret had even hugged him and then, after he had dropped the children onto the floor, she had kissed him too.

"I love you," she had said, her stern face crinkling into a smile.

"I'm not going for ever. It's only a few weeks," he had replied.

And now he was locked up in this terrible room. His eyes once more filled with tears as he stared into the gloom of his fetid cell.

A young local man called Ibrahim was squatting in the dust outside the cell, staring vacantly at the final sliver of sun before it disappeared behind the plateau. He wore dusty sandals, a futah tucked between his legs, and a loose headscarf. His face was thin and dark, tanned and leathery, belying his young age and he had a gold front tooth shining amongst blackened stubs. An ancient rifle lay beside him on the pebbly dirt. He drew a long compelling gulp from a crumpled cigarette. Exhaling heavy blue smoke into the air he noticed two men approaching and he smiled at them. He had a kindly face.

"Go," one of the men said, "go to Ali. We'll take care of the white man."

Ibrahim clambered to his feet and picked up his rifle. He was pleased his boring job was over. Handing one man the key, he threw his gun over his shoulder and sauntered off.

TWELVE

Forty kilometers west of Karim, Mahmoud, Sheikh Achmed's younger son stood on the high plateau looking at the deeply cut wadi below. He had ridden to his cousin's farm, a few kilometers to the northeast, and had walked to this spot early that morning. A warm wind was blowing across the shattered rock pavement catching dust and grit, swirling it into miniature tornadoes. Mahmoud's shirt flapped in the breeze exposing a hard chest tanned by the unrelenting sun. Deep in Wadi Qarib he could see the battered metal derrick of a drilling rig standing in the gravel plain, away from the boulders at the lower edges of the cliffs.

Around it an area had been flattened and cleared of rubble. Sacks of chemicals, bundles of wires and drilling tools lay stacked alongside metal containers and piles of rusty metal pipe. Men in silver helmets, looking tiny in the distance, were examining the equipment. A cluster of white trailers stood on the edge of the flat ground. Below the cliff a number of trucks were parked alongside a group of khaki tents. The local labourers were billeted here, many of whom Mahmoud was acquainted with personally. All had given him dollars for influencing his father, the Sheikh, and the American, Janek, to get them this job at the drill site.

Further to the south Mahmoud could see the road, a newly graded track, cleared of rubble and edged with shallow ridges like levees along a river. The track wound its way along the wadi until it disappeared around a sharp right angle bend. A truck had emerged, tiny and fragile, bumping its way towards the drill site. Bolted to the wooden bed behind the cab was a battered steel water tank. Mahmoud smiled at the sight of the vehicle, one of many he had hired. Each delivery was worth hundreds of dollars. The drivers had been told to fill the tanks only half full of water and Mr Janek had not once inspected the pit into which the consignments were piped. It had cost Mahmoud a lot to hire these trucks for the four weeks of drilling but he had monopolised the water supply to Wadi Qarib. If Janek's estimate of truck loads needed were even half accurate he would make a huge profit.

He watched the vehicle drive into the camp-site and stop at the water pit dug in the sand. The driver emerged from his cab and connected up a flexible hose to his tank. Mahmoud gazed at him for a moment and then began to climb down the steep path to the wadi, a path worn out of the plateau wall generations ago when the population of the area around Karim had been much greater and Karim had been a staging post for the incense trade from China. Although sure-footed, flurries of stones slipped down the steep incline as he descended. Three Toyota Land Cruisers were parked at the foot of the path but he ignored these and crossed to the camp of trailers, nodding at the security guard who was squatting next to an open steel container. It was carpeted and a crouching Arab inside was praying in this makeshift mosque.

One of the larger white trailers was directly facing the drilling rig. Two steps led up to a heavy door, which he pushed open. Inside the trailer the contrast in temperature was dramatic and he tucked his shirt into his trousers to help ward off the powerful air-conditioning. Sitting facing him was Dr Khaled, chewing gum behind a tidy desk.

"Hi, Khaled. What's up?" Mahmoud said in perfect English. "You wanted to see me?"

"Since you seem to run this camp you can help me. I'm almost out of medicines," replied Khaled in Arabic. "Your men are in here all the time. I'm sure they are hoarding my supplies."

"What do you expect, Khaled. Why do you let them have everything they ask for?"

"What can I do? I'm a doctor."

"Use your head" said Mahmoud, knowing Khaled's qualifications as a doctor were slim. He had spent less than two years at medical school in the capital and had come back to Karim with a certificate and doctorate almost certainly purchased by members of his family. They figured Khaled should be kept out of the family business, which involved shipping arms from Saudi Arabia to the tribes of eastern Yemen and across the sea to East Africa. What better than a doctorate to prevent others from losing their respect for the family. Khaled's certificate was displayed in a wooden frame on the wall of the trailer.

Mahmoud was surprised the American drilling company had not complained about Khaled but perhaps none of them had yet fallen sick. The agreement between Mr Janek and Sheikh Achmed had stipulated some senior positions in the camp should be held by local men. The Sheikh had maintained the security of the supply routes and the safe operation of the air strip could only be guaranteed with such an agreement. The doctor had been one of these, a radio operator offered by Captain Abdullah from his camp north of Karim, another.

The trailer door opened and Bob Janek, in dusty blue overalls, a silver hard hat and heavy tan leather boots, stepped in. Mahmoud saw dark stains of sweat at his armpits seeping outwards like the sea comes in over tidal flats. He was holding a yellow form in his hand.

"Hello Mahmoud. I saw you come in here. You keeping your men working?" he said sharply.

"Sure Mr Janek," answered Mahmoud.

Janek turned to Khaled. "Dr Khaled what the fuck's this requisition?" He waved the form in front of him.

"I need more medicines." Khaled answered sheepishly.

"What's happened to all the other stuff? Christ we haven't had any accidents. What do you need more morphine for? Nobody's fucking dying. Are you selling it, Khaled?"

Khaled stood up, and would have appeared angry himself, but for his benign expression and clumsy stance. It did little to assuage Janek's fury.

Mahmoud interrupted. "It's not his fault. I'll get the men to stop…."

"You'd better Mahmoud. Those fucking Arabs are thieving bastards."

Mahmoud didn't reply at first but he made a mental note. Janek would suffer for those words when this well was finished. Not now though, the water contract was too important.

"They see an opportunity and they take it," he finally said, "we have no medicines at all in Karim. Go see the hospital and then you would understand."

"Sure, my heart bleeds for them. Give me a list of everyone who comes to you Khaled. And Mahmoud, you make it known sick men can't work here. Control them or the trailer they pray in goes. I've bent over backwards for you. You do the same for me."

Mahmoud nodded calmly. He wasn't scared of Janek. "I'll do what I can for you. The operation must run smoothly."

"Good, we understand each other." He opened the trailer door and left.

Neither man spoke for a moment. Mahmoud walked across the room and fingered the linen sheets on the bed in the corner. "These are nice sheets," he said.

"He's right, your men are stealing the medicine" said Khaled.

"That's not the point. Americans do the same when they need something badly. We're poor. You can't blame us. He's a racist. If anyone asks for medicine don't give it to them. I'll see you tomorrow."

Mahmoud stepped from the air-conditioned cabin and the warm air pleased him. He didn't like air conditioning but he must get used to it. America was a cold country in the winter and when he had enough money to buy a green card he must be prepared. He walked over to the labourer's camp where a scruffy man in a futah and headscarf was squatting by a tent smoking. When he saw Mahmoud he jumped up and approached him, his smile exposing a gold front tooth.

"Hi, Mahmoud." He spoke with a raspy, smoke-damaged voice.

"Ibrahim? What are you doing here?"

"They came yesterday. They didn't want me to guard him. Ali sent me here to get a job."

Ibrahim was a gentle man, loyal to anyone who showed him kindness. Mahmoud thought him pathetic but at the same time he envied him, knowing Allah would take care of such a man. "Who is guarding the American now?" he said.

"Ali's men, I suppose."

Ali has no interest in the American, Mahmoud thought. Maybe he has decided to kill him.

"The American was in a bad way, always coughing."

"Yes," Mahmoud smiled at him. "You keep a look out, Ibrahim."

While he had been speaking Mahmoud had spotted Captain Abdullah in the shadow of the derrick with a soldier. He left Ibrahim and crossed the open-space between the camp and the rig, dodging the heaps of equipment.

"Give me a lift back to town, Abdullah." said Mahmoud, ignoring the other soldier.

Captain Abdullah looked at him his eyes bright in the sun. "Sure, I'm going now. Come with me."

He nodded at the soldier and they crossed over to where the vehicles were parked. Abdullah drove a battered Land Cruiser in army colours which he'd left in the centre of the parking area jamming up the exit road.

After a few minutes of driving Abdullah said, "you know the American your father is keeping in town. We all know its better he was dead. Someone will talk, I am sure of it. It will be trouble for you with this drilling and everything else."

Mahmoud agreed and regretted once again that he had saved the American's life. Everything depended on the drilling. "Yes you are right. I regret the day my half brother kidnapped him."

Captain Abdullah looked across at Mahmoud. Why did you save the American when my soldiers were going to shoot him then? You are as weak as your father. General Geshira had ordered him to make sure Turnbow disappeared. Mahmoud and Rashad had saved him and Abdullah was angry but he hid it well. He had not enjoyed the threats and accusations of cowardice the General had shouted over the phone to him when he had reported the disaster. So now there must be no mistake, the American had to be killed. Captain Abdullah did not dare disappoint the General again.

An hour and a half later the Land Cruiser bumped into town. There were few people about in the midday sun except for dusty, barefoot children playing in the road. They drew up at Sheikh Achmed's and parked under a bank of air conditioning units dripping cold water beneath the windows.

"Mahmoud, help me persuade your father to finish the American. We had a vote and he will not go back on it, but perhaps you can handle him better than I."

They entered the lobby and Mahmoud ushered Abdullah into a front room. A pair of double doors led from the lobby into the back of the house where the family lived. The only men allowed through this door were Sheikh Achmed and his sons. A narrow flight of stairs led up to the diwan where the elders had met last week and to guest rooms and bathrooms. Mahmoud went to find his father.

He found Sheikh Achmed in the ladies room along with his half-brother Rashad who had returned from Sana'a that morning. They went together to see Abdullah.

"So Abdullah you wish me to kill the American," said Sheikh Achmed, "why now?"

"It is dangerous to keep him alive. The Americans are pressuring the Government to use the army to look for him. Someone will talk and it will be bad for Karim. You must dispose of him, especially with the oil well ..."

"The oil! The oil!" Achmed raised his voice. "Everybody talks about this oil! They won't find any oil and if they do we won't get any of it here in Karim."

"Why did you vote to save his life?"

"Not because of the oil. American drillers in Karim mean trouble. Our young men get greedy," he gave a sidelong glance at Mahmoud, "and all respect for anything but money disappears."

Rashad, fidgeting nervously, interrupted. "Father. Keep him alive. It's safer."

They all turned to look at Rashad. Mahmoud was surprised by his brother's intervention. He guessed he too was planning something.

"Captain Abdullah thinks we should kill him," said Achmed. "We have to do something. Rashad, you are a good man to care about a life. But you must be practical if you wish to take the leadership here."

How little does Achmed know his son, thought Mahmoud. He is blinded by love for the mother.

"You should give him a chance," went on Rashad, warmed by the compliment, "you voted to spare him."

"I have decided. It's too risky to keep him here and there is nothing else we can do. He knows too much. Tomorrow I will send a man to replace Ibrahim and he will do it."

Captain Abdullah nodded appreciatively and stepped towards the door. Mahmoud stood still, staring at his brother.

"What are you up to, Rashad," whispered Mahmoud.

"Nothing," he answered innocently. "What are you up to my wise brother?"

"Why do you want the American alive?"

"Dr Turnbow is a human being. He may be white but it makes no difference. American's have a God too. Anyway, I must go now I have business to attend to."

Mahmoud shrugged. He was puzzled. How did his half brother know the American was a doctor and why did he want to save him. He was also puzzled about Ibrahim who he had seen at the camp. He was certainly not guarding the American now. And Captain

Abdullah too, he was anxious for the American be killed, perhaps too anxious. What is so important about that doctor?

Mahmoud hated it, hated not knowing what was going on and for the second time today he was uncertain about his plans.

Rashad walked from the room, hiding his anxiety. Once outside he ran through the dusty streets, dark now as the sun had set behind the plateau. An alley disappeared between two high mud buildings opposite the Sheikh's house and he sprinted through, past provision stores stacked with sacks of grain. He ducked behind a row of stalls selling jambiya knives and through a second alley decked with cloth. The alley opened out into a wider street at the end of which stood a large stone house with iron bars over the windows. He hammered on the door urgently.

Moments later a large bearded man in white appeared. Recognising Rashad he invited him in. "Get me your master instantly." Rashad ordered.

Rashad waited anxiously. For once he could show his brother he was a clever man. He would prove to Mahmoud he was his equal, for, despite their recent disagreements, he loved his brother and his one wish was to command respect from him. When my father is dead I must lead and Mahmoud will be my greatest ally.

Ali appeared at the door of the room and Rashad immediately began to speak but Ali raised his hand, and walked to his cushions. The manservant followed carrying a silver tray of tea cups and a pot. Ali sat cross-legged at the end of the room next to his spittoon. The tray was laid on the floor in front of him. Rashad sat near the door. After sipping his tea Ali spat powerfully into the spittoon then nodded at Rashad.

"They will kill him, sir." Rashad panted, "We must do something."

"I presume you mean kill the American."

"Yes, my father has changed his mind. He's sending a man to kill him. Captain Abdullah has persuaded him. You must go to him. Tell him no."

"Abdullah eh? What is he up to?"

"The American is dangerous for Karim."

"He is right."

"Quickly," Rashad said.

"You fool Rashad." Ali snapped at him. "If I rush to change my mind it will only make them suspicious. Could I rely on Achmed to leave the American alone when so much money depends on him? I have already moved him."

"Where is he?"

"Safe and well guarded but the Americans had better deal soon, he's in bad shape. They are weak, those white men. You know why, Rashad?"

"No." He didn't know why.

"Because," Ali said imperiously, "they don't have the true God to protect them. Americans are pathetic. Allah does not protect a pathetic, unbeliever and if it wasn't for the money I would not protect him either. And, Rashad," he went on, "our army is restless. There is talk of a military coup in Sana'a. If the southern army tries to take over Karim then Dr Gary Turnbow could perhaps be useful. If we are seen as the saviour of a snivelling American doctor perhaps the Americans will thank us, eh? Now, go and find that man your father will use to kill the American. Bring him here. I know who he is." He hawked and sent a huge gobbet of yellow spit towards the brass spittoon. It hit the rim and a stringy tongue of phlegm dangled from it like a bungee jumper leaping from a bridge.

THIRTEEN

Benjamin sat on a wall by the river and, covering his face with the paper he had bought, read about Sally Fetters murder. She had been strangled like her husband. The first reports had appeared hardly two hours after her death but they already contained a detailed description of the prime suspect, a tall, tanned man in his mid thirties with thinning light brown hair and a prominent chin. They even gave his name, Benjamin Bone, but had not yet found a photograph. The police were criticised for leaving the mother and her orphaned child alone. They and the government were as guilty as the murderer. A public statement by the Metropolitan police commissioner had promised an early arrest and the community had been put on high alert to watch out for this dangerous, careless man, who had dropped his wallet in Mrs Fetter's hotel bedroom and murdered her in front of her own daughter.

Benjamin returned to his apartment in a state of shock. He was coldly numb as he scurried through Hyde Park in the warmish evening but was alert enough to see and recognise two men waiting for him in the street outside his apartment. He doubled back and sneaked up the concealed Victorian fire escape. Inside he gathered a bag of essential items; warm clothes, toothbrush, all the cash he could find, his passport, vaccination cards and a credit card. Being a regular traveller he knew what he needed. He stuffed everything into a sturdy canvas holdall and left through the window as swiftly as he had come. He would have taken the telephone too for evidence but it was gone along with all the press cuttings he had received from Germaine. He did not notice a photograph, torn carelessly into several pieces and tossed in the bin he'd emptied that morning. It was a photograph of Tom Fetters, Sally Fetters and their smiling child. It had sat framed on Tom Fetter's desk, in Tom Fetter's office. The police, who arrived no more than an hour after Benjamin had left, found the pieces almost immediately and carefully placed them with tweezers into a plastic bag.

Natalya Cheung was unlucky with men. She had never had a boyfriend for more than two or three dates. She soon became tired of their sensitivities and sceptical of their motives. Above all she hated the flowers and dinners when they only wanted to sleep with her. She regarded most young men as pathetic and wished they would tell her straight what they wanted. She was fearful to admit it but she had begun believing all men were exactly the same. Her brother, who managed baggage retrieval at Heathrow airport, was, to her, the epitome of a humourless male and typical of those she met. She would have liked to talk about it with her older sister who was married and a doctor working in the international hospital in Bangkok, but she hadn't seen her since her wedding, over a year ago. However, Benjamin had seemed different. She had enjoyed his company and the time in the restaurant had flown by. When she went home last night she could have stayed longer, when usually after dates she couldn't wait to leave. Now, each time the phone rang in the office she had wished it was him.

On her way home from work, she had also seen the Evening Standard headline on its stand at the entrance to Holborn station. She too bought the paper, a late edition. It contained a photograph of the suspect and there was no doubt it was Benjamin. As the train clattered northwards she stared at it in disbelief. But not for even the briefest moment did she believe that he had killed his friends.

For a second night running she couldn't sleep. She wondered where he was and when the police would come to question her about the dinner she had had with him the previous night. Next morning she left for work much earlier than normal, arriving in the Strand at seven. She saw Benjamin waiting in a darkened porch below her office.

"I thought you would come," she said as they walked up the stairs together.

"How did you know?"

"Where have you been?"

"I tried to sleep under Waterloo Bridge… with the homeless."

"You should go to the police."

"I can't go to the police. They wouldn't believe me. I've been framed. The police have evidence. My wallet was planted in the hotel. People saw me running from there."

"You should still go to the police......," she repeated.

"The police want me for making them look incompetent. The public want me because of Tom's daughter and... I don't know who they are.... gangsters, want to kill me. They'll get me even if there was no evidence. Someone planted my wallet and other stuff in the hotel room and killed Tom and Sally. What the hell else do I do....?" His voice cracked.

Natalya opened the door to her offices. They entered and she switched on the lights, crossed to her desk and sat behind it. "I'll help you. What do you want?"

"Get me a flight to Yemen. I've got to find out what Outland Oil are up to."

"They'll pick you up straightaway. At the airport. You can't fly out of Britain."

"I have to get out."

"I'll get you a ticket on a ferry. Flights go from Paris or Frankfurt to Dubai and connect with Yemenia twice a week."

"Book me Paris."

"There's a flight from Paris, Charles de Gaulle airport on Saturday morning. You'll arrive in Yemen on Saturday afternoon. There is barely any passport control at ferry terminals but there are always guys watching out. Best to take a night ferry. And not Dover-Calais. I'll get you a ticket on Poole-Cherbourg. They rarely check car passengers so hire a car. You can leave it at the airport in Paris. Give me your passport?"

He pulled it out of his bag and handed it to her.

"Good, it's an old type blue one. The new EU ones have bar codes which they scan. More important though is the name. On these old passports you can alter them." She opened it. "Hmm, the picture's good, it looks nothing like you."

Benjamin looked at his headshot and nodded dumbly.

"B. A. Bone." she read. "What's the "A" for?"

"Alex."

"Okay. You are now Brian Adam. Your surname is easily changed too. See your signature. It trails off at the end. It could easily be Borne, not Bone. How about that?"

"Fine but Bone is written on the front page."

"No problem." She pulled open a drawer beneath her desk and extracted a small bottle of clear fluid. A pungent waft of aniseed filled Benjamin's nostrils as she opened it.

"We use this stuff to change tickets."

She dabbed the fine brush against the letters and Bone became Borne. Only a faint brown stain remained where the word had been altered. She smudged it with her thumb and it looked like a dirty mark on the page.

"Incredible," he muttered.

"You won't be able to do this much longer, everything will be computerised. They'll probably be checking fingerprints in future. You'll need a visa for Yemen."

"Shit I forgot. How can I get one? That's impossible."

"I can do it. I have letters of introduction for Peter Greaves. I'll blank out the name, type on yours, Brian Borne, photocopy it and courier it to the Embassy with your passport. It will look as if you are an employee of Outland Oil. We'll have to change your appearance too." She opened the passport again and looked at his photo closely. "You can come home with me. My mum's got hair clippers. She can cut your hair and you can wear my brother's clothes. He's about your size."

"Will they trust me?"

"If I tell them to. I've already told my mum."

"I'll need to pay for the tickets?"

"We'll pay them all direct. I'll bill it to Outland's account. They won't find out. We're processing loads for them right now."

"But the police could trace you. You'd be in trouble if my tickets are booked from here."

"You're innocent aren't you and anyway they don't know it's you. I'll put the purchase through our Aberdeen office. I doubt anyone will notice. You better go now before my colleagues get in. I'll see you in Ruislip station in a couple of hours. And get a hat or something, and sunglasses."

Natalya's family in Ruislip asked no questions, treating him like an honoured guest and feeding him with rice and boiled chicken all day. Her mother, a lady who wore pyjamas all of the time, cropped his hair skilfully and her brother's clothes fitted well. Her mother was kind and wise but was quick to criticise him for what had happened. She told him she believed in individual responsibility for ones actions in this life and in previous ones. The English see tolerance as a strength, the Chinese as a weakness.

He wanted to leave the country as soon as possible, even if his plane did not leave until Saturday so he only stayed in Ruislip two nights until the visa arrived. He kissed her goodbye on the doorstep and they talked about meeting up in Yemen and about how they would spend time together there.

She'd booked him a car from a company in Amersham, a market town northwest of London on the tube from Ruislip. The girl who gave him the keys questioned him about leaving the car in Paris but did not seem suspicious. He sped to Portsmouth using small roads and the A3 from Petersfield. He clutched his passport as he drove, occasionally reading the name on the front cover. Not Benjamin Bone any more, Brian Borne, Brian Adam Borne. He was no longer sure of anything.

There were no checks at either the English or French port and in the early morning he was soon racing along the auto route to Paris. He arrived in the suburbs midday, found Gilles's apartment and watched Germaine from behind a plane tree as she made her way on foot to her office. She was dressed in a khaki raincoat with buttons and tags. He followed her into the boulangerie on the corner of the street and tapped her on the shoulder.

"Germaine it's me."

She looked around startled and saw Benjamin but didn't speak at first. She collected the baguette from the counter and whispered sharply. "The police are watching me Benjamin, follow me." She looked at a brioche sitting temptingly on the display cabinet, shrugged as if deciding against purchase, and walked from the shop.

He waited a few moments before following her. She ambled down the suburban street and entered a small shop at the end. It was an arty dress shop with racks of black leotards and mannequins in dresses with price tags probably in the thousands. A pretty girl ushered him into a rear room without speaking. Germaine was standing there.

"Why have you come here? What have you done to your hair? The police came yesterday and asked me about you. Whether you had contacted me?"

"I didn't do it, Germaine. I'm innocent."

94

"Of course you didn't do it. The English police are so stupid. Your brother called me too. I spoke to Charlotte and we agreed we'll get you out of this."

"How?" he snorted, "you know it's all to do with Outland Oil. The man at the airport. The report in the case."

"You should give yourself up. Tell the police all about it."

"If I give myself up the police are going to put me in jail."

"But they'll investigate the company."

"Yes, but how long will it take for them to do thatt and what will happen to me in jail? I've got to go to Yemen myself."

"You are mad!"

"It's the only way. I need evidence and I know how to find it. You pretend you didn't see me. Don't tell Gilles. Don't get involved." Benjamin was worried that whoever had killed Tom and Sally Fetters might go after Germaine. He was pleased the police were watching her.

"How will you get to Yemen?"

"I'm flying tomorrow from Charles de Gaulle. I met a girl who helped me get a visa. She recommended I fly from Paris rather than London to avoid the police."

"She's not so smart. There are police all over the place. They expected you to come here. They have a stupid English psychological profiler who says you are bitter about the break up of our marriage, were jealous of Tom and Sally and will try to murder Gilles and myself. They listen to a psycho and they don't listen to me."

"Natalya doesn't know anything about you, I didn't tell her. She's a travel agent."

"Good. Why not?"

"It was because it would have complicated things." In truth he had been scared to tell her that he was married. He would do so in Yemen.

"She must know about me by now," went on Germaine, "it was in Le Monde this morning. I've been getting calls from journalists. You should go to the police and tell them about this Outland company."

"I've told you. They won't believe me. The British public hate me. What would happen in a jail?"

"I don't know. This girl Natalya. Tell me about her."

Before he could answer the shop assistant looked in the door. Speaking in French she told Germaine that a policeman was waiting for her outside.

"Benjamin. You better go. There's a back way out of here. Be careful."

"I will." He kissed her on both cheeks.

He didn't tell Germaine about his new name. Thank God that man called Bauss hadn't seen her at the airport. Perhaps they think she knows nothing, or now they've got the report and they don't care.

A Renault was double parked alongside his car but he managed to squeeze out along the pavement. Natalya had booked him a hotel room in the suburbs close to the airport and he drove there now. On the way he pulled in at a supermarket and purchased bread and sausage, tinned vegetables, a can opener and some bottles of French beer. He didn't mean to go out again until Saturday when his flight was due to leave. He was on the run and he had to keep out of sight.

FOURTEEN

Natalya had a lot of work to do after Benjamin left for Paris. She needed to plan her own and Peter Greaves trip to Yemen and had had little time to think. But now, in the comfort of her first class British Airways seat, she was thinking too much. Why hadn't Benjamin told her he was married? There had been so many opportunities but he had lied to her. She still knew him to be innocent of Tom and Sally Fetters' murders but she no longer wished to have a relationship with him. He was just like all the others. What really irked her was the fact that she had arranged his trip to his wife in Paris.

She looked up as a stewardess offered drinks and she ordered a coke whilst Peter Greaves at her side asked for a bottle of Australian Pinot Noir from the Barossa Valley. "It's a fine wine from the new world, but a touch too dry," he said, sipping it noisily. Natalya didn't drink wine. She rarely drank alcohol at all, only an occasional sherry and thimblefuls of Dom Benedictine which her mother called medicine. Alcohol made her sleepy and she didn't enjoy it. Her brother became red-faced after one or two beers, not merely flushed with colour but a brilliant crimson glow. Her fear of suffering similar symptoms was enough to deter her from drinking for ever.

Greaves was being intensely irritating. He persistently pleaded with her to drink wine and muttered stuff about full flavour and oaky or chocolaty aroma or some other nonsense. They had been flying for three hours, there were eleven more to go before they arrived, and she wasn't looking forward to them.

"Natalya," Greaves interrupted her thoughts.

Her skin crawled but, mindful of the hours ahead, she turned, forced a smile and nodded for him to continue. She knew that if Greaves had not been partially inebriated he could hardly have failed to notice her disdain.

"You Chinese, you appreciate money more than most people, don't you?"

"I don't know what being Chinese has to do with it."

"Now you do know, dear. The Chinese religion is money."

Natalya shivered. "Don't be ridiculous. We are like anybody else..."

"You are not and you know it. We are all different. Negroes, Chinese, Whites. The Arabs in Yemen, they are all fanatic believers in God and would kill for Him. The Chinese kill for money."

"Aren't you being racist?"

"No, of course not. There is nothing wrong with making generalisations if they are true. We Whites are as bad but in a different way."

"In what way?" She could give him a long list.

He ignored her question and went on. "Actually I admire the Chinese. It's been proven they have as high an IQ as us, much higher than Negroes."

"Proven by who? And so what. IQ isn't everything."

"I agree. IQ isn't everything. Life would be boring without diversity. Natalya, there are stupid Chinese. And even intelligent Africans. I'll tell you a good joke. A coloured cripple went to Lourdes in a wheel chair. After praying in the cave or whatever they do there, he wheeled himself out. He has a big smile on his face. He's not black anymore." He laughed loudly. "Anyway I want to make it clear how I appreciate you. And you are beautiful too."

Natalya squirmed in her seat. This objectionable man seemed to have no idea how he was alienating her. Am I supposed to thank him for the compliment? She was about to point this out to him when he gently put his hand on hers, squeezed it, and whispered in a conspiratorial way, "Let me show you something interesting."

She half expected him to pull out his penis and discuss its size relative to other racial groups and this thought made her smile to herself for the first time since the flight had begun. But he didn't pull it out. Instead he took his slim leather briefcase from the floor and opened it, extracting a glossy magazine. Natalya immediately recognised it as a copy of Outland Oil's annual report.

She shivered, thinking of Benjamin's story. Greaves let the report rest on his lap.

"You know my wife?" he went on. "She didn't want to come with me to Yemen. She likes to live in our expensive house with the children, gossip with her tedious friends and drink coffee. She thinks I'm a poor man, not much money, not much power. She makes me so angry sometimes. I'm not sure she even loves me. I tell you if she ever left me she would have to crawl back on her hands and knees. And I would put broken glass on the doormat if she did."

" I like you much better. You always listen attentively, never criticise, and, most importantly, keep your opinions to yourself. If you have any of course. My wife knows nothing about me. You on the other hand are impressed by what I am, not who I am. That is what I like about the Chinese."

"You can hardly be a poor man."

"Now you are giving me the kind of look I can feel in my wallet," he laughed. "Don't you understand? You and I are similar? We are kindred spirits. I am going to be rich, very rich indeed." He opened the report and flashed through its pages. "See here. Look at this." He pointed to the section headed 'Notes to the Accounts' below which was printed a table of names and figures.

"See this company, POG Resources." He pointed to one of the entries marked under 'Principal Subsidiaries'. "O is for Oliver. POG Resources is my company. I own it lock stock and barrel. See here, POG Resources owns 35% of Outland Oil. Are you impressed? You see I do have a lot of money. Stay friends with me, Natalya?" He winked at her and added mysteriously, "do unto others before others do unto you, as God said."

He truly does think I'll be impressed. No wonder his wife didn't come with him. He's an asshole and his middle name should have been Ivan. But she was surprised by the revelation. Benjamin had told her Greaves was not involved in any of Outland's dealings outside the UK. So she played him along. "Really Peter, you own Outland Oil. When did you buy it?"

"I didn't buy it, dear. I started the company in the US back when the oil price was real low and there were lots of cheap oil fields in the southern states. POG was my small consulting company. I started Outland and sold shares in it to raise money."

"But why so secret? Why aren't you a director?"

"I was a consultant. Had my clients known I owned an oil company I would have lost all my business. Conflict of interest you see. Then I got an American, you know Earl Rittman, to front the company in Houston while I came back to England. The oil industry is a broad church and I try to promote unity. Sometimes it is best to keep things secret. If you like, I am 'ecumenical with the truth'. He laughed overly loudly again.

"It sounds clever" she said disingenuously, wondering if anybody ever laughed at his jokes. "Can I keep a copy of the report?

I'm interested to learn more about Outland. You are one of our most important clients."

"Yes of course, take this one. You should have asked Louise for one."

"So this Yemen thing, how does it fit in? Why Yemen?"

"What do you mean, how does it fit in?" Greaves replied proudly. "It's an excellent prospect and you would be surprised who our major investor is. He's very confident."

"Who?"

"I'm sorry Natalya I can't tell even you that. Confidential you know," he tapped his nose and winked again, "But you will soon find out. Ah, good. Coffee is coming. You must have a brandy with it. I will recommend one."

Greaves slept after dinner. The peculiar rasping trill emanating from his dehydrated throat was audible even with the volume of her headphones turned up. She watched a movie called "What's eating Gilbert Grape" that had come out last year. In first class they gave you a personal video machine and a choice of videocassettes. When it had finished she was still wide awake. Disturbed by Greaves' snoring, she got up to stretch her legs and walked back towards the rear of the plane, pushing back the curtains to enter the economy section. It was half-empty and most passengers were trying to sleep. Near the back of the darkened aisle she noticed a tall man staring at her with a cheerful expression. He was in his early thirties and had handsome features. He looked a bit like Benjamin. The man smiled at her and she smiled back, her blue eyes twinkling in the low light. She noticed that he shifted in his seat as she passed, removed his headphones and turned to watch her as she continued to the back of the plane and returned down the other aisle.

The man was sitting in a row of three. Beside him was an empty seat. At the window, head back with shades over her eyes, a middle-aged woman with a puffy face and greying hair slouched against the window, fast asleep. Once the pretty Chinese girl had disappeared behind the curtain he replaced his headphones and shut his eyes. It was his first time on an overseas assignment and he was nervous, not fully clear in his mind what he was going to do when he arrived in Yemen. Mrs Turnbow by the window wasn't much help. She hadn't removed her shades since leaving London, declining all offers of food and drink.

Richard Clapton had been a reporter with the Denver Times for several years but had only recently become involved in features. He had persuaded his editor that the paper needed to be less parochial especially with the new airport and the expected influx of visitors to the Rocky Mountain city. His editor, a man who had worked on the paper all his life, had not been convinced but had given Richard a chance with a monthly feature entitled, *"Letter from out of town"*.

As soon as Richard heard of the kidnap of Doctor Turnbow he had decided this was his big chance. After persuading his editor that he should follow up the story, he had attended the oil conference in Oklahoma City where he met Earl Rittman. Then last Thursday he had followed Mrs Turnbow in her car through downtown Denver and north to a shopping mall. At a supermarket he collected a trolley and pushed it against hers, trapping her against the frozen food cabinets. She had stared at him angrily but he blurted out his prepared piece before she could escape. "I'm a journalist. Yeah, I would like a story but I can also help you. I know I can. The Government aren't helping are they? I can. Come to the Yemen with me. We'll find your husband, I'll look after you. I know people out there."

"Go away," she had screamed, "Don't follow me. I'm sick of you people."

But he had persisted and the offer to go with her to Yemen had piqued her interest. For the first time she believed she could do something. Go there and get him out, instead of sitting around brooding, waiting on her Government that seemed to be doing nothing at all.

Richard had researched Yemen and Outland Oil extensively after Oklahoma. He had found details of Earl Rittman's previous company mentioned by Sam Buckfast at the Oklahoma City convention. Rittman had been Managing Director of a family company, Rittman Oil, in partnership with his father who had struck oil while drilling a water well on his ranch in California in the 1920's. Following the death of his father Rittman had employed Buckfast, a childhood friend, to help him look for new deals. Production from the California oilfields was dwindling by that time.

Buckfast had come up with an opportunity in Texas and Rittman, who had been wrapped up in settling his father's affairs, had approved it. Buckfast raised cash from institutions in exchange for large chunks of Rittman's stock to buy acreage. It had seemed a good move until the Texan reservoirs began to water out soon after the deal had been completed. Along with the catastrophic slide in oil price at the time, the finances of Rittman Oil became seriously stretched.

Earl Rittman was ousted by the institutional shareholders and was forced to sell his entire holding in the family business to avoid bankruptcy. But, unknown to Rittman, it was Buckfast who had bought the holding. Backed by the rich shareholders wanting the return of their investment money, Buckfast engineered a take-over of the Texan group that had sold them the worthless fields. Now unsaddled by debt and cash-rich he was able to abandon those fields and pay back most of the investment. The bitterness Earl Rittman had shown to Sam Buckfast made Richard certain it had been a set-up.

Richard had also looked up newspaper articles on the Brit who had been kidnapped in Yemen. The kidnappers had demanded the release of a Sheikh from the jail in Sana'a imprisoned, according to the government, for terrorism against the state. The Englishman was an aid worker and had been missing for four weeks before turning up at the British Embassy unscathed. His wife, a Polish woman, had negotiated his release herself. Apparently not a cent had been paid and the Sheikh still languished in jail. Richard had tried to contact the couple through their aid organisation but they were now living in a remote part of the Himalayan kingdom of Bhutan. The success of this woman gave him the idea of taking Margaret Turnbow to Yemen.

But when Richard had asked his editor for his next letter from out of town to come from Yemen he had not been impressed. "When you asked me for your own goddamn column in the paper I let you have it. You flew to Oklahoma City at our expense. You were going to write about Oklahoma."

"Yes. And I did."

"Where! Show me where Oklahoma figures in this article." He threw a newspaper on the table.

"You know I was following up on the Turnbow story. I'll do you another article on Oklahoma."

"Yes, do it. Our shareholders have to see something for their money. This isn't the Wall Street Journal. We don't have a budget for maverick reporters to go swanning around the world on foolhardy missions. Leave it to the nationals to chase up this Turnbow story. Our readers are more interested in new shopping malls and traffic accidents, not goddamn Arabia."

"But it's a huge opportunity. This story is of national interest..."

"I said leave it to the nationals...."

"But Turnbow's from Denver. He lived only a few blocks from your own house."

"Where?"

"Sixth Avenue. And he has children. Two young daughters. It's our duty to help. Look I've worked it out." He pulled a slip of paper from his jacket pocket. "The expenses, apart from the cost of the flight are minimal. The American Embassy will pay for myself and Mrs Turnbow at the hotel. A story like this will put the Denver Times right up there with the best."

"If it's a good story?"

"Yes. Of course it'll be a good story."

"Can you really handle it?"

"Trust me. I've got Margaret Turnbow already. And I have contacts in Yemen. I met the CEO of Outland Oil in Oklahoma City. He'll help me."

Richard went on to discuss costs with the editor in detail. Eventually, it turned out the paper did have a budget for trips abroad. It was rarely used and had built up a large surplus.

Richard now looked across at Mrs Turnbow, still asleep, her head leaning against the aircraft window. "I hope I can do something," Richard whispered to himself. The last few hectic days and now the jet lag and tiredness was doing nothing for his self-confidence and for a moment he wished he was back in Denver. Then he looked over again at Mrs Turnbow. She was no Polish battle-axe but perhaps she was her husband's last chance. He saw the pretty Chinese girl return up the aisle for a second circuit of the plane. He smiled at her again and she smiled back.

FIFTEEN

Emmett Kraill dragged on a Rothmans cigarette, the only Western brand available in Yemen. He was waiting to meet Greaves and Natalya in the noisy arrivals hall of Yemen International Airport. It was a bleak, vacuous hangar with a high ceiling and dim fluorescent lighting. The brown linoleum was everywhere scarred with blackened holes from stubbed cigarettes. There were benches near the walls, stained with coffee and tea spilt from the foam beakers littering the floor. The outer reaches of the hall disappeared off into a murky half-light and everywhere looked dull and old.

Extended families were shoving up against the exit gate The men were small and bearded, in grey jackets and scruffy cotton shirts. Almost all of them wore futahs, a cloth skirt wound loosely round the legs with a loop of material tucked in the waistband. Many of the women were clad in black shrouds hiding their faces and bodies although some wore simple headscarves. The people were being watched by a number of uniformed guards, dark swarthy men with machine guns slung over their shoulders.

Unlike his colleague Bob Janek, Kraill felt that he was not a racist. He enjoyed living in Yemen, especially after spending many maddening years in the rich countries of the Middle East, mainly Saudi Arabia and Abu Dhabi. In Yemen he liked the cheerful poverty and respect for success. The poor people were the most trusting, least greedy. But how wrong it was to say that travel broadens the mind, he thought. Working in the Middle East made him incredibly frustrated and angry with the people, their flexible attitude to time, the uncertainty of whether something would ever be done, their certainty in their own correctness and inability to say sorry.

There were a few other Westerners in the room waiting for the daily Yemenia flight from Dubai. Kraill saw Dick Collins, the Security Officer at the Embassy, standing on his own, gloomily staring at nothing, leaning against a dusty, unmanned cake counter. There was one meagre wedge of iced cake with a cherry on top lying on a plate behind the counter glass. It looked like a warning sign.

Collins was a miserable bastard but he seemed to care about his job. He walked over to him.

"Hi Dick, you look cheerful as usual."

"Oh. Hello." Collins looked up and forced a smile. "To be frank I'm worried. There's something going on and I can't put my finger on it."

"How do you mean?"

"The Yemen army base in Hadda. We try to keep track of movements. There has been a huge amount of activity and now a satellite has picked up a column of tanks moving towards Sana'a from the old border. There'll be a fax around all the offices tomorrow." Collins went on gloomily. "We are recommending non-essential personnel be packed and ticketed for possible evacuation."

"It's not good timing. The other day you said everything was stable."

"It was. But these army movements are strange. The army's got a bunch of our aid money. The southern army too would lose out if there was any secessionist movement. I can't see why they would move tanks to Sana'a. The tribes around Marib are upset about the oil money being siphoned off. It's they who need watching." He paused. "Anyway I'm sorry. Perhaps it's nothing but you know what would happen if we hadn't warned you. The media would tear us apart."

"I suppose so but I'd rather you tried to be optimistic right now. My kids aren't here and we don't have any non-essential staff. A full evacuation would screw us up." He changed the subject. "What are you here for then? Seeing the Ambassador's wife off?"

"She won't go unless he goes. In fact I wouldn't be surprised if he left and didn't tell her." They both laughed and Collins continued. "No I'm meeting the wife of the doctor who was kidnapped."

"Perhaps Turnbow's wife can do something. The Arab men respect women. Remember that Brit..."

"He was kidnapped in the south. The tribes are different down there."

"Yes you're right," Kraill said, "but hell, if it makes her feel better..."

"I'm divorced. My ex-wife would celebrate if I was kidnapped."

"Me too. Anyway let's hope these tank movements are nothing. We're spudding in Wadi Qarib next week. The drilling won't last long but a war, even a short one won't be good..."

"I don't know, Emmett. Oh, by the way I'll be at your party tomorrow after all. The Ambassador is coming and I'm supposed to hold his hand. Curt Gawain will be in charge at the Embassy, and most of our Marines will be guarding the hotel."

"I was talking to Curt about the oil industry the other day. He seemed well-informed."

"Hmm," mumbled Collins, unimpressed.

There was a flurry of activity around the exit gate as the first passengers began to appear. Peter Greaves, his lanky body towering over the throng of Arabs at the gate, appeared near the front, pushing a heavily laden trolley. A Chinese girl walked behind him. She looked tired and pale. Kraill pushed through the crowd, waving at Greaves who was looking around for a familiar face.

They shook hands but, apart from cursory introductions they didn't speak in the noisy, echoing hall and the silence continued as they pushed through the glass doors and crossed the car park to Kraill's Land Cruiser. Greaves got in the front and Natalya climbed in the back.

"I'm taking you to the Mogul Rani hotel in the centre of Sana'a. It's about a half hour's drive," said Kraill before switching on the engine.

As they left the terminal Natalya saw a stretched white limousine appear from the VIP car park. It had the flag of the United States flying from its hood. Kraill waved at the man sitting in the front of the limo and Natalya recognised the good looking man in the back who had been on their flight. He was sitting next to a middle-aged woman staring out at the street with a frightened expression.

"Who are they?" She asked Kraill.

"Dick Collins is in the front. He's in charge of security at the Embassy. The wife of the guy who was kidnapped the other day is in the back. She's come here to get him out. I don't know who the other guy is."

"I hope she can do something," said Natalya. She surprised herself as she blinked back some tears welling up in her eyes.

Next morning Teri Mayes walked through the ballroom of the Mogul Rani hotel. She looked around at the stained walls and patchy red carpet before turning to the hotel manager at her side. He was a short Indian man who stared back at her, tugging at his beard, a big smile on his face.

"Do not worry, Miss Teri, the room will be spick and span by tonight. We know your every wish and we are doing it straight away already."

"Now Mr Patel, you promised everything would be spick and span last week." She mimicked his words. "The drinks are going to be delivered from the commissary at ten and you will need to set up the bar. How can that happen? Your staff haven't even cleaned up?"

"No problem, Miss Teri, no problem at all. The boys will be doing their business where we are putting the bar first thing. Everything is in order, I am sure."

"And the dining tables. When will they be set up?"

"I surmise you are anxious, Miss Teri, but have no fear, I am having wonderful parties in the hotel, many times. I do believe you have attended. Have you enjoyed yourself at these splendid functions?"

"Yes, but the hotel is running half empty. Why this last minute rush? You've got loads of staff."

"You are right the staff numbers are too great. These troubles in this country they are indeed not good for business. But I am hoping your illustrious company will bring many more to my hotel so I keep having too many staff. It is not so foolish to think of the future."

"Please clean up this room now."

"We are doing all you asked for just now, isn't it? The cooks are already preparing to make the food. They are always doing a magnificent job. Indeed magnificent."

Teri nodded. The Mogul Rani produced excellent Indian cuisine. "I'm sure it is fine," she said, "but I will be back at four thirty. The American Embassy needs details of all our guests and I would like a list of all the residents."

"Yes I know. The local police are protecting us very well also. My hotel will be safe tonight. I will be seeing you again at four thirty."

"Yes, thank you, Mr Patel." She shook his hand and left. Outside it was hot and dusty and she walked quickly to her waiting car. The driver, attentive as always, had started the engine and the air conditioning was pumping out cool damp air.

"Where do you go now, Miss Teri?" He asked as he roared heedlessly into the traffic.

"Back to the office," she said. A motorcycle swerved round the car, narrowly missing its fender. The rider wobbled precariously but drove off as if nothing had happened.

SIXTEEN

As Teri Mayes' driver returned her to the Outland office in Sana'a, Benjamin Bone drove nervously over the ramp at the rental car return compound at Charles de Gaulle airport. His bag, a small grey canvas holdall, had fallen as he had slammed on his brakes in front of the ramp and it now lay on the floor below the passenger seat.

The car was fully paid up, booked in the name of a fictitious travelling salesman. He parked it, grabbed his bag and walked to the rental bus stop. He was dressed smartly in a grey suit and tie and looked like any ordinary businessman but he still felt eyes watching, staring at his guilty face. The bus took just ten minutes to reach the terminal and he alighted and entered the busy departure lounge, then crossed over to one of the Air France desks. The queue was slow moving and while he waited he took note of the security guards at the end of each row of desks. Eventually there was just one couple in front of him but they were engaged in a long conversation with the girl behind the counter. Come on, he muttered to himself under his breath as they made to move off then returned again with a new question.

Finally it was his turn.

"Bonjour. I am travelling to Dubai." He spoke deliberately in English.

"Your ticket please. And your passport." The girl spoke quietly back at him, also in English but with a strong French accent.

"Thank you." Benjamin gave them to her. His palm was damp and a greasy stain had appeared on the glossy paper of his ticket.

"Monsieur Borne, have you a seating preference?"

"Window, no smoking."

She nodded and tapped his details into her VDU. Benjamin leaned over the desk to watch her.

"You finish in Dubai, yes."

"Yes."

"How many pieces."

"What?"

"Of luggage. How many pieces? Please place them on the belt."

"I only have hand baggage."

She picked up his passport and looked through it. A Dubai visa was stamped on the third page. Natalya had booked his flights to Dubai and Yemen separately. She handed the passport back and continued to tap the keyboard, looking closely at the screen. She rose abruptly pushing back her chair.

"Excusez moi, I will be back soon."

He watched her walk over to a uniformed man sitting three desks away. What if she's spotted the changes in his passport? Or seen his Yemeni visa? Maybe the police have told them to watch out for me. Why else would she just walk off? He leaned over to look at the screen but saw meaningless numbers. He sensed the restless people behind him. The check-in girl was still talking to the uniformed man and they both looked over at him. He turned away pretending not to see.

He carefully picked up his small bag and with a sidelong glance at the girl he backed away. But he failed to see the case belonging to the passenger behind him and backed into it, lost his balance and tumbled inelegantly onto the tiled floor. One person in the queue laughed. The elderly lady who owned the case helped him to his feet. As he got up the check-in girl returned to her desk. She leaned towards him, holding a slip of card.

Benjamin stared at her hand.

"Non, Monsieur, do not go. You are forgetting your boarding card." She handed the blue card to him. "The plane is full and my manager says we are pleased Air France can upgrade you to Business Class today."

"Oh, thank you. I didn't expect...thank you."

With relief he passed through emigration. The official barely looked at his passport. Nobody seemed at all interested in him, neither the passengers in the bus carrying them to the plane nor the stewardess who nodded as he stepped aboard. He sat in his window seat and after a few minutes the plane taxied to its take-off point. It roared and bumped along the runway, took off and pulled up its landing gear. Benjamin stared at the now rain-swept streets of Paris below. The ring road marked by slow moving beams of light was a pretty sight but it soon disappeared beneath stormy dark clouds which caused the plane to lurch from side to side.

They landed in Dubai a few minutes late. Benjamin went straight to the transit desk where he checked in for his Yemenia flight. He had plenty of time so he ambled about the duty free shops and completed the quick crossword from Air France's in-flight magazine. A quarter of an hour before his flight was due to leave he handed his boarding card to a girl in an orange uniform with a black silk scarf around her head. In the departure lounge he picked up an English language newspaper and thumbed through it. There was no mention of his crime in the international section. He replaced the paper on the seat and looked up when he heard a commotion at the gate at the far end of the room.

An elderly man in a gaudy blue suit and bright shirt was pushing a path to the front, ignoring the other passengers in the queue. Another man followed behind and Benjamin recognised him instantly. It was Earl Rittman. Benjamin buried his face in his hands as if nursing a headache. He heard Rittman's companion say, "First Class, make way, make way," and the two men entered the room, the loud man forcing a route past other passengers. He strutted to the departure gate and glared at the uniformed guard, demanding to board. The guard ignored him, signalling to the families with children milling near by. After several families had struggled past, the two Americans were finally allowed on the plane but Benjamin waited in his seat until the lounge was almost empty before boarding himself. As he walked along the aisle through the first class seats to the back he saw Rittman again. For a very brief moment their eyes met but no hint of recognition crossed the American's face.

The other man who worked for Outland Oil who would have recognised Benjamin was right now in the conference room in Outland's offices in Sana'a with Emmett Kraill and Bob Janek.

"I'll handle things this end, Emmett," said Peter Greaves. "You make sure the trip runs smoothly. You'll have a lot of important people flying to the wadi and it's up to you to make sure they come back with a good report. Safety is a big issue in the States."

Kraill looked at Greaves with disgust. Why should this guy, running a simple operation in London, come and order him around. In the morning Greaves had walked into the office an hour later than expected after catching a taxi to the office, despite having been told an Outland driver would be waiting for him at the hotel. His first words had been, "why was I held up?"

Bob Janek said, "Everything will go real smooth, only don't send any goddamn experts to look at the rig as it's a heap of shit."

Greaves turned to look at Janek. "It's your responsibility to drill a well. Kraill's to handle the PR. I suggest you keep your mouth shut."

"Fuck you, Greaves." Janek retorted but without animosity.

Greaves ignored him. "Now Kraill," he said, "you will commence drilling in three days. The visitors must see some drilling."

"We will follow the drilling program," answered Kraill. "However the way it's going we should be making hole the day after tomorrow."

"Excellent but I don't want the thirty inch casing run too soon."

"Tophole is shit hard. It'll be three or four days at least."

Greaves wrinkled his brow. "Rittman and I will handle reporting from here for the first few days. You should be out on the rig."

Kraill sighed. He had been expecting Greaves and Rittman to leave Yemen straight after the party.

"Splendid," Greaves went on, "I'll be back to the hotel now. I'm dog-tired, where's the driver?"

"Teri's got him but she'll be back pretty soon. Otherwise I can run you back myself."

"I'll wait for Teri. By the way Natalya will be coming to the party tonight. Teri needs all the names doesn't she? Security better be tight."

"Who's Natalya?" asked Janek.

"She's our travel agent. Keep your hands off her when you meet her, she's a nice girl. I've heard you're a ladies man." He turned to look at Kraill, smiling broadly."Does Bob attract women like mosquitoes on a steamy night in the jungle? Now I need the lavatory where is it?"

Kraill got up and took him outside, pointed him in the right direction and returned to the room. "What an asshole that guy is," he said.

"Natalya couldn't be so nice if she agrees to come to Yemen with him. He's a shithead."

"I don't know Bob. She looked all right to me."

"What's that supposed to mean?"

Natalya was sitting in her room on the twelfth floor of the hotel. It was well appointed with shower caps in leather sachets, spherical soaps and bottles of shampoo, conditioner and foam bath arranged on a folded face flannel in a wicker basket. It was a pity the carpet was stained and there was a mouldy patch on the wall above her bed. The TV was on in the corner. An Arab man with a red face was talking at the camera. She had muted the sound while methodically copying out the travel agent entries in the telephone directory, but her mind was occupied with other things.

In Ruislip she had told Benjamin she would meet him at the airport. But now she knew that Emmett Kraill would be meeting Rittman off the same flight. Although she could make up a story about visiting the airline offices, he could still ask difficult questions if he saw her with Benjamin. In any case, she had no intention of seeing Benjamin at all. She was upset with him and it had soured her trip. Benjamin had never mentioned his French wife to her, not even hinted at her existence. Her mother had even asked him in her forthright manner, "why you have no girlfriend, you not like girls?" Benjamin had blushed but dispelled her mother's fears by saying he was as manly as her husband and that Natalya was his girlfriend. The blush had been endearing at the time but now she knew it was because of his lie.

She got up from the desk, slid open the window and stepped onto the balcony. She was well covered, wearing a long cotton skirt, plain and unflattering. Her shirt was white and long sleeved. The sun was hazy but still brilliant, sparkling in the small pond at the front of the hotel below. There was a persistent, noisy drone of engines from vehicles, air conditioners and generators. The road was jammed with traffic, mostly battered saloons and motor bikes. Two women, or at least she assumed them to be women, were shrouded in black like the ninjas from the movies her brother liked so much. They stepped into the street without looking and a Hilux pickup swerved sharply to avoid them.

A row of rusty yellow taxis was parked in the hotel forecourt. Drivers were squatting together on the sandy verge smoking. Another group of taxis was parked across the road. She walked back to the desk and tore off a piece of Mogul Rani notepaper from the pad. On it she wrote in big black letters, "Brian Borne" and folded it neatly before putting it into her shoulder bag. She left her room and took the elevator to the ground.

At ground level it was hot and oppressive. The air smelt of diesel and the noise of the traffic, especially the incessant horns, gave her a headache. She watched the group of drivers on the other side of the road for a moment before crossing over. The men rose together and surrounded her, gesticulating at their vehicles and shouting. Since she was neither white nor Muslim, they treated her with scant respect. One man touched her arm and shouted in Arabic at his colleagues. "She's my passenger. I was first. I've been here since early morning."

"No, you bastard, I was here before you. You are a liar," a second driver replied.

"Come for me, my taxi good, here come," said the first, reverting to broken English.

Natalya pointed at another, cleaner taxi and said. "I want that one."

"The second driver shouted at her again, "no, you have me, I am first."

The owner of her chosen vehicle pushed him away, and was about to grab her arm, when a new voice behind her said in Arabic, "leave her alone you are frightening her. Let her choose."

The first driver shouted back, "shut up she is my fare, you mind your business." He grabbed her other arm.

Since she was almost fluent in their language, Natalya had understood most of what was being said and now she began to shout back at them. "What are you doing?" Natalya screamed in Arabic. The throng froze. "What are you doing," she repeated louder, "you should be ashamed of yourselves. I am a lady, a visitor to your country and you treat me like this. Have you no respect for a woman, do you treat your wives like this? Your wives would be ashamed at your disgraceful behaviour now go away. All of you go away."

They fell back and she turned looking for the man who had spoken in her defence. He was scrawny and unshaven and had a dirty white scarf tied round his head. "You. Did you ask them to leave me alone?" She spoke in English now.

"Yes, ma'am. I am sorry for my friends."

"I will go with you. What is your name?"

A broad smile spread across his thin face. "Of course, come with me. My name is Jimmy."

The rest of the drivers watched angrily as Jimmy led her to his battered car. The front passenger door was wired to the chassis with what looked like a clothes hanger. Jimmy held open the door of the back seat, slammed it shut behind her, then got into the driver's seat.

Natalya leaned forward and said slowly, "take me round the corner, then stop the car."

"Yes, ma'am." He cut across the traffic and stopped at the roadside.

"I am not going anywhere but I need you to pick a man up at the airport in two hours. Can you do that?"

"Of course. I will bring him straight back. Those drivers are fools but they mean no harm. They are poor. We are not bad people."

"Yes I understand. Now take your passenger to another hotel, not the Mogul Rani. Tell him to wait for a message from me. Can you recommend a hotel?"

"Yes ma'am, the Ashok is the number two hotel in Yemen after the Mogul Rani and rooms are always available."

"Take him there."

"Yes. How will I recognise him?"

She removed the note from her bag and handed it to the driver along with some money she had prepared. "Hold this name up. He's white, tall, with brown hair. But he's almost bald."

He took the money and the note. "Trust me lady. I will pick him up."

"Thank you. Now tell me, why are you called Jimmy? It's not an Arabic name."

"A man from Scotland. He gave me this name. I drove him all over town."

"Oh I see," she smiled, "and after you drop Mr Borne forget him. You never saw him."

Jimmy looked round at her, smiled and nodded. But he knew he would offer to take this Mr Borne wherever he asked for as long as he wanted. Perhaps if he had asked her why he was supposed to forget, things might have worked out better for him.

SEVENTEEN

The Yemenia Boeing 737 landed at Sana'a International Airport with a heavy bump. Several overhead lockers along the length of the plane popped open, spilling their contents onto the heads of passengers beneath. Benjamin, seated at the back, avoided the debris and peered into the dusk through his scratched and cloudy window. The plane taxied to the gate and the door was opened but he stayed where he was until most of the passengers had alighted. At last he walked up the aisle, pausing at the exit door before stepping out onto the stairway leading to the parking apron. The evening air was warm and the smells of the city were rich and heavy. Between the sky and the terminal he saw the line of the high plateau. An air force jet dipped out of the sky, its afterburners glowing red above the decrepit terminal building. It disappeared behind the plateau, in the red glare of the setting sun.

Unknown to Benjamin the jet was one of many flying over the capital that day, another of the signs concerning Dick Collins. He and Curt Gawain were talking in Gawain's office in the American Embassy. "I tell you Curt the southern army is moving troops. Tanks arrived last night and the Presidential guard has been increased around the palace. All the neighbouring streets have been closed, even the old silver souk. We need to get our people out and alert Washington."

"You're an alarmist Dick, what does the Yemeni Defence Minister say?"

"The Ambassador spoke to him this morning. He says his Guard is carrying out a security exercise. It's just a precautionary measure."

"So, don't you worry then Dick."

"The Minister is not telling the truth and you know it."

Dick Collins seethed at Gawain's lack of concern but he was more upset by the Ambassador's dismissive tone of this morning. "No use causing a scare amongst the expats," the Ambassador had said casually. "When nothing happens we don't want to be seen to be over-reacting. Americans are made of sterner stuff."

"But the French are talking about evacuating all their nationals," Collins had replied.

"Aha, talking you say. The French do that a lot, talk. They talk like crazy. Have you ever seen one of their movies? Now go and organise the guards for the hotel tonight. With all this trouble you must be extra secure."

Collins had stormed off angrily.

"Have you any news from Ali about Turnbow?" Gawain asked.

"Nope, seems he's straight and his bank checks out. I bet you anything Turnbow is in his home town, Karim, but we can't do anything out there."

"Yes," said Gawain, "the man's probably dead already. What did you say to his wife?"

"Nothing yet. She and the journalist are in the hotel. They called a few times but I was out and the Ambassador doesn't want to talk to them."

"How can the wife do anything? Best find his body and get it sent back to the States with her."

"You're pretty sure he's dead, Curt?"

"It seems likely doesn't it?"

"The thing stinks," said Collins. "If I had my way I would have all the American nationals out tomorrow."

"Well fortunately you don't. Let us career diplomats handle diplomacy."

"Sure Curt. I've got to go to the Ambassador's house now and wait for them while they get ready. Its fucking ridiculous." Collins rarely swore.

He left Gawain and walked through the Embassy building. Outside on the driveway a sleek black limousine stood on the gravel. A local driver in a suit sat at the wheel. A Marine in white uniform was standing by the passenger door, smoking.

"Sergeant Cutler, sorry about all this," said Collins. Sergeant Cutler had been guarding the Ambassador's wife ever since the bomb outside the gates last week.

"No problem sir," Cutler replied.

"Keep the Ambassador's wife safe for a few more days and we'll get you back on Embassy duty. I'm recommending the wives are evacuated."

"Thank you sir." Cutler said.

"Had any trouble so far?"

"No, not really."

"Not really?"

"Well she doesn't listen to my advice."

"They never do. If you have any serious problems contact me."

"Thank you sir," Cutler said again. Cutler liked Collins but didn't envy his job. He would bottle up his temper for a few days more.

Collins pulled out a cigarette and was about to light it when Erwin Shelterman, the Ambassador walked up. He was followed by his wife Elizabeth Shelterman, a grey woman with close-set teeth. They both greeted Collins while the Yemeni driver opened the back door. The three of them got in. Sergeant Cutler waited before getting into the front passenger seat. The driver drove the limousine out of the Embassy gates, bouncing it over the high kerb. Elizabeth Shelterman gazed out of the heavily tinted window, staring with a look of disgust at the dirty streets.

Collins, who sat facing her, was thinking about Teri Mayes. He was hoping that the Outland Oil administrator would speak to him tonight. Had she forgiven him for what had happened last month?

A battered bus took the last of the passengers on Benjamin's flight across the runway to the terminal building. He helped an old man alight from the steps of the bus and slowly walked with him to the immigration desks. He was pretty sure that Rittman and his companion would have left by now but the queue at passport control was formidable and Benjamin patiently stood in one of the slow moving lines. He was nervously aware that Natalya was waiting on the other side of the wall.

Finally through immigration, his visa unquestioned, the officers polite, he bypassed the crowded luggage carousel and walked into the arrivals hall. There were many people about, clustered around a line of rails, shoving for a better view. The dinginess of the place struck him at once, its brown walls and concrete ceiling grimy with years of decay. A throng of unkempt taxi drivers surrounded him, grabbing for his small bag. Repeatedly refusing their offers he looked about for Natalya. A scrawny man shoved a piece of paper in his face.

"Brian Borne. You are Brian Borne?"

"Yes...right," doubtful for a moment, "who are you?"

"I am Jimmy. I take you with me."

"Where to, please?"

"Your lady friend, she told me. Please follow and give me your bag."

"No, I'll take it. Where is she?"

"She is staying at the Mogul Rani, Yemen's number one hotel. Please we go now?"

Outside the terminal building sweat accumulated on his brow, in his armpits and in his pants. Jimmy guided him across a road choked with cars and vans. Children, hands outstretched, ran at his feet. Jimmy's yellow cab was parked on its own and Benjamin eased himself into the back after dropping a few English coins into some of the children's hands.

They made slow progress to the city through the crowded streets, blocked by handcarts piled with fruit, nuts and cheap Chinese trinkets, surrounded by young men wearing futahs. The few women were all heavily shrouded. The taxi crept along, caught behind a lorry belching out acrid blue fumes and Benjamin leaned forward. "Jimmy, how far is the Mogul Rani from here?"

"Not so far sir, but we don't go there, we go to the Ashok Hotel, it is of international quality. My good friend is manager. Have no fear he will look after you. I am pleased to offer myself as your driver. Anywhere you need to go, please ask, OK"

"I need money. Where is a bank?"

"No sir. Not the bank. I will change money for you in the souk. Much better rate. Sixty for one dollar."

"Is it legal?"

"Sure I make it legal. I change for you."

It took them almost an hour to get to the souk, passing the Mogul Rani hotel on the way which Jimmy pointed out enthusiastically. The walled souk lay a few blocks away in the old part of the city, unspoilt by any concrete towers. The square outside was crowded with hordes of merchants and their carts and milling shoppers. Permanent shops sold cloth and dried foods. The mud-brick buildings were tightly packed, their walls decorated with whitewash patterns and ornate windows.

Jimmy parked at the edge of the square. "You give me the dollars now."

In the car Benjamin had peeled off one hundred dollars from the notes he had changed in Dubai and he gave these to Jimmy. "You wait here, Mr Brian, I can get better rate if there is no white man around."

Jimmy disappeared into the crowds before Benjamin could object. The driver would take a cut of the money but he didn't mind as long as he returned with something. The rate Jimmy had quoted was double what he would receive in a bank.

Benjamin was just beginning to get nervous when, ten minutes later, he returned. "I got good rate," he said and handed over a wad of grubby notes, "better than I expected. It's the troubles. Our economy is no good."

"Thanks a lot," said Benjamin, pleased he had trusted the driver.

The Ashok hotel was hidden in a narrow dirt alley and the taxi had to negotiate deep ruts in the road to get there. It didn't look to Benjamin like a hotel of international quality and it was evident to him that Jimmy had never been in a Regent or an Intercontinental.

He checked in, leaving Jimmy standing in the foyer. His room on the second floor was narrow, hardly wider than a corridor. Benjamin didn't mind. In fact it was no worse than hotel rooms he had stayed in, in the north of England where running a bath could take until morning. It did not have a bath. A torn plastic curtain partly obscured a toilet bowl and a steel shower head fixed to the ceiling over the tiled floor. A metal bed ran along the wall below a small window that looked out over an alley at the side of the hotel. Next to the bed was a fridge with a yellowing price list taped to its top. The fridge was stocked with soft drinks and packets of snacks. Benjamin smiled at a nut confection called 'Mr Green.' The hotel owner had given him a blanket at the desk and Benjamin laid it over the lumpy mattress and sheet before showering.

After he had finished it had turned dark outside and he decided to take a walk to the Mogul Rani. The evening was warm, the air polluted with diesel fumes. When he reached the hotel he stood across the road. Natalya had told him Outland's party was tonight and he saw police checking everybody leaving and entering, watched by two American Marines. A stretched black limousine bearing the US flag on its radiator passed him by, its horn blaring. In the car he saw a wrinkled bitter-looking woman stare right through him, scowling at the people beyond.

Benjamin didn't dare try to enter through the front lobby so he headed for a side street to the right of the hotel. The street was flanked by a high wall bordering the grounds but he saw a metal gate swinging open and stepped through. Inside there was a dimly lit swimming pool, surrounded by fairy lights dangling from leafless trees. The dark grounds also contained a children's playground, a few ragged bushes and a patchy lawn. He walked towards a wing of the hotel where lights shone through cracks in its curtains.

He could hear the muffled beat of music and peered through a chink in the curtain, cupping his hands over his eyes. The party was in full swing. There were Arabs inside and elderly white men plus a few women. He scanned the room for Natalya. A Filipino band was performing on a stage and the muffled beat of music was vibrating the glass. Close to the window Benjamin saw an elegant blonde lady. It was his first sight of Teri Mayes but Benjamin didn't look for long at her. He started back when he saw the man she was speaking to was Peter Greaves.

EIGHTEEN

A few hours earlier Rajan Patel, the General Manager of the Mogul Rani had proved he was a man of his word. Teri Mayes returned in the afternoon as she had promised and found a scene barely recognisable from the disarray of the morning. A bar was set with acres of white table linen covering circular tables fanning across the ballroom. A stage was built and red velvet drapes hid the scaffold. Electricians, holding bundles of tangled wires, were working on the stage. The manager, standing on a now burnished wooden dance floor, was addressing a group of white-shirted waiters.

When Patel saw Teri enter the room he stepped over, smiling obsequiously. "Ah, Miss Teri. You are seeing everything is almost ready."

"Yes, thank you. I am so pleased."

"No need worrying you see. You listen to me next time."

"Yes thank you. Please could I talk to one of your waiters? Your best one."

"Of course you will be getting the best at your service." He turned to the group on the dance floor. "Ranjit," he shouted. "The lady is wanting you straight away already."

Ranjit Singh smiled when his name was called. He knew the other waiters were looking at him enviously, suspecting that the white woman desired him. Ranjit too was well aware of the simmering lusts of European women. He'd seen it in countless movies and he loved the movies, especially American ones which were so much more realistic than Bollywood melodramas. It's a pity I am married and love my wife and children, he thought. Although he was loath to admit that all five of his children were girls, the youngest just six months old.

His family relied on his income from the hotel, most of which they received back in India. The rest he saved for when he had to marry off his daughters. It was a big commitment. He intended to buy the best match possible for them. In fact he yearned to see them again soon and was happy in the knowledge that he had obtained a transfer to the Mogul Rani's sister hotel in New Delhi. He was to be head waiter of one of its most splendid restaurants and he had sent a letter to his wife only that morning telling her to look forward to his arrival.

"Yes Miss. What is it you require?"

"My name is Miss Mayes. Could you take care of the Oil Minister personally when he arrives? Make sure he has drinks and food."

"I am honoured to be chosen, Madam," he answered. Despite his wife he did wonder what this Miss Mayes lady was like in bed and was wondering whether to allow the white lady to sleep with him this one time. I am going away soon and my wife is far away. We men have urges and this Miss Mayes, in her smart suit, is just the job for me.

Three hours later Teri had finished tidying her hair in front of the mirror in the ladies washroom. She shouted through the door of a cubicle. "Natalya, I've got to be there for when my boss arrives."

"I'm coming, thanks for waiting." Teri had met Natalya with Peter Greaves in the hotel lobby earlier and she had promised to introduce her to as many people as possible. Natalya was pleased to make a friend as she had felt lonely since the fracas with the taxi drivers.

When she emerged she said to Teri, "Mr Kraill told me about a trip to your oil well on Tuesday. Would it be all right if I go?"

"You'll have to ask Bob Janek. He's in charge. The plane is pretty full."

"Can you ask him for me?"

"We don't get on so well."

"I'll ask Mr Kraill then."

"Sure. I'll mention it to him too."

"Thanks." She put a deep red lipstick to her lips smearing it on generously. "Right I'm ready, let's go."

They walked together through the hotel lobby and along the corridor to the ballroom. Emmett Kraill was standing outside the wooden double doors, thumbing through papers. He looked up when they arrived.

"Oh. Hi. Hello Natalya, how are you enjoying Sana'a?"

"It's OK."

Kraill smiled at her, fancying her. He turned to Teri. "Is this guest list up to date? How many will the Oil Minister bring?"

"He hasn't told us. I expect it'll be five or six."

"Thank God the President's not coming," he paused and then added. "They'll arrive soon. Better get inside. Where's Bob?"

"I don't know. He went off somewhere this afternoon. I haven't seen him."

"He'd better be here." He looked at Natalya, then back at Teri. "Oh Teri, you've put on a good show here."

The Hotel Manager, who was walking towards them, heard the compliment. "See, Miss Mayes, you are right for trusting me, excuse me but there is a telephone calling you right away. Please answer in my office."

She left and the Manager said to Kraill. "Yes, she is a fine lady. I am thinking like you too."

Kraill and Natalya walked into the ballroom. Waiters were milling round the tables making last minute arrangements to the settings. Three small Filipino men in maroon jackets, all with neat moustaches, were sitting on the stage with guitars. A plump Filipino girl with heaps of dark hair and full lips was adjusting her microphone. A waiter came up to Kraill and asked whether they would like a drink. Kraill took a beer, Natalya, an orange juice.

"So, how long are you here then?" asked Kraill.

"I'll be going back on Wednesday."

"You can come on the trip out to our rig then. Ask Bob Janek for a slot when he gets here. I'm sure there's lots of space."

"Thanks, I will."

"If he ever does appear. I don't know where he's got to..." He stopped speaking as the door opened and Teri came in. They watched her as she made her way towards them, pausing for a moment to whisper something to one of the Sikh waiters.

"Hi," she said. "I called Bob's maid. She doesn't know where he is. Sounds like she doesn't care either."

Natalya was about to ask why everyone was so rude about Bob Janek when she saw Peter Greaves walk into the ballroom followed by two other men. One was middle-aged, the other much older and all three were dressed in suits. Greaves and the younger of the two wore sombre, old-fashioned jackets but the older man was dressed garishly. His jacket was light blue and large, his tie was wide and multi-coloured and his trousers were hitched up over his rotund waist, half way up his chest.

"Emmett, good to see you again, call a waiter over," the old man shouted, staring at Natalya. "And introduce me to these two lovely ladies." Like his suit and tie, he was a loud man.

Kraill did so, introducing Natalya as an international executive in the travel industry.

"This is Congressman Bruce Steeples and Earl Rittman, our Managing Director," he said to Natalya.

"Oh yes, I've heard of you Mr Rittman, I've arranged your tickets before."

A waiter with a tray of drinks appeared and the newcomers chose beers. As the Filipino band began playing dance music Natalya excused herself to introduce herself to other guests. When she had gone Kraill said "Earl, I'm afraid the Oil Minister would like to visit the well on Tuesday, I couldn't dissuade him."

"No problem, if he wants to, he can."

"Peter said it would be nothing but trouble."

"What's it matter, we've got nothing to hide."

"Yes, nothing to hide," Greaves said. "Now you make sure he has a good trip." Kraill winced at the patronising tone and was thankful to see other guests were arriving. "Hadn't you better greet the guests now Earl," went on Greaves. "Ah, here's Bob Janek. Congressman he's our drilling engineer and a damned good one. Where've you been Bob?"

"Goddamn this country I was held up at a road block for four fucking hours. The Arabs were treating me like I was a fucking terrorist. I need a drink."

"What did you do?" put in Teri.

"What do you think I did? I didn't do anything. They get their kicks from screwing us up, and they're fucking tetchy at the moment."

"Sure, Bob," she answered, knowing Janek could wind up the most mild-mannered of men.

As Janek took a large beer from the waiter's tray there was a stir at the door as a US Marine walked in. He was followed by the American Ambassador and his wife. Close behind them came Dick Collins. Congressman Steeples immediately strode over to shake hands with the Ambassador.

Grunting at Steeples as he left, Bob Janek looked around the rapidly filling room. By the bar the Chinese girl he had heard about was talking to a young man he didn't recognise and he went over with his drink. "Hi," he said, ignoring the man but extending his hand to the girl. "You must be Natalya. My name's Bob Janek. Greaves told me about you. How do you like it here then?"

"It's OK," replied Natalya, "this is Richard Clapton. He's a reporter."

Janek nodded at Richard and shook hands. "A reporter, eh. So the world is interested in Outland Oil now? Don't quote me should I accidentally let out any of my opinions."

"No, I'm here with Mrs Turnbow, her husband was....."

"Oh her, I know. Her old man is probably dead."

"Why do you say that?"

"I've been out here a long time, sonny."

Natalya stared at Janek. She'd never met anyone like this American with his hollow eyes and prominent forehead. He unnerved her.

"Now Natalya," Janek went on, "I came right on over here when I saw you."

"Yes?"

"How'd you like to come out on the Twin Otter to our site on Tuesday? We're laying on a trip. For VIP's only of course."

Natalya smiled, pleased she had been asked again. She suspected Greaves would want her in Sana'a when the others were away.

"I'd like to. Can I bring someone?" She was thinking fast. "He's on an aid programme out here and would be interested."

"Sure, there's plenty of space but it beats me why these aid guys do it. The towel heads should look after themselves and if they can't why waste money on no-hopers."

"Can Mrs Turnbow and myself go too?" put in Richard Clapton.

"It's one big party. Be at the domestic airport at 7 am, Tuesday. We'll be gone all day. You won't need anything. A big lunch will be laid on. Now Natalya, how about a dance?"

Natalya would dearly have liked to say no, but nodding to Richard, she said, "see you later" and followed Janek on to the dance floor. Richard looked at them for a moment, liking the girl, before making his way across the room towards an unusually tall Yemeni from Aden he had met in the hotel earlier. He was a journalist who wrote for the local English language paper.

Ranjit Singh, the waiter, stood by the doors into the kitchen watching the guests. The Oil Minister had turned up quietly with a large group. He was now talking to the fat old American in the ugly suit who had arrived after Miss Mayes.

Ranjit was sure he had only been chosen to serve the Oil Minister because of his manly physique and good looks. He was proud to be responsible for such an important person and he liked to show off his status by standing here, directing his colleagues to carry trays of drinks and canapés to different parts of the room. He couldn't wait to tell his wife of the honour. She would certainly boast about it to all her friends. The Minister was a weaselly fellow with a bald head, its skin blotched with dark patches and moles but for Miss Mayes sake he kept his thoughts well hidden. He took a tray of drinks from a waiter who appeared from the kitchen and walked over to them. He waited behind them, looking for an opportunity to present the tray.

The shortest in the group was the Oil Minister himself but had a presence that belied his height. However it was Congressman Steeples who was dominating the other men around him. The Minister had removed his black-rimmed glasses and was staring up at Steeples' flushed face.

"So, Congressman Steeples," he said bluntly in near perfect English, "why are you here?"

"As a guest of Outland Oil. I am sure we both agree that finding oil would be good for them and yourselves."

"Of course we do. But you are well-known in America for your forthright views about your oil business. Correct me if I'm wrong but it seems to us, my advisers and I, that you disapprove of our Arab brothers selling oil to America. Although of course Yemen is a small fish compared to Saudi Arabia. Or have you now realised the stupidity of pretending America does not need Arabs?"

"Of course America does not need you. But I am here to promote better relations. Your country is on the verge of civil war and it is better we are friends is it not? If you stopped selling us oil the US army would sort you out. Why did we recover Kuwait? Because the Kuwaiti government wants to buy our American goods and we will buy Kuwaiti oil."

"My country has been peaceful for years now. We had a fair election supported by you Americans. You try to antagonise me. Why?"

"If you are threatened by America it is not our fault. As I said we support the free world and, provided the oil flows from Arab wells, we will ensure the status quo is maintained. However, any hint of anti-Americanism in your government and it will be very different."

The Minister was astonished at Steeples' attitude. "I still don't comprehend this," he said. "Yemen is not oil-rich and its production is small compared to the Gulf. Perhaps this Outland company will find a new field but it won't make us rich overnight. Why are you threatening us?" He was angry now.

Steeples smiled. "Because, my dear fellow, you are not as helpless as you make out. Although poor, Yemen is a part of the Middle East, you are all in it together. You are breeding terrorists."

"I don't know what you mean, Congressman Steeples, but if you will excuse me I must be leaving." He nodded at Ranjit, still standing with the full tray of drinks behind him, and then beckoned to his entourage.

Across the room, Erwin Shelterman, the Ambassador, saw the Oil Minister's displeasure. The Minister was an important pro-American member of the Yemeni government. "What did that buffoon say?" he whispered to his wife who was inspecting some chicken satay on the table in front of her, wrinkling her nose in distaste. "And where is Collins? He should have been with them."

"Dick is over there dear," she answered, more cheerful than earlier, having drunk several vodkas, "but who is the overdressed woman at his side?"

"I don't know the woman," he replied. "Collins," he shouted above the music, "over here."

Collins looked across at him, said something to the lady, and they both came over.

"Let me introduce Mrs Turnbow, Ambassador," Collins said when they had reached them, "…and Mrs Turnbow, this is the Ambassador and Mrs Shelterman…."

"Ah, yes Mrs Turnbow," the Ambassador interrupted. "I expect you are worried about your husband but I can assure you we are doing everything in our power to get him back for you. It's a pity he didn't listen to our advice before he travelled up the highway. We told American tourists to stay away from the tribal areas." Shelterman glanced critically at Collins. "Now I'm sure Dick will take good care of you. But its better you don't disturb his important work. We have to consider the interests of all Americans here. Your Doctor is one more problem to us." All the time he was smiling broadly.

"How can you be so dismissive?"

"Now relax. We will try to find him I assure you."

Meanwhile the Filipino band had returned from a short break and the singer began introducing the next song. Mrs Turnbow turned and looked at them for a moment. Turning back she said to Shelterman, "I can do something, I know I can. Please tell me everything you know about the kidnap..."

"Look you are not helping at all. You would probably make matters worse. We know the situation and we are doing everything we can to solve it without jeopardising American interests." Shelterman spoke firmly. "We can't talk here, can we? It's too noisy. Come and see my deputy, Mr Gawain, tomorrow. He'll talk to you and get you a first class ticket back to the States. Now I must be off, I have to talk to Congressman Steeples."

"You are brushing me off..."

"Come on Mrs Turnbow. I'm not giving you any brush-off. An Ambassador's job is not easy, is it Collins?" He turned to Collins. "Send up a good meal to her room."

"It's OK," Mrs Turnbow interrupted, "I won't bother you. Go and talk to who you like." She nodded at Mrs Shelterman, who had been looking on in an alcoholic haze, and then walked off, side-stepping a group of young Yemenis drinking beer from cans.

"I told you to keep her away from me," said Shelterman to Collins.

"I can't force her, sir. It's understandable. You were cruel."

"You've got to be cruel to be kind the saying goes. Gawain will talk to her in the Embassy tomorrow. You should know this is not the place, Collins. Poor practice to introduce us here. I haven't forgotten why you got sent here from Jakarta. I've been charged with watching you and I can't say I am pleased at the moment. I was told one mistake would be enough so I suggest you be careful. I have to run this Embassy and its no easy job without good support." He was shouting above the music. "Now you get that lazy bastard Gawain onto her and get her out of my hair."

The Filipino band played loudly, the music thumping from speakers at each end of the stage but Collins heard the words well. Although the tone of Shelterman's voice made him shake with anger he had instantly regretted his words, knowing any dissension would count against him.

Two years ago he had been a commercial attaché in Jakarta on a fast-track to an Ambassador's post. It had been a typically hot, busy day when he had arrived home late from work to find his wife had flown back to America without even saying goodbye. She had left no note, nothing to say why, nowhere to contact her. He had called her parents and they told him they didn't know where she was. For two weeks he was unable to work. He sat in his room chewing his pencil, staring into space. One day he heard from a colleague at the American Club that there had been rumours he was sleeping with prostitutes. He never found out who had started them but it seemed his wife had heard and was disgusted.

Looking for the source of the rumour he had visited a bar in a downtown shopping centre where prostitutes and transvestites hung out with Americans. The bar had an absurd name he remembered, "Spanky Wanky." He had been there for ten minutes when there was a police raid. He was arrested and spent the night and part of the next day in a police cell. The Embassy bailed him out. Close to losing his job the Ambassador in Jakarta had been good to him and kept it from the press. He was at once posted to Yemen and given a chance to redeem himself.

Collins was interrupted from his bitter reverie. The band had stopped playing mid-song and the shouted conversations all around him had also ceased. On the stage next to the singer stood Margaret Turnbow, her arms raised. She looked large, much taller than the band, who themselves looked larger than life in the spotlights. "Give me the microphone," she shouted.

The singer handed it over and Mrs Turnbow clasped it to her chest. "My husband is missing. Do you know? While you enjoy yourself with your whisky and canapés and everything else, my husband is......," she paused...."is somewhere in the desert, probably dying. Why do you do nothing? Americans playing at politics. You Yemenis let anarchy rein in your own country. Why don't you do something? I came here to get him out and what do I find but my own Embassy... yes, ignoring me, what do I have to do..." She dropped her voice. "I don't want sympathy, no, but I want someone to care, to try and..." Her voice went quiet as the microphone went dead. She stopped in mid sentence as abruptly as the band had stopped singing.

Sergeant Cutler had been standing by the door when Mrs Turnbow mounted the stage. It had taken him only a few seconds to find and unplug the electricity outlet for the sound system. Most of the onlookers briefly watched the woman then turned to continue their conversations. Sanctimonious diplomats from other embassies made a note to convey the story to their respective governments.

Ranjit Singh watched too, sorry for the old woman and for her faded looks. He had no idea who she was or why she stood there but he was touched by her forlorn expression. He watched it turn from rage to despair and her eyes glisten as she scanned the room. A young man then climbed onto the stage and led her away to the door.

"Why did you do that?" Richard Clapton said as he shepherded her outside.

"I was angry, more angry than I have ever been in my life. Shelterman is a horrible man. How could our government be so stupid to employ people like him?"

"Its not stupidity, these men have to have hearts of stone. They choose them."

"What are we going to do now?"

"I've been speaking to an engineer working for Outland Oil. Apparently there's a trip going on Tuesday to their well site. Do you want to go? We can if we like."

"What's the point?"

"The nearest town to the well is called Karim. There's a rumour your husband disappeared on the road near Karim. I was speaking to the editor of the local English language paper. See the tall man over there. He said somebody in Karim might know something. It seems crazy, Karim is miles from anywhere, but its worth a try."

"Why didn't you tell me this earlier?"

"I didn't get a chance."

"Can't we go tomorrow? Why wait till Tuesday?"

"The road's dangerous. We wouldn't get through and you need permits. Outland's got a plane."

"Where did the editor hear the rumours?"

"He wouldn't say. He's not allowed to print anything about the kidnap."

"Typical." She yawned. "Will you try and find out more. I'm going to bed. I'll see you at breakfast. I can't take any more of this tonight."

Dick Collins, who was returning from a visit to the toilet, passed Mrs Turnbow as she made for the elevators. He nodded at her but she ignored him. In the main lobby Teri Mayes was speaking to the receptionist at the desk and Collins hovered behind her hoping to catch her eye. He had been trying to talk to Teri all evening but she had been constantly engaged with her Outland colleagues. He had thought she was trying to avoid him but when she finally turned round and saw him she came over smiling.

"Teri, you're not angry with me for last month?"

"No. Of course not Dick. We'd both had too much to drink and you weren't to know it would happen. I'd rather forget it."

"How about you coming back to my place tonight for a drink after this is over? I've got excellent bourbon. It came in the diplomatic bag this morning, much better than this blended whisky you've got here."

"You drink too much, Dick. No I can't make it tonight. I've got to entertain the Congressman. Perhaps another time."

"How about tomorrow?"

"No I'm sorry I can't make it until the end of the week. We've got all these guests and the site visit is on Tuesday but I promise I'll call you next week."

She had no good reason to call him. He was an overweight loser, she was a tall blonde.

"You sure? I can call you if you'd like."

"Anything will do. I do like you Dick and even though we were both drunk I enjoyed last week until...." She paused. "I wasn't ignoring you. I was embarrassed, it was the shock."

Last month he had asked her to join him for a picnic. It was the Arab weekend, a Friday afternoon, and they had driven into the desert together to a rocky hill at the foot of the plateau twenty kilometers out of Sana'a. After eating and drinking two bottles of wine they had lain in the sun in a quiet spot surrounded by boulders. Soon Collins had rolled on top of her, kissed her and moved his hand beneath her long skirt. They had made love on the mat, her dress shoved up over her waist, her knickers still on. When their passion had subsided they both heard the sound of falling rocks and looked up to see a man, not twenty yards away, with his trousers gaping, his dick in his hand. He scrambled away over the brow of the hill. They didn't utter a word about it on the trip back to the capital and had not seen each other since.

"I'd better get back to the party," Teri said. "We've got a cake. It's about time it was brought out. The Oil Minister has left already."

"Yes, I know. Congressman Steeples is not the most diplomatic of men."

"Sure, I'll call you. But next week," she said as she left him.

Inside the ballroom she saw Ranjit Singh standing by the kitchen door. Squeezing between dancing couples, she went to him and asked him to arrange someone to bring in the cake. Peter Greaves was also standing at the back of the room, on his own, close to the curtains. After Teri had whispered her instructions to Ranjit, Greaves beckoned her over.

"So everything is going well," Greaves said, "no problems you being a woman in an Arab country."

"Oh no," she answered, "couldn't be better."

It was then that Benjamin had peered through the window where the crack in the curtains let out the light. Benjamin had started back when he recognised Peter Greaves. Although certain he couldn't be seen in the dark, even if they had been looking, his heart raced. There were at least a hundred people visible in the hall, crowded round the drinks tables or pressed against the line of windows.

Benjamin decided to go back to his own hotel. He was tired and would contact Natalya tomorrow. He stepped back onto the verge and crossed the grass by the pool. It was then he saw a large man, dressed in black, carrying a black case. The man ran through the swinging gate on the other side of the pool and disappeared into the bushes. Benjamin ducked behind a plastic sun lounger. The man reappeared moments later, his hands now empty. He scampered back the way he had come and pulled the metal gate closed behind him.

Benjamin crossed back to the line of windows, side-stepped down the narrow gap between the shrubs and stared into the gloom. Sure enough the black bag, smaller than he had thought, like the ones lawyers use to carry around papers, lay on the soil. He was well aware that Yemen was politically unstable. He was also certain many important men were inside the building, so the fact that this bag may contain a bomb was not lost on him. "Shit." he cursed aloud, "now what do I do?"

He could not leave until he had told someone about the bag, preferably one of the American Marines who wouldn't know who he was and would know what to do. He had seen a glass door set back between brick columns on the left of the run of windows where he was standing. He picked his way through the low bushes and tugged on the door handle. It was locked. He walked further along the wall, careful to keep behind the bushes. At the far end of the building was a canvas awning over a yard lined with metal bins and black garbage sacks. He made for it but stopped when he saw, standing beside one of the bins, a Yemeni man in dirty white overalls smoking a cigarette.

Benjamin backed up against the wall and waited for several minutes, crouching beneath an overhanging bougainvillea while the man finished his cigarette. He finally dropped the stub onto the concrete floor and disappeared through the door behind him. Benjamin crossed the yard and followed the man through the swinging door. Inside was a dark corridor leading to double doors with glass windows. He peered through the glass and saw a busy kitchen. At one side a tall, turbaned Sikh was standing with an empty tray, shouting orders to the cook. Benjamin pushed through the doors and the cooks and waiter looked round at him, surprised to see a white man in their kitchen. A film of grimy oil had settled on his clothes and skin like cobwebs. The Sikh waiter saw him and spoke.

"Please sir the party is this way. You are lost."

"No I am not. It was hot in there and I went for a stroll around your gardens. I saw a man leave a case by the window out there. Could you ask one of your guards to take a look at it?"

Ranjit Singh couldn't believe his luck. First the American lady had taken a shine to him and now this. "Never mind, I will take a look at it myself, sir," he said.

"Are you sure. I think a guard would be better."

"It is not a problem sir. Please show me."

"OK then. I hope it's nothing."

Ranjit placed his tray next to the cake on the nearby table and followed Benjamin out into the yard. They walked across the grounds towards the line of bushes and took a narrow path towards the windows.

"You go back to the party, sir. I will deal with this." I can make a hero of myself now, he thought, and perhaps a bonus. My wife will be even prouder of me. He pushed a shrub aside gingerly. "I will be careful. I certainly don't wish to dirty my suit."

Benjamin backed away as Ranjit stepped over the flower bed, intending to go back to his hotel now, but he hesitated, curious about the bag.

When Ranjit saw it he smiled. He had not been entirely sure of the poorly dressed white man, even concerned for a moment that he was about to be raped from behind. He had heard white men liked doing that. He supposed that was why their women were so anxious for sex. Facing the window he picked the bag up. It was quite heavy and he examined it, wondering whether to open it, or to leave and fetch a guard after all. He began to turn back through the bushes but, as a result of the vibration or perhaps because of his unfortunate timing, Ranjit, for the briefest of moments, actually observed the bag explode in his hand. A wave of potential energy tore its black leather cladding into hundreds of tiny strips, sending them floating in the air like streamers.

NINETEEN

Benjamin toppled backwards. A splinter of glass hit him above the eye and a film of blood turned the scene a hazy pink. He sat for a moment. Distant screams were echoing around him. Slowly he focussed.

It was evident the Sikh's immaculate white suit would not need to be cleaned again. Shreds of it were strewn across the grass, many still wrapped around chunks of flesh and bone. There was no sign of the man's turbaned head. The windows beyond were shattered, the aluminium stanchions supporting glass panes stove in and twisted. As the red mist in his eyes cleared he saw into the room. The heavy velvet curtains were ripped and the force of the explosion had lifted tables, hurling them against the people beyond.

He pushed himself upright and stumbled from the remains of the waiter's body towards the swinging gate where he had entered the garden. It was shut and it was locked. He wrenched at it and keeled over. Reeling, he grasped for a vine growing along the wall. Clutching his stomach he tottered towards the kitchen yard. Double gates led out of the yard but they were heavily padlocked. Nausea and dizziness returned and he collapsed exhausted onto a pile of plastic rubbish sacks. He lay there, trying to control his breathing, pondering his next move.

Inside the crowded ballroom initial panic following the explosion had subsided. A large group was pushing towards the exit, but many of the guests had already left through fire doors behind the stage. Peter Greaves and Teri Mayes had moved away from the windows before the explosion. Teri was out in the lobby and Greaves had gone to search out Natalya. But a group of Yemeni men had been less lucky. Three of them were sitting on the floor groaning, their suits torn by flying glass, blood dripping from cuts on their faces. One of them lay motionless beneath an upturned table.

Across the other side of the room Sergeant Cutler stood by the main door. A head taller than most, he scanned the room for the Ambassador who was by the stage alongside Congressman Steeples. The Ambassador's wife was sitting on the stage, her legs dangling, wide-lined eyes staring at the mayhem. Cutler forced a path through the crowd towards them.

"Are you all right sir?" he shouted.

"Nothing wrong with me. What happened to security?"

"I don't know."

"Well, find out! Where's Collins? He's responsible for this mess."

Cutler looked around the room. "I can't see him. Perhaps I should escort Mrs Shelterman outside, Ambassador."

"Do as you please, but find Collins first."

"I'll wait with you," said a now sober Mrs Shelterman.

"Congressman," the Ambassador said to Steeples beside him, "accompany the Sergeant outside, he'll get you a car to the Embassy. We have rooms there, this place isn't safe."

Congressman Steeples, a drink in one hand, the other on his hips, answered sharply. "I'm staying here, the damage is nothing. The hotel will be fine once all these people get out. What did I tell you? The Arabs are crazy. What's the CIA doing these days? I know what I would do. Friendly government? Not so friendly when they can't stop this sort of thing. The British Ambassador isn't here, nor the French. Perhaps they know something you don't."

"Outland Oil is an American company, Congressman."

"We come here, find oil for the Arabs and what do we get? Held to ransom that's what, better we take over the goddamned country."

"Darling," said Mrs Shelterman, "some men are hurt over there." She pointed to the smashed window.

Bob Janek and Emmett Kraill were already moving towards the Yemenis who had been hurt. "Get out of my way," Janek shouted as he pushed towards the young man lying unmoving beneath the table. He bent, straddling him, and began to administer CPR. There was no movement, no breathing. "Shit," Janek said, "he's dead."

Kraill looked at one of the man's companions, a pimply accountant called Hassan who worked in Outland's offices. He was still sitting dazed on the floor. Kraill had employed Hassan because of his knowledge of Karim. Was he your friend?" He asked him.

"He's my cousin but we were not close. His father is from Karim. It's not good for your company." Hassan decided not to mention who the dead man's father was for the moment.

"From Karim," muttered Kraill under his breath.

"This might cause trouble from the tribes, Emmett," said Janek as he stood up.

"You better get out there tomorrow and do some explaining. Fix up a flight on the Twin Otter and take Hassan with you." He pointed to the accountant.

"I don't want to go," said Hassan, "it's not my problem."

"Well it is now. We need your help."

As they spoke Yemeni soldiers started to flood into the room from behind the stage, several carrying stretchers. They began directing people out. Hassan got up from the floor and looked at Kraill sourly, annoyed he had to fly out to Karim tomorrow, hating flying. He scratched his face, angry with his pimples. Even his pimples had pimples.

The hotel manager approached, gingerly stepping over the debris. He had heard Ranjit Singh lay in pieces outside. "I am so sorry, so sorry, Mr Kraill. This is not a good happening, indeed no, it is truly bad. It is a bad omen."

"Has anybody been hurt," Kraill replied ignoring his remonstrations, "apart from this guy."

"I am having a good idea my most senior Indian waiter is blown up sky-high. It is looking like he is planting the bomb."

"But why?"

"I am not knowing this at all. It seems to me most strange. We must get this mess cleared away and you will not be knowing such a monstrous thing is happening. I am telling you I would like to kill Ranjit Singh, if he had not been already gone."

It had seemed like forever but it took only a few minutes for Benjamin to recover sufficiently to rise from the heap of garbage sacks and stumble into the kitchen. It was empty and he looked at his reflection in a steel unit on the wall. There was blood all over his face dripping from the cut over his eye. He splashed it with water from a basin.

He could hear a commotion behind the doors leading into the ballroom. Another set of doors at the far end of the room looked safer. He shuffled over, opened one of the doors a crack and peeped out. It led into a dim corridor of souvenir shops with dark interiors. Faded posters of Yemeni mountains and houses lined the windows. He pushed through the door. On his left he could see into a small windowless conference room. A cryptic message on a white board read 'Kindly take your seats and put them on the chair provided.' At the far end of the corridor was the hotel lobby. His only option was to walk through the lobby and leave the hotel by its main doors. Surely in the confusion he would be ignored. He walked fast and tried to slip past the crowds hanging around the reception desk. Glancing round he saw Natalya. She was standing alone with her back to him. He stopped and went towards her, brushing his tousled hair with his hand.

"Natalya, it's me," he said quietly.

She turned, startled, recognising Benjamin's voice. Her hair was dishevelled and her face was pale but she was unscathed.

"Why did you come here, now?" She whispered. "Greaves will recognise you. And you are bleeding."

"Aren't you pleased to see me?" Benjamin replied wiping his brow with the back of his hand.

"I'll talk to you tomorrow. Get out of here."

"I saw the man who planted the bomb."

"What! You bring trouble with you, Benjamin. Come to the hotel tomorrow."

"Why are you angry?"

"What do you expect? You lied to me. How can I trust you any more?"

"Lied about what?" But he knew the answer.

"Why didn't you tell me in England?"

"I was going to, I was, but ...I don't know."

"So why didn't you?"

"I don't know." Benjamin's mind was still woolly, bereft of ideas.

"I don't want to talk about it any more."

"But, Natalya you're wrong. You don't understand...."

"Behind you," Natalya hissed, cutting him off. "Greaves is coming this way." Benjamin froze. "Don't turn. Walk towards the lift. Go up one floor, there's a flight of stairs over there. Quickly." She seemed more angry than ever.

He walked stiffly away, unaware that Dick Collins, who had been standing at the reception desk, had been watching him and Natalya talking. He pressed the elevator button, staring at the metal door, not daring to look around. The door slid open and he walked in and pressed the button marked with an M, for the mezzanine floor.

Before the doors had time to close Collins followed him into the elevator.

"Looks like a bad cut, better get it fixed," he said.

"It's nothing." Benjamin answered, nervously wiping his forehead again. "Which floor?" He saw Collins glance at the lighted console.

"I'm getting off with you, too lazy to walk up a flight of stairs."

"Yes." Benjamin laughed nervously.

"I saw you talking to the Chinese girl. You know her?"

"Er, no, we just met."

"So what are you doing in Yemen? I haven't seen you around here before."

"I ....I'm a tourist, passing through."

"Not many tourists out here right now."

Benjamin nodded and the elevator door finally opened. It seemed like they had been travelling to the roof of the Empire State Building. He stepped out but Collins followed him.

"The name's Dick Collins, I'm with the American Embassy, good to meet you." He extended his hand. Benjamin shook it limply. "What's your name?"

"It's Brian Borne."

"Where did you get the cut?"

"The bomb. A piece of glass I suppose."

"Sit here a moment. I'd like to have a chat." He pointed to a sofa pushed against the railings overlooking the lobby.

Benjamin nodded. His mouth was too dry to speak. They sat side by side.

"Who planted the bomb Brian?"

"I don't know. Why should I? Fundamentalists I suppose?"

"But we've been getting reports about the army. Perhaps they are trying to disrupt this oil company's activity, make the government look bad. The south says the government is taking their oil." He paused a moment. "But what I would really like answered is what's your part in this?"

"What do you mean?" Benjamin's voice was shaky, his throat rasping.

"I saw you come into the lobby from the kitchen back there."

Benjamin didn't say anything at first but Collins waited, looking at him quietly. "I had to go into the kitchen to escape the crush."

"So you were a guest at Outland's party then. I didn't see you. I'm normally good with faces. And you know I do have a list of guests. Didn't see your name anywhere."

"I didn't have anything to do with it. I saw this man leave a bag. It was me who got the waiter to check it out." What the hell am I to do? I'm getting blamed again, he thought. He had no more excuses.

"What man, who was he?"

"I don't know, it was dark. He was a big man, dressed all in black. I didn't see his face."

"So what were you doing in the garden?" Collins said the words flatly, his soothing tone gone.

Benjamin was still dazed from the blast, completely alone, even Natalya against him. After a moment he said croakily, holding back an upwelling of emotion, "please, I have a problem."

"Then tell me about it."

So Benjamin did. He told Collins his real name and about the interview with Outland Oil in Houston and about the death of the red-haired man. He didn't mention Tom Fetters, or Natalya. As he told his story, sometimes raising his voice above the hubbub below, sometimes whispering the words, Collins listened passively. Benjamin finished by repeating what had happened in the gardens of the hotel.

Collins still didn't speak.

"Do you believe my story?"

"I'll check it out. What are you going to do?"

"Get out there and find if I'm right, if there really is no chance of oil. It's the proof I need," he said uncertainly, "I haven't thought beyond that. Can I go now?"

"I'm not stopping you. Where are you staying?"

"The Ashok Hotel. It's not far from here."

"I know where it is." Collins exhaled loudly and rose from the sofa, "I'll check you out. Here's my card. It's got my direct line at the Embassy. Call me if you find anything." He looked over the balcony and yelled to Sergeant Cutler standing in the lobby smoking. Cutler glanced up and grimaced, clearly not happy. "I'll be down right away," Collins shouted.

Benjamin remained seated for a moment, thankful the man seemed to believe him. He stood up, descended the stairs, and left the hotel without looking back. He was exhausted and needed to get back to his room to sleep.

When Collins returned to the lobby he saw Emmett Kraill standing over a stretcher. A rough green blanket covered a body. Kraill looked up and beckoned him over.

"This man is dead," Kraill said. "He was the cousin of one of our accountants."

Collins looked at the prone shape and squatted to lift the blanket from the face. He gasped when he saw the young man Rashad lying there, the man he and Gawain had met in Ali's house.

"Are there other fatalities?"

"Not as far as we know, apart from the waiter of course."

Collins looked again at the body. "There's nothing else we can do here," he said, "I suggest you make sure all your guests are OK and then go home yourself."

"Who did this?"

"I honestly don't know Emmett. It seems organised. Has anybody got anything against your company?"

"Surely it's nothing to do with us. We're small fry... no, there's no point to it, the tribes in Karim want us, there's lots of money in it for them. It must be anti-American Muslims. You were going to send us all a fax this morning about evacuation..."

"I was but the Ambassador vetoed it. But you'll definitely be getting one tomorrow after this. I'm recommending we get out all non-essentials and I'll be telling it to the other Western embassies."

"It's come at a bad time for Outland."

"It'll be safer out in the desert. Like you, I don't think it's your tribes."

Kraill nodded. "By the way I heard a rumour the doctor, Turnbow, is in Karim."

"We've heard that too. I was going to ask you formally but I'd like a trip on your plane out there. To check it out myself."

"Of course. Would Tuesday be OK? The Ambassador's wife is coming. It would be good if you could come too. For protection."

Did Kraill mean protection for her or from her? "Thanks, I've gotta go and see the Sergeant, I'll talk to you tomorrow."

Collins crossed the lobby back to Cutler whose thick-set face was sullen. "Yes Sergeant?"

"The Ambassador's real mad with you sir." Cutler was mad too, the Ambassador had shouted at him.

"Oh shit. I'll go and see him right away."

"He's gone."

"Never mind, Sergeant. You get back to the Embassy. Have the others gone too?"

"Yes sir. He told me to wait for you to turn up. There's a car for you."

"No, you go back on your own. I'll talk to him tomorrow." The Ambassador would not wait up for him. In fact he was probably already in bed.

Teri Mayes walked up. She had been over by the elevator standing with Earl Rittman and Peter Greaves but now hovered behind Collins while he talked to the Marine.

"The lady would like to speak with you, sir." Cutler said, nodding at her.

Collins turned and smiled, "yes, Teri?"

"When you've finished here," she said, "I'll take a lift home after all."

"Sure, I'm ready now. Come along." He instantly forgot Sergeant Cutler and walked with Teri out of the front doors to the car park.

Outside it was a warm, moonless night and the city was quiet. As they drove away from the hotel the roads seemed unusually deserted but groups of armed soldiers slouched at the junctions, and peered into the car as he slowed to pass them.

Teri Mayes lived about two kilometers south of the city centre. Most of the expats who didn't live in the diplomatic area near the embassies chose to rent properties in this part of Sana'a and he stopped the car at her house in a dark unlit, unpaved back street. The house lay behind a high wall topped with broken glass. At the sound of the horn, a sleepy-eyed guard opened the gate.

"I'll see you in," Collins said.

"OK, Dick, come in if you like. I'm a bit shaken."

He drove the car into the small yard. Before getting out Teri looked over at him. "In fact I would like it if you stay with me tonight, if you don't mind?"

Back in the kitchen of the hotel the celebratory cake Ranjit Singh had been about to carry into the ballroom lay uneaten on a table. An

Indian sous-chef, Chandran Gopumar, was alone there, fanatically rubbing at the stainless steel surface of the worktop. His brow was filmed with sweat and his eyes were glazed with tears. He had been a good friend of Ranjit Singh, they had spent many happy hours together discussing their families and drinking beer.

"I didn't know," he whispered to himself, "how was I to know. I'm sorry Ranjit, so sorry." It had been several days ago when the white man had approached him in the market when he had been ordering vegetables for the kitchens. The man had beckoned him over to his car and offered him one hundred US dollars to release the latch on the back gate to the hotel. It had seemed such a simple way to make so much money. The man had told him there was a girl, a hotel receptionist. He said he had slept with her and he needed to get to the party without being seen. Chandran's tears dropped onto the gleaming metal and he fiercely rubbed them into his cloth. For just one hundred dollars he had killed his friend.

TWENTY

Sana'a, being one of the highest altitude cities in the world, usually enjoyed Mediterranean temperatures despite its tropical location but this morning the air was sultry and ominous. Awnings had been erected along many of the shop fronts in preparation for a deluge. There had been no rain for months and the dusty tracks through the unpaved back streets were rock hard and pitted. The American Embassy was air-conditioned but the Ambassador was sour-faced, the heat outside tempering his mood as the surface of the tennis courts blistered in the sun.

He had vacillated about recommending evacuation, knowing he would be blamed for a decision either way. He had grudgingly approved, albeit toning down the alert to avoid creating alarm. The US primaries were due early next year and Washington would feel it was better to annoy a few Americans overseas with an unnecessary evacuation than risk a potential public relations disaster should any civilians get killed.

But most of the security wardens had read their faxes and ignored them. There were nearly three hundred American and European expats in Sana'a along with a handful of Japanese, Filipinos and other nationalities including several thousand Africans. The westerners already had thick files of warning notices. The American manager of the tobacco company didn't even inform the two expatriate Dutch men who worked for him. The Russian and Polish doctors and their three southern European colleagues at the hospital didn't for a moment consider leaving Sana'a and went about their work as if nothing had changed. Western sensibilities couldn't intercede in the squalid hospital in which they worked, with insufficient medicine, few pain-killers and equipment for only the most basic of procedures.

The oil companies, the embassies and the aid organisations all carried on as usual most having sent their wives or husbands, children and dogs back home long ago. Many of the men were on rotation, six weeks in Yemen, then two weeks at home with their families, and they were careless of the risks. The warnings were discussed and blamed on bureaucratic alarmism and incompetent politicians. Bombs had been going off intermittently for as long as most of them had been in the country.

At the embassy Dick Collins stepped into Curt Gawain's large office and closed the door behind him. He walked over and stood over Gawain's desk. "I'm sick of sitting on the fence," he said. Gawain only now glanced up from his papers.

"You look like you didn't get much sleep last night."

"No. I didn't, the bomb at the hotel kept me up," he lied. "Shelterman has refused to see Mrs Turnbow. You'll have to deal with her."

"It's no problem Dick. Would you like to sit in?"

"Of course."

"Good. Anything new from the hotel?"

"No. I spoke to the manager this morning. The army searched the grounds and found nothing. The manager blames the waiter but it wasn't the waiter."

"Why? He was carrying the bomb."

"He could have just found it." Collins had told no one about Benjamin.

"What was he doing in the garden then, Dick?"

"It seems unlikely to be the waiter. Why should an Indian waiter blow up his own hotel? And blow himself up too."

"He was probably paid to do it. He screwed up."

Collins sat down in the chair in front of Gawain's desk. "So what do we tell Mrs Turnbow?"

"We're doing our best to find her husband. We have a lead and we're following it up."

"But we're not. We're not going to give the aid money to Ali and we can't keep him hanging on much longer. What do you suggest we do now?"

"As I've always said, wait and see what the Yemeni government does."

"Both Rashad and Ali came from Karim. We've both heard the rumours about Turnbow. I'm going down there on that oil flight on Tuesday to find out. The flight's good cover, I'll be discreet."

"Sure, good idea…."

"I'll get out there and see the tribal leaders. I'll give my condolences about Rashad and talk about the oil company. They'll expect both."

"I said it's a good idea Dick, but I should go to Karim instead."

"But I have the contacts in the Yemeni army. They'll help me set meetings up."

"You can do that for me. You're needed here. You're much better placed to keep the community informed and anyway the Ambassador asked me specifically to go. We planned it together." He smiled smugly. "You get me a meeting with whoever is in charge and I'll handle it...." Gawain's phone rang shrilly.

"Yes, Gawain speaking." He listened for a moment, "OK, transfer him to me." He put his hand over the receiver. "Ali is on the line. Pick up the other phone."

"We should have planned this. What will you say...?" Gawain ignored him.

"Gawain here."

Collins took the other receiver.

"Mr Gawain, this is Ali speaking. I have bad news for you. I've heard Dr Turnbow is dead. I'm sorry."

"What about our agreement?"

"I'm afraid it's too late. I have no control. I am most upset for you."

Gawain shrugged and Collins whispered to him. "Ask him about Rashad?"

"Your friend Rashad was killed at the Mogul Rani last night. Has that anything to do with it?"

"No!" He spoke sharply and they both heard him clear his throat violently. Rashad obviously had everything to do with it. "The boy should not have been at your decadent party."

"Turnbow was in Karim, can you confirm that?"

"As I said before I do not know where he is. It is over now and I'm going back to Karim myself."

Collins' gut instinct was that Ali was agitated and hiding something.

"We would like to meet you again," said Gawain.

"No. No more meetings. Please I must go now and pray."

The line was cut. "Shit," said Collins, "what now?"

"I'll find out as much as I can on Tuesday."

"What do we tell Mrs Turnbow?"

"Nothing," said Gawain.

"She'll find out."

"Of course she will but we should be sure first."

The phone rang again and Gawain picked it up and listened. "Tell them I'll come out and get her." He rose from his chair. "Well, that's a coincidence. Mrs Turnbow is here and she's brought the reporter with her."

Collins was staring out of the window when Gawain returned with Mrs Turnbow. Richard Clapton followed behind them. She was smartly dressed in an old-fashioned pink polyester jacket and skirt. Clapton wore a bright tennis shirt, a pair of cotton trousers and brown leather shoes.

"Where's the Ambassador?" Mrs Turnbow spoke sharply as she looked around the big office.

"I'm afraid he was called away on urgent business," answered Collins, rising from his seat.

"How could anything be more urgent than the life of this woman's husband," said Clapton, "it seems to me you are not treating us properly at all. Ever since we've been here you've brushed us off. I write for a newspaper and I'm damn well going to make sure this gets into it."

"Look Mr Clapton," Collins said slowly, "the Ambassador cannot do anything from here. We have a lead and Mr Gawain is following it up. On Tuesday. Now have a cup of coffee."

"Tuesday," Mrs Turnbow said, looking at Gawain. "Are you telling me you will be flying out to Karim on Tuesday? On the Outland plane."

"There is a rumour that he's there."

"My husband has been missing for two weeks," she continued, ignoring him, "why haven't you been to this Karim place already?"

"It's a lead and we will follow it up. I'm the deputy Ambassador and I'm going there personally to check out what probably isn't true."

"We will also be on the flight and I will find my husband with or without your help."

Collins looked at them both sadly. Ali had told them moments earlier that Dr Turnbow was dead. His good mood after his night with Teri was gone now. And something else in the back of his mind was disturbing him.

On the other side of the city Benjamin walked into the front lobby of the Mogul Rani hotel. He was still tired and there was a large scab above his right eye where the glass shards had cut him. He had not got back until three in the morning but had been unable to sleep for long. Ideas were revolving in his brain, especially about Natalya and his wife. What would she have done if he had told her about Germaine at her parent's house? He had only been protecting her and now his thoughtfulness had screwed everything up. He knew it wasn't thoughtfulness really. It was fear. He should have told her, he knew, but he had been scared to do it.

Activity in the hotel seemed unaffected by the events of the previous night. A large polythene sheet had been pinned across the corridor leading to the ballroom. At the reception desk a smart, smooth-skinned man looked at Benjamin's dishevelled appearance with distaste.

"Could you tell me what room Miss Natalya Cheung is in please?"

"I'm sorry sir we aren't allowed to give out room numbers."

"Oh.... could I call her then?"

"Yes of course, use the house phone over there," he pointed to a row of phones in the corridor next to the newsagent.

Benjamin walked over and picked up the receiver. He dialled zero and a female operator answered. She spoke good English and promised to get Miss Cheung for him immediately. Benjamin tapped the shelf nervously, until the operator spoke again. "I'm sorry there is no answer for you."

"I need to speak to her urgently. What's her room number?"

"We are not allowed to give out room numbers."

Benjamin replaced the phone and crossed back to reception. "Miss Cheung was expecting me, I'll wait here."

"Miss Cheung left a package earlier. Are you Brian Borne?"

"Yes, I am?"

The man reached below his desk and pulled out a large brown envelope. Benjamin took it without thanking him and crossed the lobby to the men's room. In one of the two cubicles he sat and opened his envelope.

He pulled out a copy of Outland's annual report. It was marked on one page with a yellow post-it label. The page was annotated, an arrowed circle around a company name, POG Resources. Written by the arrow were the words, "this company is owned by Peter Greaves, perhaps it's important??" With the report was a letter written on a piece of hotel notepaper. It read: *"Benjamin, I hope this is useful. I am busy today and can't see you. I have arranged for you to be on an Outland Oil trip to their drilling site on Tuesday. I said you were an aid worker in the water industry. Be at the domestic desk in the airport by 7.00 in the morning. Natalya."*

If he had not opted for the security of the men's room to open his package he would probably have seen Natalya re-enter the hotel. He could have asked her directly why the letter was so abrupt. She walked to the receptionist who gave her the key to her room and told her the package had been picked up. He didn't mention Benjamin, who was still in the hotel, and she went straight to the elevator.

TWENTY ONE

Hassan, the pimply Outland accountant felt sick. He had met Sheikh Achmed several times when he was a boy and didn't relish arriving with news of the death of his son, even though he was sure he would know already. And now he was about to throw up as the plane lurched up and then down, and then further down and then up again on the thermals sweeping up and out of the narrow gorges in the plateau eleven thousand feet below. Bob Janek sitting directly in front of him, oblivious of Hassan's discomfort, was lolling his head back over the top of his seat, his prickly short hair almost on Hassan's lap. He was fast asleep and his sunken mouth gaped open, flecks of white spittle on its thin lips. The flight would take three and a half hours.

The Twin Otter was only half full, mostly of foreigners who had been contacted in the morning to take the special flight. The white contractors who ran the services on the rig and the black Africans who worked for the catering company were almost all sleeping off hangovers from alcoholic binges that preceded a stint on the dry rigs. The Yemeni workers at the drilling camp were all locally employed from Karim and its surrounding villages so Hassan was an alien himself in this plane. Even the two pilots were white.

Sandy, one of the pilots, was a tall man with a cheerful, confident face. He looked back at the passengers and grinned at Hassan, noticing his yellow complexion and pimply face. He had seen the nauseous look many times before and he shouted out something above the noise of the propellers. Hassan tried to smile but he yearned to be back in his home in Sana'a with his wife and five children. He dozed after that but when the plane finally made its approach to land, facing north into the mouth of Wadi Qarib, swinging around into a rolling descent, Hassan threw up quietly into the sick bag provided.

The airstrip was built on a natural gravel levee on one flank of the mouth of Wadi Qarib where it widened into the broad plain of Wadi Hadramawt along which the old road from Marib ran. The only roads visible from the airstrip were the bumpy and pitted track to Karim and the newly prepared gravel track into Wadi Qarib. The aircraft touched down smoothly, heaved to the left towards a metal hangar built on the edge of the runway and stopped yards from the building.

The passengers waited until the pilot had shut off the engines. Sandy the pilot climbed out of the cockpit and walked to the rear to open the exit door. Hassan could see three Land Cruisers waiting. Jock, Outland's tool pusher, a deeply tanned man in sunglasses, khaki shorts, thick socks and dusty boots, stood by one of the vehicles. A local driver sat inside each of the other two vehicles.

Bob Janek clambered down the narrow steps behind Hassan. "Hey Jock what's the news?"

"Everything's great, Bob. The rig's fucking junk and God knows how it's going to handle any depth."

"Yeah, tell me about it. Let's go." He ignored Hassan and climbed into the passenger seat of the Land Cruiser. The other men crowded into the remaining vehicles and Hassan followed them.

It was over an hour's drive into the wadi. The heat was intense and as the valley narrowed Hassan's body became caked with dirt and perspiration. The vehicles bounced in convoy along the newly built track and, apart from an empty water truck clattering its way in the opposite direction, they met no traffic. The driver of Hassan's car waved at the truck as it trundled past.

The drilling rig looked small, dwarfed by the cliffs on either side, hardly bigger than the water rigs he often saw in the capital. The drivers parked their cars in a row on a flattened area of land beneath the rig and Hassan climbed out relieved to be free of the sweaty smell of his companions. Janek had already ascended the metal steps to the rig floor and Hassan walked over to wait for him in the shade of one of the legs. He stared disconsolately at the drilling tools laid out in rows on the gravel. His pimples had started to itch.

After half an hour Janek descended, followed by Jock. Both continued to ignore him. He overheard Janek say to Jock something had 'a tight pattern but too much throw'. He cursed his luck for being with Rashad when the bomb had exploded, hating these white Americans for their superior attitude. But he followed them into one of the white portacabins set in a group facing the rig. Listening to more of their conversation he realised they had been talking about guns.

Inside the cabin was a radio room. A bank of radio equipment ran along one wall beside a photocopier and computer. An unmade bunk bed ran along the opposite wall. A local radio operator was sitting in an office chair fiddling with one of the dials. Janek looked round at Hassan as the heavy door slammed shut behind him and then looked back at the radio and took the mike. "Qarib to Base, Qarib to Base, come back," he said.

Earl Rittman was in Emmett Kraill's office in Sana'a reading the security file. He was relieved the fax from the American Embassy seemed positive and he made a mental note to stress to Kraill, who was currently visiting the Oil Ministry, how important it was to drill and test the well as quickly as possible.

He heard the call coming through in the radio room and walked across the corridor, picked up the handset and pressed the send button. "Base to Qarib, Base to Qarib, This is Rittman, over."

He heard the crackly voice of Bob Janek. "Hi Earl, where's Kraill? Come back."

"He's not here Bob. What's up? Over."

"I need Kraill. He needs to order some gear from Dubai. The rig's a crock of shit but it looks like we can spud tonight. Come back."

"Good, I'll get Kraill to talk to you when he gets in."

"Make it after six. They'll find me out on the derrick. I'm going to Karim now with Hassan to tell the Sheikh about his son. What the fuck's it got to do with us I don't know? Come back."

"Try to be polite, Bob, over."

"Sure I'll be polite. They asked us to employ twenty more of their men. No fucking way."

"Do what you can. Sorry the satellite phone's ringing. It'll be the States. Got to go. Over."

"Yeah, Earl. Get Kraill to call me. Out."

Earl walked back into the main reception area. A dark girl sat behind the desk. She wore a headscarf covering her hair but her face was visible. Rittman knew she was from Somalia. She was talking on the telephone and put her hand over the receiver when he came in. "It's for you Mr Rittman. He says his name's Bauss. Where would you like to take it?"

"Put it through to Mr Kraill's office."

He went into the office, and picked up the phone. "Rittman here."

"Earl it's Bauss. I heard there had been an explosion at your party."

"Things are OK. What do you want?"

"I've got bad news for you Earl."

Rittman waited for a moment but Bauss was silent. "What's your bad news?"

"Benjamin Bone is in Sana'a. He's staying at the hotel Ashok."

Rittman sat up sharply, "What! What the hell is he doing here?"

"We don't know but he has got to be fixed and you have got to do it."

"What are you talking about?"

"You got Outland into this, Rittman. You interviewed the guy. If anyone finds out about that annual report then the shit will hit the fan."

"I got Outland into this! How dare you. Bauss it was your idea and Brockley was your employee, you forced him to hide in that plane. I had nothing to do with it." Rittman was shouting down the line.

"He didn't hide."

"Well what was he doing? Of course he hid."

"It's obvious, isn't it? We couldn't let him blackmail us could we? It was because of you. You asked me to sort him out."

"Fuck off Bauss."

"And you ordered we dispose of Bone too...."

"He needed a job. You're sick...."

"...and Bone's friend...?" Rittman said nothing and Bauss went on mellifluously, "...you ordered that we kill his friend?"

"Don't be ridiculous. That guy and his wife have nothing to do with us."

"Oh, they do Earl, and you better do something about Bone before he does something about you."

"What fucking bullshit! God help me I'm an oilman not a killer. I've got nothing to gain from killing anybody?" But Rittman shivered. He had hundreds of thousands of dollars secretly tied up in Outland shares.

"If Bone says anything you are in deep shit. And so is Greaves," said Bauss.

"Leave me get on with my work here. Does Greaves know about Bone?"

"No, and don't tell him."

"He should know."

"What are you going to do about Bone, Earl? We have to deal with him."

"I don't know. Anyway he knows nothing…"

"Why is he in Yemen then?" Bauss raised his squeaky voice and a cruel wave of venom crossed the Atlantic. "You will find him and kill him," Bauss went on maliciously, "and if you don't, your son will find out his exams were fixed and he'll leave. And what's your sick wife gonna do about that, you over in Yemen away from her."

Rittman stuttered out an answer. "I don't know." Bauss didn't say anything. I'll call Jason, he thought. Tell him. He wouldn't do anything to his mother while I'm away. He raised his voice trembling. "We're not evil bastards like you, Bauss."

"Oh yes Earl and what if your sick wife also heard what happened between your secretary, Miss Claudia Pasquale, and her husband in Room 301 of the Hotel Ambassador in Oklahoma City last weekend."

Rittman gasped, clutching the receiver as if it was Bauss's neck. "How do you know? And anyway nothing happened." They had drunk a coffee together and he had left after that.

"Claudia has wanted you for a long time, hasn't she? She is trying to get your wife out of her way. She told me. Of course she didn't know I would tell you. Claudia is stupid."

Rittman was dumbstruck. Claudia, how could she be so scheming? Neither man spoke for several seconds. Finally Bauss said. "Are you still there Earl?"

Rittman's husky voice replied, "yes, I'm still here. What should I do?"

TWENTY TWO

Claudia Pasquale stood in her small, neat kitchen waiting for the kettle to boil. She lived on the south side of Houston in a suburb close to the San Jacinto River, in an area where land was relatively cheap. Flood waters regularly inundated the low-lying fields in seasons when Atlantic depressions turned into hurricanes over the Gulf of Mexico. Many of the poorest immigrants in Texas lived here in squat wooden houses. Claudia's house however, was built on an area of raised land in front of a copse of tall pines, along a broken concrete drive lined by similar buildings.

Claudia often sat on her broad veranda listening to crickets and the distant hum of traffic on the interstate Galveston highway beyond the copse. When she had been a child in the suburbs of Guadalajara the barren scrubland beyond her shack had been just as peaceful, with the restful sounds of trucks rolling towards Mexico City. She loved that peace, but had no regrets about emigrating to the United States.

As she waited for the kettle she thought about Earl, missing him, even as she remembered clearly what he had told her in Oklahoma. Earl had said that his wife was too important to him and he would not cheat on her. It had really been the end of four long years of waiting but she was strangely sanguine. She wished the wife no ill-will and she wanted Earl to be happy. She supposed that she had always accepted that his wife came first. In fact she had begun to trust Earl more than ever. On returning from the convention she had invested most of her savings into shares in Outland Oil as he had directed. Through the week she had seen them almost double in value. Earl had promised to tell her when the time to sell was right but she needed the money now and when the markets opened tomorrow she would have to instruct her broker.

She poured two mugs of coffee and carried them out to the veranda. The decking creaked loudly as she walked. Her ex-husband, Manuel Pasquale, was sitting on the swing seat staring out at the trees. He smiled at her, his dark eyes squinting under a mop of black hair.

"I honestly did not know you would be at that convention last Saturday," he said with a lisping Spanish accent. "If I had known I would not have done it."

She put the mugs on the coffee table in front of him and sat on the edge of a rattan chair. "No matter. Nobody knew who you were or could link you to Outland Oil. There was a reporter sitting at our table but he didn't find out."

"Was it a man called Clapton?"

"Yes, Richard Clapton."

"He came to see me in the jail. I gave him a story for his paper but he's from Denver. I don't know if it was published."

"You didn't mention me...?"

"No of course not."

Neither spoke for a moment. Claudia finally said, "You're always getting involved with these stupid pressure groups. Why don't you get a job?"

"God guides me in my work."

"Oh, really, its God is it?"

"I need the money urgently. They'll give me a jail sentence if I don't pay the fine."

"Surely thirty thousand dollars is too big a fine for disrupting a meeting at a convention."

"I'm sorry Claudia that's not all I did that night. You know there was a storm in Oklahoma City?"

"Yes, I remember." She shivered in the cool night air.

"When I saw the forecast I went to the convention centre before your dinner, where the exhibition was held. I loosened all the bolts on the delivery doors."

"What for?"

"The wind, it tore through the doors and wrecked some of the stands in the international pavilion."

"How did the police know it was you?"

"A guard saw me leaving the site and he recognised me from that meeting. I was unlucky. That Congressman Steeples complained about his speech being disturbed and the police arrested me."

"Unlucky! It was damn stupid. You can't destroy other people's property. When we helped the immigrants nobody was hurt. Nobody suffered and the people who got through were thankful. That's why I did it. This environment thing. It's stupid. What can you do?"

"Things will get a lot worse if we don't do something about the environment."

"Earl says that nothing is proved, that burning oil doesn't harm the environment at all."

"He would say that, he has a vested interest. This is God's earth and we weren't put here to destroy it."

Claudia didn't speak, not wishing to get involved in a religious argument, sick of his references to God and his closed mind. Her Catholicism had lapsed long ago. Unlike Manuel, as she got older she had decided that religion was an excuse not to think. But then she could not help herself.

"Manuel, those Gods like Odin and Zeus. They don't exist any more because people stopped believing in them. In the future people will stop believing in your God too and he won't exist any more either. The same holds true for all Gods." And thank God for that.

Manuel sighed, then rose from his seat and walked to the wooden rail bordering the veranda. Claudia watched him knowing if he hadn't been deported that first time she would never have left him and things might have been different. She longed for a cigarette, a habit she had kicked nearly two years ago.

With his back to her, he said, "I need to pay the money on Friday or they'll send me to jail again."

"For how long?"

"For six months but that's not the point. You see I haven't been using my real name. If I go to jail my records will be found and I'll be deported again. In Venezuela I'm a dead man for sure."

"But you said you went to Venezuela last year."

"I was using a different identity. If I'm deported the police in Caracas will know. They won't forget what I did to them. I need the money now."

"If I give you the money will you stop all this?"

He turned to look at her, frowning. "When you married me you knew what I was like. We spent years campaigning for immigrants in Texas. The environment is as important as the Mexicans." Claudia sighed, but Manuel ignored her. "Anyways you won't be giving me the money. It's a loan. I have money in a bank in Venezuela but it takes time to get at. I promise you. I will pay it all back. I promise."

They were quiet for a long time. She was seated. Manuel was standing. Finally she said, "OK I'll let you have the thirty thousand dollars but it's all I've got."

"It'll be enough. God will love you for it and you'll get it all back."

"Thank you," she said with a sarcastic tone," I'll meet you for lunch on Thursday and give it to you then. Wait at the front entrance of the shopping mall opposite my office at twelve thirty."

"I'll be there." He moved towards her and bent to kiss her cheek, then walked down the wooden steps to where an Oldsmobile station wagon was parked. Turning back he waved to her before climbing into the ancient car. Claudia left the mugs on the table and went straight to bed.

She arrived at the office early next morning, unlocked the double glass doors etched with the Outland Oil company name and logo and stooped to pick up the weekend's letters, magazines and a copy of the Houston Post. A heap of rolled-up faxes littered the floor below the fax machine on her desk and she scooped these up as well.

She first read the fax from Rittman describing the events at the hotel on Saturday night. It told her to explain to callers that the bomb was unimportant and Outland's activities were unaffected. He confirmed his return on the Wednesday night flight from London. She took the Houston Post and scanned the international pages to see if the bomb was mentioned but there was nothing on Yemen at all.

Ray Bowes, Outland's chief geologist walked in at eight thirty. "Gee, Claudia did you hear about the bomb at our party in Sana'a," he said. He was a tall, gangly man in his fifties.

"Yes, Ray. Earl sent a fax. How did you know?"

"Kraill called me yesterday. He asked whether I expected shallow gas in our well. How the heck should I know?"

"How will the bomb affect the drilling?"

"Goddamned if I know. Earl has kept everything under wraps. You probably know more than me."

"No I don't know anything but Earl's optimistic. Have we a good chance of finding oil?"

"Hot dogs! I don't know. There's not enough data. The drilling program was goddamned speculation." Bowes walked to his office but shouted back to her, "Gee Claudia, I dunno if we're gonna find oil or not but let's cross our fingers."

Claudia looked back at him as he disappeared into his room and shut the door. If Bowes was so unsure how could Earl be so sure?

After she had finished with the mail she went to Earl's office, unlocked it, and closed the door behind her. She perched on the edge of his desk and picked up the phone. Her broker answered after a single ring. She instructed him to sell all her Outland shares as soon as the market opened. She expected a handsome profit having invested most of her savings of almost forty thousand dollars. The shares had stood at 18.16 on Friday night and she had bought at 10.72. She went back to her desk at reception. There was nothing much to do this morning and she idly tapped the keyboard waiting for something to happen.

The glass entrance door opened and Micky Bauss stepped in. She looked at him and attempted a smile but it was a weak effort. She had no positive or negative feelings about this man, who was merely a business associate of Earl's, but Earl always snapped at her unreasonably after speaking to him.

Bauss padded up to her and leaned over the reception desk. "Miss Pasquale, I need to go through Earl's files. Could you please let me into his office?" His breath stank of halitosis.

"I'm sorry Mr Bauss, I am not authorised to let anybody in there."

"Surely you are Claudia," he breathed. "Earl trusts you completely. He tells me everything about you." Claudia stiffened.

"Yes of course he trusts me but I am not authorised to let you in," she repeated.

"Authorised or not you will let me in, won't you Claudia?"

"What are you talking about? You can come back and ask Earl when he gets back. He'll be back on Thursday."

"No, Claudia. I need to see the files now....."

"What are you doing?" she snapped. "Go or I'll call security from downstairs…"

"When you seduced Rittman in Oklahoma City did you know you were putting him in great danger?"

"What!" she said.

"You did seduce him didn't you?"

"How do you know what happened in Oklahoma?"

"Earl told me of course. He's so frantically worried his wife will find out. You do know she's ill? He asked me to make sure you didn't tell anyone about it while he was away. Of course you won't, but suppose his wife did find out. Who would Earl suspect?"

"Earl trusts me!"

"Then why did he ask me to keep an eye on you?"

"I....I don't know."

"So let me in his office for a half hour and we won't hear anything more of this. His wife will never know. Her health won't be your responsibility and everything will be fine." He paused. "And give me the key to his filing cabinet too."

Claudia didn't say anything. Could Earl have told him about Oklahoma? How could he not trust me? Earl's wife really was disturbed and she did not want to be responsible for anything happening to her. She hated to do it but letting Bauss into the office seemed the only option. She pulled open the drawer under her desk and retrieved the office and cabinet keys. Without speaking she walked over to Earl's office door and unlocked it.

"Here," she proffered the keys, "no more than half an hour."

"Of course. You're a bright girl."

She waited anxiously for Bauss to reappear, tapping her toes on the floor, rocking on her heels, angry with Earl. She had no idea what Bauss was after. The phone rang and she walked back to her desk to answer. It was a journalist from the Houston Gazette asking for news of the bomb. As instructed she declined to comment telling him it didn't affect them.

After nearly an hour Bauss emerged from the room carrying a bundle of papers under his arm. "You can't take those," she said, "I didn't say you could take anything."

"I'm calling the shots Claudia, I'll be seeing you."

He walked to the door and Claudia was powerless to stop him.

The phone rang again and she picked it up as Bauss walked out, "Yes," she snapped."

"Hi, Claudia, bad news I'm afraid..."

It was her broker. "Sorry I thought you were someone else."

"There are no buyers for your shares at Friday's price. The oil price is going up. The oil markets are well up for our domestic producers but not for Outland. It's that bomb at your hotel. Outland's been hit bad."

"What do you mean? How much are the shares? I need to sell now."

"Maybe 12. I don't know. It's moving all the time."

"Sell at anything above 10.72. That's what I paid," she stammered.

"Sure, if you say so but if you wait a day or two things may go up again, if Yemen settles down."

"Call me back when it's done. Goodbye." She was angry at herself and at everybody.

After a few minutes the phone rang again.

"I'm sorry Claudia. There are no buyers above 10. Outland's shares have plummeted in the last hour. There are rumours of a civil war and Outland is finished...."

"That's rubbish."

"Yeah. Most people on the floor have never even heard of Yemen, I don't know where the rumours are coming from. And the oil price is up 25 cents."

"What can you get me for the shares?"

"It's difficult to find buyers. They're at around eight. Can you handle the loss?"

"Eight! That money was all I've got, I need it...."

"You can hold, Claudia. Outland's fundamentals are solid. I've just had a look at your annual report. Based on your assets your shares are undervalued. If your boss thinks the situation is stable then the shares might readjust. Par is around eleven, with or without Yemen. I'd buy myself if I had the money." He could get the money, but he wouldn't buy. The facts pointed to a good profit but the talk on the floor was powerful.

"But I need the money now."

"It's your choice."

Her ex-husband had said he needed the money for Friday. Today was Monday.

"I'll hang on," she said.

TWENTY THREE

"I shall find who is responsible for the death of my son, and when I find him he will suffer." Sheikh Achmed shouted the words at the group of men meeting in his diwan. He had called the meeting to discuss how to protect Karim from the influence of the Americans and from the now restless government in Sana'a but he intended to force through his resolutions regardless of what the others said. He was angry, not only because of Rashad's death, but also because of what his other son, Mahmoud, had found out this morning.

Hassan and the American driller had come yesterday evening and had told him of their regrets about Rashad's death. Hassan had been diplomatic but the American was unpleasant. Neither of them could say why Rashad had been at the party, and neither of them knew whether he was drinking alcohol. Sheikh Achmed had immediately sent men to all the important houses to call together this early morning meeting.

Ali was in Sana'a and Dr Khaled was out at the oil rig in Wadi Qarib but Mutara, Hussain, Latif and Captain Abdullah had arrived punctually, wary of Achmed and careful in their words. Mahmoud, his son, was also present.

Mutara said solemnly. "We are sorry about your son and you are right Achmed. We are as one. Who do you suspect caused his death?"

"I do not know. I was expecting you to give me information, Mutara. You have many contacts in Sana'a."

"I've not heard anything."

"Find out who planted the bomb."

"Perhaps I can help," said Captain Abdullah., "there is trouble brewing in Sana'a. This bomb is one of many incidents. The President is under threat and there are factions who wish to see change."

"Do you know who planted the bomb?" interrupted Achmed, "that is what matters to me."

"No I don't, but General Geshira wishes to find out, as you do."

"What is your opinion?"

"Well we have a wide choice. Is there dissension within the army? Yes. You know those from Aden are upset about who runs the government, but I don't think it was them. A General confronts the leaders. There is no reason to target an American oil company, there is no motive, they all need the Americans whether they like it or not." He paused for a moment, sucking his teeth. "Is it Islamic terrorists? More likely. They would target the Americans and the hotel was serving alcohol. But they have no power in the city. What do they gain? Because of American support such actions increase the power of the government."

"Yes," said Mutara. "And those terrorists would have been more ruthless, the bomb would have been inside the hotel and many more people would have died. And I know they have been trying to make a deal with the President. The timing is wrong and the target is wrong."

"It could have been a small group going against their leaders," Latif spoke softly.

"The small groups do not have the skill to make such a bomb," said Abdullah. "Let us consider the tribes. Others like us." The men nodded. "Many in the north are unhappy, and around Marib where the oil is, they don't like being controlled by politicians. Perhaps tribesmen aimed to disrupt the party, upset the Americans and annoy the government. It's a threat. Give us power or we'll do it again." The others nodded again, favouring this hypothesis.

"But," said Mutara, "why has someone not claimed responsibility? What is the point in secrecy?"

"The government might be hiding what they know," said Latif.

"No. They hate speculation. They would prefer it was a tribe like us. We are small fry. We could never topple the President."

Hussain had been quiet while the others talked. He had pleaded with all of them to use the American hostage as trade for his son in jail and he was not so upset about the death of Rashad. It served old Achmed right. His own son was suffering and there were no options left. Only money would help and he did not have enough.

"Mahmoud!" Achmed said. "Go and get him now."

"Yes sir," Mahmoud rose and left the room, returning moments later with Ibrahim, the young labourer who had been guarding the American doctor. Ibrahim grinned at the seated men, exposing his gold front tooth. "This man was guarding the American for me." Achmed said.

Ibrahim was well-known. He had worked for all of them in the past. "Ibrahim, tell them what happened," commanded Achmed.

"I was guarding the American, like you wanted, sir," Ibrahim was looking at Mahmoud not Achmed as he spoke. "It was not a difficult job, he was no trouble but he was not well, he could not take the heat. Then last week, last Friday, Ali sent me away. He got me a job on the oil well. It was a good job, well paid. How could I not take it?"

"You should have told me," said Achmed curtly.

"I did tell Rashad... and Mahmoud, yesterday." It had actually been many days ago that he had told Mahmoud. "Ali has always been good to me. He brought back medicine from Sana'a for my child."

"And who was guarding the American after you left?"

"Ali sent two men. I'd never seen them before. The white man was sick. They had come to help him."

"Spare us your emotions. Did you know we ordered the man killed?"

He gulped. "I do now, but not then, I swear."

"Are we hearing," interrupted Mutara, "the American is still alive. Is that what we are hearing?"

"I don't know," said the young man.

"I'm not talking to you," snapped Mutara. "Achmed!"

"Yes Mutara. Ali moved this man."

"Why did you not find out?"

"The man I sent to kill him..., I don't know where he is."

"He's probably dead," said Hussein.

"Ali has gone against us," said Achmed ignoring him, "and he must be dealt with."

"Ali is powerful," said Hussain.

"I can rely on you, can I not?"

"Oh yes of course."

"Abdullah has his soldiers. There will be no trouble from Ali's men. It is important we find Turnbow now. There is an American diplomat arriving here tomorrow. This story must not get out. Ibrahim will be kept here until it is over. The meeting is done."

Achmed got up from his cushions. He bore no grudge against Ali for using the American for his own ends whatever those may have been. But now everything had changed. Rashad was dead and

Rashad had been plotting with Ali. He was a traitor to his own family. But traitor or not Rashad was his son. If Rashad had been killed because of Ali then Ali must bear responsibility.

"Go now," he said to the men. "Anything you hear, you inform me immediately."

He was thinking of the good times when the people obeyed the Sheikh. They had known death was punishment for disobedience. But the foreigners had come with their human rights and aid budgets. And the people demanded trivial things, cigarettes from the American tobacco companies, cars from the Japanese, guns from the Russians. Oh, how he wished he was young again.

The men rose and Mutara went up to Mahmoud who was staring out of the window. "Don't forget Mahmoud," Mutara whispered, "about the money for the water trucks. It's due Wednesday I expect you to bring it to my house at eight in the morning."

"No problem sir," Mahmoud replied instantly. "Today the American engineer will pay me and then you'll be paid in full."

Mutara had loaned the money to Mahmoud to pay for trucks for the deal with the Americans. Mutara could easily have done the deal himself but did not like dealing with white men. It suited him to use Mahmoud as a middleman.

"Some advice from me, Mahmoud," he now said. "Don't trust Americans. They talk of human rights, high morals, their God and democracy but they cannot be trusted because they talk too much. Men who talk a lot are lazy. They look around, expecting others to act for them. Have you ever wondered why our Islamic religion is strong and our people so certain of the rightness of our ways?"

Mahmoud shook his head.

"We are strong because we have real tangible beliefs...," he paused. "And this is important. We act on our beliefs. We act toughly and we act rapidly. We don't talk and talk. The white man says he has beliefs. Does he?"

"I don't suppose so."

"He talks and talks until there is no problem any more and he thinks it's solved. But it is not solved. It will come back. History repeats itself. Now we Arabs have always solved our own problems. We did for thousands of years before the white man interfered and everything went wrong. Arabs are no longer one race. Now we are fighting amongst ourselves. Look at all those bombs in Sana'a. What's it about?"

"I don't know."

"Well I'll tell you Mahmoud. It's about Western interference in our affairs. A truly Arab government would find those responsible and kill them and there would be no more unrest and the people would love the government because they love God. But our weak President craves his American aid, not caring that the foreign companies then take it all back. So he does nothing, expecting others to help him. The Americans only help themselves."

He stopped speaking and Mahmoud said nothing. He hadn't been listening. He was thinking of Rashad. Rashad had boasted of how the town would change once he became leader. He would never be leader now but the town was changing all the time.

The sun had almost disappeared behind the high cliffs as Mahmoud guided his horse into the drilling camp. The place seemed different today. Sodium security lighting shone on the derrick and a moan filled the air like the roar of tide drawing back loose sand into the ocean. Drilling had started. The water pit was almost full, its electric pump rattling noisily, sucking water through a flexible hose winding its way to the rig.

Mahmoud tied his horse to a generator next to the pit and walked to Dr Khaled's cabin. There was no one there and he lay down on one of the four beds, tired from the long ride. After a moment Hassan walked in, wearing blue overalls, looking hot and bothered. "Hello cousin Hassan," Mahmoud said, "you have forgotten what the desert is like."

"I should have flown back to Sana'a but the plane has already left. They forgot about me."

"I am pleased you are here. Tell me more about the money."

Hassan sat on the bunk opposite him. "It's true Mahmoud. My company has transferred five million American dollars from America into Yemen but the budget for this well is only around two million dollars. Miss Teri, asked me to do the transfer herself."

"The company will drill more wells. Then they will spend it. But how do we get a share, eh Hassan?"

"Some of the money is not being used for drilling. Every day thousands of dollars disappear from the account. The bank sends me copies of the statements."

"Someone must know where it's going. Find that out and maybe we can get hold of these thousands?"

"I don't want to steal it."

"What have we got to lose?"

"Our honour, Mahmoud. The money is not ours. Stealing is a sin."

"So why are you telling me about it? And stealing from Americans is not a sin?

"I want to know where the money is going. Who is getting it? Perhaps you can find out, Mahmoud."

"How can I find out?"

"Ali's bank is involved. Some of the money is transferred into his bank. He's close to your father, you can find out from him."

Ali! After this morning's meeting Mahmoud had thought Ali was finished but now he was not so sure. If he could get hold of any of this money he would keep it. He stood up and stubbed his cigarette out in a Petri dish on the desk. "Where is Khaled?"

"I haven't seen him since the morning. He said he was unwell."

"Khaled is a strange man. I shall stay here tonight. I must go and find Janek. I'll see you later." Mahmoud left the air-conditioned cabin and walked to the drilling rig. He could see Janek beside the tool pusher working high on the rig floor and he squatted in the sand and lit a cigarette, to wait for him to come down.

It was nearly an hour before Janek descended the steps and Mahmoud quickly rose to his feet. "Will you pay me now, Mr Janek?" said Mahmoud.

"I won't pay you now. You'll be paid on Wednesday like I said, when the rest of your fucking men get their wages. And I want those water trucks full when they arrive. Don't think I haven't noticed."

"How about tomorrow?"

"We have a fucking deal don't we. If I say Wednesday, it'll be Wednesday. The water better not dry up now or you're in deep fucking shit."

Janek was in a bad mood but he could not have paid Mahmoud even if he wanted to. The payroll was arriving on the flight tomorrow, including Mahmoud's money. It was going to be a busy day with the VIPs from Sana'a also coming. And the drilling was a fucking disaster. The rocks were far harder than had been predicted and the clapped out old rig was vibrating like a fucking dildo.

TWENTY FOUR

Jimmy was sleeping in his taxi outside the Ashok Hotel. He had been tipped well and now he was anxious to capitalise on every opportunity for work. Later that morning he would be taking Benjamin to the airport.

The sound of rapping on glass awoke him. A single street light at the corner of the lane was out and the lights from the buildings on either side were blocked by high walls but he could still see two shadowy men in front of the hotel rapping on the glass door.

A light came on in the interior and, after a moment, the door opened and the hotel guard appeared, rubbing his eyes. Jimmy heard him say sleepily in Arabic, "Who is it?"

"Salaam Alaikum. We wish to be let in," one of the men replied.

"No, you cannot come in!" The guard snapped back at them irritably. "What do you want? It is too early."

"You have a European staying here. We are to get him."

"Come back in the morning."

"We wish to see him now."

The men were bearded and dressed in futahs folded around their waists. They wore ornamental belts with horn handles of jambiya knives protruding from scabbards over their stomachs. For years the law in Sana'a had outlawed the carrying of ceremonial knives in public places except for weddings and on National Day but the law was generally disregarded.

The second man moved his hand to his belt and expertly drew the knife. The guard stepped back as a lethal flash of steel glinted from its wide curving blade. Jimmy, watching from his car, gasped as, with a single rapid thrust, the man deftly and almost silently rammed the blade straight into the guard's stomach, withdrew it, then dragged the sharpened edge across the dying man's throat as he fell forwards onto the steps. Not a sound issued from the guard's lips, only a sickening squelch as he hit the floor. The first man stepped over the body, grabbed its skinny legs and dragged it inside. The second man replaced his bloody knife and followed him, pulling the door shut behind him.

On the second floor Benjamin sat up in his narrow bed, woken by a loud clanging outside his window. Exhausted, he had been lying asleep arrow straight but his sleep had not been heavy. There was an early start tomorrow for the flight to the desert and even though he had asked Jimmy to give him a wake-up call he was nervous of oversleeping. He stood on his bed, wearing nothing but underpants, and opened the shutter wide to look where the noise had come from. It was dark in the alley below and he could not see clearly.

At that moment the door to his room burst open, its flimsy bolt torn from the architrave. Two bearded Arabs entered, one behind the other. Benjamin stared in astonishment at the knives they were grasping in their fists.

"What do you want?" Benjamin yelled at them.

A stream of Arabic came from the mouth of the man in front who advanced into the room threateningly. Benjamin's heart was racing but on the muscles of his arms and legs were jelly. Standing on his bed, he was stunned with fear. The front man lunged at him, the curve of the knife directed at his groin. Fortunately the aim of the man's lunge was clearly signalled and, transfixed as he was, Benjamin instinctively swivelled his hips, dodging the blade. It narrowly missed his naked thigh and drove into the plaster behind him. The man grabbed Benjamin's leg with his left hand and pulled back the knife for a repeat thrust.

Benjamin fell on his back onto the bed. He turned and crouched, parrying a second sweep of the knife with his arms. As the blade thrust forward, he managed to shove the man away who fell against his colleague behind him in the narrow room. The knife swung past him, slicing across Benjamin's forearm. A fine curving line of blood tracked the line of the blade. Benjamin was now helpless, hurt and without any form of weapon. The front attacker steadied himself and pulled back his knife for a final killing blow.

On seeing the murder of the guard Jimmy had reacted. When he was sure the two men were out of sight he had opened the door of his cab, stepped out and ran across the road. At the foot of the steps he stopped, uncertain what to do, knowing he would be powerless against such men. To the left of the hotel was a narrow alley along which the trash bins were stored. The hotel wall was on the right side of this alley and a high mud-brick wall topped by glass shards ran along the left side. The walls were blackened with dirt and grease and the cement floor of the pathway was littered with shreds of vegetables, animal bones and plastic remains, spilled from over-filled bins. Jimmy knew that the door of Benjamin's room was on the left of the upper corridor of the hotel. The window of his room must overlook this alley.

He squeezed into the narrow space, past a drain pipe jutting out from the crumbling brick wall. Ten feet further a metal bin blocked his way but he judged Benjamin's room was beyond it above the inner dark reaches of the passage. He bent his knees and pulled his feet up towards the top, pushing against each wall with his forearms. He stood up and balanced on the first bin but before he could grab the ledge above his head the bin lid slipped and Jimmy lost his balance. He fell forwards and the bin beneath him clanged against the walls.

Benjamin knew that he had only one escape route. He pushed his legs hard onto on the bed at the same time turning to grab the window ledge. Kicking his feet out at the two men he launched himself head first out of the window. His sweat-drenched leg slivered from the attacker's grip. He felt fingernails tear at the flesh of his calf. He fell the twelve feet from his window and landed on Jimmy who had woken him moments earlier. Jimmy, cushioning his fall, probably saved his life for a second time that morning. They both lay there winded from the fall until Jimmy, pinioned below Benjamin, pointed upwards. "Get up please. We must get out of here."

Benjamin looked round and saw a bony leg protruding from the window of his former room. Two hands appeared, one still grasping a knife, the other clutching at the window frame.

Benjamin jumped up, took Jimmy's arms and pulled him up. Then he turned on his heels and stumbled past the bins out of the passage. Both men ran back across the road and dived into the taxi. Jimmy fumbled with his key to start the engine. It gunned to life at once but the old car at first moved only slowly on the bumpy road.

"Come on. Drive!" Benjamin shouted as one of his assailants appeared at the hotel door and leapt down the steps shrieking in Arabic, his blade flashing. Benjamin yelled again but Jimmy's foot was already jammed hard on the gas. The Arab darted across the road and leapt onto the roof of the cab. In a single movement, he drove the shaft of his knife into the windscreen, shattering it. Splinters of glass flooded into the front seats and onto Benjamin's naked legs. A bearded head appeared from above them, upside down through the broken windscreen. The man was scowling venomously.

The car gathered more speed and the Arab slid his head and torso into the car between Jimmy and Benjamin, his knife flailing at them both, cutting Benjamin on the forehead. Benjamin clung on to the man's arm, trying to hold the knife away from his chest as the car bumped crazily.

They reached the road junction and Jimmy turned the wheel sharply left, swerving almost out of control. Unfortunately for the man with the knife the turn came just as he had begun to slide into the car, following a second sweep of his blade. His legs swung in the opposite direction to the car and the force made him slew sideways. With his left hand he grasped the window frame but only managed to hold the seal that had held the windscreen in place. This black strip of rubber unzipped in his hand and he flew out of the window and off the car onto the road. The car careered to the right then to the left, bucking violently. Jimmy pulled at the wheel, revving the engine and jamming his foot on the pedal. The clutch burned and the car shot forward again. They roared off leaving behind the Arab lying still, in a bent heap in the road.

They were silent for several minutes. At last, speeding north towards the airport, Jimmy said, "I wished to warn you sir. Were they going to kill you?"

"Thanks, you saved me."

"Why did they want to kill you?"

"I don't know." He paused and then added, "I need clothes, Jimmy."

"I will take you to my home and get you some."

"Thank you."

"You are a guest in my country. Those men have no right to be killing a guest."

They continued through dark, almost deserted, streets then left the high road, passed through a deserted vegetable market and turned into a bumpy unpaved street before finally pulling up at a partly-built dwelling with a single naked bulb shining above its gate. The land around it and parts of the road were littered with breeze blocks and heaps of loose cement.

"This is my house. Stay here."

Benjamin waited, watching him disappear through a gap in the unfinished wall. He looked at his arm which was bleeding slowly but fortunately the cut was shallow. Jimmy returned a few minutes later carrying a bundle of clothes and a pair of dusty leather boots which he handed to Benjamin. "My wife wishes you well," he said.

The clothes were clean and ironed and Benjamin took them gratefully. "I cannot pay you. All my money is in the hotel."

"Tomorrow I will get your money and things and when you return I will take you to the Mogul Rani hotel. It is better for a foreigner to stay there."

"No, it's all right. I'll get my own things tonight when I get back."

"It will not be safe for you. The police will take all your money if you wish to be free."

"What do you mean?"

"The hotel guard is dead."

Benjamin had grown used to surprises. "They killed him?"

"Yes."

"Won't it be dangerous for you to go back to the hotel?"

"No, not for me, they are not after me. I am not a foreigner."

Benjamin was dropped off outside the airport terminal. In that early hour the airport was deserted and the car park was near empty. One lone guard stood by a locked door, staring at him. Benjamin slumped on the floor and waited for the building to open. The clothes fitted well but the blue jeans were cheap with a low crotch and the shirt was gaudy. His hands still shook from the fear that had overwhelmed him in that tiny hotel room and he clutched his legs tucking his knees up under his chin for comfort. My only chance lies with that American from the Embassy, he was thinking. But in the state he was in he did not wonder for a moment how those men had found him at the hotel. It did not cross his mind that, apart from Natalya and Jimmy, only the American knew where he was staying.

TWENTY FIVE

Al Hulver and Kenneth Letniowski descended towards Sana'a airport in Business Class seats on the flight out from Dubai. They were engineers working for an oil well testing company and both had been called at short notice from their vacation.

Al, a Canadian, had come from Bangkok. Since his divorce two years previously he had rotated out of Bangkok living in his vacations with his girlfriend, a bar girl at the Pink Panther club who waited for him and his money. He had been brought up in Calgary and had spent much of his life working on rigs in Western Canada, then in the North Sea, and now in the Middle East. He had been married for ten years when his wife, who remained in Calgary and had seen him only during his leave periods, wrote to say she was having an affair with a neighbour. Al had not been back to Calgary since. He was lonely and didn't much care that his girl in Bangkok serviced other clients when he was away. She often gave him letters to read to her, with envelopes stuffed with cash from Germans who promised to bring her to Frankfurt or Munich and marry her. She said it was the Japanese she liked the best though, they were quick and didn't fall in love.

The aeroplane dipped in a thermal and Al, holding his beer steady, took a sip almost by accident. He turned to his colleague "What gets me about being called onto this job right now is the oil price. Its picking up and the market looks good. I was going to buy stock but I didn't get a chance to tell my broker."

"I don't know anything about it Al. I spend everything I get."

"Gee, Ken you've got to save for your pension, it's a financial imperative."

"What are you talking about Al? You swallowed a dictionary or what?"

Kenneth was five or six years younger than Al, in his mid-thirties. All his life he had been blessed by an incapacity to worry about the future. Stress didn't exist in his vocabulary, and nor did most other words. He had never lost his temper, only becoming slightly impatient with his wife if she nagged him about saving money. His wife who lived back in their home town of Austin in west Texas took care of anything that required forward planning, including organising everything for their children, all of which were, of course, unplanned. She had been an airline hostess and he'd met her on a flight into New York. She was the prettiest of three sisters whose names were Cuddles, Bubbles and Boop Boop. Kenneth wasn't a man to take precautions and so far he and Bubbles had had six children, three boys and three girls. But Kenneth was genuinely good at his job and his powers of concentration ensured no safety option was ever overlooked when he was testing oil and gas wells.

They landed at Sana'a airport and, as the two men emerged into the sun, Al pointed to Outland Oil's Twin Otter plane standing on the apron. "That must be ours," he said. The blue-black plateau dominated the skyline behind the plane. "And that's where we'll be going."

After passing through immigration they followed the yellow signs to the domestic departure gate. A young, sun-tanned man was leaning against the coffee bar in the departure hall. He was wearing reflecting sunglasses but Kenneth and Al recognised him immediately as one of their pilots. He had often taken them to jobs around the Gulf. The pilot casually directed them into a room to one side of the building.

They walked into the small lounge and Kenneth looked around, his eyes alighting on an unkempt white man in the corner. "Look at him over there," he said, "that shirt takes some beating eh?"

"Gee, Ken it sure does. Who the hell are this crowd anyway? Don't look like oil field to me. See the blonde broad talking to Sandy."

Sandy, the other pilot working on the flight, was also well known to oil workers in the Middle East. He was a charismatic, tanned and handsome Englishman in his mid-forties with a small tightly clenched bottom women couldn't resist. He was clutching the passenger manifest and Al, with Kenneth following, walked towards him.

"When's take-off, Sandy?" said Al.

"About an hour, but security is tight so I can't promise anything." He was half looking at the blonde lady as he spoke.

"Are these people flying on our flight then? What's cooking?"

"We have a VIP trip to the rig today," said the blonde "they're mostly expats, diplomats. I don't know most of them myself."

"Who are you then?" Kenneth asked her.

"Teri Mayes, I work for Outland Oil. Who are you?"

"Kenneth Letniowski. And this is my mate Al Hulver."

"We're test engineers," put in Al. "We were called out to test your well for oil."

Benjamin, who was the man in the gaudy shirt, was watching the two men, guessing they were oilmen. He had sat in the corner hoping to avoid the gaze of the other passengers but, as they walked in, they all stared at his shirt and bruised face.

Natalya had arrived earlier with Emmett Kraill and Teri Mayes. Benjamin watched her now, deep in conversation at the far end of the room with a good looking man and an older lady. He recognised no one else in the room and sat alone, head bowed, glancing occasionally at Natalya, the young man and the older woman.

The doors to the lounge burst open and a bristle-headed Marine walked in carrying two small bags. The Marine held the door for two ladies, one middle-aged and dressed in an all blue viscose trouser suit, the other slightly younger in a green cotton dress, the buttons of which bulged in a line perpendicular to her breasts, like a badly stitched scar. She had curls of platinum grey hair shading her face.

"This is the lounge where you should wait Mrs Shelterman," said the Marine to the blue woman. "I must go. I'm needed urgently at the Embassy."

"No, Sergeant Cutler. Wait here with our bags until we depart." She turned away towards her taller companion.

"Come Gladys we'll sit over there." She pointed to the empty seats next to Benjamin. Sandy, the pilot with the clipboard, intercepted the two women and ticked them off on his board while Sergeant Cutler leaned against the wall and lit a cigarette. His face remained impassive but his body language, with hips stuck out and chest expanded, appeared resentful.

The ladies crossed the room and sat next to Benjamin. "Hello," he said to Mrs Shelterman. "Are you with the American Embassy?"

"My husband is the American Ambassador, Erwin Shelterman. This is Gladys Plectrum. She's the wife of the commercial attaché." Gladys looked at him and smiled, releasing her pout, uncrinkling the wrinkles and taking years off her age.

"My name is Brian Borne. I'm an aid worker," he said, warming to his new altruistic role, "I work on water supplies. May I ask why you two ladies are on this flight?"

"Our husbands were invited but they're too busy. We thought it would be jolly to come anyway, didn't we Elizabeth," answered Gladys.

"Perhaps you did Gladys dear but Erwin ordered me to go. The sooner we are back the better."

"Oh Liz, cheer up. I have a bottle of vodka in my bag."

"Shhh! Gladys. You are not supposed to drink on this trip."

"I'm new here," interrupted Benjamin, pretending he had not heard about the vodka. "I don't know anybody but there is a man from the Embassy I once met. Collins, Dick Collins. Do you know him?"

"Oh yes. He's supposed to be in charge of security but between you and me, and you Gladys of course, he doesn't know what he's doing."

Across the other side of the room Richard Clapton, Margaret Turnbow and Natalya were still waiting together.

"As soon as Gawain arrives, "Mrs Turnbow said, "collar him and persuade him to take me to Karim."

"I'll try Margaret but I didn't have much luck with him yesterday. He maintains he'll be doing 'delicate negotiations, strictly for professionals'." He spoke sarcastically.

"Professionals! I want to meet this Sheikh myself. Gawain is a creep."

"But Gawain is right about one thing. The Arabs are funny about women."

"Actually the Arab men have a great respect for women," put in Natalya. "I expect you would be very safe if you visited the Sheikh, but I doubt whether he will tell you anything. Respect comes at a price."

"What do you mean?" said Clapton.

She glanced across the room at Benjamin, "you men will give us flowers, open doors for us but when it's time to tell the truth..." Her voice trailed off. "And look at the way Margaret has been treated by your diplomats."

"I don't want to defend them, but..."

"...but you are about to," Mrs Turnbow interjected.

"...well they do have a difficult job. We don't know all the facts."

"Are you really a journalist, you don't sound like one?" said Natalya.

"We in the States don't behave like your tabloids in England."

"I'm a Singaporean actually. In Singapore the government controls all the papers and we don't get ridiculous gossip."

"But filtered local news."

"Perhaps, but Singapore is not corrupt."

"Can you two stop arguing," interrupted Mrs Turnbow. "There is Gawain." He had stumbled into the room alone and was talking to Sergeant Cutler still at his post by the door. "If you won't do it Richard then I will." She left them and marched over to Gawain.

"She's some woman coming over here like this," Natalya said.

"She has changed even in the few days I've known her."

I've changed too, she thought. Unlike Mrs Turnbow she was more vulnerable, more easily hurt because of Benjamin. She glanced over at him and their eyes met for the briefest of moments.

As Mrs Turnbow headed for Gawain, Teri Mayes came over to Natalya and Richard. "We should be away soon. Is everything all right with you two?"

"Yes fine thanks," said Richard.

"How far is it from the landing strip to your rig?" asked Natalya.

"It's about an hours drive, about fifteen miles, the road's bumpy. Every Land Cruiser on the site will be waiting for us..." She stopped speaking as she heard Mrs Turnbow raise her voice by the door. "What's up with her?"

"Margaret wants to go with him to Karim."

The three of them looked across at Mrs Turnbow. She had her hands akimbo and was shaking her head. Gawain was smiling, nodding occasionally.

Gawain was trying to get away from Mrs Turnbow and when a tall grey-haired man with a pasty face introduced himself, interrupting Mrs Turnbow's tirade, he used the opportunity to slip away. He walked over to Mrs Shelterman and, ignoring Benjamin, who was still sitting beside her, said to the two women, "Mrs Shelterman, Gladys. How are you both? The trip should be good."

"Isn't it about time we left? It's gone eight."

179

"They've got trouble with fuel. Everything will be in order soon. This is Yemen."

"I'm not going to forget that, am I? Now go and ask Sergeant Cutler to see if he can hurry them along."

"Before you go this is Mr Borne," put in Gladys, "he doesn't know anybody."

Gawain shook Benjamin's hand. "Pleased to meet you Mr Borne." He spoke off-handedly glad the women had latched onto someone other than himself. He would be driving straight to Karim when they landed and had no time to nurse the Ambassador's wife. He would also be going alone whatever Mrs Turnbow did. He now needed an excuse to lose her and avoid a scene in the desert.

"You can let Sergeant Cutler go now," he said to Mrs Shelterman, forgetting Benjamin, "we should be leaving soon and Collins needs him for Embassy work. There'll be a lot to do today... after our warning."

"What warning" asked Benjamin?

Gawain turned to him again. "Your British Embassy has circulated the same. Haven't you received a fax from your warden?"

"No."

"We've advised that all non-essential personnel are evacuated. Mrs Shelterman and Mrs Plectrum will be leaving on a flight tomorrow. But there's nothing to worry about. It's only temporary."

Mrs Shelterman nodded keenly, but she was still angry her husband was not leaving too. If anyone wasn't essential it was him.

"Are you essential?" Gawain asked Benjamin pointedly.

"Yes, essential," he said and laughed nervously.

He was pleased to be interrupted by the pilot in sunglasses who had returned and shouted above the voices in the room. "We can board now, please follow me through the door on the right."

The passengers began to file through the glass doors but Benjamin hung back watching the assorted men and women collect on the hot tarmac by the small plane. Finally he followed them, walking over to Natalya who was now talking to Teri Mayes. The two oilmen he had noticed in the lounge earlier stood nearby.

"Hi," one of them said to him as he passed. "Where are you lot going then?" This is an oil flight." Kenneth spoke as if he had forgotten what Teri Mayes had just told them.

"It's a special trip. We're visiting to have a look around the site. Outland had a party on Saturday to celebrate." Benjamin said.

"They should have waited till we tested the well before celebrating," Al interjected.

"No, the party was to celebrate spudding the well, replied Benjamin."

"When did they start drilling then?"

"I don't know, today maybe."

"Why the shit did they call us?"

"How should I know? What do you do?"

"We're test engineers. Do you know anything about drilling?"

"Not much," lied Benjamin.

"When you drill a well, see" said Kenneth, "if you find oil you have to test it. Check it'll flow fast enough. There's gotta be enough oil to payback the cost of putting in pipelines and shit."

"They can't have found oil. They have only just started drilling," Benjamin said stupidly.

"That's my point, isn't it," said Al, "why did they pull us off our holidays? It'll be weeks before they hit pay dirt."

"Beats me," said Kenneth, "wasting money."

"You know," said Al in a conspiratorial tone, "I once heard of a company exploring for oil in Borneo, a country near China." Al believed himself to be an expert on the geography of Asia having visited Thailand so many times.

"It's not a country, Borneo is an island. Three different countries own parts of it," advised Benjamin.

"Oh, well they were drilling this well back in the eighties. Engineers like us were flown out to test it and there were reports in the press about it. Turned out they were floating a company in London, selling all the shares to the public at the same time as the well was drilling. The share price shot up because everyone thought they had discovered a big oil field. But it was all bullshit, they'd found fuck all. They called in those guys to make it look like oil was there."

"Did it work?"

"The directors made heaps by buying and selling at the right time but they got rumbled by your English authorities. Dunno what happened to them. Didn't you read about it, Ken?"

"Nope."

Benjamin hadn't read about it either. The pilot appeared from the door at the side of the plane and beckoned the passengers to enter and they began to board in single file up the four steps. There were seats for twenty people each side of the narrow aisle.

Benjamin found an unoccupied pair of seats near the front and sat by the window facing the terminal. Benjamin's mind was focussed on the engineers. Didn't Outland Oil know there was no chance of finding oil in Wadi Qarib? Who called in the test engineers? He turned and looked at Emmett Kraill standing at the back by the stairs.

And Natalya's report said Greaves owned a big chunk of the company. This place would be perfect. A country where few westerners lived or visited. No geological data. Bad communications. Put together an inflated valuation. Add in lots of publicity, the party last night and this trip. The Outland shares would surge and those who already owned shares would be rich, provided they were sold at the right time. Before the truth came out.

A distinguished-looking Arab man who Benjamin had noticed talking to the American diplomat on the tarmac outside the plane sat beside him. The man nodded at him and put out his hand. Benjamin shook it, feeling its roughness.

"My name is Ali. Do you work with Outland Oil?" He spoke with a thick cloying voice as if his palate was coated with treacle.

"No, I'm an aid worker. Hydrogeology, you know. Water supplies."

"Ah, you are English. Your clothes, they look American. That is a nasty cut. Did you fall?"

"Er, yes and the clothes...I borrowed them. Mine were in the laundry." Benjamin looked out of the window, embarrassed by his cut face. A stretched limousine with dark windows was coming towards them from a building to the left of the terminal. Its lights were flashing and continued to do so after it had stopped. The driver, who wore a peaked black cap, got out and opened the rear door. A neatly dressed Arab man appeared and made his way towards the steps.

"He's the Oil Minister," said Ali. Benjamin watched as two further men, larger, more sturdily built, appeared from the car. "He doesn't need those guards. Nobody in Yemen has a grudge against him."

"Why not?"

"He is a religious man. He has no enemies."

Emmett Kraill and Teri Mayes greeted the Minister, directing him and his men onto the aircraft. The flimsy plane rocked gently as the guards entered. Ali was silent now, apart from the sound of phlegm stirring in his throat. Sandy, the English pilot, closed the door and walked down the aisle checking everyone was wearing belts. Stooping, he squeezed through the opening into the cockpit and flopped next to his colleague. After flight checks the engines fired and the propellers began to turn, at first slowly, then spinning invisibly. Sandy shouted safety instructions back to the passengers above the roar in the cabin and within minutes they were airborne.

Benjamin was tired and sleep came soon. But before nodding off a nagging doubt troubled him, a nagging doubt about the killings and the attempt on his own life? Tom was dead. And Sally too. And someone had tried to kill him. Did corrupt businessmen mixed up in fraudulent share scams murder people? Benjamin had never met such men but he doubted it. Benjamin shivered despite the heat.

The other occupants of the plane were quiet too, unable to talk above the roar of the engines. Even the oilmen were queasy as the plane lurched in the thermals. The winds were picking up.

A good few sick bags had been used by the time, three hours later, the plane bounced to a halt on the makeshift runway in Wadi Qarib. Benjamin was jerked awake and through the window he saw six Land Cruisers lined up on the compacted gravel. An Arab driver stood next to five of the cars. A white man with closely cropped blonde hair and bony features got out of the nearest car and walked towards the aircraft to greet the two pilots.

In the plane it had become hot and humid. When Benjamin finally emerged outside into the hot dry desert air it felt refreshing. His skin tingled in concert with another tingling, the tugging hollowness of apprehension.

TWENTY SIX

Dick Collins, feeling cold in the artificial atmosphere of the American Embassy, steeled himself to knock on the door of the Ambassador's office. Shelterman was expecting him, it was a regular morning meeting, but this one was different. Collins had news guaranteed to upset him and there was also something else, something the Yemeni journalist on the English language paper had told him earlier this morning.

Collins was tired. He had been awake much of the night collating and checking information arriving at the Embassy from his local contacts during the day and from the States through most of the night. He used his contacts in the Yemeni army, his own staff who scoured the town for information from other embassies, and he used satellite photos pouring into the computer on the secure link to the Pentagon. They all confirmed the suspicions he had had for a week or two and he was glad he had sent out the warning to evacuate. The expatriate residents of Sana'a who had ignored this warning awoke unaware of activity in the Yemeni camps but to Collins the pointers were clear. The southern army was planning a coup. He knocked and entered Shelterman's office.

"Come in Dick." Shelterman put down the briefing documents he was reading. "I'm glad to see our people are not over-reacting. Let's get all the women out."

"As you know sir I think the situation is really unstable. In fact our satellite photos are unequivocal."

"Come on Dick, a few tanks. You've been wrong before. In Indonesia. What's to say you won't be wrong again? Once you've opened Pandora's Box you can't shut it again, can you?"

"You know what happened in Indonesia was nothing to do with my job," Collins replied, ignoring Shelterman's clumsy aphorisms."

"Maybe the Mayes girl has influenced you."

"What about her?"

"You have been seeing her. It would surely be bad for her employers should the Americans all have to leave in the middle of their drilling."

"She wouldn't influence me. And in any case I want the Americans to leave."

He sighed. Teri Mayes was so different from his ex-wife. He loved Teri. He would tell her so as soon as she returned from the desert, maybe tonight. He had been a fool to be so lacking in confidence, so scared she would reject him. "You're right sir, I was stupid in Indonesia."

"Good Dick, that's what I like to hear."

Collins reflected a moment. "I have something else to tell you."

"Be quick about it, I've got a tennis match with the Swedish Ambassador at ten."

"It's about Congressman Steeples. It seems he's arranged a meeting with the Yemeni Defence Minister tomorrow morning. You must go with him. He's a disaster waiting to happen."

"Damn that man. About this you are right. I want Steeples here this afternoon. We must find out what he's up to."

"There's also another thing. From the editor of the Yemen Observer."

"What now?" Shelterman stood up. He didn't trust journalists.

"There's talk we're supporting the southern Yemenis, funding them directly."

"Don't be ridiculous. What talk?"

"There's money, lots of it. Army officers have become rich. He says we're giving them money."

"Nonsense," Shelterman said dismissively, "get Gawain on to it when he returns. Is my wife booked on tomorrow's flight to Dubai?"

"All the American's who want to leave are on that flight. Steeples is on it too.

"Good, now get me Steeples. I want to see him after my tennis game." He started to riffle through the papers on his desk. As Collins got up to leave he continued, "...and if Steeples won't come, tell him the Pentagon will hear about it."

Collins left. In the corridor he spotted Sergeant Cutler who had returned from the airport. "I want to talk for a moment, Sergeant. Are the ladies OK?"

"Yes sir."

"Good. Since you are free of Mrs Shelterman I have something for you to do. She's leaving the country tomorrow so you can get back on Embassy duty."

"Thank you, sir."

"The country is a hot potato Sergeant. We need our men to be alert at all times."

"It won't happen again. I'm sorry."

"It's not your fault. Now go and get Congressman Steeples for a meeting with the Ambassador at two o'clock. I expect he's at the Mogul Rani. I'll get my secretary to check. Take a driver and go to the hotel. Call me on my direct line when you get there."

Cutler nodded and marched away. Robocop, thought Collins.

Meanwhile Earl Rittman sat in Emmett Kraill's office reading a drilling report that had arrived on the radio PC linkup a few minutes earlier. He didn't care about the exceptionally hard drilling. As long as everything was proceeding smoothly he was happy and, on the rig at least, it was. He smiled when he read Janek's footnote which would have to be deleted from the version sent to the Ministry. It read "a few fucking bombs in Sana'a won't affect us in the middle of the goddamned desert, drilling ahead, Janek." The drilling campaign would be short, the reservoirs were shallow, and all necessary commodities were already on site, so Rittman remained confident.

He was also thankful he had decided not to listen to Bauss's threats. He had suffered his wife's problems for too long and they wouldn't go away if he tried to kill Benjamin Bone. If Bauss knew him better he would have understood. Soon he would be back in Houston and he could tell his wife everything. Claudia was history. She couldn't frighten him. But he was disappointed after so long with her as his secretary. In any case Benjamin Bone didn't deserve it. What had he done? What could he do in Yemen? How could one Englishman influence Wall Street? The guy was a loser, he'd seen it himself. He can't get to the drilling site with those bandits out on the road and what could he do there anyway? What is Bauss so scared of?

He hadn't seen much of Greaves. The man made him sick. I've only stuck it so long because of the money, he thought. When I get my oil company back Greaves and Bauss can fuck off. He had to call Houston and he picked up Kraill's phone and dialled. He would talk to Claudia about all this sometime but he decided not to confront her now. It could wait until he returned. He certainly didn't want her ringing his wife in a fit of rage.

It was nearing the end of the day in Houston when Claudia picked up the phone on her desk. "It's Earl," came the terse response to her acknowledgement. She had decided not to tell Earl about Bauss's visit. She would confront him when he returned. Demand to know why he didn't trust her. She asked him about drilling progress and listened patiently to his requests to check the mail, fax any articles in the press and fax the oil reports. Then she told him about the call from Sam Buckfast.

"He asked whether I wanted a job after Outland goes bankrupt," she said.

"What did you say?"

"I said Outland is as strong as ever, the Yemen well's looking good." She gave him the news about the oil price and how the Outland shares had fallen. She listened attentively when Earl told her to hang on to her shares.

"They'll shoot up when the discovery is announced," he said

"If you are sure?"

"Yes I am sure, goodbye. I'll see you on Thursday."

But she wasn't so sure he was as confident as he made out. He sounded anxious and there was something else, an offhand manner, something she had not heard in all the years she had been his secretary. She regretted she had tried to seduce him in Oklahoma City and she resolved to apologise to Earl next time he rang. She also had to tell him about the files Bauss had taken. She was clutching at straws but years of infatuation couldn't be discarded overnight.

She called her broker again before leaving for home. "What about my shares?" she said. "You were supposed to call me."

"The price has stabilised Claudia. I can probably get you 8 now, they were six at midday."

"What do you think?"

"I don't know. Outland shares are not following the market. Oil futures are well up but Outland is suffering because of its association with the Middle East. The trends point to destabilisation and the US has a real domestic supply shortage. The Democrat's have been running down stocks and the government will be in big trouble if there's a shortage. They've been doing nothing about it for years. But my guess," he continued, "is Outland will bounce back if they find oil. It's your call. I shouldn't tell you this but your boss has a lot of money wrapped up in it too. The shares have to improve for him or he's bankrupt."

Her ex-husband needed the money by Friday. There wasn't enough now, there would be a five thousand dollar shortfall so there was no point in selling. Earl seemed confident. "How long would it take to get the money after I sell," she said.

"Sell before midday and I'll get it to you the same day. Provided there are buyers of course."

"Thursday then, she said, I'll see what happens and talk to you on Thursday."

TWENTY SEVEN

After getting his windscreen replaced by a backstreet mechanic Jimmy returned to the Ashok hotel but was unable to retrieve Benjamin's belongings. The place was swarming with soldiers and the bloody body of the guard still lay sprawled across the lobby in a mist of buzzing flies. He waited in a nearby coffee shop for a couple of hours, returning when the soldiers had gone. Benjamin's former room was unlocked and clean, all trace of his existence removed and the manager could not tell him where the luggage had gone.

Jimmy returned to his cab and sat for a while, considering the Englishman. Who is Brian Borne? Who is the Chinese girl? What are they doing in Yemen? Why is someone trying to kill him? Could it be the girl? Jimmy's mind sifted the evidence but the questions entering his head were unlinked, like multiple choice questions in an exam and Jimmy had never taken an exam in his life. There was only one thing that he was sure of. The two Arabs were hired killers.

He decided to go back to the Mogul Rani taxi rank. As he left the Ashok he did not see the man with a knife in his belt watching him from across the road and also failed to notice an old car clattering behind him on his journey. Outside the hotel he stood with the other taxi drivers unaware of the same old car parked in an adjacent side street. In it sat two men, both chewing qat, cheeks bulging. The driver of the car was one of last night's assailants, his jambiya now returned to its scabbard at his waist. This man had only revenge on his mind, revenge for the death of his younger brother who had broken his neck as he flew from the taxi in the early morning. The body had been removed from the road long before the soldiers had arrived and it would be buried before sundown but it would not rest soundly until vengeance had been wrought on the taxi driver and the white man who had caused his death.

Sergeant Cutler arrived at the Mogul Rani moments after Jimmy. He called Collins from the hotel phone and was told that Steeples had agreed to a meeting with the Ambassador and would see him outside. He stood on the steps by his car and lit up a Marlboro. Curls of blue smoke rose into the already polluted air and he observed through the smoke a group of taxi drivers loitering across the road.

He particularly noticed, as he was trained to do, the occupants of an old car in a side street across from him. Two men were inside and they looked shady, plotting something perhaps. He dismissed the idea as wishful thinking but touched his gun for reassurance. He had doubted the Marines this morning, almost wished he had stayed in the States. He had been so angry with those women at the airport, making him stand there like a security guard. He liked a man's discipline, none of this bullshit of old women pushing him around. The Marines was for men and now at last he had a chance to prove he was a damn fine soldier.

Cutler was on his third cigarette when Congressman Steeples finally appeared at the door, beckoning to him arrogantly, wearing the same crumpled blue suit he had worn on Saturday. "You're my driver, are you? Put the cigarette out. Where's the car?"

Cutler directed him to the black limousine and he held a rear door open and Steeples got in without acknowledgement.

The journey to the Embassy through heavy traffic was conducted in silence. On arrival they passed through the embassy gates, swept round the drive, and halted in front of the main doors. Steeples waited for Cutler to open his door and, ignoring the Marine who stood to attention by the car, entered the building.

"The Ambassador." he demanded at the desk.

"Who," said the American receptionist, "do you wish to see?"

"I said the Ambassador. And I don't wish to see him. He wishes to see me."

"Write your name here." She pointedly omitted a please and passed him a book of name labels. "And give me your passport."

He handed it over and she checked the details and compared the photograph with his face. After receiving the completed name card she called Dick Collins.

"Congressman Steeples is here to see the Ambassador."

"I'll be right out."

She replaced the phone "Take a seat over there and wait."

Steeples grunted but before he had reached a seat Collins appeared through the door behind the desk and waved him through the X-ray machine. They walked down a long corridor and entered a room at its end. Inside Erwin Shelterman sat alone at a round table with a set of coffee cups on a tray in front of him. He stood up and extended his hand. "Congressman I am pleased you could come."

"You didn't give me much choice did you," Steeples replied. He lowered himself slowly into a chair as if he had something uncomfortable lodged in his trousers.

"Yes, I hear you have arranged a meeting with the Defence Minister. How and why?"

"I'm a Congressman by God. I'll meet who I like."

"There is no need for loud words," said Shelterman. "I need to know if you are acting in the best interests of the US government. I should accompany you on such a meeting but unfortunately I will be unavailable so I need to know what you will be discussing."

Collins rolled his eyes. Unavailable, why? Surely a meeting between a Congressman and a Yemeni Minister was more important than a tennis appointment. "You see," Shelterman continued, "my wife will be leaving Yemen tomorrow and we have business to attend to."

"Of course. I'll be on the flight too," Steeples said. "I shall probably see you at the airport. Look Ambassador, I arranged a meeting to discuss Yemeni oil policy. Outland Oil might be successful in their search. I have to make sure exports to America are assured. You know my main interest don't you?"

"Yes Congressman. But I would appreciate a full briefing after the meeting, verbal and written."

"Sure. Could you get the Marine to take me back to the hotel?"

"Of course. I'll see you at the airport tomorrow."

After Steeples had left, Collins stared at his Ambassador. "That was rather brief," he said disagreeably.

"You know Dick, I don't trust that Congressman. When I told him I was unavailable did you see how he changed his attitude? Policy bullshit. You saw him with the Oil Minister on Saturday. Let's see what you can find out between now and then. Of course I'll turn up at his meeting. Steeples is much more likely to reveal what this is all about if he isn't prepared."

"Yes, good idea," answered Collins surprised at the Ambassador's plan. How quickly we change our views on people. Or was he just a terrible judge of character.

Collins spent the rest of the afternoon ringing round his contacts, checking and re-checking information. He had arranged for a biography of Steeples to be faxed over from the States but found nothing of interest in it. Towards the end of the afternoon his mind wandered to Teri. When she got back he would ask her to marry him.

For Collins things were going slowly but for General Geshira at the army camp they were running ahead of themselves. His payment from the American had been received. One million US dollars in cash was stashed in his office, the rest disseminated to his trusted staff. But the bombing at the hotel had not been planned. It was hugely damaging to his plans and he had no clue who was behind it. Because of it the Yemeni Presidential Guard was alert and the expatriates were on the verge of panicking. If the American, who he was scheduled to meet tonight, could not offer any help he would be forced to move a lot sooner than planned. The American had said timing was important but Americans don't know what is important.

The million dollars in his office was particularly worrying. He would have to hand carry it to Switzerland on his next trip out of the country. But he couldn't do it yet, the situation had gone past the point of no return and he couldn't leave the base now. "This coup is now as inevitable as night follows day," he muttered to himself.

TWENTY EIGHT

Margaret Turnbow stood staring at the army jeep as it disappeared into a cloud of sand and dust. She turned to Richard Clapton and said angrily "Why didn't you stop him?"

"How could I Margaret? They planned it. The Embassy don't want you out here. It's obvious."

"It may be obvious but I'm disappointed in you. You should have demanded he wait for me."

"Come on, be reasonable. The soldier had a gun."

"Damn it."

"He will probably find nothing and..."

"That's the point!" She interrupted, "they're not trying. They are resigned to the fact my husband is dead. I know I could find out something from these people. I know it. I'm going to ask the Arab to give me a lift into town."

"Is he safe?"

"How should I know, but I've got no other choice."

The man she was referring to was Ali who had accosted her as she left the plane. He had helped her down the steps and she had been charmed by him, in his white robe and ornamental belt. After ushering her to the rear under the shade of the tail wing he had said in his deep throaty voice, "Madam I am pleased to welcome you to my land." He waved both his arms at the cliffs beyond, "it is beautiful is it not?"

"Yes it is. Do you live here?"

"I have a house in Karim and a house in Sana'a. I divide my time."

"You speak good English."

"I was at college in England. In Birmingham, perhaps you know it?"

"Oh no. I have never been to England. Birmingham in Alabama yes, for a medical conference with my husband."

She had turned to see Richard standing on the far side of the runway, a Yemeni soldier glaring at him. Gawain was sitting in the front seat of an army jeep next to another soldier. As she watched, the jeep sped away in a cloud of dust.

She and Richard now looked at Ali who was leaning on a battered Toyota pick-up parked away from the rest of the group.

"It's not a good idea, Margaret, you don't know who he is." Mrs Turnbow ignored him and set off towards Ali and he hurriedly followed.

As it turned out Richard need not have worried about Mrs Turnbow. The Arab was charming to them both but, apologising, told them he was not going anywhere near Karim but to his farm in the hills in the opposite direction where he had urgent business to attend to. Mrs Turnbow resentfully returned to the group huddled around the vehicles.

Richard was unimpressed by Ali. He watched him spit phlegm onto the gravel and drive off along the same track as had been taken by Gawain, towards Karim. He didn't mention it to Mrs Turnbow but he had seen Gawain and Ali talking back in Sana'a airport and suspected she had been deliberately accosted by him so that Gawain could leave without her.

The Outland vehicles were filling up with people and cargo from the plane and the two of them climbed into the back of one of the cars, squeezing in with the Deputy British Ambassador and his wife. Bob Janek, who drove one of the vehicles, had ensured Natalya sat beside him. Once again Benjamin had no opportunity to speak to her and, in any case, she continued to deliberately ignore him. Benjamin got into another of the cars and Mrs Shelterman and Gladys climbed in next to him. The German consul, another guest on the flight, wedged himself in, on the other side of Benjamin. All the vehicles set off at once in a convoy.

Meanwhile Gawain was on his way to Karim. Although the track from the airstrip was an old well-compacted surface and the soldier who had picked him up was a skilled desert driver it was slow going and it was past midday when they finally roared into the narrow streets of the town, scattering the children playing in the dust.

He arrived at Sheikh Ahmed's house and a small bony servant beckoned him to enter, pointing towards a meeting room to the left of the cavernous lobby. Sheikh Achmed was sitting there and he rose from his cushions. The two men shook hands. "I am pleased to see you Mr Gawain. It is not often we have the pleasure of a visiting American diplomat in Karim."

"Hello Sheikh Achmed. There are stories in Sana'a. Are you keeping the American man Turnbow in this town against his will?"

"You surprise me Mr Gawain. It is not proper to discuss such things without first taking refreshments."

"I am sorry but I don't know about what is proper in Yemen but I do know I need an answer now. Do you know where Dr Turnbow is?"

Achmed, concealing his rage at the American's abruptness, made a mental note to tell Mahmoud to forget about America, he would never allow his son, now his only son, to be tainted by such vulgarity. The American driller and now this Gawain today, they are beyond redemption. With a steady voice he said, "I do not know anything about this man. I have heard the same rumours as you but my people here have nothing to do with it. Know nothing about it. If you do not wish to take refreshments then please leave now. We have nothing more to say."

"If that is your last word on it then I agree we have nothing more to say but I would appreciate it if you would not be so abrupt with me. I was told you desert Arabs were a hospitable race. I am upset by your attitude. It seems you are trying to hide something."

"Hide something? I am an honourable man. Please do not accuse me of such things."

"Fair enough, pleased to talk to you," Gawain stuck out his hand and Achmed, after a moment's hesitation, preferring to draw his knife, extended his own hand.

"Goodbye, Mr Gawain."

Gawain left the house and got back into the front seat of the jeep. "It's gone one o'clock," he said, "drive fast, I mustn't miss the plane." The driver started the engine and bounced off the concrete driveway onto the road leading into the centre of town. They roared through the crowded market and turned left down a narrow alley. At the end of the alley the road opened out into a dusty track winding northwards towards the cliffs. They travelled for ten minutes up this track. The brick buildings of the town gave way to corrugated iron shacks and then nothing but sand and rocks except for the occasional derelict house. Low thorny shrubs and stubby cacti were the only vegetation. A couple of miles out of town they reached a high barbed wire fence stretched limply across the track. A pair of flimsy wood and wire gates blocked their path and two soldiers were squatting in front of the gates with guns slung over their shoulders. They both rose as the jeep approached. The driver called to them and one of the soldiers opened a gate, the other waving them through.

Inside the compound there were more soldiers slouched in the dust, smoking. The car drew up at a low mud-walled building, shaded by the cliffs, and an officer appeared. He walked up to the car and spoke through the open window. "You must be Mr Gawain. My name is Captain Abdullah, please come inside. You are late."

Gawain accompanied him into the building. Its whitewashed interior was pleasantly cool and they sat on cushions on opposite sides of the room. A small man in a robe brought tea in glass cups.

"General Geshira suggested I see you," said Gawain.

"Drink first." Captain Abdullah said, as he cupped his hand around a glass and sucked at the hot fluid. After a minute or two Abdullah spoke again. "You should have come to me first," he said, "before Achmed. I know as much as he does and I know where the American is. And I also know he is still alive."

TWENTY NINE

Benjamin sneaked off whilst the other visitors were given a tour of the rig. He walked around the water pit and climbed up a gravel bank onto a cracked terrace of dried clay. Although bare and hard it showed signs of cultivation with low ridges to capture water running off from the plateau during rainstorms. He skirted the field and dropped into a man-made mud gully that ran up to the cliff's edge. The gully was also designed to channel water into the parched fields. Now completely out of sight he relaxed, relieving himself against the mud wall.

The ground was hard underfoot, the clay cracked into polygons. They were peeling, like the skin of an onion, from the gully bed. The ground became stonier near the cliff, below which a pile of boulders blocked his path. He scraped the sand off the surface of a boulder. The rock was a young limestone, barely ten or twenty million years old, laid down when the country had been inundated by sea. These hard limestones formed the huge flat pavement of the plateau.

Benjamin knew that rainwater, as it falls, cuts through limestone pavement along surface cracks, progressively widening and deepening them into the dry river valleys called wadis. The walls of a wadi record the history of the sediments below the pavement rocks, the oldest exposed along the present-day wadi floor. The cliffs here were made of the same young limestones down to the top of the boulder wall but he needed to look at the rocks below these boulders. The geological map he had seen in London had shown outcrops of hard basement exposed in the wadi floor indicating that the limestones had been deposited over a surface where oil fields could not possibly exist. But there was no evidence for such basement at this site and to the left and right along the length of the cliff the boulders, yellow sand and gravel obliterated any sign there might ever have been. He brushed the sand off a ledge in the cliffs and shrugged as half of it ended up in his ill-fitting boots. It would be impossible for him to prove anything here and he wondered, not for the first time, at the truth of the old map he had seen.

Disillusioned he started back to the rig. A horse appeared around the bend ahead. It was ridden by a young and handsome Yemeni. He had a friendly face and Benjamin nodded at him in greeting.

"You are lost?" the man spoke in English.

Surprised, Benjamin answered, "No, I'm out for a stroll. I'm going back to the site."

"You will find oil. My town needs your American money."

"I don't work for the oil company. There's not much chance of finding oil here though."

"I am sorry. My people are hopeful."

"Your people?"

"I am the son of the Sheikh. My name is Mahmoud."

"Pleased to meet you Mahmoud but I better get back."

"And what is your name?"

He hesitated. "Brian. I'll see you around." He edged past the horse, waving to Mahmoud as he rounded the bend.

When he arrived back at the rig he spotted the visitors standing below the rig floor. Gladys, Mrs Shelterman's friend, turned and watched him as he approached. "Where have you been Brian, you've missed half the tour," she shouted above the sound of the rig and the others turned to look at him.

Emmett Kraill, who had been talking to the assembled group, paused for a moment before continuing. "The rig is shaking so much because we are drilling through rocks much harder than we expected," he shouted. "We don't know what's causing it but are hoping to get through the worst of it by the end of today, isn't that right Bob?"

Janek looked at him accusingly. "Sure," he shouted back at him.

"We'll go now to the mud logging cabin, it'll be quieter in there," went on Kraill. They followed him to a white trailer adjacent to a row of tanks. He shouted as they walked. "These are the shale shakers that separate out the drilling cuttings from the mud and water. Water, mixed with chemicals called mud, is pumped continuously into the hole and out again to lubricate the drill bit."

The trailer was similar to those parked in the camp but larger and heavier with thick electrical cables connecting it to an external generator. There was no one inside and the party squeezed in between banks of computer equipment. The sound of drill pipe and the roaring of the draw works and pumps were muffled once the door had been slammed shut.

"This is where we decide whether we have found oil. The readings show how the drilling is going, the speed of bit rotation, and other things. There is also gas detection equipment and the loggers will collect samples from the shakers outside and check them under the microscope. There is nobody here now as it is early days and, as I said, drilling is real slow." He pointed out each piece of equipment in turn and, noting a lack of enthusiasm in his audience, finally said. "If there are no questions we can go and have lunch." There were none and the visitors trooped out into the sun. They followed Kraill and Janek across the shadow of the rig to the living quarters.

Benjamin hung back. When the people were almost out of sight he climbed onto the walkway next to the shakers, reached into the falling stream of mud and shoved a handful of the wet crushed rock into his trouser pocket. He wiped his dirty hands on his legs and ran towards the group who were now disappearing into the restaurant cabin.

A buffet had been laid out on two rows of tables. Directed by Teri Mayes, two black chefs were putting finishing touches to a dressed salmon, the centrepiece of the spread. "Please help yourself," Teri said. "Enjoy the food." The group had cheered up, buoyed by the sight of a heavy meal and a cool breeze from the air conditioning.

Benjamin wolfed down a sandwich while he watched Natalya talking to the German consul who had sat beside him in the Land Cruiser. A woman's voice beside him said. "You work for an aid organisation then?"

"Yeah I do." Benjamin spluttered masticated bread at Teri Mayes who stood there, big and blonde.

"I haven't seen you around town. Don't you go to the expat clubs?"

"No. I keep to myself. I haven't been here long. I'm a consultant."

"Who's employing you?"

"The UK Government, I'm a hydrology expert. Excuse me this sandwich is making me damn thirsty. I'll get a drink." His cheeks were burning with the feeble lies and he pushed his way to the orange juice dispenser. Whilst swigging on a glass of juice, he slipped out the back through the kitchen, stepped gingerly over some pipes and electric cables running from the generator and walked swiftly back towards the rig. Behind was the mud logging cabin where they had been earlier. He entered and slammed the door shut behind him. It was deserted. There should have been at least a geologist collecting and examining samples and an engineer monitoring the drilling. Most of the equipment was turned off, the LED displays flickering zeroes.

He pulled up a swivel chair and sat in front of a binocular microscope. Pulling some of the wet grit he had collected from his pocket he sprinkled it into a Petri dish on the microscope stage. Turning on the light he peered into the lenses, his heart picking up a beat in anticipation. Most of the sample was made up of fragments of the same limestone he had seen in the cliffs. Poking with a pair of tweezers he noticed amongst it pieces of greenish, platy rock that glittered in the light. This was greenschist, the rock that the Victorian geologist had mapped, the rock that had been heated to a temperature in the distant past that would surely have destroyed any oil. He smiled, certain of himself. The scraps of rock in his pocket were the evidence he needed to show Dick Collins in Sana'a.

He was startled by the door opening behind him and knocked the microscope painfully on his nose. Natalya stood silhouetted in the doorway

"Natalya! I've got it, the evidence."

"You have?" She spoke coldly.

"Yes, this well will never find oil. I know it and Outland must know it too. It's bloody obvious. And there were two guys on the plane who are test engineers. Nobody would send test engineers on a well so early. It's all a fake."

"Teri Mayes asked me about you. She said you were in here and wants to know why."

"She knows I'm a hydrologist," he panted. "Don't you see Natalya, this will prove it. The photocopied annual report in the red case was true. The published one gives exaggerated valuations to boost Outland's share price. I gave Tom the report and they killed him for it. It's all a scam, don't you see?"

"I'm not so sure," she said flatly, "I don't see how Peter Greaves could kill your friend. And a few pieces of rock. You won't convince anyone with that."

Benjamin stared at her, unable to accept she wasn't as excited as he was. He got up and looked into her blue eyes, his heart still pounding, "please Natalya I told you it was a mistake. I was going to tell you about my wife honestly. She means nothing to me. We were separated before I met you." Although he was emotionally wrapped up in the conversation he was careful to keep his voice steady. His teacher at college had once told him that he tended to drop his voice at the end of sentences, and that it sounded like he did not believe in what he was saying. In truth he had dropped his voice because he really did not believe what he was saying. But he believed in himself this time.

"I am on your side, Benjamin," said Natalya finally, "but I've been hurt before and it's not going to happen again. We don't know each other at all. You are mixed up in this... this problem ...and I will try to help. But that's all."

"But I don't love Germaine, she is nothing ..."

"Your wife's got nothing to do with it. It was a mistake I fell for you." Her voice was trembling."

"What can I do?"

"There's nothing you can do. I'll clear you with Teri. Where did you get those ridiculous clothes?"

"It's a long story, Natalya. I'm not going to give up ...."

"That's all, Benjamin." She turned and left the cabin but not so fast for Benjamin not to see her eyes glistening with tears.

Ali arrived at his house in the middle of the afternoon in an angry mood. His car had broken down on the road to Karim, the fuel pump gone, and it had been two hours before another vehicle had passed by. Eventually a battered truck laden with haberdashery had given him and his driver a lift into town.

He walked into his house to find his wife in tears. "Our son has been taken by Captain Abdullah's men," she wailed. "They came here last night looking for the American, asking our son about him. What are we going to do?" She was screaming the words, tears pouring down her face beneath her veil. "He will have told them you were on the oil plane this morning. You must go and hide or they will kill you both."

"Our son has nothing to fear, they only want the American hostage."

"And what about you?"

"Not me you fool," he shouted at her, even angrier but for the first time uncertain.

"There's more." she screamed "they say you caused the death of Rashad. These lies are spreading. My friends won't speak to me." She wailed louder at this final shame.

"What!" Ali hawked and spat into the spittoon in the corner of the room, missing it for the first time in years.

"I told you..."

"Shut up woman." How did they link me to that stupid boy?

When he had told Rashad to go to the hotel to make Collins move on their deal he had not expected him to get drunk and then get himself killed. Ali had many enemies. If it got out he had sent the boy to a decadent American party, it would ruin him. He cursed the day Rashad and Mahmoud had brought that American to Karim.

THIRTY

It was a bumpy ride for the visitors back to the airstrip. Benjamin sat in the back of the Land Cruiser with the German consul who introduced himself as Hans Brotenwurst, and a Yemeni with a spotty face called Hassan. Mrs Shelterman and Gladys bounced up and down in the front alongside the driver.

Benjamin was preoccupied, mulling over what he would do next. The obvious solution would be to go to the American Embassy and show Collins the samples stuffed in his pocket. He knew it was naïve but what else could he do? He had no explanation for the murder of his friends. Could any of the people he had met in Yemen be murderers? Only Peter Greaves was wholly unpleasant but Benjamin was sure he was not a killer. Both Earl Rittman and Emmett Kraill seemed like typical oilmen. And Bob Janek was a caricature of a drilling engineer. It had to be someone else.

He leaned over the front seat and said to Mrs Shelterman, "Have you got someone to take you back to town from the airport?"

She turned back. "Yes, we have a personal guard, a Marine. I'm sure we can give you a lift if you are in difficulty. Don't go in one of those taxis."

"No. They're horrible," put in Gladys, "I'll tell you a story about the one I went in."

Mrs Shelterman stared at her. "You've been in one?"

She proceeded to tell her story but Benjamin could not hear above the roar of the diesel. He would ask the Marine to take him to Collins. And he would persevere with Natalya too; persuade her that Germaine was nothing to him any more. He needed a chance to have a long uninterrupted talk with her.

Those killers at the Ashok hotel had been looking for him, he was sure, but who knew where he was? Jimmy, his taxi driver, had saved his life. He couldn't have had anything to do with it. Of course Natalya might have mentioned it to someone, but to who? He was sure she believed him innocent. What worried him now was Collins. Benjamin had decided to depend on Collins. For sure it was a coincidence he had met him at all, but was it? Collins had watched him, followed him, befriended him, and Collins had wheedled out his story. Benjamin realised that he couldn't trust Collins and his plans for sanctuary in the American Embassy were in tatters.

By the time their Land Cruiser bumped onto the airstrip at the mouth of Wadi Qarib it was gone four o'clock and he was surprised to find the air had cooled considerably. A light gusty breeze was blowing from the north, funnelling down Wadi Qarib and out into the plain of Wadi Hadramawt. There was even dampness in the air. He could see the pilot, still in his sunglasses, in the cockpit tinkering with the controls. Sandy, the other pilot, was loading bags into a luggage compartment beneath the wing.

Hans Brotenwurst had also noticed the drop in temperature. "It is colder, ja. It is good I brought my coat." He spoke with a strong German accent.

"I've no coat," said Benjamin.

"You see the clouds. It is looking like we will be having a storm."

Benjamin followed him to where the pilot was stowing baggage. "Excuse me Sandy" said Hans, "the wind is picking up. Will the weather be bad, many people were sick before. Me too."

"It won't be any worse than when we came in. The storms are local. It might be pissing down in one wadi, brilliant sunshine in the next. But we'll have to get off the ground pretty soon if we are to beat this one. I've seen them like this before. They roar up the valleys."

"We can wait until it passes?"

"We'd rather not. We need to get back to Sana'a in the light."

"We all would I expect," Benjamin put in, "shouldn't we be boarding?"

"Soon, but there's another passenger to come." As he spoke a strong gust of wind lifted the plane a fraction and its rivets creaked. "No, you're right, we'll start the checks. You go on and find a seat."

The group was pleased to get out of the wind but Benjamin hung back by a propeller, waiting for Natalya to board. He followed her onto the plane but she sat at the back next to Teri Mayes so he walked through to the front of the plane and sat in the same window seat behind the cockpit as before. In the distance he could see a huge black cloud emerging, moving across the plateau top like a massive haematoma. Above it and towards the mouth of the wadi the sky was a deep crimson blue and below it the cliffs were red and threatening, striped with angular shadows of orange. Benjamin watched fascinated as balls of black cloud billowed over the plateau top, tumbled into the wadi beneath and rolled along the plain.

The aircraft was quiet but for the whistling of the wind outside. Sandy climbed in and pulled the cockpit door closed. The wind continued to buffet, softly at first, then with increasing violence. The plane lifted and settled as each gust of wind swept out of the valley. The first pilot, his eyes masked by his dark sunglasses, looked back at the passengers and they returned his gaze, nervous of the movement. "The wind's picking up," he said. "Mr Gawain can take tomorrow's flight. Bob Janek will wait for him here."

The passengers nodded their heads, but Teri Mayes spoke up. "Can't we wait a few more minutes?"

"It doesn't matter Teri," said Kraill, "the Embassy will understand if we have to leave him." He looked at Mrs Shelterman behind him, "Is that OK, Mrs Shelterman?"

"Yes, of course. Let's get in the air."

"Wait!" interrupted Mrs Turnbow who was sitting with Richard Clapton. "I can see a car on the horizon." The day had been a write-off for her and despite her distaste and distrust of Gawain she did need to learn what he had found out in Karim. The rest of the party peered through the windows on her side. Benjamin could see the line of dust thrown up by a car on the open plain.

Another severe gust of wind hit the aircraft. Vibrations slammed past the wings and over the fuselage and the plane lifted into the air. It seemed to jump several feet down wind. Heads pressed to the windows were jerked backwards and Benjamin bumped his already bruised nose painfully.

"Sorry, we're gonna have to go," shouted Sandy looking back out of his cockpit window and flicking switches. The other pilot responded and in a moment the engines were fired into life, their sound increasing to a roar during the pre-flight checks. The sun was completely covered by the black cloud. It was almost dark within the cabin, only the aircraft controls glowing brightly through the cockpit door.

The propellers then picked up speed, the blades disappearing into a spinning haze, and the plane started to struggle against the wind sheer as it crept forward. The pilots revved the engines, let them idle for a moment and then revved them again. The propellers were roaring now, drowning out all other sounds, and Benjamin watched the two pilots struggle with their joysticks as another strong gust of wind lifted the aircraft on its suspension and then, side-stepping on the gravel surface, thumped it back down again on its wheels. All the passengers were gripping their seats and, despite the deafening sound from the propellers, there seemed to be a deadening hush in the cabin. The plane was inching forward but the buffeting wind seemed to be getting stronger as they gathered speed. Both pilots gripped their joysticks, fighting with the wind smashing into the rudder.

By now most of the passengers were terrified and even Benjamin with his long experience of flying to remote oilfield sites was nervous. They continued to drive forward but the plane was still travelling far too slowly for take-off and Benjamin saw the spinning propeller to his right reappear. The pilots had cut the throttle and the plane was slowing. But as it did so the fuselage began to turn despite their efforts. Its nose veered into the wind and Benjamin's view through his window spun through forty five degrees. The jeep carrying Curt Gawain swung into vision, much nearer now.

The plane slewed crazily. It jerked further round to the right, the pilots unable to hold the tail as the power of the propellers dropped. There was a loud bang from the rear. Someone screamed and most of those seated next to the aisle on Benjamin's side tumbled out of their seats onto the floor. Benjamin clung onto a rail in front of him, watching through the rain spattered window the clumsy figure of Curt Gawain struggling out of his jeep. He saw what looked like a scrap of paper carried on the wind but it was actually a wafer thin sheet of metal the size of a man torn from the rear of the fuselage. It sailed drunkenly towards Gawain and hit him full on. He fell to the ground and lay in a heap, slumped like a beggar.

The plane continued its slewing turn and Gawain disappeared from Benjamin's view. It slowed, nose pointing into the wind, wings at right angles to the force of the storm. Then it tipped over, a wingtip touched the ground and the jolt threw a number of the passengers from their seats on the other side. It tipped back and stopped, the propellers now turning at a puffing beat, the wind still roaring outside. But the plane seemed quiet, despite the wind.

For a long moment no one spoke. "Shit," said Emmett Kraill at last as he stood up shakily.

Passengers picked themselves from the floor. Natalya helped the Oil Minister up. He had been sitting in the seat across the aisle and had received a nasty blow on his chin. Also hurt was the German consul, a deep gash across his forehead dripping blood which he wiped from his brow until his sleeves and hands were drenched in blood.

"It seems I am hurt, ja," he said as he stood up and watched drips spatter the dress of Gladys sitting in front of him. She looked up horrified and was set to burst into tears before Mrs Shelterman put her arm around her. "Don't worry dear we'll get the boy to wash it."

The German sat down again in an empty seat nearby, dizzy from the blow. The plane, for him, had not yet stopped spinning.

And then the rains came. Huge drops hit the metal skin. The noise was tumultuous, a clattering, banging serenade drowning out the groans of the hurt. At first rivulets of water ran down the round windows. These turned into sheets as rain beat on metal. After three or four minutes of cacophonous noise it slowed to a thin drizzle as abruptly as it had started. The interior of the aircraft was now soaked in condensation and the windows were steamed up like a mirror after a hot shower. Benjamin rubbed the glass of the window with his shirt but all he could see was misty gloom. Nobody had tried to talk above the clamour of the rain but now everyone started at once.

"You should not have tried to take off in the storm," Teri Mayes said.

"It was worse than we expected," answered Sandy. "We've taken off in winds like that before. But you're right I'm sorry."

"We better get out of here," said Kraill. He pushed on the rear door and a cool breeze entered the cabin.

Natalya and Teri, who were first to climb down the steps, ran splashing in puddles of muddy water to Bob Janek who was kneeling over the slumped figure of Curt Gawain. Teri knelt and cradled Gawain's head while Natalya checked his pulse.

Benjamin was one of the last to emerge. The first thing he saw was the teeming river of water running in a channel below the airstrip. It had torn chunks of gravel off the escarpment, a testament to the power of water which had eroded the network of wadis in the plateau. In Wadi Qarib the sky remained a brilliant blue and the crew at the rig were probably unaware of the downfall. He saw Natalya tending to Gawain and ran towards them, the two pilots at his side.

"Let me have a look at him, I'm a trained paramedic," Benjamin said when he reached them.

"He's bleeding, there's blood everywhere," said Natalya, "but he's conscious."

Benjamin looked in Gawain's eyes and leaned close to his face.

"Help me," whispered Gawain, terrified.

He tore off his shirt. There was a deep cut across his chest. Perhaps some ribs were broken, Benjamin didn't know. He stood up and said to Sandy, "we need to bind him up and get him back to the rig as quick as possible. The doctor's got to look at him."

Mrs Turnbow stood above them, Richard Clapton at her side. Ignoring the others she looked at Gawain's pasty face, his head still cradled in Teri Mayes' arms. "What did you find out about my husband?" she said but Gawain didn't answer. "Did they tell you anything?" He shook his head slowly.

Meanwhile the other pilot had been examining the sheet of metal that had hit Gawain. "It's part of the tail fin. You'll all have to go back to the rig. We'll radio into Sana'a from there and ask for a part to be flown in. There'll be no tail in the country. It will have to come from Dubai. We'll get a replacement plane to fly you back tomorrow. Sorry."

"But Curt's seriously hurt," said Teri.

"There's a doctor at the rig, isn't there? He'll look after Mr Gawain."

Benjamin was standing close to Bob Janek and he heard him curse under his breath. Seeing Benjamin's stare, Janek glared back at him with his sunken eyes and muttered hoarsely. "Dr Khaled hasn't a fucking clue. God help the man."

THIRTY ONE

One pilot remained with the plane at the mouth of Wadi Qarib while Sandy returned with the passengers to the rig where he could radio for help. It was past midnight when he finally managed to contact his engineer, summoned from his lodgings near the airport by Earl Rittman. The engineer promised to contact Dubai and organise a new tail to be flown into Sana'a on a second Twin Otter. The news was good. The company had a plane on contract which could be used. After passing through Sana'a airport's customs it would leave direct for the rig. Rittman, after hearing the news, informed the Embassies. He was anxious to seem unconcerned. It had been a minor incident. No one was in any danger.

Discussions with the American Embassy however, took a different course. The injury to Curt Gawain could not be glossed over. What's more the chartered 737 special evacuation flight out of Sana'a was due to depart in the afternoon of the next day and there was concern that Mrs Shelterman and Mrs Plectrum would miss it.

There were now eighteen visitors at the drilling camp and bunks had to be found for all of them, doubling up with the drillers who would work through the night. They ate a late dinner together. The workers were kept out of the canteen during the meal and conversations were subdued.

Natalya and Teri took Bob Janek's cabin. It was larger than most with a desk, bunk bed and ensuite shower. During the day the room was also his office. They hadn't spoken much since retiring to the cabin after the meal, taking turns in the shower, putting on the long white tee-shirts supplied from the work-stores. As Natalya lay awake in the dark in the top bunk she was thinking of Benjamin. He alone was her connection to home.

Teri spoke from below. "That man, the one with the bright shirt, who is he?"

"What do you mean?"

"I don't trust him. You know him, don't you?"

Natalya looked up at the ceiling a few inches from her face and sighed. She had been bottling up her emotions and had wanted to talk about Benjamin ever since she had left England.

"He's in trouble," Natalya confided.

"He's a good looking guy. His clothes are weird though."

"I don't know where he got those. In London he was well dressed."

"In London?"

"I met him there. I haven't known him long but I liked him straight away."

"Oh yes?"

"He's married. He kept it from me and I cannot forgive him … and I was going to sleep with him."

"What a bastard."

"He says he's split from his wife. Perhaps it's true…, but he didn't tell me anything about her."

"Bastard," Teri muttered again and then was quiet. After a minute or two she said. "Why is he here. How is he in trouble?"

"A friend of his was murdered and he thinks your company is involved."

"What. How could we be involved?"

"The British police want him for murder, of his friend and his friend's wife."

"He didn't do it then?"

"No, I know he didn't. Peter Greaves is something to do with it but Peter couldn't have killed them."

Teri said nothing.

"I don't know but Greaves owns Outland Oil, doesn't he? Benjamin says your oil well has no chance of finding oil, that's why he's here. He says the rocks can tell him."

"You're worrying me Natalya. I'll talk to him in the morning. Thanks for telling me."

"OK, but don't tell anyone else please." Had she had created new problems for Benjamin?

"Of course not. I suggest you don't mention this to anyone either. I must admit I have been suspicious of Greaves. They are all fucking idiots."

Natalya didn't answer, surprised at Teri's cursing. She realised any one of Outland's employees could be guilty, any or all of them. Emmett Kraill, Bob Janek, Earl Rittman or Peter Greaves. She lay quietly, unable to sleep, the sound of Teri's shallow breathing in her ears.

Benjamin woke after an uncomfortable night on a mattress on the floor of the tool pusher's cabin amongst cigarette ends and sand, the constant grind of drilling reverberating in his ears. He was still in his clothes. As he slept he had kept his hand in the pocket of his trousers clutching the grit he collected from the shale shakers yesterday. The cabin was empty now, the tool pusher out on the drill floor. He rose, washed cursorily at a stainless steel basin in the corner and attempted to clean his teeth with his gritty finger. Then he opened the door and stretched his arms wide, feeling the warm morning sun with pleasure.

It was a beautiful morning. It was difficult to comprehend yesterday's storm. He walked over to the canteen trailer from which aromas of grilled bacon and coffee were emanating. Inside the canteen there were a few of his companions from the plane but Natalya was not amongst them. He collected a plate of fried food and a mug of coffee from the kitchen and sat at a row of tables near the young man he had seen talking with Natalya yesterday.

"Hi, I'm Richard Clapton, pleased to meet you."

"Brian Borne." The name was beginning to roll off his tongue. They shook hands. Benjamin began eating. After a minute or two Clapton said, "so what brings you here then?"

"I'm looking at water resources in the region. An aid project for the UK Government."

"What's the budget?"

"Oh, I don't know those details," Benjamin said. "Are you in aid too?"

"Oh no, nothing so altruistic. I'm a journalist following up on the kidnap."

"What kidnap?"

"You don't know? Where've you been?"

"I haven't been in Yemen long. Who's been kidnapped?"

"An American tourist. See the woman over there, that's his wife." Benjamin had seen the women in Sana'a airport departure lounge talking to this journalist and to Natalya.

"Is he here?"

"We think so, but the latest news is he's dead. She doesn't believe it though."

"What are you going to do?"

"Dunno. The Embassy guy who was hurt at the plane was supposed to check it out yesterday. Mrs Turnbow wants to see him but these guys won't let us."

The door opened and Emmett Kraill walked in. He looked around, spotted them both and came up to the table.

"Mr Kraill," said Richard, "thanks for your help. Are you going to let me see Gawain now?" Richard needed to do something to get Mrs Turnbow's confidence back.

"No, not yet. It's this man I need to see."

"Me!" Benjamin choked on his toast.

"Yes, excuse me. You said you are a paramedic."

Benjamin looked up at Emmett Kraill. "I've done some first aid."

"Could you come with me? It's the American, the one hit by the tailfin, he's seriously ill."

"I'm not sure I can be of any help, I'm not a doctor."

"Come along anyway, we need another opinion."

"Sure." Benjamin got up and nodded at Richard Clapton.

As they walked across the gravel to the medical cabin Benjamin said, "I thought there was a doctor on the rig?"

"There is, but he's a useless son of a bitch. Curt Gawain is in a bad way and Dr Khaled doesn't know what to do."

"Won't a plane be coming this afternoon to take us back? Can't it wait?"

"We won't be getting back until tomorrow morning, I'm afraid. I spoke to the engineer in Sana'a this morning. The spare Twin Otter arrives at around three in the afternoon. The pilots won't leave Sana'a if it'll be dark when they get here."

"What about overland?

"It's a day's drive, and dangerous. There are bandits on the road for about three hundred kilometers. The soldiers at the checkpoints can't be trusted either."

"Are there any hospitals in the nearest town? Karim isn't it?" The town had been marked on the map he had studied in the Geological Society Library in London.

"I wouldn't wish my worst enemies in one of those places. They have no medicine and anyway the only doctor for miles is in here and, as I said, he's fucking useless." He gestured at the trailer.

Inside Benjamin was surprised to see the Yemeni man he had spoken to yesterday by the cliffs. He was sitting in the corner of the room with another Arab man who was wearing a western suit. He assumed this was Doctor Khaled. Gawain lay in a bunk at the end of the room and Natalya was by his side. She looked up at Benjamin as he walked in.

"I suggested you have a look at this man," she said.

"Oh, yes." He stepped over to the bed, directing a hopeful smile at Natalya.

Gawain was lying flat on his back, his face pale. A white sheet was tucked around his neck like he had been prepared for the barber. He was awake and his eyes were flecked red and filmed with moisture.

"How are you?" said Benjamin.

Gawain opened his mouth but didn't speak. There were specks of blood on his lips. He kneeled by the bed and looked at his skin, which had a bluish tinge. The veins on his neck were unnaturally prominent. He listened to his breathing, tapping his chest gently. Gawain's injuries were far too serious for his basic medical knowledge. He got up, turned to Khaled and said. "He doesn't look good. What do you think?"

"I don't know what to do, his blood pressure is too low, he will die…"

"You've got to try to do something," Natalya said.

"I don't know what to do, I have no equipment. Inshallah he will live."

"I think he's got a collapsed lung. It may have been punctured by the impact," said Benjamin. "The space between the wall of the chest cavity and the lung could have filled with air. The pressure in the lung cavity then slows the return of blood to the heart from the veins. This lowers his blood pressure. He will need emergency treatment, maybe a tube in his chest cavity to release the pressure. A syringe could do it. But I'm only guessing."

Natalya looked at Kraill, "Get the pilot to persuade his guys to come out today."

"I'll try, but I don't think they'll be able to do it. They've never been here. It'll be tough to find in the dark…" His voice trailed off.

Benjamin stepped back so that Natalya could speak to Gawain. "We'll get you help somehow," she said into his ear, "the doctor here doesn't have the experience but we'll get you on a flight out of here soon. The pilots have a new plane arriving in Sana'a today."

"It'll be too late, we need someone who can drain his lungs," interrupted Khaled.

Natalya turned to him and snapped. "Who do you suggest then? If you've nothing useful to say keep quiet."

"I know. I know." It was Gawain, his feeble voice, barely a croak. Benjamin and Natalya both bent towards the bunk.

"What did you say?"

"Get Turnbow," muttered Gawain breathlessly, "Turnbow. If you are quick you can find him. He may still be alive…," Gawain was whispering hoarsely. As he spoke he turned his head and looked at the young Yemeni man, the man who was called Mahmoud, "…he'll know, he'll know."

THIRTY TWO

As the sun rose above Sana'a, Jimmy heard the wail of sirens. His face was pale and he failed to register the warmth from the sun, its rays magnifying and spreading out into a glittering chiaroscuro on his newly fitted windscreen. Jimmy had had a loving wife. He had also loved his younger brother, who was his friend and lived with them as he was unable to get work in the family village two hundred kilometers to the south. On the back seat of the cab, Jimmy's ten year old son lay sound asleep undisturbed by the encroaching day.

Yesterday evening Jimmy had set off for the airport in the late afternoon. It had been raining. The first drops of the season had fallen and the road was churned into a muddy quagmire. Despite the slow traffic he was on time and expected to see the oil company plane land. But as night fell it became clear the plane was cancelled and Mr Borne would not appear. He returned to his cab, unable to find a fare and, late in the evening, arrived back at his half-built house.

Something was wrong. His outside light was always on, but the naked bulb was unlit. The metal door swung open on its hinges, creaking in the breeze. Black puddles of muddy water had collected in the rutted surface behind it. He parked opposite his house, got out of his cab, stepped through the gate and picked his way across the building waste in the dark. The front door of his house also swung open. He flicked the light switch but no light appeared. "Hello" he shouted out, "Where are you?" His voice echoed round the hall and came back to him in a whisper. There were candles and matches in the cupboard by the door, and he scrabbled for them and struck a match repeatedly until it spluttered to life. His candle flickered, dimly lighting the bare cinder blocks of the hall. Ahead of him was the living room, the only decorated room in the house. Here was where his family lived, ate and slept.

His wife lay slumped on the carpeted floor. A dried pool of blood by her head looked like spilled jam. His brother was slouched against the table by the far wall, his eyes staring in fear, his mouth twisted in a half smile. "What has happened, what has happened?" Jimmy cried, softly at first but his voice rose with the bile in his throat. His brother did not speak and, as the candle flickered towards him, Jimmy saw that blood had spread and congealed around his gaping throat.

Jimmy, open-eyed, emitted a wail of anguished pain, gripping his candle so hard it split. Hot wax ran onto his hand. The door from the living room led to a small bedroom where his son slept. He stepped towards it unable to think. In the room his son lay sleeping in his bed. Jimmy had thought him dead too but the blanket covering him rose and fell in the rhythm of sleep. He picked his son up in his arms and ran out of the house, placing him gently in the back of his cab. He had sat until dawn in the driver's seat unable to move at all.

A few minutes previously a young bearded man had walked past his car. Jimmy had beckoned to him. "Go inside please, see what has happened and tell me if it's true?" The young man had looked at the open metal gate and then at the cab driver. "Please will you do as I say?" pleaded Jimmy.

"All right," answered the man. He seemed carefree as he ambled across the road but a moment later he returned and Jimmy at once saw the expression of revulsion on his face. The young man had run to the end of the street and disappeared around the corner.

The wail of sirens was loud now and two shabby police cars drove up. Uniformed officers alighted from each car. Three of them went into the house whilst another pulled open the cab door and tugged at Jimmy.

A policeman reappeared and ran to the cab. He pushed his colleague out of the way and grabbed Jimmy's shoulder. "Get out you murdering bastard."

The noise woke the boy, who was still asleep in the back seat. "What is it Daddy, what's happening?" he said weakly. The two policemen continued to pull at Jimmy's arms and shoulders, cursing, wrenching him out of the cab and pushing him onto the muddy road.

General Geshira had waited in his office in the military compound in Hadda, south of Sana'a, for most of the night. He slept on his bunk in the corner of the room wearing his uniform and now, in the shadowy morning light, he looked unwashed and dishevelled.

The camp was not peaceful. The dozen or so tanks parked on the hill above the barracks were revving engines and spinning turrets, preparing for action that everyone was expecting soon. The camp was bursting with soldiers transferred from outposts in the south. The General knew he was exposed, dangerously so. If the President decided to use his Guard in a pre-emptive strike, his plans would collapse. Geshira had many enemies, even on his own side, enemies who would welcome his removal, with or without the President.

There was a knock at his door. "Enter," he said roughly.

A handsome young captain, the General's personal aide, came in. He was wearing a new-looking uniform flopping over him untidily, much too large for him. A silvery sheen glowed from his high creased brow and sparkling droplets hung on his upper lip. "The officers are getting cold feet," he said at once, "they say you are dithering."

"I know this, Captain Hadran," the General said exasperated, "what do they want? Tell me straight."

"To name a date. They are tired of waiting and if it is not soon they will return to their bases and their families."

Geshira looked at his captain, glad to hear his men were enthusiastic for a fight, but annoyed by their impatience. As a young captain, he had spent a year living in a sand covered tent on the eastern border without complaining at all. He had served his commanding officer without question. These days the men were soft. At that camp he had also met a young boy in the village who had illicitly serviced his burgeoning lust. Without him perhaps the year might have been less rewarding.

And Captain Hadran is good looking, he thought, a promotion prospect. These men need me and the country needs me. I must do it. It's now or never. The palace knows too much. The Presidential Guard in Sana'a is almost as strong as an army battalion, but the tanks, they'll see me through and make the difference. The American owes me more cash, but money or no money I have no choice. I have the million dollars still under my bunk but there's the new oil from the east. When I am President it will all be mine. I don't need their dirty money. They will have to buy my oil. The Americans will back anybody who promises them oil.

"Captain Hadran," General Geshira said slowly.

"Yes sir?"

"Call in all my tank commanders. We'll hit the palace tomorrow."

"Tomorrow?"

"Get them he snapped. And come back here tonight, I want you … here." As the captain departed General Geshira was certain this was the only way. He glanced at his watch, it was eight thirty. Surprise, the ultimate weapon. It was the only way he could win.

THIRTY THREE

At nine thirty next morning Congressman Steeples and the manager of the Mogul Rani stepped out of the hotel.

"I am most sorry to hear you are not enjoying your stay Mr Congressman. We try hard to please but sometimes our pleasing is already too much."

Steeples huffed and said. "Spare me the apologies and get me my limo."

"I am certain your car will be well on time. No problem. I check myself it is waiting and spick and span for your transportation needs." As Patel spoke he was surprised to see a black stretched Cadillac with the stars and stripes flying on its hood draw up in the hotel drive. Sergeant Cutler emerged and climbed the marble steps. The Congressman confronted him. "I will not be needing a car. I have made my own arrangements. You are dismissed."

"Congressman Steeples," Sergeant Cutler interjected, "I have been instructed to escort you to your meeting with the Defence Minister."

"No need sergeant I have arranged a hotel limo. Please go."

"Those are my instructions. The Ambassador is waiting for you. I am carrying out orders."

"Well carry them out somewhere else!" Steeples blustered out the words but he had already seen Dick Collins emerge from the back of the Cadillac.

Patel stared at them dejectedly. Oh dear, it is looking like my car will not be needed already and the trouble I went to in order to please this objectionable man will be wasted. Nothing is going right for me these days. I am still shell-shocked from my telephone call to New Delhi and the poor wife of Ranjit Singh. She had been wailing at me louder than a siren. He looked at Steeples and said. "It seems you will not be requiring my hastily arranged vehicle. I will cancel it straight away so the cost is not great for you."

Collins had reached the top of the steps. "Excuse me Congressman, the Ambassador wishes you well. Please accompany me to the car."

"You leave me no choice, Collins, but I will make reports about the appalling way this Embassy is run as soon as I get back to the States. I shall be speaking to Senators about it."

"If you say so sir." Collins was not concerned. The Congressman had no right to arrange appointments without consultation. He nodded at Cutler who, impassive as always, followed them to the car.

The Ambassador was waiting inside. "Before you start shooting your mouth off Congressman," he said after the door had closed, "I would like to make it clear we are here to help you. We appreciate your concerns about Middle East oil and we share some of them but Yemen is our patch. We are responsible for American interests in the country and we can't have maverick politicians running the show."

"Rubbish!" blustered Steeples, "you are a little man in the pay of the Democrats. You can't possibly understand how important oil supplies are to America or you would not be doing their dirty job. Appeasement is wrong, something else is needed."

"What else?" Collins asked.

"Something to make the people of America realise we have no control over the most important asset in the world. The Arabs will dig their own graves. Come to my meeting then. I don't wish to talk about it."

"Why are you seeing the Defence Minister?"

"I am not hiding anything from you," Steeples repeated.

"Why didn't you inform us?" asked Shelterman.

"I don't need you. We'll meet him together but you don't understand politics. I need nothing from you."

"We will be observers."

Steeples grunted, settled back in his seat and stared out through the tinted window. Collins also stared out at the streets, wondering why they seemed much quieter than usual.

The Foreign Ministry, where meetings between foreign and Yemeni Government officials took place, was a large plain concrete building. Next door was the Presidential Palace, a grander building with pillars and ornate windows. They drove past two armoured cars and parked in the palace drive where several soldiers were standing to attention behind high railings. On the other side of the road the bleak concrete Defence Ministry was also well guarded.

Sergeant Cutler remained next to the vehicle, and took out a cigarette as the others entered the building. They were greeted by a thin man who introduced himself as the Minister's secretary. He directed them upstairs to a dimly lit, wood-panelled ante room. After a moment the door opened and the Defence Minister appeared. He was tall for a Yemeni, standing inches taller than even the Ambassador. He had a squashed dark face and there was an oily sheen on him. Extending his hand he said in a friendly voice in impeccable American English, "Hello Ambassador. It is nice to see you again, and Mr Collins too." Shaking their hands he turned to Steeples, "Congressman, you said you would come alone but I am always pleased to see my American friends."

"It's an informal visit," said Steeples.

"Thank you, please sit. It's a bad thing about this plane being grounded in the desert. Your wife is there, Ambassador?"

"Yes, that's true but I'm sure she's all right. Your Oil Minister is there too. They should be back tomorrow morning."

"I thought they would be back today."

"Immigration and customs have to authorise the parts required for the aircraft. And the plane cannot land in the wadi in the dark." The replacement Twin Otter had yet to arrive in Sana'a and a flight to Wadi Qarib would be out of the question, customs or no customs.

"Yes. Now Congressman Steeples please tell me what you wish to discuss, I am unfortunately busy today and have not got long."

Collins was surprised at the briefness of the introductions. He had met this man a few times and there had always been coffee and small talk before business.

Steeples sucked in deeply, exhaled and said. "As you know I am in Yemen as a guest of Outland Oil who are drilling for oil in the east of your country. I am concerned any oil they discover, along with the rest of your reserves, will be used as a lever to influence American policy."

"I am pleased you rate Yemen so highly but the oil we have is like a drop in the ocean compared to the OPEC countries. We have no influence and, in any case, I am the wrong person to talk to."

Steeples ignored the Minister's words."America will be unable to support you if you withheld oil from American markets?"

"You give us aid and we are thankful but Yemen has little oil to export. Why should we withhold oil? I do not understand you...."

There was a distant noise of thunder and the Minister paused for a moment before going on. "Our industries are operated by North American and European companies. I do not know what you are talking about Congressman."

"I have the interests of the American people in my mind."

"I have the interests of the Yemeni people in mine. It is important for me but I am not so arrogant as to believe it is for you."

"Let me add sir," interrupted Shelterman, "the Congressman is not speaking for …"

He stopped. There was muffled shouting outside, like a crowd cheering at a football match. The Minister looked at the curtained window.

"What is that?" he said, more to himself than to the Americans.

"A rabble…" Steeples began, and then there was loud bang from nearby, closely followed by another which rattled the window.

"Sounded like an explosion," said Collins.

"We know what it sounded like," scowled Shelterman, "but where's it coming from?"

They listened and heard the ratatatat of a machine gun followed by several more muffled explosions, closer now. Collins rose and walked to the window but a high parapet blocked his view to the ground. The telephone rang and the Minister picked it up. He squinted and nodded repeatedly into the receiver before replacing it. "I'm sorry gentlemen but this meeting is at an end. It seems we have some troubles. There would appear to be tanks in the main street, please stay here for your safety until we can resolve this problem." As he spoke there was more gunshot, this time much louder, sounding as if it was coming from right outside the building.

"What!" blurted out Steeples, "tanks? What are they doing?"

"I don't know but you must stay in this office. You will be safe here. You must not get involved." He rose from his chair and added, looking directly at Shelterman, "I know we can count on your support. I am only sorry you did not visit sooner, while this threat was mounting." He left the room rapidly.

Collins looked at the others. "What does he mean?"

"I don't know," said Shelterman.

But Collins could not help feeling a little smug. He had been right to warn of a coup. The Defence Minister's veiled plea for help would be accepted. But the American Government would only support him with words and cash. Yemen had little strategic importance and would not be another graveyard for American troops.

"We should stay here," put in Steeples.

"I better get to the Embassy," said Collins, "someone needs to take control. The evacuation flight is supposed to leave at six."

"No Dick. You stay here with the Congressman. I'll go."

"I know all the security wardens sir. I have to go. I'll drive myself, Cutler should stay with you."

"I suppose you're right. Be careful. It's a damn good thing you didn't go on the trip to the oil rig like I wanted."

"What? Curt said you asked him to go."

"No, but he was right. You're needed here."

Despite the mayhem Dick Collins was feeling exhilarated. After sending Cutler upstairs he removed the American flag from the hood of the limousine, started the engine and inched towards the soldiers at the gates. They held their guns ready as he slid his car through the cordon of armoured vehicles. Collins had mapped out a route in his head. He had many times pored over classified maps of the city, devising new and tortuous routes for the Ambassador to get to his meetings. It was US policy every journey should be different, minimising opportunities for terrorist attacks.

The roads were mostly clear of people and vehicles but there was scattered debris and a burnt out car opposite the Bank of Yemen, which had been hit by a missile. He drove past the bank and turned west, following narrow, almost deserted back streets to the north of the souk. After half a mile he turned a corner and came upon a tank trundling towards him and swiftly reversed into a side street to let it pass. The tank moved rapidly, its caterpillar tracks splitting the already crumbling asphalt. It slowed and stopped when it reached the junction of the street where he had parked up, but only for a moment. He guessed other tanks would be moving on all fronts through to the palace. Timing must be important, the attack carefully synchronised.

He opted to cross the high street at its western end where it divided into the airport road and the trunk road running west towards the highway to the port. The high street was largely deserted but he saw four men loading boxes of videos and TV's onto a pick-up truck.

One man turned to look at him and began to run towards the limo, drawing a gun from his belt. Collins rammed his automatic shift into reverse, slamming his foot on the accelerator. The car wheels spun, the car moved backwards, the man chasing. Collins shoved the gearshift into drive and, narrowly missing his assailant, the car careered back across the street. A shot rang out behind him as he spun into a side street.

The road turned a corner and then narrowed and he could go no further. He locked his doors and selected reverse. He backed out of the alley very slowly but nobody had followed him. The looters have other things on their mind he thought. He revved the engine and roared north along the dual carriageway that led directly to the diplomatic sector. He reached the gates of the American Embassy without further incident but it still had taken over an hour for him to drive the five miles from the Ministry.

The Embassy was well guarded. Floodlights, powered by two large generators in the grounds, lit the road outside. Two Marines stood outside the gate and they readied their guns as Collins drove inside.

Across the city the offices of Outland Oil were also peaceful with only a few staff remaining in the building. The power was out but an emergency generator ran in the yard. Rittman and Greaves sat in the conference room in dim light. Rittman had been in the office most of the day in constant communication with the rig and later fielding enquiries from embassies and companies about their nationals or employees who had been on the site visit. Since three o'clock however, the phones had gone quiet. Greaves had arrived from the hotel in a taxi, the driver paid more than he would normally get in a week. He had summoned Rittman into the conference room.

"This is going to screw up everything," said Greaves angrily.

"The fighting will be over in a day or two and everything will be back to normal."

"What about my oil well, my shares are going to plummet."

"Short term only," Rittman said with false confidence. "In a week they'll hit the oil reservoir, you'll be sitting on a goldmine, coup or no coup."

"We won't find any oil, you idiot." Greaves sneered.

"Of course we will. The reports from the consultants were clear. Nothing's changed." He had pored over the originals of those reports many times in his office back in Houston before filing them away in his cabinet.

"Sure Earl. We are going to find hundreds of millions of barrels of oil. And our annual report told the truth. The company is worth every penny of our investor's money."

"The report understated it. We'll be worth twice what it said when the well strikes."

"I'm being sarcastic, you moron. You lost your own company Earl, didn't you? Why?"

"I was tricked by a double crossing bastard."

"Please listen to me then and don't let yourself get tricked again. You are not a clever man. I suppose it was why I gave you a job, but it's time you were told the truth. After driving through that bloody war outside I need to talk to someone. I am going to let you in on the secret, although I thought you knew already. I've no one else to tell, my wife's not interested. You know I almost told the Chinese travel agent. I fancied her, thought she would be impressed, but I didn't tell her after all."

"What are you trying to say?" Rittman's heart had begun to beat like the time Bauss had threatened him, fast and furious.

"Those consultant's reports were fiction. The valuations were dreamed up. Mick Bauss suggested it. It was a great plan, he would value the company based on geological reports that I made up and raise a bunch of money to drill a shallow, cheap well and announce an oil discovery. The share price shoots up and we sell our shares, pocketing the rest of the cash and make a killing..."

Rittman was dumbfounded, "You mean there's no oil out there?" he stammered.

Greaves ignored the interruption. "Then we say the discovery is smaller than we thought. The share price slides, the oil we have found becomes too expensive to develop. We sit on it, who'll find out?"

"The Yemenis will know."

"Come off it Earl. They'll kick us out. Good for them. We haven't done anything illegal in Yemen."

"What about your valuations?"

"That's Bauss's problem. He did them. My reports are an opinion based on geology. Nothing can be proved I faked them. You know as well as I do there's no such thing as certainty in the oil industry."

"The valuation by Bauss's employee, Brockley, that was certain."

"That was his scam."

"He was trying to blackmail us. It was a fake. He was going to send it to the press."

"That report's been destroyed," said Greaves.

"But how did he know?"

"It was bad luck. His wife's grandfather was an English geologist who worked out here back at the turn of the century. She'd inherited some maps. The maps disagreed with the data I gave Bauss. The bloody fool checked them out and used his own information to do his valuation. To blackmail us."

"You killed the man in England to get the report, didn't you?"

"No, of course not, that nutcase Bone did that."

"Don't you know?" It was Rittman's turn to shock Greaves, "Bauss got back the report and killed the Englishman and his wife...."

"Rubbish." Greaves spat out the words.

"And Brockley was killed at the airport too."

"He would have messed everything up. Anyway it was an accident."

Rittman looked Greaves in the eye, thinking him completely mad. Any sane man, knowing what Greaves knew, would have concluded long ago the deaths of those people were too fortuitous to be an accident, but Greaves had blocked his mind from the truth.

But he had done the same. They were both in deep shit. Finally he said. "There were no accidents. We'll tell Kraill to stop drilling and set casing. It'll take a couple of days to resolve. By that time this mess in Sana'a might be sorted. The government will win and we'll be back on course."

"Good idea, Earl. Let's do it and get to the airport. If there is no drilling we don't have to stay here. We can take that flight and be outta here. We'll radio the rig now."

Rittman had been planning to stay in Sana'a while Kraill was in the desert but he also needed to get back and sort out his investments. They walked to the radio room. A Yemeni engineer with a young face was fiddling with the controls of the receiver.

"What are you doing here?" Greaves said curtly.

"Oh sorry sir, excuse me, I was trying to contact the rig. It's important I talk to Hassan. His house is near the presidential palace. I've taken his family into my father's house."

"Can't you operate the radio?" said Greaves incredulously. "We need to contact Kraill."

"Of course I can sir, but I can't get through. At this time the reception is normally clear, we sometimes have bad reception early in the morning but not now. I can't pick them up at all. There's no response on any of the frequencies."

Rittman took the handset from the young man, who rose to give him a seat. "Base to Qarib, Base to Qarib, over." He let go of the transmit button and waited. All they heard was a crackling hiss. He repeated "Base to Qarib, Base to Qarib, over," several times, turning the silver dial a notch at a time through the frequencies Outland had been allotted by the Defence Ministry.

Rittman looked up at Greaves who stood over him, "He's right, they are not responding."

Later in the day Sergeant Cutler stood on the flat roof of the Foreign Ministry and saw two MIG 29's, their afterburners glowing red and yellow, roaring across the sky. Above the high buildings to the north the planes simultaneously wheeled westwards and two missiles, incandescent white streaks in the darkening sky, fired from the wings of the first jet. The missiles dipped towards the airport in the west. Houses blocked his view but a glow followed by a hollow boom indicated a target had been hit.

More planes came out of the night sky behind him, so low there was a rush of air on his stubbly hair as they overflew him. He ducked into the doorway and made his way back down the narrow flight of stairs to the Minister's office.

Steeples and the Ambassador were seated where he had left them in the candlelit gloom. "All hell's breaking loose. There's tracer fire in the air and it's not safe to go out. There are tanks on the main street outside and the Presidential Guard has erected a barricade in front of the palace."

"I've got to catch that plane out of here," said Steeples.

"Nothing took off while I was up there. The airstrip is a target for the MIGs. I saw two hits."

"We'll sit it out here Congressman," said Shelterman. "Collins will take care of our people."

"We should have gone with Collins."

Shelterman ignored him. "Well done Sergeant," he said.

Cutler couldn't believe his luck.

Inside the American Embassy there were few people about when Collins had walked in. The receptionist told him the evacuation flight had departed early, soon after the first explosion, with most of its scheduled passengers. The commercial attaché should have taken charge but he had gone to the airport to see off his family and had not come back. It was the Ambassador's secretary, Cathy, a middle-aged lady from North Carolina, who seemed to be in charge. She was sitting implacably in the Ambassador's chair in his office when Collins stepped in.

"What's been happening," he said to her perfunctorily.

"Thank God you're here," she said, getting up from the desk and walking to her more normal position on its other side. "Where's the Ambassador?"

"He's still at the Ministry. We have to check every American in the country. Get into the files and pull off a list of all contact numbers and addresses."

"Yes, of course, but..."

"That'll be a good start. I assume the phone lines are all down."

"Yes, the Yemeni ones, but we've got the satellite links to the States."

"Good, now get those files now."

"Sure. But have you any news about Curt?"

Collins shook his head.

"A Mr Bauss from Houston has been trying to get Curt for the last hour. He's calling on his private line. I wasn't sure what to say."

Collins recognised the name but could not place it. "Did you tell him about the accident?"

"No, I was told not to say anything, but he's due to call again in half an hour."

There was a knock on the door and a man's head appeared around the door. "Oh! I'm sorry. The Middle East Secretary is on the line from Washington again. Will you speak to him, Mr Collins?"

"Yes put the call through to this office. Go and do the list now Cathy, the sooner the better."

The phone rang on the Ambassador's desk and Collins leant over the desk to pick it up. "Good morning sir, Collins here."

"Hello, so you are Dick Collins, are you?"

"Yes."

"We've never met but I've heard all about you. Where's the Ambassador?"

"He's stuck in the Ministry with Congressman Steeples. It's unsafe for the Congressman outside. There are looters and tanks on the streets."

"OK, then you tell me what's going on. What do you make of all this?"

"Did you see my report last week, sir? I could see this coming....."

"I want to know why," the Minister interrupted, "these guys are rebelling. We thought it was all sewn up in Yemen. This could destabilise the rest of the Middle East putting us in the shit with oil supplies. The oil price is already up nearly five dollars."

"I sent a report, it...."

"We know about your report. Why is the army doing this? What has happened to common sense? Don't they know we won't back them? They will lose all the arms aid and the American investors will pull out. We've gotta show we're behind the Sana'a government or Saudi will get cold feet. And OPEC. Remember those Houthi rebels are supported by Iran and if they see an opportunity the shit will hit the fan."

"I know but it seems the army don't have 'common sense' as you put it. And it's not the Houthi. It's the south I'm sure. I've seen the photos."

"So why? What's going on?"

Collins was thinking on his feet. In truth he had no idea. America was giving millions of dollars in aid and investment was growing. The Yemeni President made sure a lot of this money went to the southern army to keep them happy. True, Aden was not happy about oil revenues but the President had seemed to be in control. If this had been a fundamentalist or tribal uprising it would be different. They didn't give a shit about American support.

"The Russians perhaps," he said at length.

"The Russians are spent. They've enough troubles in their own republics."

"I don't know then, sir."

"OK," the secretary sighed, evidently disappointed at the lack of enlightenment coming from his staff. "What's this about Curt Gawain getting hurt?"

"He was hit by the tailfin of an aeroplane, out in the desert, at a rig site. It blew off in a storm. We don't know how badly he's hurt although I gather he's fully conscious. Emmett Kraill, the Outland manager, was supposed to give us a report today but the phones are dead."

"And he's still out in the desert?"

"Yes, the plane's damaged. They need a replacement part." Shit, he had forgotten. Had the new plane arrived in Sana'a before the bombing? "The desert's the safest place to be," Collins added. He was glad Teri was out there too.

"How long?"

"Before they get back?"

"No. When will this fighting finish? Who's going to win? I need to tell the Secretary of State."

"It won't last long. What I saw out in the streets suggests there's going to be one hell of a battle this evening. The southern army's got tanks in the city. But I don't think they can win."

"Do all you can."

"Of course sir," answered Collins but he was wondering what the hell he could do.

"And Collins, one more thing, I hear you've been enquiring about an Englishman called Benjamin Bone."

"Yes."

"How did you get this man's name? He's wanted for a double murder in England."

"A double murder?" Collins was shocked. Benjamin had told him of a dead American in a plane, no murders. "Who did he ...?"

"There's more, the police in London are not blaming Benjamin Bone. Seems this Bone guy got financial information about Outland Oil that he shouldn't have and he gave it to the guy who was murdered."

"You said a double murder."

"The wife bought it too and they had a six year old kid."

"Shit, who killed them?"

"The English police are fingering this Outland company. It sounds implausible but we gotta follow it up."

"It does," Collins spoke off-handedly.

"Where did you come across his name?"

"I spoke to him. He's in Yemen. What you are saying figures all right."

"So where is he now?"

"He went on out to Outland's drilling site, the same place Curt Gawain went."

"Do the Brits know about this?"

"No, nobody does. Look sir, I trusted him. Seems I was right to trust him. If he's onto something then best let him find out."

"When he gets back grill him before the Brits get to him. How the heck he got out of England to Yemen beats me. Their security must be shit. And where'd he get a visa?"

Collins was not listening. "I've been thinking, sir, about what you said before. This coup here. If it messes up our relationship with Saudi and the Gulf States it could seriously disrupt our oil supplies. Prices are going up already. The oil company lobby in the States would be shouting, I told you so?"

"Yes?"

"And the environmental lobby have been screwing them into the ground."

"What are you driving at?"

"You know a disruption to oil supplies would suit someone who had predicted it."

The line was silent for several long seconds.

"And the primaries are coming up. Dick, I know what you're driving at. I've gotta go now. Goodbye and thanks." He replaced the receiver.

The implication was definitely there. Outland, Yemen, and Congressman Steeples. Was it just a coincidence? Was Steeples involved? No impossible, Steeples had been genuinely surprised by the fighting this afternoon. And scared as well.

The Ambassador's secretary, entered without knocking carrying a sheet of foolscap with a list of all the Americans in the country. There were over two hundred of them. Twelve were on the Outland rig and another thirty eight employed in oil operations in the southern and western part of Yemen. Collins was pleased to see many of the others had left on the flight, heeding his warning or leaving at the last minute as the tension had increased in the city. He recognised most of the remaining names but eight had no address listed. He marked each one.

"See what you can find," he said. "By the way Cathy, who is this Bauss?" The name was bugging him.

"Mr Bauss has spoken to Curt before. I'll get the log of his incoming calls. Curt keeps a printed log and deletes the file copy every night."

"How can you get it then?"

"It's in the trash box on the network. They're not deleted when you press delete, they hang about on the hard disc for ages."

She returned fifteen minutes later with the printout for Gawain's satellite phone. The number Bauss had used today was a Houston number and it appeared nine times over the last six months. There were also calls from Gawain's home in the States and from other numbers Collins recognised in Washington. All were long calls. Another Houston number, appearing three times, and a recent call from London caught his eye. "Do you know these ones?"

"Yes, its Congressman Steeples' office. I had to call him before he arrived Friday."

"But these three calls came in before I knew he was coming."

"Maybe Curt was handling it."

No, I was handling Steeples' trip for Shelterman. What the hell's Curt been up to? "Can you get me the key to Curt's office? It's important."

"I could get you the master from the safe but it has to be authorised by the Ambassador."

"Isn't there a spare key?"

"No, Curt kept the only copy. He wouldn't even let his secretary have one."

"Well I'm standing in for the Ambassador, I'll authorise you to get the key."

"I'm not sure whether its allowed under procedures."

"Christ, forget procedures Cathy."

"Yes sir. But I'll have to give you a form. You can sign it."

"Get the key, OK."

When she returned ten minutes later she was carrying a fob holding a collection of master keys that opened all the rooms in the Embassy. She dangled them round her chubby forefinger. A form was in her other hand.

"Bauss called again. I asked if he wanted to speak to you but he refused."

"Did he say anything else?"

"No, I tried to find out. He just asked me to get Curt to call him when he got back. Here are the keys. Please sign the form."

He signed and followed her to Gawain's office. The room was tidy, the desk clear apart from a phone, in trays, a desk diary and an unwashed coffee cup. He sat in Gawain's chair and opened each of the desk drawers. They contained stationery and routine files. One of the larger drawers was locked. "Go and do your work Cathy. Leave me here for the moment."

As soon as Cathy had shut the door Collins took a penknife from his pocket, a knife he had carried since he was a boy. He forced the lock on the drawer. Inside he found a wad of dollars, a black track suit and a torch. He closed the drawer again.

Noticing the appointment diary he picked it up and flicked through its pages. If Gawain had anything to hide it would not be in here, visible to all the secretaries in the building and true enough there were only brief scribbled notes written in Gawain's clumsy hand, referring to routine meetings and telephone calls. He checked the entries for May. He was about to close the book when he noticed something unusual. An entry for Thursday May 28th, scribbled, almost unreadable, was a local Sana'a number. Collins didn't recognise this number but he did the name underneath. It said *"Dr G. Turnbow. Meeting tomorrow."*

Gawain had told no one of this, not once when they discussed Turnbow after the kidnap. Collins flicked over the page to May 29th. The page was blank apart from the words *"Embassy Meeting run by Collins."* Collins remembered he had told the diplomats at this meeting about the Yemeni army troop movements. The Ambassador's response had been lukewarm and Gawain had left early. Did he keep the appointment? Did he go to see Turnbow?

Collins closed all the drawers, closed the diary and left the room. He was sick of Gawain.

In Houston Claudia arrived early in the office as usual and read the daily Reuters news agency fax. There was a short report about fighting in Yemen and she stared at it in horror. There had been nothing about it in the Houston Post or in the other US papers and she was terrified about the impact it would have on Outland's shares. She tried to call Sana'a but failed to get through. As she looked through the rest of the faxes two men in dark suits stepped through the door. Neither was wearing dark glasses but she had an uneasy feeling they should have been.

"Are you Miss Claudia Pasquale," the man on the left said.

Not waiting for an answer the man on the right continued. "We work for the United States Government. The FBI." They both flashed badges. "We have reason to believe Outland Oil may possess information that will assist us in our enquiries."

"Enquiries about what," whispered Claudia, scared by the two men.

"About your company's exploits in the Middle East, a country called the Republic of Yemen."

"What do you need to know?"

"My department has reason to believe there have been financial irregularities in Outland's accounts with regards to your business in that country. Have you ever heard of an Englishman named Benjamin Bone?"

Claudia did remember Bone. He had been interviewed for a job. He had been good looking and had flirted with her. It had crossed her mind he was gay.

"Yes, he was interviewed for a job here. Would you like to know when?"

"We would."

She checked the register. "Tuesday two weeks ago, in the afternoon, he left at four."

"Did you notice anything about him? Was he strange at all?"

"No, I don't think so. He had an English accent."

"Thank you, said the man on the left. Now we will search Mr Rittman's office. Please give me the key."

She retrieved it from the cabinet on the wall and also fished around in her desk drawer and handed them the key to the filing cabinet. They took them and disappeared into Earl's office. She tried to call Sana'a again. The line was still dead.

She had suspected something was wrong even before Bauss had taken the files. It had been Ray Bowes the geologist. "Hot dogs!" he had said. "The drilling program was goddamned speculation." Coupled with Earl's confidence it hadn't seemed right. She was wondering where the gay Englishman fitted in when the two FBI men reappeared. They were carrying nothing and, although she detested Bauss, she was relieved he had removed those documents, whatever they were.

The men walked over to her together. The one on the left, although she was by no means sure he was the same one on the left as when they had first arrived, said sinisterly, "Miss Pasquale, one more thing before we leave, don't tell your boss about us, not yet."

"How can I, he's in Yemen. The lines are down."

"When they are up, please don't tell him."

She was sure these men could not stop her from telling Earl anything, not legally anyway. Earl should be on his way home by now.

Then she had an idea. "I won't call Earl. I won't tell him anything if you do one small thing."

THIRTY FOUR

The road to Karim had been damaged by the rainstorm blowing in from the airstrip and it took over three and a half hours for the group of men from the rig to arrive on the outskirts of town. It was past six thirty when the dusty Land Cruiser arrived at Ali's house. In the front of the Land Cruiser sat Emmett Kraill and Benjamin Bone. Khaled and Mahmoud were in the back. Natalya had also wanted to come but Kraill asked her to stay with Gawain. He also advised her not to mention Gawain's revelation to either Turnbow's wife or to Richard Clapton.

When they left the rig it had already been too late for the new plane to arrive at the airstrip before nightfall. Gawain was semi-comatose and his muttered, exhausted suggestion about Dr Turnbow seemed to be his only chance. Mahmoud had been questioned and he admitted to having heard about the missing doctor. Khaled too said he had heard rumours. Of course, both maintained they had nothing to do with the kidnap, agreeing that the rich banker Ali was the culprit. Sheikh Achmed would know nothing they assured Kraill, there would be no point in troubling him.

Mahmoud did not let on to the Americans or to Khaled he was as stunned as the white men, fearful for the town that such a high ranking diplomat knew for certain Turnbow was hidden there. He secretly hoped Gawain would quickly die and Turnbow would already be dead.

However, despite this he was happy to have received his payment for the water from Janek. He did not dare keep the money in the labourer's tent where he slept so he hid it in one of the cabinets in the medical trailer. Whilst the rest of them were discussing what to do outside he had removed the envelope from beneath his shirt, counted the bundles of notes and placed the envelope at the back of an overhead cabinet. Gawain, moaning quietly, had stared at him with glazed eyes from the bed. He would return to the rig later and carry the money back to Karim on horseback when he got the chance.

As the Land Cruiser drew to a halt Benjamin saw a heavily veiled woman sitting on the steps of Ali's house. She rose quickly and disappeared inside her compound. A teenage boy appeared and spoke to Kraill through the open car window.

"Ask him where this man Ali is," Kraill said to Mahmoud in the back seat. "I don't understand his dialect. Tell him we need to speak to Ali urgently."

Mahmoud nodded, opened his door and got out of the car. He acknowledged the young boy, shook his hand and talked to him. The boy answered back, gabbling out words, clearly agitated. Eventually Mahmoud turned back to Kraill. "This boy is Ali's son. He says his father has gone to my father, Sheikh Achmed, to sort out a disagreement between them."

"What is the disagreement?"

"My father blames Ali for the death of my half-brother Rashad at your party in Sana'a."

"What. Why Ali?"

"My father has found out Ali was responsible for kidnapping the American and perhaps the two are linked. We should go there and leave this boy alone with his mother."

"Not so fast. Does he or his mother know where Turnbow is?"

"No, they know nothing."

Benjmain wasn't so sure but could not do anything. Mahmoud, as interpreter, was protecting the scared boy. "OK, we'll go and see your father." Kraill said.

They bounced through the narrow streets of the darkening town. Empty of people, the shops were shuttered and only a man herding scrawny goats, devouring edible rubbish piled at each street corner, slowed progress. A few years ago these goats were perfect recycling systems but the advent of plastic bags and bottles had stopped all that. Trash lay everywhere.

At the Sheikh's house, Mahmoud opened the door, led the party into the visitor's room and left to find his father. Benjamin and Kraill paced about waiting for him to return while Khaled lay on the cushions, exhausted by the journey. Sweetened tea arrived and they sipped this from small china cups. After around half an hour the Sheikh eventually appeared at the door, dressed in a white robe and head-dress. "Welcome gentleman," the Sheikh said. "I am so glad to be of assistance to my esteemed guests."

"We wish to find Dr Gary Turnbow," said Kraill at once, "Do you know of his whereabouts?"

Sheikh Achmed was unperturbed by the abruptness. He was beginning to accept such rudeness from Americans. He answered at once, "You are in luck. I have found out that Dr Turnbow has been in Karim ever since his loss. I am sure my son has told you that Ali, my former ally, was responsible for kidnapping your countryman. I am shocked and upset."

Benjamin was pretty sure the Sheikh was neither shocked nor upset, at least not about Turnbow.

"Where is he?" said Kraill.

"Inshallah, he is still alive. Ali has not treated him well I am afraid. Ali is not a kind man but I offer you my house to rest in for I am a generous man."

"Thank you. We must get him. Please, where is he?"

"Your operations. Are they going well?" said Achmed. "I hear the plane is damaged."

"We have a replacement on the way. The operations are fine."

"It could be days before you get a new plane. I believe nothing can land at the airport."

"The airport? Which airport?

"In Sana'a, the runway is damaged."

"What do you mean? How is it damaged?"

"The fighting..."

"What fighting?"

"Have you not heard about the fighting?"

"No! In Sana'a?"

"It would seem so, we have an army camp here in Karim and the officer in command, Abdullah, is my cousin. He is in radio communication with Sana'a. But never mind he says it will be over soon and we will have a new government." One shouldn't give in so easily to these white men, he thought, satisfied he had been the one to tell them this thing. "Yes..." continued Achmed, "I'm sure it will be over soon. Now about this kidnapped man...," he thought for a moment and then said, "...our workers on your rig..., from Karim..., are they doing a good job?"

"Yes, an excellent job." As soon as Kraill had said it he regretted it.

"Then I'm sure you can raise their hourly rate, say twenty percent, please pay the money to my representative in the normal way and he will distribute it fairly."

"You are right the workers should be better rewarded but I am sorry twenty percent is not possible. Outland Oil is not a rich oil company but when the oil begins to flow then of course twenty percent will be an option. I suggest a rise of five percent."

"Too little. I agree when the oil flows the wages will be much, much better but the work is hard and, as you say, my men are doing a job better than can be expected of them, an excellent job, you said. Fifteen percent will not be a problem for your finances."

"Some do an excellent job, others are not so good. Since you distribute the money, give the good men more. We can manage ten percent."

"I will accept twelve percent, but when you find oil my men will expect more."

"Of course. I accept." Kraill would try later to recover some of this money from the American government who will surely be grateful for Turnbow's release.

"Good. Now you wish to know where the American is. I have told Mahmoud. He will take you to him. He's locked up near Ali's house."

"We will go there now."

"Yes, and come back here when you find him. We must eat together."

Mahmoud was waiting for them outside and they retraced their route through the town, headlights blazing in the dark streets. A battered Land Cruiser preceded them, and another followed them, each carrying four of the Sheikh's men.

The house where they stopped was in darkness. Its front wall had one shuttered window and a closed wooden door at ground level with two shuttered windows on the second floor. It looked deserted. Two of the men from the leading car started to batter on the door under the light of its headlights while the others, including Kraill and Benjamin, got out of their vehicles and watched.

There was no response to the battering so, with shouting and gesticulating, an axe was produced and the door was demolished. Two men disappeared inside while another stood guard. A moment later they returned followed by a man, naked but for a torn pair of shorts. He stumbled out into the light and covered his eyes with the back of a hand blackened with dirt, holding onto the doorframe with the other. He was blonde-haired with yellow skin, a drawn face and cracked, peeling lips. He squinted at them with round bloodshot eyes. Nobody spoke. Kraill and Benjamin just stared, elation at their find mingled with horror at seeing a man in such a condition.

At length he seemed to become accustomed to the light and, looking at Benjamin's white face illuminated amongst the others, he opened his mouth. "Hi," he said, his voice hoarse. "I'm Gary Turnbow."

Kraill, in the darkness, looked across at Benjamin and muttered under his breath, "Christ he looks worse than Gawain."

An hour later Dr Turnbow was sitting slumped on cushions in the whitewashed ground floor room of the Sheikh's house. A servant was collecting up the tray of plates and a mug lying at his feet. Kraill walked in. "The car's ready. Can you take the journey out to the rig now? It's bumpy as hell."

"No problem. If he needs my help the sooner we get there the better."

"Do you know what this Ali was going to do with you?"

"I didn't know anything at all. Nobody spoke to me. Nobody said a word in English. I couldn't even keep track of the time. And I couldn't eat, even when they gave me food..."

"Why did you come here in the first place," interrupted Benjamin, "didn't you know it was dangerous?"

"Yes I did know. I wouldn't have come.., I shouldn't have come but the Embassy assured me it was OK. They arranged my trip well. My driver was armed. The diplomat assured me it was safe. How wrong he was. I suppose you know my driver was shot dead when I was taken."

"No we didn't know," said Kraill. "You say the Embassy arranged your trip. The American Embassy?"

"Yes of course."

"A diplomat in the Embassy? Who? Who was this diplomat? Was his name Dick Collins?" went on Kraill, astonished.

"No, it was someone else, Graham, Green, something like that. He's a big man with a moustache."

"Gawain?" Benjamin and Kraill gasped in unison. "Gawain, was it Curt Gawain?"

"Yes that's him."

"But he's the one who's been hurt. The Embassy kept that quiet. He was out here looking for you."

"I'll do my best for him."

"Who knows about this?" Benjamin asked Kraill.

"Well I didn't, but everybody's going to damn well know when I get back. They are a useless bunch of clowns."

"Clowns you say? Who are clowns?" Sheikh Achmed had appeared at the door.

"I was talking about our politicians," said Kraill expeditiously.

"Ha, clowns, yes, and so are ours. You are better now Dr Turnbow?"

"No I am not better, but I am recovering. When can we leave?"

"I am not stopping you, not me. Ali was to blame and we will punish him. Do not be afraid of me, I am the Sheikh."

"I have one more question for you before we go," said Kraill to the Sheikh as they watched Turnbow weakly get into the car. "Your son told me Ali was responsible for the bomb at the Mogul Rani Hotel. Why should he wish to bomb our party?"

"No, you do not understand what we are saying. Mahmoud only told you Ali caused the death of Rashad, my other son. He would not have wished to blow up your party. Why? What for?" Sheikh Achmed spoke eloquently. He found this man much easier to talk to. He was friendlier than both Janek and Gawain, easier to dominate. "Ali is not a politician," Achmed went on "he is a banker, but he sent Rashad to the party and Rashad died. For this he must pay. Rashad should not have been drinking alcohol. Your Yemeni staff perhaps yes, the politicians perhaps yes, they needed to be there to keep you Americans happy, but Rashad did not need to be there. Ali sent him. He is responsible."

"Why did he send him?"

"To bargain for the release of your Dr Turnbow, of course. To bargain with your American diplomats. We poor people in Karim knew nothing of this man but the Americans knew. Oh yes. They knew Ali kidnapped him."

"And they didn't tell us, or Mrs Turnbow?" Kraill spoke incredulously.

"No, of course not. The day I trust Americans is the day I become a Christian." At this the sour-faced Arab burst into guffaws, tears of laughter welling from his eyes.

Kraill waited, embarrassed, until his laughing stopped. "So where is this Ali?"

"You don't need to see him. You have Dr Turnbow alive and now it is time for you to leave." He moved to the car door and beckoned the two men.

Benjamin shook hands with the Sheikh and asked, "if Ali didn't, then who did? Who did plant the bomb?" Who was that mysterious man in black?

"I do not know, but when I find out he will be dealt with too."

Achmed smiled to himself as he watched the car bounce away lit by the powerful security lights fixed above his wall. It was if the soul of his dead son had returned and entered his own tired old body, rejuvenating his passion for power. He had surely accomplished a lot today. He had skilfully manoeuvred the stupid Americans to think Ali was the culprit. Gawain asking for Turnbow was perfect, unplanned but perfect, surely a gift from Allah. Mahmoud had handled the situation brilliantly. Perhaps I shall forgive him after all. Thank goodness Khaled hadn't spoilt it.

And Ali will be destroyed. Shall I let him go? Shall I show him the mercy he has never showed to others? One thing I won't do is have a vote. That is certainly not the way to solve matters. Perhaps Rashad's death was for the good. Allah works in ways men cannot comprehend. Achmed turned and re-entered his house. I need more sons, he thought. It's time I got another wife. He closed the door behind him.

Turnbow sat in the front of the vehicle and Benjamin sat in the rear next to Mahmoud who had appeared just as they were about to leave and insisted on returning to the rig. Khaled had disappeared in Karim.

They drove in silence, the occupants dozing. Kraill several times had to shake his head to keep awake. After about an hour and a half they left the damaged track at the airstrip and started down the new road along Wadi Qarib. Turnbow, who had been sleeping, opened his eyes and stared vacantly out at the darkness ahead.

"How are you feeling?" Kraill asked him quietly.

"Terrible, but I'll survive."

"There'll be questions to answer when we get back to Sana'a."

Kraill was angry at Collins for not telling him what the Embassy had done. Outland Oil was badly exposed. "But I'm afraid we are stuck here for a while," he went on, "there's a war, a coup by the southern army it seems. In Sana'a. We won't be able to land a plane."

"Yes," said Turnbow. "I told Gawain all about it."

"What?" said Kraill. "How did you know?"

"One of the patients in the hospital was an army doctor, a major. We became friendly and he told me. He said a general in the army was going to do it and he was a stupid man because the Americans wouldn't support him. I was carrying a note about it in my pocket when I was kidnapped. I told it all to Gawain at our meeting. It was all I had to read in the cell and I read it over and over again. It eventually crumbled to dust," he laughed as if to cover up a sob. "I expect I will need counselling when I get back to Denver."

It was past midnight when the Land Cruiser bumped into the camp and drew up beside the row of cars. The rig was brightly lit and the sound of crashing metal and the shrill grind of crushing rock cut the unusually warm night air. As soon as the car came to a halt Bob Janek appeared on the rig catwalk and made his way down the steps and across the yard towards them. Kraill opened his door but before getting out he put his arm on Turnbow's bony shoulder.

"There's something we haven't told you Doctor," he said softly. "She's probably asleep now. Could you help Gawain before seeing her?"

"Who are you talking about?"

"Your wife is here, Doctor."

Bob Janek was walking towards the Land Cruiser. "The radio's fucked up," he shouted.

"How come?"

"The software's been corrupted...." Janek stopped speaking when he saw Turnbow. "Shit, are you the Doctor?"

"I'm Dr Gary Turnbow." He extended his hand.

"I'm Bob Janek, drilling manager," they shook hands, "so they fucking found you?"

"They did." He turned to Kraill. "Why is my wife here?"

"A journalist brought her. She's fine. Please you must check Gawain first."

"Where is he?"

"In the medical trailer over there."

"I'll take him," interrupted Benjamin who had got out from the back of the car. Janek nodded to Benjamin, with distaste. He didn't much like the smooth Englishman. He had noticed how both Natalya Cheung and Teri had looked at this man and he resented what an English accent did to a woman. On the rigs in East Texas the women went for the rugged types like himself. They all want poncy Englishmen these days, he thought.

Benjamin directed Turnbow towards the trailer camp and they disappeared into the gloom. Mahmoud followed a few steps behind.

"How did you find him?" shouted Janek to Kraill above the noise of the drilling.

"I'll tell you later. So what's this about the radio?" yelled Kraill. "Christ the drilling doesn't sound good."

"It's not fucking good. Yeah, the radio. The software's been corrupted. It looks like a virus. The radio operator doesn't know how it happened. Did you hear there's fighting in Sana'a?"

"Yes, the Sheikh told us, let's hope it doesn't last."

"At first we thought something had happened to the connection in Sana'a when it crapped out but there's no fucking signal and the radio op's convinced it's a fucking virus. He's good. They're not all fucking headaces like that fucking Doctor Khaled? How would a virus get into the computer?"

"Somebody's got to load it, somebody on the camp. Who would have done that?"

"Fuck knows. But the radio room is empty half the time. An operator's gone sick, gone back to his camp or somewhere. Anybody could have walked in."

"How soon can it be mended?"

"Apparently it can't. Not until we get some backup software."

"Shit," exclaimed Kraill, "any news on the plane?"

"I haven't heard anything from the fucking pilots. God knows if the plane can land if there's a fucking war going on. By the way I let the Oil Minister and his two cronies take one of our Land Cruisers. They were giving me all kinds of shit. They're driving back to Sana'a."

"I suppose they can get past the checkpoints. I wouldn't want to risk a trip, not after what happened to Doctor Turnbow."

"That Minister's a powerful man." Janek paused. "You know we're gonna have to change the drill bit in the morning. These rocks are too fucking hard. We're only making a couple of metres an hour. This well is gonna take forever unless we get through the top layer faster."

"We weren't expecting such hard drilling."

"It's not in the program. I told you we needed a proper ops geologist instead of fucking Bowes. We're gonna have to change the make up of the drill string."

"I'll design a new one for you. It wasn't my fault about the geologist, Bob."

"And another thing, Emmett," Janek went on, "we've got two test engineers on the rig. They're asking when we're gonna test. Who sent those guys out here. It's fucking crazy?"

"That asshole Greaves. It was the first thing he did when he arrived. It's a waste of money. Those guys are on six hundred bucks a day. And we don't have proper testing equipment."

"This well is a fucking disaster."

"It's looking like that. How's Gawain?"

"I'm keeping out of it. Those two women are nursing him. I don't like having fucking women on my rig. It's...... Christ!"

As he spoke there was a roar from the derrick. It shook as if every weld, every rivet, and every nut would snap. Both men looked up at the drilling pipe suspended ninety feet above the drill floor. It had stopped rotating and was spiralling like a corkscrew. Seconds later it jerked, and with a shrill grinding, popped back to its former shape, to begin spinning once more. The noise returned to its earlier rattling, crashing symphony.

"Shit we lost a few fucking teeth from the bit. I better get up there."

Kraill watched him dash up the metal steps under the floodlights. He then walked over to Janek's cabin in the darkness intending to catch an hour's sleep. Inside the room there was a folded pile of clothing on his desk, amongst his papers. He had forgotten Mrs Shelterman and Gladys were billeted in there. He quietly picked up his documents, a drilling manual and a calculator, and left, walking between the trailers to the radio room. The night seemed oppressively hot, the air thick with moisture. No wind at all. To the south, away from the lights of the drilling rig, the sky was clear of cloud but the stars were hazy specks.

Dr Turnbow stooped over the unconscious body of Gawain while Teri and Natalya peered over his shoulder. Turnbow pulled back the sheets recognising the man who had sent him to the old city. The man's heart was beating fast. He tapped his chest and shone a pen torch into each eye.

"He's not too bad but his left lung has collapsed. I'm gonna have to try and release the pressure. We need painkillers."

Benjamin reached for one of the cabinets and tugged at the handle. It was empty. "They are all empty. There are no medicines. Khaled gave them all away." Mahmoud spoke quickly.

"Damn. We'll have to do without," He looked at Gawain as he did so, "or he will."

"Do you need me for this? I'll come back next morning." Teri interrupted.

"No. Brian can help. Both of you girls can leave."

"Thanks," Teri replied.

"I'll stay," said Natalya, "you go and get some sleep."

Teri left the cabin, the door slamming behind her. Mahmoud had been waiting to retrieve his money from the cabinet. He would also have to come back in the morning. "I'll go too," he said.

Turnbow was bent over the bed but hearing Mahmoud made him look up. He recognised him then as the quiet man who had sat on his horse impassively while a soldier had shot the driver of his Land Cruiser. But he didn't say anything. His eyes returned to the patient. "OK, we must do this quickly."

"Wait, I can get something for him, I'll be back in a few minutes," said Benjamin. Five minutes later he returned with a half full bottle of vodka. "This should help," he said.

Natalya took it from him and, as their eyes met, he was sure she smiled.

Hours later it was dark in the trailer except for a small desk light pointing to the wall. Turnbow lay on the upper bunk, sound asleep, and Benjamin sat by Natalya watching the patient.

"You seem to be able to handle yourself out here," she said.

246

"I was trained..." Benjamin's heart began to beat faster. Natalya was speaking to him. He waited for her to go on. She was silent so he whispered, "you know Natalya I was going to tell you about my wife. And I am separated from her. I didn't know how to handle it. You know what I'm like."

"I don't know what you are like." She glanced at the clock. It was three in the morning. "But yesterday I was impressed."

Benjamin took her hand and squeezed it, watching her in the low light of the trailer. Natalya did not respond to his touch. Her hand remained limp in his but she didn't pull away. "There's a war in Sana'a now. Give yourself up to the British Embassy. You have to."

Gawain shifted in his bunk and they both turned to look at him. They were surprised to see his eyes wide open, looking towards them, but glazed with incomprehension. "What did you say about a war?" He spoke groggily, "It's too early. Does she know?"

"What do you mean, too early, does who know?" said Benjamin back to him.

"It's too early," mumbled Gawain still drunk from the vodka. "We've got to get back and stop it. Geshira can't win yet, he needs us."

"What do you mean?"

There was no answer. Gawain's eyes were closed again.

"What was he talking about?" said Natalya softly, almost asleep herself.

"I haven't a clue." They sat silently, motionless until Natalya's head began to drop.

"Where did you get the vodka?" Natalya spoke sleepily.

"It was the American Ambassador's wife and her friend. I took it from their room."

"How did you know....," she said as she drifted off to sleep, her head on his shoulder.

Benjamin was unable to sleep himself. He carefully rested her head on the padded arms of the doctor's chair, rose and left the trailer. It had remained warm through the night. The sun had just begun to rise over the cliffs east of the drilling rig. There were none of the usual horizontal sheets of mist in the valley and the sultry atmosphere persisted, the air so thick that noises seemed muffled like in a winter fog. The sweat was sticky under his shirt as he crossed the yard to the canteen. Inside Emmett Kraill sat alone, an orange juice in his hand, a cigarette in his mouth, papers strewn around the table. He looked up as Benjamin entered. "How's Gawain?"

"He's all right. Turnbow's good. Have you been up all night?"

"Yes, the drilling's going bad and the Ambassador's wife is sleeping in my cabin. I'm designing a new drill string. That's the different pipes we use to drill the well. The rocks are unexpectedly hard and we need to change it."

"Oh," said Benjamin unsurprised. He collected a cup of coffee.

Kraill continued his work, tapping calculations into a pocket calculator and puffing on his cigarette. Finally he stubbed it out in a full ashtray beside him, flipped the lid of the calculator and pushed his papers to one side. "Brian," he said, "you heard what Janek said about the radio?"

"Yes, what's wrong with it?"

"We need new software, it's got a virus."

"How did that happen?"

"Brian, you are the only one I can trust. I trust Bob for sure but I'm finding it difficult to believe anything any more. You seem an OK sort of guy, despite being a Brit," he smiled ruefully.

Benjamin nodded eagerly. Perhaps he was going to learn the truth at last.

"I've been thinking all night," Kraill went on, "not only about the drill string, about other things, and I've come to some damn weird conclusions. I don't know why I'm telling you this, hell I've only just met you but, as I said, I like you. I don't trust anybody on this goddamn rig."

"When I was first employed by Outland Oil a guy named Earl Rittman in Houston employed me. I was working in the Persian Gulf, well paid, my kids at the American school, my wife spent all day at the club, she had a great tan. Everything was fine and then I joined Outland Oil. I still don't know why I did it...," he paused reflectively, "...of course I do, it was the money. Too much money."

"We weren't happy with the International School in Sana'a so my family went back to the States, while I worked out here. I'm telling you Brian your family should come first, not money. Since I joined this company a year and a half ago, everything has screwed up. My wife had an affair with a guy from New York, my eldest boy was busted for drugs and my dog got run over by a truck. He was still a puppy." He paused for breath as if the thought of his puppy was too much for him. "Well Brian, what it seems to me is all these things happened for a purpose, they are telling me this job stinks and I should get the fuck out of it. You know I decided over six months ago to get out but I'm still here, stuck in a fucking civil war, all because of a few lousy dollars."

"Sure the money was good, too good for me to jack it in but there was something else, something else was bugging me, so I stayed. I stayed because I was curious.....," Benjamin remained quiet, listening intently, "....sitting here last night, listening to that god awful noise from the rig, got me thinking different. I don't know if you know anything about drilling rigs, but I'm telling you this one is no good. It came from Somalia real quick and cheap, no crew, that's why we've so many locals employed. And I had to use it despite my screaming about it being shit."

"Secondly, the location out here. Is there a more stupid place to drill a well, in this goddamn crack in the ground surrounded by cliffs, miles from anywhere and miles from water even?"

"Thirdly, we've got no geologist. This well is costing millions of dollars and we don't have a geologist to check out the rocks. You know we had an operations geologist all lined up to come out here, a Brit like yourself, and at the last minute Rittman decided not to send him. It wasn't because of the cost. We've got plenty money. Our account in Yemen has millions more than we can spend. And where's all the money coming from for this screwed up fucking well?"

Benjamin said nothing.

"And we had a party a few days ago," Kraill continued. "This guy Congressman Steeples turned up. He's a big cheese in the States but he's against American companies investing in overseas oil. He's the last person you would expect to be supporting Outland Oil. What's he here for? And now the radio's fucking broken."

He paused again and Benjamin said "You didn't mention the plane losing its tail, Gawain getting hurt."

"No I'm not talking about accidents, they were accidents. We saw them happen. The passengers, the women, diplomats, you and I are not supposed to be here at all. You know, Brian, I think we don't have a hope in hell of finding oil out here, and the ops geologist was pulled because he would've told us so ..."

Benjamin was hardly surprised. The cuttings in his pocket would have given it away immediately. "Then why did this Rittman guy interview a geologist in the first place?"

"I suppose because I nagged him about it. Maybe I'm wrong, I don't know."

"So what you're saying is Rittman could be pretending, pretending you have an oil field. And this Congressman, he's involved too?"

"I didn't say that but hell it makes sense. Rittman or Greaves? It was Greaves who sent a couple of test engineers out here. A waste of fucking money..."

"You said Outland has plenty of money and these guys Rittman, Greaves and Steeples. None of them are here. Who broke the radio then?" And who got those men to try and kill me at the hotel, he thought.

"Someone who knows how a radio works. Someone who knows computers."

"The radio operators?"

"Yes, there were two of them on twelve hour shifts but one went sick yesterday. I've talked to the one who was covering. He's a good guy, even Bob said so."

"And the other?"

"I don't know but he left before the radio went down and the room is often empty, there was lots of opportunity for anyone to do it."

"So you don't know?" Benjamin said.

"In fact I do have an idea but it's not a nice one. It's not an idea I'm gonna share at present. I'll check it out first." He paused, "Bob's stopped drilling. I better talk to him."

Benjamin had also noticed the unusual quiet outside. "Tell me who....." he said but stopped speaking as the door to the trailer opened. Hans Brotenwurst, the German consul walked in looking flushed. He had a huge blue bump on his forehead where he had knocked it in the plane. "Guten morgen," he said "it is damned hot outside. I will be looking forward to getting out of here. But I have built up a big hungry appetite for my breakfast."

"Christ I need some sleep," said Benjamin as the German disappeared into the kitchen to give the cook his order.

"Me too. I'm gonna take these sketches up to Bob on the drill floor." He began to collect up his papers then said, "I'll tell you later but I've got to check it out before I say anything." Benjamin nodded and got up, leaving Kraill to pack away his drawings.

Outside he walked to the tool pusher's cabin, passing the two test engineers, Al and Kenneth. Like the German they had also risen early for breakfast.

"Morning" said Al to Benjamin "Gee, you look all in, what you been doing."

"Oh, nothing. I'm off to bed now."

"Sleep well" said Kenneth "I slept like a baby."

"You sure don't look like one," retorted Al and they were both laughing loudly as Benjamin walked away.

"Who's that guy over there," Kenneth said to Al, pointing to a thin stick of a man standing beneath the drilling rig watching lengths of pipe being pulled. Above him they could see Bob Janek on the drill floor directing the operation, stacking them in upright racks one by one in the derrick.

"Never seen him before. Looks like he also needs breakfast," and they were still chuckling as they disappeared inside the canteen.

Dr Turnbow, who was standing beneath the rig, was not hungry and, despite the exhausting night, was now wide-awake, anxiously waiting for his wife to appear. He had woken with a start when the drilling had stopped, cleaned up in the doctor's shower and crept out after checking on Gawain. He had left Natalya asleep in her chair. He was looking at the rig when Kraill climbed the steps to the drill floor.

Moments later Richard Clapton jogged by, dressed in a T-shirt and a pair of grubby shorts he had borrowed. He ran past Turnbow glancing at him casually and then he stopped and turned back. Richard had seen many photographs of Dr Gary Turnbow. Wedding photos, holiday photos and full face shots for his passport, but none looked as real as this. He was thinner for sure, with sunken eyes, less hair, but he was unmistakable. "You....., you're Turnbow."

"If you mean I'm Gary Turnbow, yes I am. Who are you?"

"I'm, Richard Clapton. I'm a reporter on the Denver Post. I came out here with your wife. Have you seen her? How did you get here? Where've you been?"

"I'm waiting for her to get up."

"So how'd you get here?"

"The guy who runs this rig and another man got me out last night. They told me you brought Margaret out here. What could she do? Give you a better story I suppose?"

"No you're wrong," Richard said quickly, "she's brilliant, you'll be proud of her. She wanted to come. Can I have an interview with the both of you?"

"I'm gonna sell my story to the highest bidder."

"That rules out the Denver Post."

"If Margaret says you're OK I'll let you have first shot. You can file a story before I get back to the States."

"Great, you don't go away. Margaret will be up soon. She'll confirm everything."

Richard gave up on his morning jog for the first time in years. He left Turnbow and made for his trailer to pen a draft of the story. He was sharing his room with Sandy, the pilot who was already at the only desk, poring over the Twin Otter's manual. Lines of copy were rushing through Richard's brain so he retrieved his notebook and pen and walked over to the canteen to use a table there. Ahead of him he saw Teri Mayes crossing the yard and he waved at her, wishing he could make love to her. She looked attractive in the morning sun, her blonde hair shining but she seemed not to notice his wave, intent on an errand of her own.

Benjamin fell asleep in the tool pusher's bed almost immediately. Now the drilling had stopped the air-conditioned trailer was blissfully peaceful. He dreamt he was being interviewed for a job by Earl Rittman. Rittman was asking him difficult personal questions about his relationship with his wife and the separation. Benjamin was sitting in a swivel chair completely naked and he crossed his legs hoping Rittman wouldn't notice. When he refused to answer a question about Natalya, Rittman rose from his desk and came over and Benjamin was terrified he would see he was naked.

A hand shook his shoulder and he opened his eyes. Hair tickled his unshaven cheeks and he saw, was it still his dream he wasn't sure, a woman's face, a pretty face with blonde hair, looking at him. His groin tingled with pleasure and he turned over. He then felt a sharp pain in his head and he opened his eyes again. It wasn't a dream. The blonde was Teri Mayes and she had a gun pressed into his temple.

"You are Benjamin Bone, aren't you?" she said.

He was wide-awake now.

"Yes I am," he gulped, "what are you doing?"

"You're a nuisance. Get up!"

Things popped into place in Benjamin's head. "It wasn't my fault. Your annual report...."

"Don't be so pathetic!"

He remained lying on his back, the gun at his head. "Why did you damage the radio? How can you report an oil discovery without communications?"

"I don't care if this company has a discovery or not, I'm not a cheap fraudster like Peter Greaves."

"What are you talking about?" Benjamin had thought he understood everything but now he was floundering, "why are you here then?"

"To shoot you."

"Why are you in Yemen, on this rig, anyway it's too late, Emmett Kraill knows everything. And Dick Collins. I told him too."

"Told him what! Nothing! Kraill knows nothing about me and I know what you told Collins. He doesn't know the half of it, you idiot. Collins would tell me anything, he trusts me, loves me..." her words faded away for a moment and then picked up once more, "...he told me you were at that hotel."

"So you....."

"Yes, I sent those men to kill you. You were going to ruin everything. Looks like they failed but it didn't matter, did it? You came straight to me."

Kraill does know, of course he does. That's why he was so reticent, he thought. "Kraill told me it was you," he said.

"I don't believe you." Benjamin could tell in her voice he had rattled her.

"It's true."

"It won't help you."

And Benjamin knew it would not help him. And now he was scared. "It's too soon, isn't it? The war in Sana'a is too soon."

"What are you talking about," Teri snapped back at him.

"Gawain told me. It's a waste of time. The coup will fail without Gawain in Sana'a."

"Rubbish, shut your mouth. Sit up."

He pulled himself up as Teri inched backwards. He sat on the edge of the bed naked but for the blanket wrapped around his waist. She was pointing the gun directly at his head, staring into his eyes. His forehead started to bead with a cold sweat, chilled by the air-conditioning unit whose hum had become a roar in his ears. He was suddenly not so scared. Looking at the gun was no worse than the Yemeni knife at the Ashok hotel in Sana'a or that thug's fist in the elevator of the Venice Hotel in London. He was becoming used to threats, but this time he had no idea what to do. And he was scared again. This time he was a dead man.

But the shot never came for moments later the world seemed to fall in on both of them.

THIRTY FIVE

The last flight to leave Sana'a before the runway was put out of action landed in Dubai late in the evening. It was full of expatriate evacuees who had reached the airport before the roads were closed. Yemen is not on a main air route and, besides one or two flights from North and West Africa, all planes from Sana'a finish at Dubai, the tiny but wealthy Emirate a short hour and a half hop away.

Dubai was once oil-rich but progressively turned itself into an entrepot trading centre even as its oil reserves depleted. Now the Hong Kong of the Middle East, it boasted many large, international hotels, putting the service of the Mogul Rani to shame. A few of the evacuees from the flight caught taxis to the most luxurious of these hotels. Only the diplomats, civil servants and employees of government aid organisations could afford rooms, financed by taxpayers back home. Most businessmen had more frugal budgets and less time. They stayed at the airport waiting for connecting flights, while private aid workers had to double up in small hotels in the suburbs.

If one of the lucky few had checked out the swimming pool at one of the best hotels in Dubai they might have spotted two pale-skinned men lying on sun loungers. The men, plain clothes detectives from Scotland Yard in London, were sipping cold beer by the pool. The last flight had left Dubai for Sana'a hours previously and the two detectives were now stuck, waiting on word from their superiors. They had been sent to find Benjamin Bone and bring him home, but now, unable to depart for Yemen, they burned in the sun but did not curse their luck.

Most of the evacuees from Sana'a continued their journey homewards, either travelling west to India and Southeast Asia or east to Europe and the States. From Dubai the busiest route to Europe flies direct to Paris. On the early morning flight were Peter Greaves and Earl Rittman who had abandoned the Outland office and its dead radio. Tired and irascible, they waited in Dubai airport lounge for nine hours, stretched out on the bench seats, unable to buy business class tickets on the fully booked flights. Now in the air after the discomfort of the night, they found economy class cramped and breakfast over-cooked.

"So, Rittman, what do we do now?" said Greaves petulantly as he forked a rubbery heap of scrambled egg into his mouth. "The oil price is up, but Outland shares are down. All the other fucking oil companies in the world are laughing all the way to the bank and we're in the shit. Why didn't you warn me this would happen?"

"How was I to know? The American Embassy thought Yemen was stable..."

"Useless fucking Americans...."

"Come on. Even Congressman Steeples was convinced."

"That bloody Congressman. Where the fuck's he got to then? Thank God it was his fucking money."

Rittman sighed, but contained his anger. He did not like Greaves. In fact he was beginning to detest him. Greaves used to be polite, acting like a distinguished English gentleman at the Outland Oil board meetings, but now he was acting like a moron.

In the middle of the night Rittman had called his broker from Dubai airport. The fighting in Yemen was not front page news, but it was covered in the international section of the evening Houston Post and Outland's shares had dropped to below three dollars. Rittman had bought two weeks ago at nearly eight fifty and he was in big trouble. He didn't have the money to pay his broker and would be bankrupt. What was worse he had also sold forty thousand Buckfast Energy shares short, expecting them to fall in price. The reverse had happened. Buckfast was a domestic producer and the high oil price had sent its shares up twenty five percent. Rittman was now looking at a million dollars of losses on each of his two gambles and he couldn't pay for either of them.

Of course at the time they hadn't been gambles at all. Only last month he was sure he had a fail-safe system to beat the market. A year ago Greaves had presented the plan to him. Micky Bauss had promised to raise full financing from an investor for a well in Yemen, a well certain to find oil which would lead to a surge in Outland's share price. Greaves showed him geological reports to prove it. Buy and sell Outland shares at the right time and big profits could be made.

The opportunity was too good to pass on and it was his best chance to shaft Buckfast. A few days later he had innocently agreed to lead the operation. He hadn't known then, of course, that the well would never find oil and those geological reports were fictitious, concocted by Greaves himself.

Sure the annual report had overstated the value. Bauss had told him Outland could only be certain of the sort of trading volumes it needed if the company was prominent in the market and the share price started out high. Rittman had argued for days that this was risky but Bauss had persisted and Outland had already been spending cash. Emmett Kraill and Bob Janek were in Yemen and Teri Mayes, seconded from Bauss's company, was due to fly out soon.

But those exaggerated accounts had caused nothing but problems. Not only with Brad Brockley, the red-head who had tried to blackmail them, but with Benjamin Bone too. And it had been because of Bone that Bauss had threatened him. What's more, Rittman cursed to himself, it's probably because of Outland Oil that the oil price in Texas had been so affected by this stupid war. If Outland hadn't been exploring in Yemen, if it hadn't looked like we were in it so big, if it hadn't looked like we were putting big amounts of money into a venture in a crumbling country, the oil traders wouldn't have even noticed what was happening right now and this war would have been over by the time any of them had. Well we haven't got any oil. Insider trading, that's gonna screw me, he thought. He would destroy all his files, especially those geological reports. Bauss won't tell. He's in it deeper than me. And then there was Claudia and his wife to deal with too.

Rittman finished his breakfast and finally said to Greaves, "Looks like you and I are in a lot of trouble unless this coup finishes quickly and Outland's shares pick up again."

"I'm in no trouble," replied Greaves curtly, "I haven't done anything. There's no reason for our shares to be so weak. I've decided we'll delay the drilling until the heat's off, but let's make it two weeks not two days. Everything will be back to normal by then."

"We can't delay the well for two weeks." He needed to pay for the shorted shares before then. "If anybody finds out the operation was a con you'll be in deep shit, Peter."

"It was Bauss's idea. Nothing to do with me and who's gonna find out. Two weeks is good."

"But you own a chunk of Outland and you made up those geological reports, you're in the biggest trouble of all." Saying that cheered Rittman. If he went under he'd make damn sure Greaves did too.

When the plane touched down in Paris they both waited for their connecting flights in the business class lounge. Greaves slowly got himself drunk, knocking back miniatures of neat Scotch whisky whilst Rittman thumbed through the American papers reading the news about the rising oil price. In the Washington Post there was a long article about its impact on the forthcoming primaries. The oil price rise was bound to have a positive impact on the Republican vote.

But it was the last few paragraphs that left him numb. There was a long write-up on Congressman Steeples and the fact that he had been predicting an oil shock for years. In fact, the journalist wrote, it had been leaked that Steeples would stand as a presidential candidate for the Republicans.

Rittman read the article twice and thought some more about Steeples. The man would lose nothing from this coup, nothing except money, and he was a man with too much money. But he could gain, fuck it, he could gain. He realised then that both he and Greaves were fall-guys, nothing else but fall-guys.

Like Greaves a number of evacuees needed to fly north from Paris. They caught connecting flights taking them the short distance across northern France and the English Channel to London. To get from Paris to London it was now as fast to take the tunnel as go by air. In fact five days ago Germaine Bone had done just that, travelling by car on Le Shuttle to Folkestone and then driving to the capital. Nobody knew she had left Paris. She had not even told Gilles.

It had been Saturday night. Gilles was in Lyons attending a mushroom grower's convention. She was shaving her armpits with the shaver that had arrived by post in the morning, when the splutter of a match outside her open bathroom window made her stop abruptly. She switched off the light and peered out into the yard to see a man lurking in the shadows, smoking a cigarette. The man was not one of the two detectives who tailed her night and day. He did not even look French. He was a hard man and English for sure. She had also seen him that morning in the Paris Metro. She had particularly noticed the green sailing shoes, just like the ones Benjamin had told her about.

Germaine had been keeping track of developments in London. She had read all about her husband in the English papers. A psychological profiler from Scotland Yard had produced a character map of him. It had made her laugh out loud for it bore little resemblance to Benjamin. The psychologist had told a tabloid newspaper that Benjamin was dangerous. After all he had murdered two innocent people ruthlessly, in cold blood. The evidence was there for everyone to see. Benjamin Bone's marriage had broken up and he was unemployed. He had a history of depression. He had never been violent the paper said, proving he had oppressed those urges. The breakdown, when it finally came, was all the more severe. There was hard evidence too. Benjamin had torn up a photograph of the Fetters family and discarded the pieces in the bin in his flat. Witnesses had seen him running away from the Venice Hotel and later, many more witnesses had come forward. It seemed he had been stalking women throughout London and the Home Counties for months.

Germaine wanted to help Benjamin so when she had seen the green-shoed man outside her bathroom window she knew the time to do it had arrived. She hastily dressed, packed a small overnight bag and crept out of her flat through the building's delivery door. For a day or two her disappearance from her Paris home confirmed the psychologist's worst suspicions, Benjamin was a maniac and had now killed her too, cleverly disposing of the body under the noses of the French police. There would be much argument about this, the British accusing the French of neglecting their duties and the French criticising the entire English race for their social ineptitude and the disproportionate number of psychopaths and, for that matter, homosexuals in their ranks. For a time relationships between the two forces would be on a Napoleonic footing.

It was late Sunday morning when she found the address in Ruislip, West London that Benjamin had given her. Natalya's brother and father were both out when she rang the bell but her mother answered and stared up at her suspiciously.

"Hello, I am looking for Miss Natalya Cheung. Do you know her?"

"I'm her mother."

"She knows a Mr Benjamin Bone. Do you know where she is?"

"How you know Benjamin? You police lady?"

"No, I'm his wife, Germaine. Can I come in?

"His wife? Ayeeyah, I knew he was hiding something. So you are his wife. You good looking one too."

"Thank you. Yes, I'm his wife but we're separated. He's single."

"Come in. You want Chinese tea?"

They sat in a warm kitchen that smelt of fried chillies, making her eyes sting.

"I've come here to help Benjamin. He is innocent of course."

"I know he is. Natalya told me. I can see he is a good man."

"Where is your daughter, I need to talk to her."

"Ayeeyah, you not know. She in that country. She not back till next Wednesday."

"She went too?"

"Yeah lah, of course. You can stay here in Natalya's room tonight if you wish."

"Thank you but no need. I have already booked a hotel. But can I use your phone?"

"Can."

Natalya's mother showed her to the phone in the front room and stood over her as she dialled. It rang three times and a woman answered.

"Charlotte, it's me, Germaine. How are you?"

"Germaine! I heard on the radio you had disappeared. They say Benjamin killed you...... Where are you?" Benjamin's sister-in-law sounded relaxed, as if she had been expecting the call.

"I'm in London."

"You're all right aren't you?"

"Of course."

"What are you going to do?"

"I was being watched... and I have a plan. I want to get into Tom Fetters flat and I need you to help me?"

"Sure, how?"

"It's an idea. I know what Tom Fetters was like. I'll meet you at Notting Hill tube tomorrow at 8.30."

The next day she met Charlotte at the underground station and walked with her to the Fetter's flat. The converted Victorian house was unguarded and they waited for someone to come out so they could enter the building. Fetters had lived on the top floor. His door was taped up and a yellow and black no entry sign was fixed to the wall beside it. It was locked but Germaine had a steel jemmy hidden in her coat, purchased from a hardware store in Ruislip.

Inside the flat they found Tom's computer but the hard disk had been ripped out from the back. Charlotte opened the leather case she had brought with her and pulled out a laptop computer. While it booted up the two women rooted through Tom's drawers and shelves and it wasn't long before they found a box of storage tapes. For all his annoying habits, Tom had been a thorough man and backed up his computer regularly. In fact one of the tapes was labelled 'backup'. It was password protected but Charlotte was sure she could bypass it. Since this would take some time she suggested they leave with the disk but Germaine, who was impatient to finish the job, tapped in, Cindy, the name of Tom's daughter.

It took Charlotte a quarter of an hour to unzip and download all the files into her laptop. She soon found what she was looking for, a version of Tom's report on the Outland Oil accounts and an analysis of the figures. It contained everything they needed and it was clear Benjamin and Tom had been onto something.

The two women left the room as they had found it and made their way back to Charlotte's house. She printed out a copy of the report and Germaine placed it into a large brown envelope and caught the tube to St James's Park station. Here she walked the short distance to Scotland Yard and hand delivered the envelope, marking it in bold with the name of the chief superintendent in charge of Benjamin's case. She then returned to Charlotte's house and the three of them, including Benjamin's brother Bertram, got rather drunk.

When Germaine had left the report at Scotland Yard she had not counted on the inefficiencies of the police postal service. It languished in the mail room unopened for half a day. After being seen by a junior police officer who neither appreciated its importance nor understood a word, it had sat in the in-tray of the chief superintendent for a further day. Not until late on Tuesday, when the officer read a Reuters report about a bomb going off in a

Yemeni hotel, at a reception of the Outland oil company, did bells ring in her head and she called her boss directly.

From then things moved fast. The Americans were contacted and talks continued for most of the night. After two days of arguing, promises of future favours and agreements of confidentiality, the Americans told them a diplomat had met Benjamin Bone in Sana'a. Two Scotland Yard detectives were told to go to Yemen to pick him up. Meanwhile later next day, before the first of the evacuees had arrived in London, detectives from Scotland Yard raided Peter Greaves' London office in Lincoln's Inn. Louise, his plump American secretary, let them in without complaint and watched as they took away his filing cabinet on a trolley, bumping it loudly down the narrow stairs.

In a way she was pleased. She had wanted to return to Texas for months and this was all the encouragement she needed. The policemen told her she could not leave until permission was granted from a court but not wishing to waste time she picked up the phone and dialled the Hi Ho Travel Company. She bought an open dated first class ticket to Houston and asked them to bill it to Outland Oil's account.

The North Atlantic, London to United States air route is the busiest in the world. Most flights go to the East Coast cities of New York, Washington and Boston so to get to Houston direct it is necessary to travel to London's second airport, Gatwick, in the countryside thirty miles south of London. On Thursday morning the daily British Airways flight was already overflying Iceland by the time Claudia arrived at Outland's offices at seven thirty. A uniformed guard stood outside the glass doors of the reception area. The big chrome handles were fastened together with a loose chain and padlock. She stared at it in disbelief.

"I'm sorry ma'am you are not allowed in," said the guard. "No one is. People will be in touch. Go home and wait for a call."

"Why. I've got to go in. My things..."

"I'm afraid you can't."

She stared incredulously at the man, who looked impassively back at her. The elevator pinged behind her and Ray Bowes stepped out.

"Morning Claudia," he said then saw the guard and the chain. "Hot dogs, what's going on?"

"I don't know Ray. Looks like we're locked out. The FBI is going to call us."

He didn't step out of the elevator. "Hot dogs," he muttered to himself again as the doors closed., leaving her behind.

Outside it was a warm day. Instead of going home she walked up the road to the shopping mall. She hung about in the shops waiting for her ex-husband to arrive for the midday meeting they had arranged.

He finally appeared twenty minutes late. They kissed on each cheek and sat down in a fast food Mexican restaurant overlooking the ice rink. After ordering she said, "I haven't got the money, Manuel, I haven't sold my shares and I've lost all my money. I'm sorry."

"I don't need the money anymore. They let me go."

"They let you go?" She faked surprise.

"This morning, two policemen turned up at the apartment. I thought they were going to arrest me. They didn't look happy at all. The charges are dropped, they said. I am no longer a suspect. I didn't ask why in case they changed their mind," he laughed nervously. "It's too good to be true."

"Have you any idea why they did it?"

"I have an idea." He smiled broadly.

"Yes," nodded Claudia, pleased that she would get credit at last.

"Well you see, Claudia, as I have always said, if you pray to God, He will look after us. You should try it, I mean it. God saved me," and he sat back in his chair, a satisfied grin on his face as if to say I told you so.

She would have dearly loved to hit him or at least tell him the truth. But she didn't. The opportunity had come out of the blue to do a deal with the FBI and, of course, he would say that was a gift from God too.

They finished their meal without talking about it any more. Manuel was uninterested in Claudia's savings, how she had lost them and why Outland's share price had dropped so dramatically. He talked about himself and about how God would help him decide his next mission.

They made their farewells, another cursory kiss on each cheek, and then she walked by herself back across the main road and down a long residential street to the office block where her car was still parked in the basement. Although hot the weather was lovely, a light wind was blowing from the east and it cooled her, drying the sweat from her dark skin. Few people were about on the street, just one black cleaner pushing his cart and a couple of schoolchildren in the distance standing at a bus stop. Despite losing all her money and probably her job too she was cheerful. Her home was paid up, secure, she had no worries at all. She would go back home and watch talk shows on TV. Perhaps later she would walk up to the river and watch the sunset, forget Rittman, forget Outland Oil, and tomorrow she could look for another job.

To travel to the Middle East from the United States most flights go via Europe but those who live and work on the West Coast prefer to fly across Asia. The overnight flight to Tokyo used to stop over in Honolulu before crossing the International dateline but now the journey is unbroken. From Tokyo a few flights go direct to Dubai but a stop is usually required and New Delhi is an important destination. Planes leave Tokyo full of Indians with large cardboard boxes of tax-free electronic equipment.

In New Delhi the house of Ranjit Singh, the former waiter at the Mogul Rani hotel in Sana'a, was located in a working class suburb where the streets were rutted and the air dusty. His small house had one room for him and his wife and one for the children, a shared outside toilet and a tin shower in the yard. Although small and poor it was homely, with thick carpets on all the floors and the smell of spicy cooking coming from its tiny kitchen.

That day the widow of Ranjit Singh directed the removal men to carry her few possessions to a pickup van parked in the nearest street while her four daughters played in the alley and the baby cried in her wooden crib beneath the awning in the yard. Ranjit's widow was proud of her husband, a hero in Sana'a, sure soon to be recognised by the Indian government with a medal. His bravery saved the Indian Ambassador in Yemen who, she had heard, was attending the oil company party when the bomb had gone off.

But a week ago when she had heard about his death after reading about it in the New Delhi papers she had been distraught. For one terrible day she believed she was a pauper. Who would pay for the house? Where would she get food? The children might have to beg for a living. Her friends in the alley had comforted her but it did little to assuage her misery.

It was funny though how her friends had now become so unlike her, so lower class. When she had found out about the life insurance policy Ranjit had taken out and the income she would receive for the rest of her life, and a lump sum as well, they had been so rude and unpleasant. And it wasn't long before she began to notice other things about her friends, they kept their houses dirty, their clothes were unfashionable, they ate with their fingers, not like the movie stars from Bombay.

The cash was sufficient for her to move from this slum to a better part of town, so why not. Ranjit had looked after her so well in death proving he was a great man. She must be a great woman to have been chosen by him. Never mind she thought. I will make new and more sophisticated friends in my new house.

The short flight from New Delhi to Dubai took two hours and from here there are two connecting flights a day to Yemen. Of course these had to be cancelled because of the military coup, news of which was prominent in the headlines of the local morning Arab and English language papers. Sitting on the tarmac in Dubai was the replacement Twin Otter destined for Outland Oil's camp in the desert, a tail fin wrapped and stowed in its cabin. But it could not leave because Sana'a airport was closed. Flying direct to Wadi Qarib was an option but the Yemeni authorities had refused permission and the pilots would not enter Yemeni airspace without authorisation.

Dubai airport is rarely crowded and the taxis are smart and fast. They can whisk passengers into the city in air-conditioned comfort to the top class hotels lining the Creek. The price for Dubai crude was sharply up, business was swift and the big hotels were thronged by Arab and Western businessmen. Now at lunchtime, the two English detectives from Scotland Yard had finished soaking up the sun. Dressed in suits, they walked into the coffee shop and collected a buffet meal. They felt safe in the knowledge that no scheduled flights would be leaving for Sana'a that day.

THIRTY SIX

The flash flood that hit Wadi Qarib early Thursday morning was the most powerful flood in the area for over twenty five years. In a plateau dissected by wadis flash floods are a rare, though regular, occurrence. They are rare because the rainstorms feeding them are sporadic, governed by the seasons, their run-off controlled by the lie of the land. Rain water channelled through crevices and ditches will, in time, fill one of many rocky channels cutting the plateau. One wadi may be dry while the one next to it is a seething torrent. But flash floods are regular because the existence of wadis depends on them. Over the millennia repeated floods cut them into deep, tortuous ravines.

It began on the coast even before the drilling site had been bulldozed, white wisps of cloud in a brilliant blue sky over the Gulf of Aden. Over several days, the clouds coalesced into cumuli blowing onshore over the southern plateau. As hot wet air lifts over the land, it cools, vapour condenses and the plateau rains begin, but this year there had so far been no rain. The winds blew to the northwest and the clouds tracked west of the plateau in the low lying plain along the Red Sea, finally veering to the east, north of Sana'a. The clouds multiplied during their long journey and as they began to rise over the plateau the children in the few remote villages clinging to the cliff walls saw thunder and lightning even their grandparents said was more spectacular than ever.

But the rains didn't fall at once. The dark clouds had travelled many miles inland before they poured their huge droplets of rain over the rock pavement below. Here there were narrow cracks and joints funnelling water into culverts along which it poured southwards. And so it built and ran and ran until a steaming, foamy torrent of muddy, debris-laden water reached the upstream entrance of the wadi known as Wadi Qarib.

Bob Janek, of course, knew all about flash floods, having drilled in several wadis in other parts of the Middle East. He had to drill where he was told but had sited as much of the camp as he could on higher ground. He had never seen a flood but Bob Janek was unlucky today, for the remote chance had come. Water cascaded into the narrow valley gaining power every moment and it wasn't long before the wall of water turned the final bend and came upon the camp, the drilling rig and the people. It powered towards the rig beneath which Dr Gary Turnbow, newly released from his foetid cell, stood waiting patiently for his wife to rise from her bed.

The first thing the torrent encountered was a pile of casing in the centre of the wadi upstream of the camp. Metal pipes were picked up and hurled downstream. The two test engineers, Kenneth and Al, were sitting drinking coffee in the canteen when several of the pipes hit its wall. One penetrated a window, shattered the glass and flew like a missile across the room towards Al who was sipping hot coffee right in its path. Al would never know he was HIV positive, having picked up the disease from a prostitute in Manila he had visited over a year ago. The casing severed his head before thumping against the wall on the other side of the room. Kenneth, sitting opposite him, looked at the headless body of his partner, and screamed.

There were five people in the canteen, Richard Clapton, Kenneth and Al, an African cook and the German consul, Hans Brotenwurst. The German was the first to react.

"We have a problem, for sure....," Hans shouted with no trace of fear in his voice. But he was cut short by a flow of water beginning to gush through the smashed window, and by Kenneth who continued his shrill, piercing scream. The pipe, surrounded by a torrent of water, divided the room in two, one end jammed in the window, the other in the opposite wall. Al's body and the cook were on one side, Al's head, Richard, Hans and Kenneth on the other.

Hans pulled Kenneth by his shoulders and tugged him to the door, pushing aside floating plastic chairs. Richard followed behind them and they leant hard on the door. It wouldn't move, jammed solid by the weight of water outside. Behind them on the other side of the pipe the cook had abandoned what was left of Al and made for the kitchen. The canteen was tilting away from the open kitchen as the water continued to pour through the window. Thousands of gallons a second were filling their half of the room rapidly while the cabin sank into the soft sand beneath.

"Scheissen, we must push on the door together hard," Hans said to Richard, ignoring Kenneth, who was still screaming. It would not budge, the water was rising and they were trapped.

In his own cabin Benjamin's mind was a shambles of colours, movements and sounds. Unaware of what had happened outside, unable to even speculate, he had been sure Teri Mayes was about to shoot him when the trailer had overturned. But, whatever it was, he was thankful for the catastrophe. The toolpusher's trailer lay close to the canteen and to the rig but it was not as heavy or as sturdy. The first wave of water lifted it off the ground and flipped it over on its side. Teri fell backwards, gun in hand, with Benjamin, naked, falling on top of her, tumbling across the floor of the cabin and landing with a thump on the opposite wall now horizontal with the ground. The mattress, a desk and other odds and ends landed on top of them. As the trailer continued to turn Teri let go of the gun, scrabbling for a hand hold, tearing at Benjamin's skin with her nails. Benjamin was fortunate to be on top for as she tumbled her blonde curvaceous body provided a soft landing. He saw the gun spin away.

Upside down now the cabin continued to rock steadily and Benjamin grasped both of her slim arms in his hands, straddling her, pinning her to the floor which was previously the roof. "Who killed Tom and Sally, was it you? Tell me!" he puffed out the words in anger.

She had hit her head as she fell and blood dripped from a cut in her forehead, "No, she panted, no, it was Bauss. Let me up, what's happening?"

"Why did Bauss kill them?"

"You're hurting me..."

"Why did he kill them? What are you doing out here?"

"You're hurting me…"

"Tell me. You and Curt Gawain, you're both mixed up in it. What is it?!" He was shouting in a crazed frightening way and he watched the cut on her head grow to a blue bruise as he spoke, spindly lines of blood creeping through beneath the soft skin of her brow.

"Curt's my husband, he's my husband. Let me go, I'm hurting." and then the trailer jerked and turned again, crunching on the gravel below. As it did so Jock's heavy desk fell on them both and he was sure that the loud crack he heard was the sound of splintering bone.

Emmett Kraill, Bob Janek and Jock were high up on the rig floor discussing the new drill string when the water hit. Two local men were with them, roustabouts who were greasing the giant tongs used to tighten the joints in the drill pipe. One of them spotted the torrent as it thundered round the bend in the wadi. He shouted crazily to Janek in Arabic. The three white men turned to him, recognising the anxiety in his voice, but not understanding him. Then they heard the sound too and turned and saw the wall of foaming water lift a pile of casing like matchwood. It poured towards them.

Janek spoke first. "Mother fucking son of a bitch."

"Christ," said Kraill, "hold on to something."

There was no time for them to get out of the way. The small cabin holding the drilling control console was bolted to the rig floor behind them and the three men dived into it followed by one of the two Yemenis. The other man, the one who had shouted out the warning, stood terrified, rooted to the spot, watching the water approach them all.

"Get in the fucking cabin you crazy son of a bitch," shouted Janek, but the man didn't seem to hear and, as he stared, the first waves hit the legs of the rig. The water level was not as high as the drill floor but the rig was located right in its path. It shifted on its legs, scoured by sand and silt. The structure settled again at a tilt and as it tilted, the tongs, supported by chains connected to the top of the derrick, swung across the rig floor. On the second swing they hit the petrified Yemeni on his shoulders and he fell, screaming in pain, tumbling downwards along the sloping floor.

The four men squatted down in the cramped cabin and hung on to anything they could as the tongs swung back, ramming into the glass above them. The window smashed, showering them with shards. The tongs swung back again and then returned, hitting the metal stanchions of the cabin, crumpling it above their heads. They swung away again and Kraill, who was crouched on the floor, peered out of the smashed window. The downed roustabout, clambering about on all fours, was sliding towards the edge of the rig, forty feet from the turbulent waters below.

Natalya had been asleep in the medical trailer. Like the canteen it was a large heavy trailer on wheels parked in the sand. Although partly protected from the direct force of the first wave of muddy water it was much closer to the rig than the canteen. As the stream deepened, the cabin began to lift at one end, its wheels rising from their wooden supports. It shifted violently and its door flew open. Natalya was thrown from the chair in which she slept and Curt Gawain's bunk toppled towards her. He fell from the bed, crying out in agony. Natalya picked herself up and scrambled towards him across the unsteady floor.

Gawain was alert, the effects of the vodka of the night before gone. "Help me, I'm bleeding," he said deliriously, bubbles of blood popping from his lips. "I'll give you money, anything. Help me, I'm in pain. I have lots of money."

She stared at him, unable to speak. Gawain was in a panic-stricken state and shouted at her again. "Save me, its the Muslims, I hate them…"

She stared back at him as he kept on talking, her face wrinkled with fear, her blue eyes sparkling in the light from the open door. Then she saw the water begin to gush into the trailer and flow around Gawain's prone body. All the trailer wheels had now lifted from the sand and it began to float. She grasped the fallen bunk, trying to hold on as it rocked to and fro before being thrown forward into the wall. Through the door she could see they were careering towards the tilting drilling rig. More water then rushed in, totally engulfing Gawain in its path.

As the medical trailer hit the rig it tilted further downstream, its front legs sinking deeper into scoured sinkholes. Kraill, still cowering in the cabin up on the rig floor, was thrown forward, hit the driller's console, and was showered by spray. Outside he saw the injured roustabout slide further towards the edge of the platform clutching helplessly at the greasy metal floor beneath him.

"I'll help him," Janek shouted to Kraill, releasing his grip on the cabin wall. The tilt of the rig was now so great that water was lapping over the lower edge of the drill floor. The prone Yemeni, hanging on with his fingers jammed into the floor grill, was partly engulfed. Janek crawled over to him grabbing at any handhold he could find, keeping low, avoiding the still swinging tongs. He reached the man who was almost totally immersed and pulled him up and out of the water, bracing his legs against two of the posts supporting the safety rail at the edge of the floor. The water rushed around their feet and spray soaked them both. With a huge effort he pulled the man onto his shoulders and began to clamber back using the rail for support, the roustabout clinging to his neck.

They had almost reached the cabin when Kraill, who had been watching with growing apprehension, heard an ominous sound behind him. The upright stack of drill pipes removed from the hole and arranged by Janek in their rack earlier that morning was shifting. Up till now these had stayed fixed despite the crazy tilt of the rig but now the entire rack of pipes began to loosen from their chains and slide under the supports, to tumble randomly towards the two men.

"Bob, watch out," screamed Kraill but his words were lost in the tumult of rushing water. Too late Janek turned, saw the pipes, and his sunken eyes, for the first time, showed real fear. There were too many. He had no chance to dodge them. The first gave him a glancing blow on the head, the second knocked the roustabout from his shoulders, who slipped back over the wet floor, the third and fourth bowled him over and he fell backwards, grasping out for a handhold. He hit the Yemeni with a thump and they both tumbled into the turbulent, muddy water. The power of the stream would have been too much for a champion swimmer and they were swept into the main current and away.

Benjamin saw the two men fall from the rig as he clambered out of his trailer. It had not been his own bones crushing when it had grounded but those of Teri Mayes, whose limp body he had left behind. She had been alive, moaning, but he could do nothing for her. He had risen unsteadily and quickly pulled on a pair of Jock's trousers and a white T-shirt he found amongst the debris.

From the top of the trailer he watched the two men flounder in the water, then sail by. He stared at them as they were carried downstream then turned away shocked as both men were thrown like rags into newly fallen rocks torn from the cliff walls by the force of the water. They disappeared for a moment and then Janek's body reappeared and was tossed further downstream and around the bend in the wadi.

Benjamin's trailer had come to rest upside down against an old stone wall above a narrow sand bank winnowed by the fast flowing water. The wall had been partly demolished but the waters ran slower here, protected by the mass of the rig upstream. On one side of it was a turbulent current beyond which, on higher ground, was the local's camp which seemed untouched. Further upstream many of the white trailers also stood undamaged, but surrounded by flowing water.

Benjamin did not look at the remains of the camp for long. In the foreground the tilting rig dominated his view. Some men were clutching pipe work but he ignored them. He was staring at the medical trailer rammed up against the lowest part of the structure. He knew Natalya was in the trailer but he could do nothing but look helplessly as the howling continued. The rig, slowly at first, was toppling towards him, the derrick looming large. With a grinding screech it toppled forty five degrees, the central frame landing on the heavy mud logging cabin where he had examined rocks two days previously.

The medical trailer had now shifted position and he saw Natalya appear from its upturned door. She looked around and clambered out. Benjamin spared the briefest thought for Gawain trapped inside but was then distracted by his own predicament. The rig was no longer protecting him from the flood water and his trailer was beginning to move again. He clambered onto the remains of a stone wall below him just as the sand bank holding the trailer in place was completely winnowed away. He watched it float in the current, pick up speed, and then turn into the middle of the stream, the injured Teri Mayes still inside.

Benjamin did not watch it go. He was staring at the sinking medical trailer battered by a new force of waves and debris. It spun around hitting an upturned leg of the toppled rig and the force threw Natalya into the water. She was swept under the rig's metal frame where iron rails and bars, some with jagged edges, poked from the foaming torrent. She collided with a length of drill pipe wedged between the rig legs. Benjamin watched in horror as she clung to the pipe, wrapping herself around it as waves of water and debris tore into her.

Back in the canteen Richard, Hans and Kenneth were waiting for the water level inside to rise far enough to equalise the pressure outside so they could push open the door. The force of water from the window and the length of casing straddling the room made it impossible for them to move towards the kitchens. In any case Kenneth was shaking with fear and both Hans and Richard would have been unable to pull him across the barrier even if they could get across themselves.

They did not speak. The sound of the water was too loud for them to be heard. Richard was thinking about an article, in fact a string of articles. He could write riveting stuff about his experiences and couldn't wait to get back to Denver to do so. He was a strong swimmer but was scared for the other members of the party trapped at the rig and, in particular, the Chinese girl who was sleeping in the medical unit nearby. Ever since their eyes had met on the darkened plane flying over to Sana'a he had been unable to get her out of his mind. Perhaps she would come back to Denver with him. His girl friend back home was a distant memory.

Hans was thinking only of survival, for himself and these other two men. He had dragged the largest table close to the door of the room and all three of them were standing on it as the water rose. Kenneth was calmer now but white as a sheet.

"Do not worry, we soon will be svimming to safety, under the vater and away. You can swim, ja." He shouted and then laughed out loud, his German accent stronger than ever.

The water had risen to their shoulders and the noise had died down inside. The broken window was now completely submerged. But they could still hear the screeching sounds from outside. "It sounds like an Armageddon out there," shouted Hans.

"Yeah," said Richard, "I'll try and open the door again." He took a few deep breaths and disappeared under the murky water. Minutes later he returned.

"Shit, I can't get it open, it's jammed solid. We can't do it."

Kenneth was about to scream again but Hans slapped him in the face hard.

"We must use the window. I know I could reach the kitchens, but he can't," Richard shouted. "We'll take him between us."

Kenneth started to struggle but Hans hit him hard again. The water was now almost at their necks and even Kenneth was conscious enough to know there was no choice. They took deep breaths and slipped underwater. In the murky depth Richard could not see the broken window but the casing straddling the room lay there like a sunken submarine. They surfaced above it into a small gap between the roof and the water, and drew long breaths. Kenneth spluttered and coughed.

"Ok, here goes," said Richard and he dived again leaving Hans holding Kenneth, their faces pressed against the ceiling.

He still could not see the window but he scrabbled with his hands to find the opening. Blood in the water, coming from cuts on his hands from the broken glass in the window frame guided him. He tugged on Hans's leg beside him. The window, three-quarters blocked by pipe, was big enough for a man to squeeze through and there was light above the water on the other side. Hans pushed Kenneth, who was beginning to panic again, under the water and Richard shoved him into the gap before following himself. He surfaced, sucking in huge gulps of air, and saw Kenneth clutching the side of the building, coughing out water.

Richard had been underwater for nearly a minute and he took another minute to recover before realising Hans was nowhere to be seen. He dived back into the water, grabbed the rim of the window and pulled himself inside. Hans was still there, his leg trapped between the pipe and the refrigerator that had stood under the window. His arms were outstretched, his eyes and mouth wide open. Richard struggled to pull him out but could not free him. He finally swam back to the surface and took huge gulps of air before diving in again. Hans was swaying in the water floating like seaweed, his leg still wedged. He was drowned.

Outside again Richard clambered onto the roof of the building where Kenneth now stood shivering. The sun was dazzling and the sloping metal roof sloshed with water. They squinted as they made their way to the far end of the building where the water ran slower. Richard's hands were dripping blood.

"We should swim for it," said Richard.

Kenneth was shivering, head bowed. Without a word Richard shoved him in the back and he dropped head first into the water. Richard then jumped and swam freestyle to him, expertly flipping him over, and dragging him the fifty metres to the edge of the flood waters where they could wade to safety.

Emmett Kraill, still trapped in the cabin high above them was shaking uncontrollably. He had watched his drilling manager die. Their own position was relatively safe now. The water level had stopped rising although it continued to flow below them. The rig, although tilted on its side, seemed stable.

He carefully rose, wedging his feet into the angle between the cabin wall and drill floor, and scanned the area below him. It was then he saw Benjamin crawling along a ladder barely inches from the water. What the hell is he doing? He thought. He had no idea that Natalya was down there too.

The wall on which Benjamin had stood after escaping from his trailer was crumbling away but part of the derrick of the drilling rig had fallen within his reach. He waded into the water, the sand beneath his bare feet sucking through his toes. Pulling himself up on to the rig he climbed over to a metal ladder, bolted to the superstructure. It lay almost horizontal, above the flowing river. He crawled along it, ducking through hoops surrounding every ten steps. He was moving directly towards the main body of the rig, below which the maelstrom was at its most violent. To his right above him he saw the driller's cabin, below him to his left there was a raised catwalk snaking towards the point where Natalya struggled.

He leapt onto the catwalk bruising his bare feet on the sharp metal floor. The water was roaring below, spouting fountains through the grating. He sprinted towards Natalya shouting at her as he saw another surge of muddy water engulf her. "Hold on Natalya, a few more seconds…," but she could hear nothing, the roar of the stream was deafening.

The pipe she was clutching began to move away from the catwalk, yielding to the full power of the water. She slid along the greasy pole away from him. Then she saw him. "I'm slipping," she screamed, "I'm slipping!"

"Hang on," Benjamin shouted back, leaning out across the railings as far as he could, his right arm outstretched. He couldn't reach her from here so he climbed over the rail and perched his feet, now cut and bruised, onto the edge of the catwalk. Grimacing with pain he clung to the outside of the rail and leaned into the stream to grab her. For a moment he felt his fingers brush through her hair before she slid further along the pipe. Every second she slipped further away.

"Benjamin!" she moaned as she sank into the stream still clutching the bent pipe, her head almost under water. The force was too much for her. It would hurl her downstream.

"No! It will not happen!" Benjamin stood up, his heels wedged into the thin, sharp ridge of metal running along the outside of the railing. Opposite him, in the direct path of the water, but beyond Natalya's reach, was a length of grill suspended by a thick metal girder spanning the torrent. When the rig had fallen part of the catwalk running from the mud logging cabin to the shale shakers had torn apart and now it was bent over across the mud pumps submerged somewhere beneath them. He stared at the grill, taking several huge breaths as he did so. Filling his lungs to capacity, he roared and, summoning a strength and courage he did not know he had, bent his knees and leaped. He flew through the spray flailing out his arms. With the tips of his fingers of his left hand he brushed past the grill but his right hand, almost by chance, hit the girder above him. It was a painful blow and for a moment he hung helplessly like a monkey, his feet dangling in the stream. Conjuring up all his reserves of strength, he used his forward momentum to hoist his legs up and around the girder and he grasped it tightly.

He was exhausted but there was no time to lose. Hanging by his crossed legs he shouted. "Let go Natalya, let go now. I can't hold on like this for long!"

She turned. Instantly the water swept her away from the catwalk where Benjamin had been standing. She disappeared under the water but Benjamin grasped, missed her, then grasped again and held her wrist.

"Climb up my body, Natalya, I can't pull you out."

"Yes, yes," she shouted as her mouth gulped the air and she grabbed his arm with her other hand, hoisting herself up onto the metal grill beside him. Crouched on the platform she pulled Benjamin by his shoulders and he swung over and dropped down beside her.

The water had stopped rising but it was still running fast and the old rig screamed and whined in the torrent. Natalya clutched Benjamin close to her on their tiny sanctuary, both of them panting uncontrollably, soaked in spray. The bent grill on which they were crouching began to sink under their weight, inching downwards into the water.

"We've got to get higher," yelled Natalya.

"How?"

"Follow me along the girder." She pointed. "We can get to that cabin and climb on its roof."

She stood up and walked along the narrow beam, then jumped into the water directly onto some steps hidden just below the water line.

He followed her on all fours. "Go on quickly, I'll catch you up," he yelled.

She reached the roof of the mud logging cabin and yelled back at him. "Hurry, it's still shifting. Can't you go faster?"

The rig above them, although supported by the cabin, was sinking slowly as the power of the water continued to scour its feet. The steps had disappeared into the fast flowing water which had now reached his waist. He lost his balance and dived at the vertical ladder on the side of the cabin. As he climbed the rig shifted again, sliding along the edge of the cabin, grinding its way into his path. Natalya was ready, leaning out over the edge of the roof. Benjamin could have taken her hand but he did not, instead grabbing a pipe running up the wall, opening up the gash on his forehead as he did so. He clung on, pulled himself up and, with a final effort, dragged himself onto the roof, blood pouring down his face.

"Why didn't you take my hand?" she said, wiping the blood from his face with her sleeve.

"I didn't see it," he lied, gasping for breath, "thank God we're safe."

The speed of the water slowly abated. It had reached six or seven feet below the top of the cabin where they were perched but now the level began dropping almost as fast as it had risen. Metal girders of the rig and the equipment below them reappeared like a kraken arising from the depths. But Benjamin was not now looking at the water, but at Natalya, her blue eyes shining under a canopy of lank wet hair.

"I saw your driller fall." Benjamin said to Kraill an hour later. They were standing with Natalya in the area of the car park. Two Land Cruisers were parked next to them, the only two to survive the flood, and Kraill had the keys to one of them in his hand.

"Yes, Brian," answered Kraill, "Bob was an enigma. He was a racist bastard but he died saving a Yemeni." He betrayed no emotion in his voice as he climbed into the driver's seat. Benjamin got in beside him and Natalya in the back.

Kraill started the car. It spluttered and started, ejecting water from its exhaust pipe. He manoeuvred it over the damaged track avoiding the rocks littering the area. They could see Jock's trailer lying on its side about a mile downstream.

"You were going to tell me it was her," said Benjamin, "Teri Mayes damaged the radio?"

"I don't know now. I don't want to say anything."

"You were right, it was her," Benjamin said, "she had a gun to my head when the flood hit, she told me she's married to Curt Gawain...."

"What!" Kraill interrupted him and Natalya leaned forward also astounded. She was the one who had told Teri who Benjamin was.

"Benjamin," Natalya interjected, "Gawain said something to me about hating Muslims." She leaned forward between the two front seats as she spoke.

"They are husband and wife," said Benjamin, "and they are... were, engaged in something criminal. I thought it was to do with this well, some way to make money but now I don't know."

"I did think it was her," said Kraill. "We have an accountant called Hassan. After the radio was damaged he told me Teri was stealing money from our account. He had told his cousin Mahmoud as well, so I guessed she spoilt the radio to stop them telling anyone. It sounded ridiculous. Last night when you and I spoke, Brian, I was going over the accounts Hassan gave me. Everything he said was true, money had been disappearing ever since she arrived. Large sums, tens of thousands at a time. And why did we have so much money in the country anyway? It was much more than we needed. After I spoke to you I searched her things and found a disk in her bag. I told you I wanted to be certain."

"Did you call Sana'a?"

"I didn't get a chance to load it. I still don't understand why she did it" He stopped speaking while he manoeuvred around some fallen rocks in the road.

Benjamin of course suspected that she had destroyed the radio on his account, afraid that he would call somebody and tell them what was going on. Ironically, he had had no inkling that she or Gawain was involved and he knew nothing of any money. If the plane had

278

not been trapped in the desert she would never have been compromised. It was Dick Collins he had doubted.

"When we get back to Sana'a," Kraill went on, "we'll find out maybe. Anyway, here we are. I'm not looking forward to this." He parked the car close to the upturned trailer and they clambered over to it. It had come to rest against a pile of rocks. The door was easily accessible.

They found Teri Mayes inside, her body bent at an impossible angle, her face twisted in pain. She was stone cold, and no longer looked beautiful.

Natalya went outside, sickened by the sight but as Benjamin made to follow her, Kraill gripped his arm tightly.

"Why does she call you Benjamin, I thought your name was Brian. Who are you?"

"Oh, she's mistaken....."

"No, she's not. You said Teri had a gun at your head. I'll ask you again. Who are you?"

"I'm sorry, it's a long story, my real name is Benjamin Bone but you can trust me Emmett. Let's go to the car and I'll tell you everything."

They returned to the drilling camp and parked in the shadow of the fallen rig. Mrs Turnbow was standing there, pale and drawn but unhurt by the flood. As soon as they got out she came up to them. "Richard has told me, you found him. You found Gary. Where is he?"

Natalya looked at her before turning to Benjamin. He remembered now. Turnbow had been standing directly in the path of the full force of water.

THIRTY SEVEN

The sun rose over the hills outside Sana'a as the flood in Wadi Qarib was at its highest. It was an unusually quiet city that morning but, as light found its way into the room in the Ministry where the Americans slept they were awakened by a loud bang that shook the building, rattled the windows, and rocked the crystal chandelier above them.

Shelterman rubbed his eyes vigorously, rising from the sofa on which he had slept. Steeples lay wide awake, lying on the rug in front of the Defence Minister's desk. His eyes were rimmed with a blue-grey shadow and his white hair was in disarray. He looked old and sick, his fat face a yellow pallor, jaundiced like a preserved corpse. "Where's Collins. And where's the Marine?" he said. There had been no word from Dick Collins or from anyone else. The guards on the door outside had been uncommunicative.

Sergeant Cutler was on the roof. The sound of guns coming from the north of the city had continued sporadically all night and every hour or so he had risen from his vantage point by the door and made his way up the back stairs. Through the night the sprawling town had been dark apart from the odd yellow glow in parts of the city, flashes of explosions and the sounds of rumbling tanks, occasionally punctuated by gunshots.

He had been smoking his last cigarette when the explosion woke Congressman Steeples and the Ambassador. Loath to stub it out he pulled quickly on the soothing blue smoke, then tossed it over the parapet and ran past the guards inside the main office door, who turned to watch him threateningly. He looked as fresh as he had the night before, his uniform spotless, his short, stubbly hair well groomed. He was enjoying himself.

Steeples sat up and remonstrated when he stepped in. "What are you doing, Sergeant. You should be protecting us, not running about the building like a fucking moron."

"Sorry Congressman," he said and then looked at Shelterman. "Good morning Sir, the fighting's concentrated in the northwest. We can't leave though. The guards have orders to keep us here."

"What was the noise?" Steeples said sourly. All his muscles ached and the intermittent pain in his groin and hip he had been feeling over the last few months had returned.

"A rocket. It came from the army camp and landed about a hundred yards to the west of here."

"We need food, Sergeant, see what you can do."

"Sure sir," he said and left again.

Shelterman stood up, walked over to the president's desk and looked at Steeples, still sitting on the floor. "Now Congressman it's about time you told me what's going on. What are you really doing in Yemen and why did you arrange a meeting with the Defence Minister without my knowledge? I've had the night to think about it and it's quite obvious to me you came to Yemen to talk to the government for a specific reason. It's my business to know what the reason is."

"What do you mean, Shelterman?" Steeples spoke without his usual strength of will.

"Look, we are prisoners in here. It's no coincidence all those soldiers arrived outside last night. We can't leave and it's because of you. Tell me the truth and perhaps we can get the hell out of here." He could see Steeples was still squirming. He raised his voice. "We are hostages, Congressman. Whoever started this thing cannot win this fight without us. You know as well as I do that if we let a southern army faction take Yemen, the rest of the Middle East will be watching. They'll think America has lost its nerve, Saddam could invade Kuwait again. With the Russians so weak, Iran could go for the Caucasus." He raised his voice, "Then Iraq will attack Saudi and what's that going to do to oil supplies in America? America would be screwed, including your precious Outland Oil company. We must offer our full support to the Yemeni Government. You're a Congressman, you should do it."

Steeples got up and walked over to the sofa, a tired old man. He looked hard at Shelterman, long and hard. "I don't have to say anything to them." He spoke fiercely and bitterly. "I am a US Congressman and I am answerable to no one. So cut the crap and think about America, not your own fucking job. Do you want us to depend on these fucking Arabs?"

Shelterman stared at him, then walked to the window and pulled back the curtains. It was now fully light outside. Answerable to no one? What about the electors? But he didn't push it, Steeples was not going to help.

There was a commotion outside the door and gunshots. He turned around as the door was flung open and a senior officer of the Presidential Guard stormed in. He was well-groomed. His vest bristled with campaign medals but his uniform was crumpled and dusty. He was followed by two uniformed men dragging Sergeant Cutler between them. Blood was dripping from Cutler's mouth and a blue bruise surrounded his left eye. Behind them came several more officers.

Then the Defence Minister walked in with two civilians. He ignored the Americans and sat down at his desk. He looked at Shelterman. "I have no argument with you Mr Ambassador," he paused "but we need information. This man...," he pointed at Steeples on the sofa, "...this man has information."

"No," Shelterman said quickly. "You tell me what is going on first. What has happened to the Sergeant?"

"A foolish mistake. He misunderstood what our men were doing. He fired a shot at them and they responded. I am sorry." Then in Arabic he said. "Put the Marine on the sofa."

"Sorry Sir", said Cutler softly. "I was defending you in here."

Steeples stood up to make way. He wrung his hands. His right leg was shaking. "What information can Congressman Steeples give you?" said Shelterman. Urgent appeasement was required.

"I have it on the best authority..." said the Minister. He paused, "...this man", he pointed at Steeples, "has been meddling in our politics, disrupting our country. It seems nine months ago he was in contact with General Geshira. You may be interested to know that Geshira is responsible for this outrageous insurrection."

"Who told you this?"

"He and Geshira met in Switzerland in October last year. I am sure you remember your meeting in the Lake Hotel, Geneva Mr Steeples?" Steeples shrugged his shoulders but did not respond either way. The Minister smiled and went on, "so Ambassador, you wish to know the source of this information. It comes straight from the Pentagon." He paused again. "It was Mr Collins who passed me the news not two hours ago. Mr Collins is on his way here right now and will verify it."

Shelterman looked at Steeples. "Did you see the General in Geneva?"

Steeples shook his head, refusing to answer. The Minister smiled again and indicated to the two soldiers who had been holding Sergeant Cutler, "The Congressman will stand here, in front of me." The soldiers moved towards Steeples and took an arm each. They shoved him towards the Minister's desk.

The rough handling seemed to awaken Steeples from his dark mood and, for a moment, he returned to his old self. He looked at the Ambassador, "are you going to allow this, you fucking cowardly bastard? I demand to be released. I am a United States Congressman."

Shelterman looked at him distastefully. He didn't speak at once. The man had come to Yemen and upset the whole bloody political applecart. And he had disturbed his tennis training for the championships next week although at the current rate there would be nobody left in Sana'a to play in them. But Steeples was an American and his job was to support Americans whatever they had done.

He turned to the Minister. "We should talk about this reasonably..." but his words were cut short as one of the two soldiers gave a vicious slap to Steeples face. Deeply shocked, Steeples brushed his temple with the back of his hand. Blood seeped from a cut above his eye.

The Minister snapped out words fiercely, spittle flying from his lips, "What is this man, this so-called Congressman doing then?"

Shelterman changed tack, "Congressman Steeples, please tell us why you are here, it is best for you." He was alarmed now.

"I was going to warn them, of course. Warn them of the threat from Geshira." Steeples spoke shakily, "I was going to offer my help..."

"Bullshit," snapped the Minister and the soldier slapped him again

Steeples mumbled, "I would have double-crossed Geshira. I should not have been here."

There was a knock on the main door and a junior officer entered. "Excuse me sir there is a man outside to see you."

"We are busy!"

"He's one of them." He pointed at Shelterman. "And he has an officer from the army with him, one of Geshira's men. Captain Hadran."

"Ah, good. Send them in." The officer returned moments later followed by a neatly dressed Yemeni army captain in a uniform much too big for him. Behind him Dick Collins walked in. The room was getting crowded.

Collins looked at Sergeant Cutler lying on the sofa, then looked at the Minister and said "I have brought the captain as promised. I also have the assurances you need. It's time to let them go."

"Go ahead, what are your assurances?"

Collins had been busy during the night. What he had unearthed about Curt Gawain was enough to put him in jail for life. Last October Gawain had been careless, he had used the Embassy travel agent in Sana'a to book an air ticket for General Geshira to visit Switzerland And Congressman Steeples appeared in Gawain's telephone diary several times in the month. A quick call to the US confirmed Geshira's trip overlapped with one made by Congressman Steeples. It hadn't been difficult to find the link between the two but the meeting, in the hotel where Geshira had stayed in Geneva, was just a guess.

There was other news from the States. After Collins had checked with Washington it hadn't been long before a senior official with the Inland Revenue Service had called back. The millions used to set up an office in Sana'a to and drill Outland's well had come from one of Steeples' companies in Houston. Collins had not been surprised but the extra information that Steeples was also a director of the accountancy company that the mysterious Micky Bauss ran was a revelation. A brief glance at the list of employees of this company in both its US offices and in London was enough to show accountancy was not all the company did. At least ten senior employees, probably more, had no qualifications at all but had been soldiers from elite US and UK special services.

It had been three o'clock in the morning when the editor of the English language newspaper in Sana'a, had arrived at the Embassy. He had an interesting story to tell about his cousin Hadran, a captain in the Yemeni army. The captain had come to the editor at midnight with his own story about an American who had been a regular visitor of General Geshira in the southern army camp. Over the last nine months, Gawain had helped General Geshira plan and mount a coup against the Yemeni Government, supplying millions of dollars to pay off officers. But Captain Hadran knew that many of the southern Generals liked Geshira even less than they liked the Government. Although resenting the northerners and the Presidential Guard, with its superior American equipment, they tried to use Geshira too. First get power and then destroy him when it was all over.

Collins could not guess why the captain had told his cousin this story now, but he acted on it at once because it fitted with his own evidence. He called the States and retold it to the officials in the Pentagon, embellished with ideas of his own and within an hour they had agreed to his plan. Steeples was expendable, the CIA, the US Government and the Embassy must be protected at all costs. It must be made absolutely clear that Steeples was working alone. Collins contacted the Yemeni President on the satellite phone via Washington and then left for the editor's house to fetch the captain.

Now in the Ministry the Defence Minister waited for him to speak. "I am confident you can win this battle," said Collins. "Many of the southern officers are on your side. Captain Hadran has come to warn you, he is not alone."

"Of course we will win this battle, but this man, this Congressman, says he came here to warn me about Geshira. Of course I was well aware of Geshira's plan. I was ready for him. And I knew you Americans were scheming to help him. Geshira has become rich lately. Where did he get the money, but from you?"

"It was not from us, it was not sanctioned by us. It came from the Congressman. He was playing politics at home. We were unaware of this money. The Secretary of State has made it quite clear to me. We wholeheartedly support your government. Steeples is a renegade. America offers you our total support."

The Minister looked at Captain Hadran and then back at Collins. He spoke in Arabic. "If Geshira had won, if he took power in this country, would you Americans support him too?" The Minister spoke sarcastically.

"Emphatically no." Collins replied in English. "As I said I have been in direct touch with the Secretary of State. Should General Geshira or any other army general take power by force they would be subject to sanctions, from us and from the European Community." The latter was a lie, only Britain had agreed to sanctions unequivocally. France in particular did not want to upset the Arabs. "We would impose a no fly zone along all Yemeni borders. Anything the Congressman has ever said to General Geshira to the contrary is untrue."

Collins had been told this in no uncertain terms. Of course there had been no doubt they would deal with any new Government in the future. Everyone could be bought, and what Collins had heard about General Geshira made him no exception. But the White House wasn't thinking long term. They were terrified the oil price would keep on rising before the elections. Oil shortages and gasoline price rises could destroy the Democrat vote.

"Why should we believe you?" asked the Minister.

"When Steeples returns to the States he will be indicted. He will not be a Congressman for much longer. Now it is time to go. Captain Hadran should get back to his unit. Tell them it is over. And your men must contact the other Generals."

"You are right but Steeples stays."

"I am afraid our offer is conditional. No Americans get hurt, imprisoned, anything. We must all leave together."

"Agreed…" The Minister knew about Caucasians and their strange need to defend the rights of their criminals. But to save face he added, "…but the Ambassador and the Congressman must stay here until the fighting is over and Geshira has been detained. You can go to your Embassy, call your Secretary of State. We will provide an escort."

The Minister rose and stared at Captain Hadran. "You have a job to do. Do it well and you can expect promotion."

The Minister's entourage began to file out of the room. Collins immediately went over to Sergeant Cutler who was still lying on the sofa. "Can you walk Sergeant? You better come with me if you can."

But Cutler didn't move even when Collins shook him. Then he saw the redness through the Marine's uniform, spreading out over his chest, soaking the sofa beneath. Cutler was dead. A bullet had penetrated his heart and his massive internal bleeding was now external, seeping into the Ministry's upholstery.

It was hardly three hours before all the guns had stopped. There were the occasional pops from the city centre where the looters worked but even these ceased when government troops once again took control. Through the night the tanks had failed to co-ordinate the attack on the palace and Geshira's troops had taken many casualties. When they heard a ceasefire was being negotiated they were grateful.

Meanwhile the two Americans remaining in the Defence Ministry waited silently. Steeples continued to stare at the dead body of the Sergeant, unable to take his eyes off him. Collins arrived back with a limousine at four o'clock followed by another Embassy car with two Marines inside. The cars were flanked by six motorcycles ridden by officers from the Presidential Guard. The sullen-faced Steeples sat meekly in the front seat of the limousine while Collins and Shelterman got in the back behind a glass partition. The dead body of Sergeant Cutler was carried into the car behind them. As they drove away Collins looked across at the Ambassador and said, "You haven't heard everything sir. There's more. And it's about Curt Gawain."

"What about him?"

Collins told his boss what Captain Hadran had told him and then went on to tell him what else he had learnt through the night, about Micky Bauss's firm and about how the Englishman Benjamin Bone had alerted him to the peculiarities in Outland Oil's accounts. "You know the American hostage Dr Turnbow?" he went on.

"Of course I do."

"It was Gawain who sent him on a trip to the old town. An Embassy driver and a Land Cruiser are missing. Gawain reported the driver stole it, but that's not what happened. He organised the trip knowing Turnbow would not be coming back."

"Why would Curt get rid of Turnbow?"

"Turnbow knew something. My guess is he found out about a link between our Embassy and Geshira from one of his patients and went to Gawain with the news. So Gawain had to get rid of him. It was stupid and unnecessary because it wasn't long before half the Yemeni army knew." In fact we all knew there was trouble brewing except you Ambassador, he thought.

"And there's more. On the night of the bomb at the Outland Oil party Gawain left the Embassy. He left for about an hour in his own car. I checked the register at the gate."

"So where did he go?"

"I found a black tracksuit in Gawain's desk. Benjamin Bone told me he saw a man dressed in black before the bomb went off. I think Gawain planted the bomb. In fact I'm sure of it."

"Why?"

"To scare us, to scare the westerners in Yemen, to get us to evacuate so it looked like we were deserting a falling Government. It was another thing that boosted the oil price."

"Why did you tell the Yemenis about Steeples in the first place? That Marine died because of it."

"Yes, I'm sorry, but I had to tell them something otherwise they'd think we were all scheming against them. The Pentagon authorised it. It is far better the Yemenis know nothing about Gawain. The Yemeni Captain will keep his mouth shut. He was involved himself until recently. That's why I talked only about Steeples not Gawain. If it was reported that an American diplomat living in Sana'a was responsible it would put the frighteners on every goddamned Embassy in the Middle East. If it's a politician from the States looking for votes it's a different matter." He paused and added reflectively. "Which of course it is. The fewer people who know the better."

"Will it get out?"

"The FBI is investigating Benjamin Bone, Micky Bauss and Congressman Steeples but the link with Gawain has not been made."

"Good, you've done damn well." He paused and then added. "Another thing I don't understand is why the Congressman came here in the first place. Why did he want to meet the Defence Minister?"

"The captain told me the coup had been planned for next week. I guess that when the fighting started out here, and he was back in Houston, he was going to tell the newsmen how he had foreseen it all, how he had been here and had tried to stop it all by himself. He had even witnessed a bomb in his hotel. He was going to say that no one would listen to him because the Democrats don't care about oil prices, they don't care about US dependence on Middle East oil supplies, and they don't care about the American people. Yes, I can hear him now. He would accuse our President of ignoring the needs of the common man. A car needs gas and a car is the most basic of our needs, isn't it. Gas prices going sky-high. That was going to swing it?"

"You sound like a politician yourself. It all fits doesn't it?"

"Yes. Steeples and Gawain were going to screw up this country so they could ridicule the Democrats."

"And the money to pay off Geshira and the others came from Outland Oil, not the Embassy?"

"Bauss's company is some mercenary outfit with accountancy as a cover. It was involved with Outland and was working for Steeples. Benjamin Bone told me Outland has no hope in hell of finding oil. They are only here to get money into the country to finance the coup. The Outland company was a way to get money into the country without raising eyebrows. Steeples' plan rested on links to oil, the power of oil."

"Who the fuck is this Benjamin Bone? You've mentioned him several times."

"Oh yes. Well it's a long story."

"Tell me, please."

So Collins told him but he was only half concentrating. The fighting had lasted only twenty four hours. The papers in Washington would say American diplomacy had saved the day, but it had been American diplomacy that caused the war in the first place. He didn't care though, he had done a good job and soon Teri would be back. In fact, for the first time in years, he was looking forward to the future.

THIRTY EIGHT

They found the body of Dr Gary Turnbow amongst boulders at the foot of the cliffs three miles downstream of the fallen rig. His emaciated body was contorted, his skin white. Nearby was the body of a grey-haired lady who ran the UN offices in Sana'a. She had been unfortunate to be billeted in a flimsy plywood cabin that could not withstand the might of the torrent. Further downstream they found three more bodies. One was an African cook who had been smoking outside the canteen when the flood had struck and the other two were Pakistani technicians who had also shared a plywood cabin. There was no sign of Bob Janek or of the roughneck he had tried to save. Their bodies could have been carried miles and nobody had the inclination to look for them.

The medical trailer containing Gawain reappeared as the flood subsided. His body was spread-eagled on Khaled's desk, drowned, his eyes wide open, staring in fear and pain. Including Teri Mayes, Al Hulver, Hans Brotenwurst and the two missing men, the flood had killed eleven people.

None of the Yemenis in the local camp were reported killed or hurt and most had deserted their tents within an hour of the water level beginning to subside. They had plundered anything of value they could find. Mahmoud, however, remained behind. While the foreigners were searching for bodies he picked his way through the mud and debris to the upturned medical trailer. Climbing onto the roof he dropped into its wet, dripping interior, ignoring the body of Gawain. The door of the cabinet hung open above Gawain's body, the money gone. Mahmoud stared at it, his heart thumping unnaturally. He had packed his fifty thousand dollars from Bob Janek in a thick manila envelope and stowed it there but now there was nothing, no envelope, no money, absolutely nothing.

He had many creditors. He owed the jeweller Mutara many thousands of dollars, the man who owned the water well was expecting a payment of two thousand dollars, and there were payments due to the truck drivers. The rest would have been Mahmoud's profit and, along with future payments he had expected from Janek, was to have funded his emigration to America. Staring dumbstruck at the empty cabinet he frantically ran his hands round its walls and rummaged about the cabin, upturning everything, even scrabbling around Gawain's lifeless body, hoping the envelope would be concealed amongst his clothes. But he failed to find any trace so he knelt and, with his head in his hands, prayed to Allah. He was beginning to hate Americans.

The new road leading from the camp out of Wadi Qarib had been badly damaged but the road was their only lifeline so Emmett Kraill and Sandy, the pilot, took one of the Land Cruisers and set out for the runway. It was slow going for the first ten miles, taking the best part of three hours, but further south where the wadi widened into a flat plain, the damage was less severe and they accomplished the final ten miles in less than an hour. They arrived before sundown but by now the shadows were long and the wings of the damaged plane threw a dark cross over the sandy runway. The other pilot, who had spent a day and a half working on the Twin Otter, had removed the broken tail section, cleaned all the connections and greased the bare metal. It shone redly in the setting sun. He was shocked to hear the news from the rig. Although he had seen the water flow in the wadi channel below him, it had been gentle here. The flood had petered out by the time it had reached half way along the wider part of the gorge.

The two pilots tried to radio Sana'a airport on an emergency frequency from the Twin Otter but were unable to communicate for long on the crackly connection. They did hear, however, that the coup against the Yemeni government had fizzled out and bulldozers had already begun repairing craters in the runway in anticipation of flights beginning to arrive next morning. The damage had only been superficial. The airport promised to contact Yemeni air traffic control and the relevant embassies at once.

It was gone nine o'clock and dark when Kraill finally returned to the devastated camp alone. Despite the lateness of the hour, there was unanimous agreement that the remaining men and women who had been on the original trip to the rig along with non-essential workers including Kenneth Letniowski, still in shock, should go straight to the runway to be ready for arrival of the replacement plane in the morning.

Each of the two working Land Cruisers could carry eight passengers so two trips were required for the evacuation. Kraill drove one and Benjamin the other. The drive was long and arduous in the dark but the night was cool and Kraill had already picked out the best route through the boulder-strewn plain. On the first trip Benjamin followed Kraill closely. The American Ambassador's wife and her friend, Gladys, sat quiet by his side, both of them suffering from a lack of alcohol, still wondering where their vodka had gone.

On the second trip Natalya sat at his side. They didn't speak much. He was concentrating on his driving in the dark. Dawn was an hour away when he finally followed Kraill up the narrow track onto the runway for the last time.

The first group of passengers had spent an uncomfortable cold night trying to sleep in the damaged plane. They had mostly paced about outside to keep warm, not wanting to think about the horror of the flood. Mrs Turnbow stood alone, motionless at the far end of the runway looking out at the shadowy cliffs beyond. She had told Richard to go away when he tried to comfort her so he returned to the back of the plane and scribbled notes in his book under the dim lights from the failing aircraft batteries. He was still scribbling when the sun came up and Benjamin appeared at the door to ask if anyone needed breakfast. He had filled his Land Cruiser with loaves, cubes of butter and bottles of jam he had found in the camp freezers. Now defrosted, he distributed these to all who wanted them. Benjamin ate greedily for he was ravenously hungry.

It was after ten in the morning when the replacement Twin Otter passed overhead, earlier than had been expected. Sana'a airport had alerted the American Embassy and Ambassador Shelterman had called the Defence Minister who had personally sanctioned a direct flight from Dubai to the wadi.

Before landing, the plane flew along the line of Wadi Qarib. The pilots were experienced men having flown in most countries in the Middle East but they had never seen anything like the devastation below them. From the air the drilling site looked like a scrap yard, but a scrap yard contravening all environmental regulations. Rubbish littered a huge area and debris lay scattered miles downstream along the narrow cutting of the wadi. They thought it a miracle anybody had survived at all.

The plane carried a powerful radio fixed on the frequency of the American Embassy in Sana'a and so they were able to report safe arrival and list out the dead. While they talked Benjamin helped unload the replacement tail section from the cabin and other provisions for the people remaining at the camp. The pilots, along with an aircraft engineer who had accompanied them, set to work unpacking the cardboard crate while the passengers boarded the new plane.

Emmett Kraill said goodbye to each one of them apologising for the events of yesterday as if they were his fault. He would return to the camp, staying behind with Jock to sort out the mess. As he shook each of their hands firmly, he yearned to be going with them. He shook Benjamin's hand last, then, as he watched him walk to the plane, called out, "We'll meet again some day. Perhaps you'll be the geologist on one of my next wells."

"Perhaps," Benjamin replied but at the moment he had no intention of doing the job again.

"Whatever happens we must meet. When I'm next in the UK I'll look you up."

Mention of the UK depressed Benjamin. "Yes, I'll send you my address."

Then Kraill turned abruptly away and walked back to his Land Cruiser.

It was lunchtime on Friday when the Twin Otter landed at Sana'a airport. The runway had been hastily repaired and they were able to land without difficulty. The first commercial jet was not due from Dubai until the evening but the Twin Otter was not the first plane to arrive. There was a US air force transport plane parked by the terminal, its propellers turning slowly. Benjamin climbed out onto the tarmac and walked swiftly to the arrivals door hoping to find Dick Collins before the others got there. A large welcoming party of expatriates and Yemenis thronged the hall but he could not see Collins. There were two US Marines, but neither was the one who had seen Mrs Shelterman and Gladys off on the trip. A tall white man in a suit stood next to them and Benjamin walked up to him.

"Excuse me. I would like to get in touch with Dick Collins. Do you know where he is?"

"He's in the Embassy. I'm afraid he couldn't make it here. Who are you?"

"Er Brian Borne..."

"Ah, good, yes. I know all about you. It's Benjamin isn't it. My name's Erwin Shelterman, I'm the American Ambassador here. Unfortunately Collins couldn't make it. The dead Americans you see, the girl, he's got a lot to handle. We'll look after everything, we've got to talk, and, of course, to thank you. Yes, good, please go with the Sergeant to the hotel. You'll be well looked after. OK sergeant, there's my wife. You take Mr Bone with you to the Mogul Rani and we'll go with the two women in the limo." He waved his arm, "Elizabeth dear, over here."

"But how do you know....?" stuttered Benjamin.

"Later, we'll talk later."

Shelterman left and another white man came over, also wearing a suit. "Are you Benjamin Bone?"

"Yes I am."

"Please come with me. We need to ask you some questions."

"No, I'm going with the Marine."

"I represent the British authorities...."

"Oh, but I would prefer to go with the Marine."

Meanwhile Shelterman, his wife walking behind him, had returned. "What's the trouble Benjamin?" But he didn't wait for an answer. Turning to the Englishman he said, "the American Embassy will be putting Mr Bone up at the Mogul Rani. I suggest you talk to him later. We are in contact with your foreign office. Check with them first."

"Foreign office. Oh." The man paused. "Well as long as we know where he is. There are two detectives flying in from Dubai who need to see him...."

"OK Sergeant let's go," said Benjamin and he turned on his heels.

As they drove out of the airport Benjamin saw the US air force plane again across the fence. "Do you know what that plane is for?" he said to the Marine next to him.

"Evacuating personnel sir." He grimaced, his cheeks puckering. There would be just the two evacuees on the flight, one alive, one dead. Congressman Steeples and Sergeant Cutler were on their way home already.

Benjamin showered as soon as he got to his room in the Mogul Rani. He was lying on his bed, about to nod off, when there was a knock on his door. It was the American Ambassador.

"Hi, Benjamin. Feeling better? Can't stop long but need to tell you a few things and ask a few questions. First I want to thank you. Dick Collins has told me it was your, er, confession after the bomb here that put him on the track of Curt Gawain. He's real grateful to you."

"What was Gawain up to then?"

"Oh, blackmail. Well he's dead now so no more worries."

"Did you know Gawain was married to Teri Mayes?"

The Ambassador stared at him, but only for a moment. "Well, no I didn't know. I suppose there's the link. They kept it secret all right."

Benjamin went on to tell him how Teri had damaged the radio and threatened him, and about the men who had tried to kill him at the Ashok hotel. "Dick Collins told her I was staying at the Ashok."

"I see," the Ambassador nodded at him slowly.

"Where is Collins?"

"He's busy, but what you say about Teri Mayes might help. He was in love with her you know."

They talked some more. Benjamin asked again about Gawain's motives but the Ambassador was cagy. "Those English detectives will need to see you tomorrow. Any problems we'll sort it out. Good luck now, I must get back to Elizabeth. She thanks you too by the way, goodbye." He left the room with a wave.

After the Ambassador had left Benjamin called Natalya on the hotel phone, asking her to join him for dinner. She had been fast asleep and sounded disgruntled at being awoken but said she was hungry. Benjamin took the elevator to the ground. The restaurant adjoined the ballroom where the Outland party had taken place. He pushed aside the plastic sheet over the door and looked into the large empty room. Only the damaged window gave a clue to the bomb.

Like the ballroom the restaurant had a small stage, the tables clustered below it around a polished pine dance floor. Natalya arrived soon after he had sat down. She was wearing a simple white dress and the sight of her cheered him up. Richard Clapton, sitting on the other side of the room, was eating by himself and he also smiled at her when she came in.

Benjamin was unable to talk in his usual carefree way. He was dwelling on the terrible events of the day before, and Natalya too was pensive.

"You're safe now?" she asked as she finished her main course. "They know you didn't kill your friends?"

"Yes, I've got it all figured out, Peter Greaves owned most of Outland Oil. I can thank you for finding that out. Earl Rittman was his employee, Bauss was the accountant. Teri Mayes handled everything out here. They concocted this plan to drill a well in the middle of nowhere. It didn't matter whether they found any oil. They were going to pretend they had found a huge oil field by sending out a couple of test engineers, cut off communications, create rumours. Their shares would go up, they'd offload the lot at a huge profit and then they'd buy them all back later. They wrote a fake annual report to get the punters interested, make it look like Yemen was worth a fortune. The red-head at the airport was going to mess it all up and I was going to mess it up too. So was Tom. We had to be got rid of. They got Tom but they didn't get me, but what did mess it all up was the flash flood."

"And the fighting here."

"Yes and the fighting here."

"All this killing. It seems too much." She paused. "Peter Greaves may be an objectionable man but he's not a killer and I quite liked Earl Rittman. There must be more to it. And why Yemen? What about the American who died? He was secretly married to Teri."

"You're right Natalya, there's another story here. There's the Outland story I've told you but there's another one, something to do with Congressman Steeples. The American Ambassador knows. I'm going to try to find out the truth."

"Tell me when you do." After another long pause she spoke again, "why was that red-haired man on the tarmac in Houston airport?"

Benjamin was surprised at the question for he had not considered this at all. "Shelterman told me he was an accountant with Bauss's company. But why was he out there? I don't know."

Coffee arrived and, at the same time, a Filipino band now on stage began playing loudly. It was too noisy to talk and they silently watched couples dancing on the hexagonal floor below the stage. Benjamin was unable to ask Natalya to dance, much as he would have liked. His injuries, especially his ankle, hurt too much. After a while Richard Clapton came over and sat with them. They talked about Denver but Benjamin did not join in. Eventually he got up and shouted over the music he was going to the toilet. When he limped back, after again being surprised in the mirror by the bruises to his face and the blood that had once more begun to ooze from the cut on his forehead, Natalya and Clapton were dancing. He went to his room meaning to clean his wound and return to the restaurant. But he lay on his bed and fell fast asleep.

As had been promised by the British Security officer the two detectives from London, sun-tanned and flushed with success, arrived at Sana'a airport. They were on the first scheduled flight from Dubai but it landed several hours later than usual in the early morning. They had no wish to stay longer than was absolutely necessary and had already booked themselves and Benjamin on the same plane out of Yemen. They were driven from the airport directly to the Mogul Rani by two guards from the British Embassy and Benjamin was shaken awake at five.

He didn't complain, meekly rising and brushing with his hands the drab, crumpled suit the Americans had given him. He asked to see Natalya before they left. The two detectives agreed but when he knocked on her door there was no answer. Had she spent the night with Richard Clapton? He did not know, but he could do nothing now and he wasn't going to knock on Clapton's door like a pathetic loser. All he could think of in the dark bleak corridor was how he had refused to take her offered hand as she had reached out to him from the mud logging cabin during the flood.

He wasn't afraid of the detectives. He was certain the Americans would see him right, but there was the dull pain of anti-climax. He dreaded returning to the cold and loneliness of London and his empty flat. As they drove in a British Embassy car through the silent city, arriving at the airport as dawn broke he silently thanked Yemen for giving him back his self esteem, and he was sad to leave. He found it incredible that less than three weeks ago he had hardly heard of Yemen. During the days since Tom had died he hadn't once thought about his future but now it was over, the future loomed large.

The plane was almost empty. It took off on time and Benjamin gazed at the twinkling, early morning lights over Sana'a as they disappeared beneath the thin cloud. Far to the east, glimpses of the dark red cliffs of the plateau could be seen, cut by the mouths of wadis. Above the cliffs the land spread out as far as any passenger on the aircraft could see, the dry streams in the sand merging and lost in an endless plain.

EPILOGUE

Rajan Patel, the hotel manager, came out of the Mogul Rani and stood on the steps smiling broadly. He was carrying a suitcase and was a happy man today. His annual leave was due and he had received payment from the insurance company for rebuilding the ballroom wall, a sum much more than he needed. The quote from the builders had been grossly inflated so he could take a large cut for himself. What's more, since the brief war, the President had put a stranglehold on the army and the Americans were doubling aid into the country which would improve occupancy. Aid workers and businessmen as well as tourists would return to Yemen now the Americans had declared the country safe. He had already had a call from a tour operator in Italy block booking rooms for the winter season. He was expecting a fat bonus payment next year.

The last few days had only been disturbed by the mystery of his sous-chef, Chandran Gopumar, who had been acting strangely of late, upset by the death of his friend Ranjit Singh. Chandran had last been seen by one of the hotel waiters at the old market. The waiter had watched Chandran talking to a distinguished Yemeni gentleman before getting into a taxi with him. The waiter had told him that the Yemeni had repeatedly spat gobbets of phlegm onto the ground, which remained there in a shiny yellow-white heap after the taxi had driven away. The manager wondered if Chandran, a devout Muslim, had got mixed up with local gangsters. Never mind, he thought, he could always get another chef from India.

His stretched black hotel limousine was waiting in the car park below the steps and he waved for it to come to him. The chauffeur had already been instructed to take him to the airport from where he would fly to New Delhi for a three week holiday. He certainly deserved this holiday. He might even go and visit the wife of Ranjit Singh in India who had had the good fortune to have benefited from a big life insurance policy. What a strange man Ranjit was. He hadn't seemed the sort to be so caring, instead always eyeing up the girls. Anyway his widow was said to be lonely in her new house and he could cheer her up.

The limousine drew up in front of the steps and the hotel chauffeur stepped out. He was smartly dressed and held open the rear door of the car professionally. The manager was pleased with his new chauffeur, Jimmy. Not only was the limousine now spotlessly clean, but he had also received a large sum of money from the American Embassy to take him on. The poor man had been in prison, wrongly accused of the murder of his own wife and brother, but the Defence Minister himself had given him a full pardon.

He thanked Jimmy and was about to get in the car when an American Embassy vehicle drew up and two ladies got out. "Good morning Mrs Shelterman," he said, "you are back from the States already. You couldn't be bearing to be outside Yemen for long."

"Good morning Mr Patel, yes we are back. Funnily enough we missed Yemen, didn't we Gladys?"

"Sure did. It's pretty boring back home, no adventures for the likes of us."

"Ha, you are liking to come to my hotel too. I am honoured. Please be enjoying yourself, but no bombs today, except bombe Alaska, of course."

The two women looked at him as if he was mad, bade him farewell and disappeared inside. The manager knew they were making for the bar, one of only three bars outside the embassies licensed to sell alcohol in the city. He slid into the limousine, leaving his suitcase to the chauffeur.

The drive to the airport was slow. There seemed to be more cars than ever in Sana'a and the untidy, undisciplined streets were choked with traffic. Despite this, by the time they reached the airport the manager's cheerful mood had still not waned and he gave a big tip to Jimmy as he handed over his luggage.

In the bleak airport terminal he spotted the Twin Otter pilot, Sandy, who had regularly stayed at the Mogul Rani. The pilot waved to him cheerfully and, in an unusual show of friendship, the manager walked over to him. He rarely spoke to white men except professionally but the pilot was an easy-going man and his good mood brought out a sociable streak. "Where is it you are going to already then sir?" he said.

"I've been offered a job. With Cathay Pacific. I'll be flying Jumbos."

"That is indeed good. So you are pleased to be going where now?"

"To Hong Kong of course. Great, isn't it? I always wanted to join a passenger airline. Get out of this oil lark."

"Good for you, indeed. And your partner? Where is he going?" The manager spoke politely but was already bored by the conversation. These white men insisted on talking about themselves all the time.

"He's gone to Saudi, poor bugger. Six month contract. No women out there. He'll be pissed off."

The manager smiled wryly. Caucasians have one thing on their mind. Ranjit had always said the same. White men and white women wanted sex all the time. Not wishing to hear more about this man's sexual exploits and successfully masking his envy he was wondering how he might arrange some action for himself in India. "I'm being gone now sir," he said to the pilot, "thank you for our interesting chat." He followed a family of shrouded women into the departure lounge. Yes, he was thinking, Ranjit's widow might look on me well if I become her good friend.

Jimmy did not park after he dropped off the manager but left immediately to drive back into town and pick up his son from the American School. He liked to spend as much time as possible with the boy because only his son could help him come to terms with the death of his wife and brother. He still wasn't sure why the Defence Minister had pardoned him, nor why the Americans had been so helpful, but he did know the white man, the one who had been attacked in the Ashok Hotel, had something to do with it.

Three weeks previously a Marine had visited Jimmy's house to return the clothes lent to Benjamin Bone. A policeman was on guard outside the deserted house and he told the Marine of the awful murders that had happened there. The American Embassy contacted Benjamin Bone and a high-powered Embassy delegation, including the American Security Officer, visited the Defence Ministry. There was no question of Jimmy's innocence and a pardon was signed that day but it took some time for it to filter through to the prison service who always resented releasing anyone.

Jimmy remembered the day he had finally walked out of jail after his release to see a grim-faced Marine in an Embassy car who offered to take him to his home. Although apprehensive he had accepted. When they arrived he had been thrilled to see that professional builders, at least as professional as you can get in Yemen, had completed the building and decorated it, inside and out. The Americans had paid for everything. It was a huge surprise but what had lifted his spirits most was the sight of his son standing in the doorway.

Awakened from his reverie, Jimmy slammed on the brakes as a truck stopped in front of him outside the military compound near the airport. The truck swung left, halted at the gates and blocked the road. He waited patiently knowing it would be unwise to remonstrate with the soldiers. The army were very sensitive these days. Two uniformed corporals climbed out of the driver's cab, walked round to the back of the truck and pulled back the canvas. They shouted inside before dragging a man out, a southern man wearing the clothes of an army private but soiled and torn, his face blackened with bruises. One of the soldiers shoved him in the back at gunpoint while the other went to the gates of the compound and rattled the rails. Moments later two guards appeared, opened the gates and followed the soldier back to the truck.

They walked past Jimmy's car but didn't look at him, turning away to watch one of the soldiers high-kick the prisoner in the backside. "Bastard," the soldier shouted, and laughed at his companion. A guard also aimed a kick and the four of them started shouting abuse together. The commotion had alerted a senior officer, a lieutenant-colonel, who appeared from a building within the compound. The officer walked through the gates and over to the vehicle, watched for a moment while the guard kicked the prisoner again, then raised his hand. The victim, who had had his back to the limo up until now, turned to glare at the officer and Jimmy recognised him immediately. General Geshira's fat face had been splashed across the newspapers for days.

The Lieutenant-Colonel looked at Geshira disgustedly then said loudly, in earshot of Jimmy and the drivers of the other cars nearby, "this is what happens to men who shame the Yemeni army." He ordered the guards to take the prisoner into the compound and they frog-marched him away, the officer following. The two grinning soldiers climbed into their truck, reversed, made an untidy turn and headed away in the direction of the city. Jimmy and the queue of cars behind him followed but keeping their distance. Jimmy had not liked seeing the violence but it hadn't spoilt his mood. After picking up his son he would return to the hotel and eat a slap-up supper.

Lieutenant-Colonel Hadran, recently promoted from Captain, also returned to his place of work, strutting through the compound to his office. The money he had retrieved from Geshira's former room in the army camp was now safely in his house and he would keep it and not spend any of it until the prisoner was dead and all links between them were forgotten. It may be years but he was a patient man. When he had seen his former General hide the money he had wanted it dearly but it wasn't until Geshira had tried to fondle him later that night that he decided to destroy him completely. His cousin, the editor of the English language paper, had been ideally placed and his plan worked perfectly. In fact the promotion, gifted to him by the Defence Minister, was a bonus even he hadn't dared hope for.

He looked up as he crossed the compound and saw a soldier slouching in the yard. He cursed him, threatening him with a charge. Reaching his office he shouted at his private secretary to bring him Turkish coffee and sat down, putting his feet up on the desk.

While Jimmy ate his supper and Lieutenant-Colonel Hadran drank his fourth cup of coffee, Rajan Patel, the hotel manager and Sandy, the pilot, were eating airline meals high up in the sky above Wadi Hadramawt. As their plane veered northwards to Dubai far below them they could have seen, if they had been looking, the peaceful town of Karim and its bumpy streets quiet in the dark. The only lights visible from the air were in the centre of town sparkling from the windows of Sheikh Achmed's palace. The lights were brightest at the highest floor where, in the diwan, a meeting was in progress.

The usual elders were present. Dr Khaled in his polyester suit was inattentive as usual. Hussain was cheerful. His son had been released from prison under a general amnesty for minor criminals. Mutara was also there. He was happy too, though he didn't show it, paid off in full by Mahmoud and soon to benefit from increased tourist trade in jewellery sales. He was thinking of opening a tourist shop in Marib and even Karim itself. Captain Abdullah was standing by a window, smiling about his new responsibilities. He had been given a battalion to guard the highway and ensure tourist cars were not disturbed by tribesmen. He expected to be promoted soon. Finally, Latif the farmer sat in the corner. He had neither lost nor gained from recent events but, in any case, he was always cheerful.

Sheikh Achmed, with his booming voice, said "we are all agreed then, a new member of council to replace Ali, a new man who is now my only son, a man we can trust." There were nods from all of them. "He is waiting outside, I will beckon him in."

No one disagreed. Sheikh Achmed did exactly what he wanted these days. Only Khaled was fidgeting, his index finger buried in his ear, turning to extricate the wax. Moments later Achmed returned followed by Hassan, the pimply former accountant of Outland Oil. Hassan, who hated the desert, had been made an elder of the town.

It had been two days after the coup was over and a semblance of normality had returned to Yemen when Hassan, after making sure his family members were safely back in their small house near the Presidential Palace, had returned to the Outland Oil offices. Of course no one was there. The secretaries and drivers with nothing to do stayed at home. The two Government secondees were in the Energy Ministry fearful for their jobs. And Emmett Kraill was still in Wadi Qarib. So Hassan had spent the best part of three days sorting out Teri Mayes accounts. There would be heavy costs involved in the clear-up, and he needed to ensure adequate funds were available. He was also able to access the secret holding account which contained over one million dollars. It was General Geshira's final uncollected payment, ready for encashment. There was no record of the money anywhere in Outland's books. Only Hassan knew of its existence.

Hassan had been heavily influenced by his cousin Mahmoud while in the desert. Mahmoud had persuaded him that he should grasp any chance in life and chances were rare indeed. Mahmoud had given him the courage to take the opportunity the money presented. After leaving Outland's offices for good, his work in Sana'a finished, he returned to Karim with his family.

In turn, Hassan had been good to Mahmoud. He paid off all Mahmoud's debts to Mutara and his other creditors and bought him a visa and a one way ticket to the States. Although it was an altruistic act, Mahmoud was the only person in Karim who knew where Hassan's money had come from so it was better he was far away. And before he left, telling no one of his final destination, Mahmoud did something for Hassan in return. He suggested to his father that a rich young man like Hassan, a man who was a close relative too, should be made an elder. It was easy to persuade Achmed for Hassan's money meant power and it was better to control that power from within.

So, as Hassan, now almost pimple-free, walked into the room where the elders sat, he smiled at the seated men, knowing it would not take long for a young man to dominate this group of has-beens. He would control the town, run the businesses. Perhaps a small private army would be a useful asset. But first he would build a house, a house to make the Sheikh's look ordinary, and in the currency of power in the desert he would make sure the number of windows was double, no treble that of Achmed's.

As for Ali he no longer lived in Karim. He had finally brought back from Sana'a the last man alive responsible for the death of Rashad, the pathetic sous-chef from the Mogul Rani hotel. Achmed had been grateful but it was not enough. Ali's life was spared but all his assets in Karim were seized. With his wife and son he was thrown out but, although it cost him half his fortune, Ali felt he had got off lightly. They left town in a battered Land Cruiser, laden with as many belongings as they could carry. If anybody had been watching them leave in the early morning they would have seen a huge spray of phlegm fire from the window and land in a stringy lump on the prickly pears. Ali left his signature.

As the elders of Karim welcomed Hassan into their midst Mahmoud was on the other side of the world lying stark naked on his bed, reading a newspaper. He had rented a small room in south Houston, close to the San Jacinto River. He had obtained an evening job selling burgers and applied for a pilot's license. His days were mostly free and he often spent them like this, reading and watching television, improving his English. He was happier than he had ever been in his life even though he was uneasy about the fanatical, racist Christians he had met in the country. The weather was hot and he loved it. The air was clean, everything was clean and he could breathe freely without sand and dust invading his nose and mouth, without his skin becoming gritted and powdery.

He had come to Texas partly because of the promise of hot weather for most of the year but it had mainly been because of Emmett Kraill, his only white friend. Kraill had guided and helped him during those few days out in the destroyed camp, while he had toiled, one of the few locals to do so, clearing up the destruction after the flood, hoping to find his money somewhere, and avoiding Mutara and his other creditors. He never did find the money but he did see Hassan again who had helped him. But it was Kraill who had treated him particularly well, even finding this room for him.

There was a knock on his door and a voice said, "I'm doing lunch, Mahmoud, would you like some?"

"Yes thanks. That'll be cool," he shouted, pleased with the American accent he had been practising after watching daytime repeats of comedy shows on television. "I'll be right out." After a few more minutes reflecting on his good fortune he rose, pulled on a pair of jeans opened the door and walked out onto the wooden veranda. The planks creaked under his feet, loud in the quiet road, and he stretched his bronze muscular body in the clean air. A small table had already been laid with two plates, two glasses and two forks and he sat at his usual seat and waited for the food to appear.

"Hi, have you been sleeping," her voice came from behind him.

"No, Claudia. I was thinking about luck, how bad and good things link together."

"Yes, the same has happened for me," Earl was now out of her life for ever, she had a new part-time job and extra money from this man. She smiled across at him. Emmett did me a good turn suggesting I let out a room. She put the plate of paella onto the table and sat opposite him, gesturing him to eat.

"You're a good woman, Claudia. Back home in the desert it's no good, in fact you cannot meet any woman."

"This is your home now, Mahmoud."

"Yes thank you, this is my home."

When they finished their meal they both went inside to escape the heat leaving the plates on the table unwashed. In the hall, Claudia smiled at him, took his hand and guided him into her room.

Earl Rittman would have been glad for Claudia if he had known she was happy but he had not seen her at all since he got back. He and Greaves had argued in the lounge in Paris after Rittman finally guessed Congressman Steeples' real motives for financing his well in Yemen. Greaves had sworn back at him, blaming him for everything and Rittman had aimed a blow at Greaves' head.

The police had arrested him when he landed at Houston airport and he was remanded in custody without bail. But, two months later all charges were dropped. The prosecutor said there was no evidence that he had been involved in insider trading and was convinced Rittman had known nothing about the false accounts and hopeless oil well. He had lost a fortune and the FBI found nothing incriminating in his files. He was declared bankrupt but fortunately his house was in his wife's name. He was now penniless and jobless and Buckfast Energy and Sam Buckfast would have to wait until another chance came for him to get his own back.

As Rittman had languished on remand his son, Jason, had left the country. Two letters had arrived from Micky Bauss, one for him and one for his mother. When Jason learnt his father had fixed his exams he took all his money and caught a plane to Europe as he had been threatening to do. His mother pleaded with him to stay. But his mother reacted differently to the news of her husband's alleged liaison with Claudia. She made a remarkable recovery. It was a panacea, the shock made her realise she was mad, her impossible character would make her lose the husband she loved, and lose him forever. Of course, when her husband had returned from jail she had shouted and thrown things at him for she didn't want him to think he could get away with it. But then they went to bed and made love. She had her first orgasm for years.

Peter Greaves was arrested a few days after arriving back in the UK. On bail in England Greaves was due to stand trial for share manipulation and false accounting with a maximum jail sentence of ten years. The only plea his barrister could come up with was that he had a mental illness. It had worked before, he said, it could work again. Greaves was at first sceptical but there seemed no other course of action. One morning in late June he ran along Weybridge high street stark naked shouting obscenities at all who looked at him. He got five years in Ford open prison but would probably serve just two.

On the same day Congressman Steeples was indicted by the Supreme Court for corruption. The case would take years to complete and nobody expected him to be found guilty for Steeples was a powerful and rich man and there were many on the right of the party who said he was innocent. In fact a significant section of the public was convinced his actions in Yemen were something for which America should be proud. Covering the first day of the trial Richard Clapton wrote in the Denver Post that Steeples was a racist and the white Americans who supported him should be ashamed of themselves. They were no better than the terrorists who tried to bomb American cities. The paper had more letters of complaint than it had had the entire year previously and the editor was not pleased. He told Richard there would be no more foreign trips for him and instead sent him to cover the opening of a new shopping mall in the west of Denver.

After writing his report on the mall, and the exceptional retail experience to be had, Richard Clapton returned home to his new Chinese girlfriend and told her he had decided to move to Washington where he was confident he would be able to get a proper job as an investigative reporter. There he wrote an article on Congressman Steeples and submitted it to the Washington Post. The article detailed the Congressman's life and also reported on the man's unwelcome news. The pain Steeples had suffered in his hip and groin over the last few weeks had been diagnosed by his private doctor as secondary tumours on the bone, a result of a prostate cancer that explained the impotence he had been suffering over the last year. The Congressman's frustrated wife, who would inherit many millions of dollars, couldn't wait for him to die.

Curt Gawain's funeral was held in Washington with full military honours, attended by the Secretary of State for the Middle East as well as by Erwin Shelterman who flew over from Yemen especially. Few people knew the truth. It would have been a public relations disaster for the US Foreign Service and they were making it their business that as few as possible would ever know. Before Shelterman returned to Yemen he and the Secretary of State discussed the cover-up in detail, planning a complicated strategy to keep the media ignorant of Gawain's part in the affair. After the meeting they repaired to the tennis courts for a game of doubles with two young girls from the typing pool.

But they had one unsolved problem, one person knew all about Gawain who could not be bought. He was the accountant Micky Bauss but Bauss had disappeared. Soon after Rittman had been arrested the FBI had raided his offices and found them empty, wrecked, all the files shredded. There was no trace of Bauss at his home, or any record of his whereabouts anywhere else. He had simply vanished.

In London Benjamin Bone left the American Embassy after his final debriefing and walked up Oxford Street and then down the hill to Trafalgar Square. It was lunchtime and he climbed the steps into the National Gallery, walked through the rooms full of pictures and descended the short flight of stairs to the canteen. She was waiting for him, holding a cup of coffee in both her hands blowing on the surface to cool it.

"Hi," he said grinning, "its over. They don't need me anymore. I'm free..." he paused. "I mean, we're free to go anywhere we like."

"Great, call the waiter over. Where do you want to go?" she laughed.

"Sure. I'm hungry now, really hungry. To Singapore, where else. You know today I found out why the red-head was on the runway in Houston. It was his wife, she worked there..."

"Benjamin," said Natalya her voice serious, her blue eyes crinkling into a frown, "tell me later, first there's something important I should tell you. I kept it to myself up to now. I didn't want to compromise you with those Americans."

"Yes, what?"

"In the flood when I was in the trailer and Gawain was pleading for help he told me he had money, plenty of it. He told me to look in the cabinet above his head. Well when he drowned and before I left the trailer, before you rescued me, I forced open the cabinet and true enough there was an envelope containing fifty thousand dollars. I stuffed it in the pocket of my jeans, didn't tell a soul. Was that wrong? Should I have kept it?"

"Gawain doesn't need it, nor does his wife. He gave it to you."

"Yes I suppose so. But I still feel guilty."

"Don't, it's yours."

"Well first thing I am going to do is buy air tickets to Singapore, for the both of us."

"Thanks, that's great," said Benjamin and he held her hand tight, staring into her blue eyes.

Four days later at Heathrow airport Benjamin's brother and sister-in-law, Charlotte and Bertram, and Natalya's mother and father saw them off. Dick Collins was also there, transferred to London and promoted to Middle East advisor at the American Embassy. He had been responsible for Benjamin's debriefing over the last few weeks.

It had been hard for Dick Collins when he had found out about Teri Mayes's death. For a few brief hours he had been happy, anxiously awaiting her return from the desert and preparing his words of proposal to her. Then he had learnt she was dead. To his colleagues, who didn't know the strength of his feelings, he seemed to have hardly flinched. But the Ambassador, with a shrewdness unsuspected by his staff, watched alarmed while Collins continued to work as before but unresponsively and unimaginatively just like he had been when he had first arrived from Jakarta.

It was with relief Shelterman had found out the true story about Teri, that she had been Gawain's wife for four years, that she had flunked her accountancy exams and turned to prostitution, that she had worked for Congressman Steeples, then for Gawain, that in her early twenties she had been convicted of arson after trying to burn the offices of the Democratic party in New York, that she had a passionate hatred of authority, of government, any government, a psychological disorder that the prison service said was completely cured after she had completed her three year sentence. Shelterman told Collins all of this. He didn't break it gently. He called him to his room and blurted it all out and Collins had gone crazy swearing and cursing, but afterwards he had begun to recover.

At Heathrow Airport Collins introduced Benjamin and Natalya to a blonde girl who looked very like Teri Mayes. But she was English and her plummy accent couldn't have been more different from Teri's New York twang. They took the escalator to the departure gate together. When an extended Arab family, with an extended family of suitcases created a hubbub in front of them Collins took the chance to whisper in Benjamin's ear he had had his new girl friend fully checked out, there were no skeletons in her cupboard.

The non-stop flight took Benjamin and Natalya southeast across Europe then across the Empty Quarter of Saudi Arabia north of Yemen. Benjamin nudged Natalya, whose head rested on his shoulder, pointing out the lights in the desert and the deep red sky ahead prefacing the rise of the sun in the east. But she was fast asleep and didn't respond. In the dark he recalled their conversation soon after she had returned to England.

"How could you think I'd gone off with Richard Clapton," she had said angrily, I hardly knew him."

"Well you were with him."

"I've been with lots of men. It doesn't mean I sleep with them."

"Yes but there was no answer from your room..."

"I was fast asleep, shattered. You'll soon find out when I'm tired. I don't wake for anything."

She must be shattered now, he thought. Although he needed to tell her something urgently, he decided not to try to wake her again.

It was raining outside as the plane touched down at Changi airport in Singapore. Silver drops of water sped across the windows of the British Airways 747, leaving a sparkling web of moisture on the surface of the glass. A neat row of flame of the forest trees lined runway two in front of a high grassy verge. In stark contrast to the yellow sand and rock of Yemen, the place looked lush and green. Despite this, the heavy thunderclouds above the trees reminded Benjamin of the violent storm that had rocked their light aircraft in the mouth of Wadi Qarib.

As he gazed out at the tropical scene Natalya leaned across to see for herself the country where she had been brought up. "When I first landed in England," she said, "it was mid-winter. There were no leaves on the trees and I thought they were all dead."

Benjamin turned to look at her, his face inches from hers and laughed, "I don't believe you..."

"I did, it's true." She paused and then added, "I'm glad to be back, I'd like to stay here longer."

"You can."

"No I can't, I've got to get back to my job. He'll fire me if I take out longer than a week."

"Natalya, I've got something to tell you. You know the fifty thousand dollars that Gawain gave you. You've spent a chunk of it on this holiday haven't you..., on me."

"Yes, don't worry about it."

"Actually I'm not worried because you didn't need to. I know you think I haven't any money, but things are changing, things have changed."

"What's changed?"

"Before I left Yemen I told you I would try to find out what was really going on out there, you know, the other story, the story Greaves and Rittman probably knew nothing about."

"Yes?"

"Well I did find out and the Americans have given me five million dollars to keep my mouth shut. I can't get at the capital yet but as long as the story doesn't get in the press, then I've got the income for life. I'll never have to work again. Nor will you."

"Why didn't you tell me sooner?" she sounded disappointed and Benjamin had a terrible feeling she thought she'd been deceived again. Like when he had kept quiet about Germaine.

"I wanted to be sure. I only got the first payment yesterday. I checked at the bank in the airport."

She smiled at him and clasped his hand firmly, "I wondered what you were up to. For a moment I thought you were calling Germaine...."

The plane halted at the terminal and the passengers rose to retrieve their belongings. Benjamin, with Natalya in front of him, waited in the aisle. He leaned across and whispered in her ear, "I'll tell you what," he said, "you'll know everything from now on, yes everything, as soon as it happens, you'll know all the facts."

Natalya looked up at him and her smile was enough to convince him she didn't believe a word but, at least for now, she didn't seem to care.

After passing through immigration they took a hire car to the centre of town. It was starting to rain and, as Benjamin drove the car along the East Coast Parkway, he stared out to sea past the palm trees running along the edge of the artificial beach. There were hundreds of moored ships and drilling rigs dotting the skyline offshore. Although he did not have to work now, he was oddly anxious, almost wishing he was on his way to a job on one of the rigs. He was being foolish. Even in the warmth of the tropical rain with a girl at his side and money in the bank he could not be satisfied. Perhaps, when he looked back on this day, the moment would seem better. Or perhaps not, the day was not over yet.

SOURCES

This is entirely a work of fiction and all the characters are invented. However, many of the oil field incidents described in the novel have happened to me, albeit perhaps in a less dramatic way. And there was indeed an account of an oil strike, actually in South East Asia, reported falsely in an effort to raise stock prices in London. And, of course, it is certainly possible to conceive of politicians in the United States, or anywhere else, trying to manipulate the oil price to their own ends.

In terms of Yemeni history, the army personnel, politicians and tribes in the book are fictitious. Nevertheless, although it did not happen in quite the way described here, there was an attempt by the southern army to break up the country in 1994. In May 1990 the southern communist state of the Peoples Democratic Republic of Yemen had merged with the northern Islamic State of the Yemen Arab Republic. The latter's capital, Sana'a, became the administrative centre of the new country, now simply called the Republic of Yemen.

Despite free elections the relationship between the two former states, with their differing ideologies and new oil wealth, remained strained and in 1994 the country erupted into civil war. A tank battle occurred in Amran, near Sana'a in late April and both sides bombed their respective capitals in May. Aden, the capital of the south, was eventually captured by the northern army in July 1994. The southern military and political leaders fled into exile.

Unfortunately the optimism at the end of the novel did not last. Tensions continued to build and civil war returned in 2011 after the country's long standing President had been deposed during the so-called Arab Spring. Factions supporting the north, the south and the tribes people continued to fight each other and Yemen fell into turmoil. Sana'a was finally captured by the Iran-supported Houthi tribe who were subjected to incessant bombings by a Saudi-led coalition. Children began to starve and Yemen became a terrorist refuge. President Saleh, who had ruled the North since 1978 and then the unified country from 1990 to 2012, was murdered in 2017.

In the past large volumes of oil were produced in Yemen although significantly less than the other big countries of the Middle East. The Soviets had been first to find oil in the south around Shabwa near the old border of North and South Yemen back in the 1980s. They failed to develop any of the fields. It was North American and French companies that turned the country into an oil exporter, at first from the northern Marib region and later from the southeast plateau near Wadi Hadramawt where Outland Oil is drilling its well.

Production increased rapidly in the 1990s but everywhere is now in decline. A liquefied natural gas plant was opened in late 2009 exporting gas to Europe. However, pipeline flows of both oil and gas were regularly cut by local people, angry at the government in Sana'a and infiltrated by Islamic extremists. By 2016, most production had stopped.

I was once a geologist working with oil companies and consultancies around the world but now forecast oil and other energy supplies. For many years I have been interested in the true outlook for oil and the future energy transition. I would ask any interested reader to visit globalshift.co.uk or a guide to the industry and advice about what the future may hold.

If you would like to receive information on new books when released, or discuss anything about this book or about the website please email: michael@globalshift.co.uk.

Printed in Great Britain
by Amazon